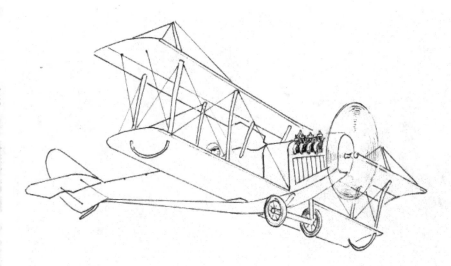

Praise for other books by Jim Moore:

Ride the Jawbone

"When you read Jim Moore's *Ride the Jawbone*, you have to constantly remind yourself that it's fiction and you haven't slipped into Montana 1902. One heck of a read!"
—Craig Johnson, author of *The Cold Dish* and the rest of the Longmire Series

Election Day

"Jim Moore knows the law, and he knows politics, and he's brought both to bear in this crackerjack of a read."
—Craig Lancaster, author of *600 Hours of Edward* and *Edward Adrift*

The Body on the Floor of the Rotunda

"There is a Montana way in everything Jim Moore does. This book is an example of his dedication to a good story under the Big Sky."
—Neil Lynch, Former Majority Leader, Montana State Senate

The Whole Nine Yarns: Tales of the West

"Jim Moore loves the landscape of Montana. Ride beside him as he tells his tales from then and now with humor and the tempo of a real Montana gentleman."
—Florence Ore, author of *The Road Between*

THE JENNY

a novel

Jim Moore

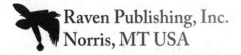

Raven Publishing, Inc.
Norris, MT USA

The Jenny
Copyright © 2015 Jim Moore
Cover art © 2015 Ryan Scott Weber

Published by Raven Publishing, Inc.,
P.O. Box 2866, Norris, MT 59745, USA

Library of Congress Cataloging-in-Publication Data

Moore, Jim, 1927-
The jenny : a novel / Jim Moore.
     pages ; cm
ISBN 978-1-937849-29-0 (alk. paper)
I. Title.
PS3613.O5626J46 2015
813'.6--dc23
                                                    2015001763

For Kay, who flew with me

1 Olive Breen was sixty years old and burdened with a bad disposition. She arose each morning at four o'clock and trudged the four blocks to her restaurant on Main Street in Two Dot, Montana, to prepare for the first customers of the day—some of whom would arrive before five. On the fourth of June, 1920, she rounded the corner of the bank, head ducked down into her collar against the cold northeast wind—and spied the body of a man stretched on the boardwalk half a block away and near the front of the saloon. Olive muttered words that she wouldn't use in polite society, coarse words to describe drunks who passed out after slurping the stuff that Lippy served for whiskey now that Prohibition was in effect. Debris from the previous night's revelry littered the boardwalk and blew along the street, adding to her disgust. Well, she'd just kick life back into the worthless wretch and chase him out of sight. As Olive approached the prostrate form she saw something protruding from the man's chest. Two steps closer and Olive lurched backward, clutched at her stomach, gasped, and muttered, "My God! It's Merci Bruce's young man. And he's deader than last week's cod fish."

Olive didn't scream or cry. She was too practical for that. Instead, she retraced her tracks up the street and around to the back of the general store building where she pounded on the door. Stefan Steiner, half-dressed and bleary eyed, pulled the entry open. "Merci Bruce's boyfriend's dead on the walk in front of Lippy's place. Call the sheriff," Olive snarled. The old woman turned on her heel and trudged again toward the restaurant. There would still be people coming for a morning meal—maybe more than the regulars, considering what she had just found.

Steiner stumbled to the telephone attached to the rear wall of the store and turned its crank once to ring for the operator in Harlowton. He had to yell to make the woman understand that she should connect him to the sheriff's phone.

2 Just the day before, twenty-year-old Merci Bruce had stood with her back to her aircraft and had scanned the crowd gathered along the roadways—one leading south to the ranches along Big Elk Creek—the other leading west to the Bruce ranch and on to Martinsdale. The gawkers, the curious, and the bored lined the space behind the fences that bordered each road. Something new to the ranch country was about to happen. Many of them had arrived on horseback. A few just walked up the hill from town. Some had come in buggies. Others had driven to the field in automobiles. Among them were men, women, and children. Nearly all were people from the ranching community that Merci knew so well.

Nate Hamilton, friend from childhood, leaned his back against the side of the large Ford truck. His black, bushy eyebrows, pulled together in a frown, told of his displeasure at her foolish venture. But then, many of those who stood and watched were certain the attempt at flight would end in disaster and the pilot would soon be dead and buried. Those would be the morbid ones, she thought. That idea brought a small smile to her lips. A glance toward the west reminded her of the short distance she had for a takeoff run. Such a short distance to get the ungainly machine into the air. The smile disappeared. The crowd was right. She might not survive.

The June day was cloudless and cool with a slight breeze from the west. A perfect day for flying. A perfect day also for the excitement that the strange machine brought to Montana's cattle land.

Merci turned her attention back to the focus of the gathering—her proud possession. The aircraft, a Curtis JN4, built to train pilots during the recent war in France, squatted near the fence corner with its tail to the ground and its blunt nose pointed upward into the air. The two wings gave it the look of an ungainly insect—an insect rather like a huge dragonfly, or, she sometimes thought, if not a dragonfly, some other monstrous insect that could never lift itself into the air. The machine appeared to be held together with wires that crisscrossed from the fuselage to the wings and back again. Merci patted the fuselage once. She was about to trust her life to it.

The young woman's attention turned to her brother. Just the sight of him brought a warm smile to her face. Spencer was of a muscular build, just over six feet tall. He had regular features that most would call handsome. Today a western hat covered his thick, dark hair. He appeared to be at ease as he leaned against the fender of his Hudson Roadster. That appearance, she knew, belied his anxiety—anxiety that Merci understood. After all, she was his little sister, the one he'd protected and cared for from earliest childhood. Now, she knew, he was wondering again if she could really get the ungainly flying machine into the Montana sky. What if she couldn't?

The elevation of the flat tract of land where she stood was about forty-four hundred feet above sea level. No one really knew if a Jenny, as the aircraft was ordinarily called, could get off the ground in the thin air of that elevation with such a short takeoff run, a run that was only about fourteen hundred feet in length. At her request, Spence had used his automobile odometer to measure the distance from the fence corner to the end of the tract of level ground. He'd measured it again by pacing it off on foot.

Fourteen hundred feet—slightly more than one-quarter mile. Merci's eyes swept once more from the aircraft westward to the place where the flat land dropped down into the shallow basin created by Alkali Creek. Such a short distance—with so much at risk.

The aviatrix put the thought from her mind. She had chosen the location because the land was flat, the takeoff would be to the west into the prevailing wind, and there were no obstructions near at hand. But of most importance was the drop down into the creek bottom. Should the machine fail to achieve flying speed in its dash across the quarter mile of flat land, that drop into the shallow valley might yet allow it to become airborne.

Merci had purchased the aircraft in California and arranged to have it shipped in a railcar to Montana. The disassembled parts were unloaded at the railroad siding in Two Dot and hauled to this location just to the south of town. The reassembling was then completed in the fence corner where the airplane rested. It was Arnold Masters who put the pieces together with some help from Merci and a little from Lyndon Morgan, one of her father's ranch hands.

Merci walked one more time around the airplane to assure herself that it was indeed ready to fly. Masters, who had traveled from the airfield in California, was checking the water in the radiator of the huge OX5 engine. She ambled along the wings, strumming the landing and flying wires as she went, making certain that each was tightened to the proper tension. She met Masters at the front of the airplane as he pulled the propeller into its correct position for cranking.

He turned to Merci with a smile and a wink. "The Jenny's ready, Merc. How about you?" Masters was only about an inch taller than Merci. His body—slim but muscular through the shoulders—was covered this day by baggy coveralls, stained with grease. His complexion was ruddy. Dimples flashed when he smiled, and he smiled often.

Merci, seemingly flush with confidence, grinned at Masters as she made a wrap around her neck with a white silk scarf. "Damn right I'm ready. I'll show the locals what a woman can do!" She flashed a winsome smile over her shoulder at her brother while buttoning the heavy fleece lined jacket. The smile grew brighter when Spencer waved one hand in acknowledgment.

The bottoms of her jodhpurs (She'd heard one woman in the crowd scold that a woman wearing trousers was scandalous.) were encased in heavy boots that laced to the tops of her calves. She pulled the flaps of the flying helmet down over her ears and fastened them securely under her chin. Merci settled the goggles over her eyes and drew a pair of warm, tight-fitting gloves onto her hands. One last stretch and twist of her body to loosen the clothing under the jacket and she was ready to be the first woman to take a Curtis Jenny to the air in Montana.

The flying clothes concealed a lithe body, graced with curves that ordinarily caught the eye of every man who passed her way. The hair, now under the flying helmet, was honey colored and worn in a bob, the most current fashion. Merci's eyes were more green than blue. Her nose could best be defined as pert. Full lips that smiled easily seemed to invite a smile in return. Few, if any, women in that part of the world were more attractive, but right now her looks didn't matter to anyone. Would the Jenny fly? Or crash?

She tossed another reassuring smile in Spencer's direction before jumping lightly onto the aircraft's lower wing and stepping gracefully into the rear cockpit. From there she waved both arms high in the air. Better give the crowd a show! Folks in the throng responded with whoops and hollers and shouts of encouragement. A man hurried forward with one of the new, small cameras to snap a picture. Her eyes caught those of Nate Hamilton, who was still wearing the frown. Merci poked one hand in his direction and widened her smile.

The aviatrix then waved to the crowd one more time before grasping the sides of the fuselage to lower herself slowly into the cockpit. Once seated she took a deep breath, then clasped the joystick and wiggled it from side to side while watching to assure that the ailerons alternated up and down as they should. Good! Merci moved the stick back and forth while looking over her shoulder to the rear to make certain that the elevators raised and lowered in the proper manner. Also good. While still facing the rear she pumped the pedals and watched the rudder move freely from side to side. Everything good.

For a moment she sat quietly, then took a deep breath. Her outward appearance did not reflect the churning in her stomach. A look at the short distance to the creek drop-off reminded her of the possibility that she might not survive. But here she was, ready to go—with all those people watching and waiting. After a muttered, "Well, Merci, just do it!" she raised her eyes to look toward Masters standing at the propeller, gave him another grin, jabbed two thumbs into the air, and yelled, "OK, pull the prop. You know how to do that, don't you?"

The broad-shouldered young man laughed. "I've done it a time or two." He grasped a blade of the huge wooden propeller with both of his hands. Masters kicked one leg into the air and jerked it back to gain leverage and momentum as he pulled downward on the propeller with all his might. The motor turned but failed to fire. Merci clenched her jaw and shook her head. She pumped the throttle and then signaled from the cockpit for Masters to pull again. Another mighty heave. Again, there was no response from the OX5 engine. Merci mumbled something unintelligible and signaled again. On the third attempt the motor coughed once and thundered into life. The mechanic scrambled to the side to get out of the way of the turning propeller.

A loud cheer—that Merci couldn't hear—arose from the throng of onlookers. Horses, frightened by the sudden roar, reared back against the reins that tied them to the fences. Spencer inhaled and clenched his fists.

The aviatrix sat absolutely still while she muttered a silent prayer. Though not ordinarily very religious, she suddenly and instinctively decided the prayer couldn't hurt. Finally, after one more perfunctory wave in Spencer's direction and another thumbs up for Masters, she gritted her teeth and pushed the throttle to the stop.

The engine thundered. Dust and dirt blown by the turning propeller enveloped the spectators standing directly behind the machine.

Slowly, ever so slowly, the plane began to move, tailskid dragging as it went. Yard by yard the speed increased, but at a painfully slow pace. Merci leaned forward as though that act would help the machine increase its speed. After a bit she began to ease the stick gently forward. Not enough speed to lift the tail. The damn tail skid continued to drag on the ground slowing the acceleration.

To Spencer, watching with clenched fists and a clenched stomach, it seemed there was no chance the machine could gain flying speed in time to avert the wreck that seemed certain to come.

Merci was holding her breath. Leaning farther forward, she muttered, "Come on! Come on!" About half way to the place where the land dropped off into the creek bottom she was able to coax the tail skid from the ground. As the rate of acceleration increased, she began to breathe again. At two thirds of the distance to the drop off, the speed exceeded that of an automobile racing on a smooth road. She pulled back ever so easily on the stick, but the wheels seemed tied to the ground. At three-fourths the distance she eased back more firmly on the stick. The machine broke free from the earth and lifted gracefully into the air.

The young aviatrix pumped a fist and yelled. Exhilaration—even greater than during her first solo flight. Merci whooped and hollered.

She wouldn't admit that the feeling might just be relief. What did it matter? She'd done it! She was airborne! Over the Musselshell Valley! In her own airplane! The first woman in Montana to do it by herself!

On the ground, men jumped and whooped and pounded one another on the back. Women hugged and laughed. Spencer Bruce stared after the Jenny as it climbed into the sky. Then without really thinking, he clasped his hands at his waist, closed his eyes, and muttered a heartfelt prayer of thanks.

Nate Hamilton puffed out a long breath. She'd made it. Then the usual thought replaced the anxiety—maybe soon she'll get this foolishness out of her system.

Merci flew westward in a shallow climb as the airspeed slowly increased. Then she moved the stick to the right and pressed lightly on the right rudder to bank the Jenny to the north and out over the river valley. The aircraft continued to gain altitude as it circled over the town of Two Dot, over the Mason Ranch buildings, and then completed the circle to pass above the crowd.

Some on the ground were still trying to quiet the horses, so frightened by the odd machine. Others continued to shout and wave. A couple of cowpunchers threw their hats upward toward the airplane as it passed overhead. In 1920, the ranch country of Montana had finally entered the modern era. That was something worthy of celebration.

Merci banked the plane and looked down to see Spence already in the seat of his Hudson two-seater with Arnold Masters clambering into the passenger side. With a grin she knew he couldn't see, she waved once from the cockpit and pointed with her hand toward the Bruce Ranch.

Spence waved back, then shifted the Hudson into gear and sped west along the dusty county road. His worries wouldn't end until Merci was safely on the ground.

Merci could hardly contain her emotions. She pounded with her hand on the small instrument panel. Her grin widened. She pumped a fist and shouted, "Hallelujah!" Finally, she quieted enough to focus her attention on the panorama spread before her.

Below and to the right the Musselshell River wound along to its confluence with the Missouri River, two hundred miles to the east. The Little Belt Mountains on the far right marked the northern boundary of the Musselshell Valley. The Crazy Mountains towered to the southwest. The Castle Mountains rose directly before her. The world was green this June day. Hay fields along the river and along Little Elk Creek, lush with new growth, offered colors that varied from ivy to olive. Leaves on the cottonwood trees along both the creek and the river shimmered in the breeze. The sky, now dotted with the beginnings of billowing cumulus clouds, seemed too blue to be real. And just ahead, the house in which she'd grown to adulthood stood large among the barn, sheds, the bunkhouse, and other outbuildings that were so necessary to the Bruce Ranch operation.

Peering through the windscreen, she could see her parents, T. C. and Felicity, as they stepped out onto the wide front porch and peered upward at the approaching aircraft. Each held a hand to the forehead to dampen the glare of the morning sun. She'd been disappointed when they said they wouldn't watch her take to the air, but she understood their reasons. Felicity couldn't bear the thought of watching while her daughter foolishly risked her life. Her father stayed at home to comfort her mother—in the event that comfort might be required.

Merci pushed forward on the joystick to lose some altitude in preparation for her pass over the ranch compound. She wobbled the wings and leaned over the side of the cockpit to wave at the people below. Ranch hands in the barnyard were busy preparing for the summer haying season—some shoeing horses, some repairing equipment.

All stopped their activities and threw their arms in the air in a kind of salute. She could even see old Olaf, the choreman, dancing a foolish jig.

Beyond the buildings and across the creek was the long stretch of level ground that she'd chosen for her landing field. A flat roofed aircraft hangar had been constructed near to the east end of the field, ready to house the Jenny when it was at home and at rest. Merci's eyes swept the area as she passed overhead. This was, after all, the first time she'd seen the field from the air. She concluded both the field and hangar would serve the purposes for which they were intended.

The air was smooth, the day was bright, and the engine was running smoothly. Too nice to end the flight so soon. Merci pushed the throttle to increase power and pulled back on the stick to climb higher into the air. She circled to the south and up the course of Little Elk Creek. About a mile upstream she passed over two men with shovels spreading irrigating water that ran from the creek through ditches to the hay fields. Very little snow remained on the face of the mountains. Soon the flow of the creek would be insufficient to provide water for irrigation, so the men were covering as much ground as possible as fast as they could.

Once she'd gained enough altitude, she turned again to the east to fly over the northern sloping shoulder of the Two Dot Butte. Cattle grazing on the grasslands below appeared as dark red spots. Banking to the north she passed above an uneven section of land that had been taken up by homesteaders, each claiming one hundred sixty acres of ground. The last three years of severe drought had driven all but one of them to abandon their homestead claims. Only the Morgans—Hiram, Sophia, and their son, Lyndon—remained. Sophia, standing near the barrels with which they hauled water to their house from a distant well, waved once at the Jenny as it passed overhead. Each day or so, Hiram or Lyndon would hook a team to a stone boat, go to the well and fill two barrels with the precious liquid. From the air Merci could see that the grain Hiram had planted in anticipation of a bountiful harvest was already beginning to shrivel. The drought continued, and the outlook for all the dry land farmers was dismal.

Dust rising behind Spencer's auto as he raced westward along the county road caught Merci's eye and brought a grin to her face. He would arrive at the ranch just in time to watch her first landing.

Once again the aviatrix turned to the west, throttled back on the motor, and began the approach to her chosen landing field. While passing over the ranch buildings she applied enough power to assure that the plane would clear the tops of the trees along the creek. Near the ground Merci pulled the throttle all the way to idle and tugged the stick back between her legs to raise the nose of the machine and reduce the airspeed. The wheels of the Jenny touched once, bounced, and then settled solidly to earth. She allowed the aircraft to coast along as the speed diminished and the tail skid sank to the ground. She gunned the engine to turn the plane around and taxi to the hangar. Once there, Merci hit the switch to kill the engine.

As the propeller whirled to a stop, the aviatrix scrambled from the cockpit and leapt to the ground from the lower wing. Overflowing with exuberance, she couldn't contain herself. She waved her arms above her head and danced once around in a kind of pirouette. After a moment, feeling foolish, she dropped her arms and took a breath to calm herself.

Spence clambered from the Hudson. The two, brother and sister, ran together. Spence grabbed her at the waist, hoisted her off the ground and twirled her around and around. "You did it, Merc! You did it!" Merci just hugged his head to her mid-section before he dropped her to the ground.

T. C. arrived in the Ford Model T Runabout. He hurried from the vehicle to clutch Merci into another hug, not one quite as vigorous as that of her brother. "Thank God, you're safe."

Arnold Masters, who had been standing quietly to the side, re-frained from giving Merci a hug. But his grin was wide as he grasped her hand. "I knew you could do it, Merc. Never a doubt in my mind."

The men shifted their attention to the flying machine. Together they moved it backwards into the hangar. When finished, T. C. pulled the two metal gates together to block the broad opening. Merci checked the arrangement to assure herself that the precious machine was safe. Her father touched her arm. "Let's go to the house and celebrate with a glass of the iced tea Felicity's fixing right this minute."

Merci didn't wait. She jumped into Spencer's sport car for the short ride back to the ranch house while Arnold climbed into the Runabout beside T. C. Just before the vehicles began to move, Merci hollered at Masters, "After the tea, either Spence or I'll take you back to Two Dot. But let's relax for a bit. We've both earned it."

They savored the tea in comfortable companionship with much talk about the modern age in which they lived. After a time Spence began to fidget. Finally, he clambered to his feet. "I have to get back to my office in Harlo. Olaf Larsen is buying a house, and the bank asked me to review the abstract of title. That's a time consuming task."

Masters pushed the chair back to stand. "Can I ride with you as far as Two Dot?"

Merci followed them to the automobile where she gave her broth-er a final hug and the mechanic a warm handshake and a smile.

Still feeling the exhilaration that came from the first Montana flight after the noon meal, Merci helped her mother clear the table and wash the dishes. Those tasks completed, she found it difficult to either sit still or stand without pacing. Her father saved her. He poked his head from his office door. "Are you there, Merc? I have a letter that needs to be put in the mail this afternoon. Would you drive down to Two Dot and drop it at the post office?"

She walked to the office doorway. "Of course, Dad." she said with a grin. "I may spend some time visiting, if you don't mind. There'll be folks in town who'll want to hear all about the Jenny and what it's like to fly."

"It's fine with me, but before you go, please tell your mother."

The grin widened. "May I use the Packard?"

T. C. smiled at his daughter in return. "Of course. But be careful with it."

She walked to the desk and reached an arm around his shoulder. "As always. And I won't be late."

3 Merci was alone in the kitchen the next morning when the phone hanging on the wall in the corridor jangled two short rings and one long ring—the signal that the call was for the Bruce Ranch. Merci, rushed to answer. Steiner's voice, shouted into the telephone at the Two Dot store and then carried over the one wire telephone line, was garbled. Merci was able to understand enough to realize something had happened to Arnold Masters. Without a word to her mother, who was as usual cleaning an already clean house, she grabbed a coat and a scarf for her head, scrambled into her parents' Model T Runabout, and sped eastward toward Two Dot.

Merci parked the auto at an angle in front of the general store and hurried to the group that was clustered a few yards down the street. She pushed her way through the onlookers to Spence who stood hunched with his hands stuffed into the pockets of his overcoat. Her eyes shifted immediately to the prostate form that was the focus of the gathering. The sight of the body of Arnold Masters, his lifeless eyes staring upward, caused her to gasp and then to gulp. The bitter cold wind whipped at Merci's skirt as she instinctively grasped Spence's arm for protection. Without question, the mechanic was dead. My God! How could this have happened to someone as much fun and as gentle as Arnold Masters?

One more gulp and she was able to turn her attention to the store-keeper. That stumpy little man completed his monologue by pointing to the body. "That's just the way I found him—after Olive Breen rousted me out." Merci turned again toward the body lying face up on the boardwalk. Only yesterday Arnold's eyes had sparkled with the excitement of the flight of the Jenny. Now those eyes were dull and unmoving. Yesterday his skin glowed. Now it was gray and blotched. The second look nearly caused her to lose her breakfast. Acting on instinct, she jerked off her coat and covered Masters' face. A sob racked her body as she leaned against her brother and clutched at his arm. He wrapped his arm about her shoulder to pull her close. Merci dropped her head and let the tears ran down her cheeks. Spence held her even more closely.

The crowd of onlookers was gathered on the boardwalk along the west side of the main street that ran north to south through Two Dot. The business district, if it could be called such, consisted of a bank, a general store, a hardware store, a barbershop, a saloon, a small house, and a hotel along the west side of the street. A blacksmith shop, livery stable, jewelry store, and a cafe were on the opposite side.

Merci's tears began to diminish. Wearing only a plain gray house-dress of cotton material, the scarf over her head and now without a coat, she began to shiver. With her arms clasped about her body, she looked more carefully at the surroundings. The body was lying directly in front of the barbershop. The sheriff, the storekeeper, Spencer Bruce, and the other onlookers, most of whom were also shivering in the chill, were standing quietly in a circle around it. She finally cast a questioning look upward to Spence's face. He appeared to be waiting for the sheriff to ask questions—to make decisions—to give orders.

The law officer, a former homesteader, was about fifty-five years of age. Small eyes peeked out of a face that was lined from years of toil in the weather. He was short of stature and burdened with a large belly now covered by denim pants held in place with broad suspenders. Unlike other law officers, he wore his sheriff's star pinned to a belt loop on the denims. His western-style hat was misshapen from hard use. Despite the cold, the sheriff wore only a light jacket, unbuttoned to the gusty blasts of cold air.

Sheriff Lester Graves was well liked. He possessed common sense and was quick witted, but his agricultural background provided little assistance to him in the performance of his recently acquired duties as sheriff. As the others huddled in the wind, he remained mute, chin in his hand, and with his eyes locked on the dead body. When he didn't speak, Spence felt a need to help. He asked of the storekeeper, "It's been a couple of hours since you called, Stef. Anyone move him?"

"Nope. I got here first—before anybody but Olive. And I made sure everything stayed the same as I first found it." The merchant scowled toward the townspeople crowded together with their backs to the wind. "A couple of them folks wanted to check to find out if he was really dead. But I didn't let them. It's easy enough to see that there's no life in that one."

His statement was accompanied by a jerk of his thumb toward the corpse. Merci felt a tinge of anger at the off-hand manner in which the man talked about the body near their feet, the body of her friend. The anger led her to grasp Spence's arm and cling tightly to it. Since their earliest childhood he had provided comfort and support. Right now she really needed both. She pulled a handkerchief from the sleeve of her housedress, dabbed at her eyes, and took a deep breath. Tucking the handkerchief back into its place, she vowed to herself that she would keep her emotions under control and not allow anyone to notice her distress. How she felt about Arnold Masters was the business of none of the others standing there in the cold.

Merci huddled closely to Spencer who was dressed as he would on any workday in his law office. The suit beneath the heavy topcoat was black and tailored to fit. The white dress shirt bore the kind of soft collar that had only recently come into style. The black tie was perfect-ly knotted. A fedora covered his head and the coat offered protection from the elements. With a start, he seemed to notice his sister's shiver-ing. He shed his coat and wrapped it around her shoulders.

Spencer's eyes followed the storekeeper's gesture to more closely scrutinize the body. Merci's eyes followed those of her brother. Arnold Masters was sprawled on his back with his head, now hidden by Merci's coat, turned slightly to the side, his mouth hanging open, his tongue protruding. His arms were parallel to his body and the ankle of one leg was tucked under the other. The corpse was clothed in the same kind of pants, shirt, and jacket that had been his daily attire since his arrival in Montana. Now, however, the collar of his shirt and jacket were but-toned tightly around his neck. Merci remembered that the stiff north wind, chilling them now, had arisen late the evening before. Most of those who were at the party and out on the street had done their best to bundle and button up to stay warm.

She took a step closer to the body. Someone had driven the bay-onet completely through the man's upper torso, perhaps through the two-inch plank beneath the body. Any blood from the wound must have drained through the planks and onto the dirt beneath, since little was visible on the wood surface of the boardwalk. A ragged square piece of white cardboard about ten inches in size was pinned to Mas-ters' jacket by the blade of the bayonet. The words "SHE'S MINE" were printed in crude black letters on the cardboard. What could that mean, she wondered.

This was the first dead man that Merci had seen, but she knew it wasn't the first for Spence. He and others who endured combat in

France during the recent war saw far too many of them. Merci watched as he seemingly forced any such remembrances from his mind and focused on the sheriff, "That's a German bayonet." When the sheriff remained mute, he added, "Some of our men carried them home from France as souvenirs."

Everyone within earshot, including Lester Graves, focused on the bayonet. Graves merely nodded to acknowledge the comment. He'd never dealt with a murder in his short tenure as sheriff of Wheatland County—a county created only four years before—and seemed unable to decide what he should do. For the moment, the man chewed on the inside of his cheek in contemplation, then gestured toward the cardboard with his thumb. "What do you make of that?"

Merci, like the others, stared at the crude lettering. Spence frowned, blew out a sigh, and silently shook his head. As he scanned the many onlookers, he felt reluctant to venture a guess. Finally, he spoke softly, "Hard to say." Then, while addressing the sheriff, but loud enough for all to hear, "We should get the body to Harlowton so Doc Scanlan can take a look." He looked at his sister and asked, "That all right with you, Sis?"

"Yes." Merci, still shivering in the cold, turned away. "Get him away from here."

A gust of the wind blew something in the sheriff's eye. He squinted and brushed at it with his hand. With a nod, he said to Spence, "You're right. But anyone can see what killed the guy. I don't think Doc will find anything that will tell us who did it." He turned toward the men standing near at hand, lifted his arm as though to get their attention, and raised his voice one notch. "All right, gents. Let's boost him in the box on my Model T."

Merci grasped the sheriff's arm. "Sheriff, get a blanket or sheet to wrap him. And please do it gently."

Sheriff Graves turned to her, eyebrows raised, like he just realized she was there. "Of course, Ma'am. You're right. He should be covered."

Spence spoke up. "And, Sheriff, don't you think you should pull the bayonet from the body? Using your gloves? And then wrap the bayonet carefully in a cloth of some kind? There might be fingerprints on the grip. If so, we shouldn't mess them up."

Lester Graves frowned as though offended by the suggestion, but shrugged and turned to the storekeeper once again. "Stef, you must have something we can use to wrap the body. And maybe a couple of towels to wrap the bayonet. Go fetch them, will you?" He blinked at the man's show of reluctance. "Oh hell! I'll find some way to get you paid for the material."

At that remark Spence looked from the storekeeper to Graves and shook his head. "Don't worry about the cost, Lester." He turned to Stef. "Just put the amount on my father's bill. We'll take care of it. After all, the man was a family guest."

As Steiner hustled back up the street toward the general store, Sheriff Graves pointed at two of the younger men. "How about you, Arch? And you, Clem? When Stef gets back with the cloth, help me get this guy wrapped. Then we can load him up." He waved a hand in a dismissive manner and growled, "Why don't the rest of you go on about your business? There ain't going to be any more excitement here today."

The onlookers began to drift away, most after taking a last glance at what was left of a once vital and handsome young man. Spence watched them go before turning to the sheriff. He spoke with some hesitation, "I'm sure you'll want to question Olive Breen to find out what she can tell you. After all, she was the one who found the body."

"Yup. I'll go see her as soon as we get your sister's friend to Harlo. And I'll talk to any of the others here in town who may know something—starting with Lippy Lippencott."

"And I suppose you'll be looking carefully at the area around the boardwalk for anything that might help in learning who did this?

"Of course, dammit! I don't need you telling me how to do my job."

"Didn't mean to intrude, Sheriff. And I'll get out of your way." He paused in thought. "While you're doing that, I may as well go back to Harlo. Shall I report what we've seen to the county attorney? He may want to take a look at the body before Doc Scanlan starts to work on it." When Graves nodded his assent, Spence continued, "And I'll tell Doc what's happened so he can be ready."

Spencer touched Merci on the arm. "Do Dad and Mom know about this?"

"No, they don't know." Merci grasped Spence's sleeve once again. "They don't know because I couldn't understand the storekeeper when he called. The morning dew was on the phone line. Stef's voice was garbled. I just understood him say that something was wrong with Arnold."

Spence seemed to suddenly notice her trembling. "My God, you're freezing." Spence hoisted her coat from the body, helped her shed his coat, and held hers as she slipped her arms into the sleeves.

She shrugged once to settle the coat. "I'll head back to the ranch right now." Merci Bruce took a deep breath as a look of resolve settled over her face "Whoever did this is going to pay!"

Merci turned to walk to her car. As she reached for the door handle she saw Sheriff Graves struggle mightily to pull the bayonet from the body. Once it was free the law officer stared for a moment at the end of the blade. Finally, he shoved his hat onto the back of his head and exclaimed, "Well, I'll be damned. The tip's broken off."

Spence murmured, "That bayonet belongs to Nate Hamilton."

Merci climbed into the Packard, backed it away from the storefront to turn around in the street and head south up the hill, then west for the Bruce Ranch. Her mind was flooded with remembrances of the mechanic she'd brought to Montana—only so someone could murder him. The tears flowed without stop.

4 Merci crumpled in the center of the davenport and huddled next to her mother who held her close. From time to time she offered a handkerchief so Merci could wipe at the tears that flowed without apparent end. Her father, T. C. Bruce, six feet tall, slender of build, and graying at the temples, sat quietly on her other side with an arm resting on the back of the couch behind her. When at last the tears began to diminish, T. C. asked, "How was it done?'

Merci crumpled down even farther. "You mean, how was he killed?" She stared at the floor before answering. "There was a bayonet stuck clear through his body." Then she slumped forward, elbows on her knees, hands covering her face as she broke into great racking sobs.

Felicity quickly gathered her daughter into her arms. Slowly, she began to rock from side to side, rather like she had done when holding Merci as a small child. The grief stricken young woman turned her head to bury her face against Felicity's shoulder, her whole body shaking as the sobs intensified.

T. C., a deep frown on his face, elbows now on his knees, leaned to the side as though wanting to get closer to the stricken girl but reluctant to do so.

After a long couple of minutes the tears subsided. Merci straightened and wiped her face with the handkerchief. While continuing to look at the floor rather than at her parents, she moaned, "It's my fault."

"Your fault? Why your fault?" T. C. straightened as he asked.

"Someone must have thought Arnold and I were more than just friends. Some man who thinks of me in a romantic way. That has to be what the death note meant."

Felicity thought for a moment. Her voice had a tentative tone when she asked, "Did you have a romantic attachment to Arnold?"

Merci pushed herself upright, wiped an eye with the back of her hand and frowned. "No, Mom. He was just the guy who could put the Jenny together. That's why I asked him to come to Montana." She snuffled. "And he was a nice person—always smiling—fun to be around.

T. C. sat even more erect with his hands now resting on his thighs. "Is there any man who has a serious interest in you and might be angry at the attention you've given to Arnold? Any fellow who might believe your feelings for Arnold are romantic?"

Merci turned to look her father right in the eye. "Daddy, I haven't given any man that impression. I've never met one that I thought deserved it." Her look softened. "Maybe it's because you've spoiled me. I've never met a man with your qualities."

T. C.'s embarrassment was apparent for only a flash as he exclaimed, "Nonsense!" The embarrassment turned to a smile. "But thank you for the compliment."

Felicity cast an eye at her husband, then turned back to Merci. "We know that Lyndon Morgan thinks you're something special."

"Mother, Lyndon's just a child.

"He's a year older than you are."

"Well, he just seems so young." She shook her head. "Romantic interest in Lyndon? Not a chance."

T. C. shifted in the chair. "You may not have had any romantic feeling for Arnold, but did Arnold have a romantic attachment to you?"

The young woman shook her head. "No, he was just a friend." Again, she rubbed at her eyes with the hankie. "He never once gave any indication that he was interested in me in that way." A glimpse of a wry smile crossed her face. "Maybe I should have been offended that he didn't find me attractive."

T. C. reached over to pat her knee. "You're very attractive, child. That has never been in doubt. We know of several young men who've exhibited an interest in you. Is there any one of them you might have encouraged and who might feel that Arnold was a threat?" He paused. "Perhaps Nate Hamilton? We know that he once suggested you two should marry."

Merci shook her head. "That was in a letter that he wrote from the battlefront in France during the war. I'm sure lots of men did something like that at the time." She shook her head again. "He seemed kind of embarrassed after he came home." She turned to her mother. "Nate's good-looking, and he has a pleasant personality. We went to the Two Dot School together. Yes, I went to a couple of dances with him. And we've done other things—almost always with others—a group thing. None of it means there's anything between us other than friendship."

Felicity frowned. "You may believe that's the case, but Nate has made it plain that he has other ideas about you."

"Mother, he's just a friend."

Felicity shifted on the davenport to more directly face her daughter. "Tell us. What happened in town last night?"

Merci looked down at her hands as she rubbed them gently together. "Well, you know that I wanted to celebrate my successful first flight or at least talk about it with some friends." She straightened, thrust out her chin, and a flash of grin replaced the frown. "I did it. I got that airplane into this thin Montana air and landed it here at the ranch." Merci cast a look from one to the other of her parents and added, "And

I'm proud of myself!" Then, sober faced again, Merci continued. "Well, when I got to town I dropped your letter at the post office. Some girls were at Olive's café so I visited with them for a while. Since I was there and it was getting along to suppertime, I ordered a meal." She chuckled. "It was about as good at Olive's food always is." Serious once more, she added, "For some reason a crowd had gathered at Lippy's place. You know how it is. Since prohibition came along, Lippy's doesn't call his joint a saloon any more. He calls it a cafe. He serves candy bars, crackers—other stuff like that—and soft drinks in the front. But he pours out liquor in the part of the back that's partitioned off. There seemed to be a lot of the stuff he calls whiskey going out the back door."

Felicity interrupted to ask T. C., "If that man Lippencott is breaking the law by selling alcohol, why hasn't the sheriff done something about it?"

"It's a federal law. I imagine that one of these days some revenue agents will appear and shut Lippy down."

"I wish it was sooner rather than later."

When her mother scowled in silence after making that pronouncement, Merci resumed. "Anyway, the crowd got so big that most of us were outside. Some of the men hauled Lippy's old piano out to the street, and a man I've never seen before began to play dance music. In a few minutes some guy with an accordion joined him. The music was really good. They played all of the popular tunes—*Dardenella, A Pretty Girl is like a Melody, Mandy.* They even played Paul Whiteman's *Whispering.* It's his latest. Someone began to dance and before long we were all doing it—right there in the street. There were more men than women in the crowd so I was kept busy. I danced with Nate twice." She glanced at her mother. "And with Arnold a couple of times. I even danced with Lyndon Morgan once." She paused as she remembered. "We were all just having fun."

T. C. asked, "Did you notice anyone quarreling with Arnold?"

"No. Arnold'd had some of Lippy's liquor, and he was all smiles." She thought for a moment. "As usual, when the boys have been drinking that stuff, there was some shouting and cussing and some shoving, but no real fights that I'm aware of." She thought some more. "Of course, there could have been fights out back. I didn't go back there."

Felicity asked, "What was Arnold doing when you left? Did he go to his room in the hotel?"

"No. About eleven o'clock the wind came up and it got real cold. I was ready to leave anyway so I grabbed Arnold and told him I was leaving. He'd been dancing with Irma Lewellyn and said he wanted to dance some more. I was kind of worried because it was apparent that he'd had a lot of Lippy's hooch, so I asked if he was sure he could make it to the hotel by himself. He just grinned and said he'd be fine. Then he grabbed Irma for another dance." Merci's face was red and blotched from all the crying. Now some more tears appeared. She shook her head. "I left just left him there. And someone killed him."

Felicity wrapped an arm about Merci again. "It isn't your fault, child. Arnold Masters was a grown man. He could do what he wanted."

"I know, Mom. But if I'd insisted he go to the hotel—made sure he went to bed, this wouldn't have happened. He'd still be alive."

"If. If. If. If won't change anything."

T. C. leaned forward again. "You may not be the one."

Merci's eyebrows went up. "One what?"

"The one the printing on that piece of cardboard refers to. The words 'She's mine.'"

Merci frowned. "But who else? Everyone knows that I brought Arnold to Montana."

"You said he danced with Irma Lewellyn more than once. Maybe some sport has his eye on her."

"I didn't think of that." Merci leaned against the back of the davenport. Her face brightened. "Maybe it isn't my fault after all."

T. C. rubbed at his cheek, rose, and began to pace. At last he looked at his daughter. "I really hate to mention this, but the sheriff or the county attorney may make the same assumption that we did and think the message was about you. If so, they'll want to ask questions of you. When they do, it's important that you tell the exact truth—as I'm certain you will. But it's also important that you try to remember everything that could have any bearing on this terrible thing that happened. That applies not only to last night's events, but to anything else that might be helpful to the authorities."

"I understand. When will they want to do it?"

"If you feel up to it, we could drive into Harlo today."

Merci was on her feet. "I'd hoped to fly again today." There was a long pause as she glanced out the window. "But the wind has come up and Arnold won't be here to pull the prop." She wiped at her eyes once again before nodding her head. "I'm up to it, Dad. I'll get dressed. Let's get it over with."

T. C. looked down. He had on the denim pants and flannel shirt worn by most ranchers. "I should put on some cleaner clothes, too."

Felicity Bruce was younger and much shorter than her husband. Her hair remained the caramel color of her youth. Now, however, she was forced to use spectacles to see clearly. Today she wore the usual flowered cotton dress that she favored in the summer months. She grabbed at the skirt. "And this dress will never do to wear to town."

5 The original roadway that soon came to be called Main Street ran along a flat stretch of land overlooking the river. The transcontinental Milwaukee Railroad reached Harlowton in 1907. Its tracks ran east and west along the river bottom below the bluff upon which the original buildings of Harlowton were constructed. A roadway, north and south and perpendicular to Main Street, soon developed. It led southward from the original town on the bluff site to the railroad depot near the river. That street, called Central Avenue, became the town's principal business thoroughfare.

The two-story sandstone courthouse was located at the corner of Main and Central. First a bank, it was one of the original buildings bordering on Main Street. The other buildings along that street included some residences, a general store, and the Catholic Church. The Weber Arms, the first hotel in town, was across the street and to the east of the courthouse.

Many of the business buildings along Central Avenue were constructed from sandstone that was quarried from the bluff that underlay the town. Among them were the Graves Hotel, the Times Block, two banks, and a couple of mercantile establishments. The other business and professional establishments, including the one that housed the law office of Spencer L. Bruce, were of wood construction.

Spencer, back in Harlowton, hiked the three blocks up Central

Avenue from his office to the courthouse, hunched against the cold wind. Time to discuss the death of Arnold Masters with the county attorney.

Roger Davidson was forty-five years old. He was tall, slight of frame, balding, and walked with a perpetual slouch. In the hallway on the ground floor of the courthouse he offered Spence the customary lawyer-to-lawyer handshake, then waved his caller in to his private office. When both were seated, he listened to Spence spill out the tale of the body on the boardwalk. Davidson leaned back with his hands behind his head. "A bayonet, you say? A German bayonet?"

"That's what it was. Took a heck of a thrust to put it all the way through his body and into the planks underneath."

"Nothing a woman could do?"

"Not a chance. Had to be someone with considerable strength. But there are lots of men around here that could do it."

Davidson raised his eyebrows as he asked, "And the note? It just read, 'SHE'S MINE'?"

"That's right. In capital letters. Crude printing. Nothing else."

"Who's the 'she' do you suppose?"

Spence shifted around to cross his legs. "The note would seem to indicate that someone killed Arnold because of a woman—a woman the killer thinks is his." He leaned his elbow on the desk and looked at the county attorney out of the corner of his eye. "You're wondering the same thing that I am, aren't you? Does that note refer to Merci?"

"Seems logical, doesn't it? Masters came here with your sister and her flying machine. He hasn't been here long enough to get well acquainted with any of other the local gals. Everyone in the community knows that he and Merci spent time together in California while she was learning to fly. And I hear they've been together almost constantly while they were reassembling that Jenny."

Spence leaned back and stretched his legs. "It does seem likely that the killer meant Merci."

Davidson mimicked Spence by stretching out, still with his hands grasped behind his head. "Which of the local gents have shown an interest in Merci?"

"Oh shucks, Rog. There's been lots of them over the years." He grinned at the thought. "You know my sister. She's about as attractive as any girl can be. She's personable and witty and vivacious. Ever since she was about sixteen, there have been boys mooning over her."

"But anyone more serious than others?"

"Not that I can recall." Spencer rubbed his hand along his jaw. "Well, there's Lyndon, of course. Lyndon Morgan. Hiram Morgan's son. Ever since he came to work at the ranch it's been obvious that he's attracted to her. But I'm not sure she even realizes it. And I don't think he's ever spoken to her except about ranch matters."

"Who else?"

"Maybe Nate Hamilton. Merci went to a couple of dances with him last summer." After a second of reflection, he added, "But it never seemed to be something serious, at least with Merci." Spence chuckled. "She never says much to me about such things, but she confides in our mother. If Merci ever had serious feelings for any man, Mother would know."

"Nate reputedly has a temper. He's supposed to have whipped on a horse at the Mathers' branding a couple of weeks ago. Harley's wife saw it and wanted me to charge him with cruelty."

Spence cocked his head. "If every cowpoke that whipped on a horse is charged with cruelty, the jail would be full, and there wouldn't be anybody to work the cattle. Whipping on a horse and running a bayonet through a human being are totally different. Hard to think that one of our ranch neighbors could do such a thing."

"Well, maybe the note isn't about Merci at all. Maybe your California friend smiled at another of the local belles, and her boyfriend took exception."

"I certainly hope so. Merci will hate the thought that she's the reason Arnold was killed."

"So the killing apparently happened after a party that night. It would be helpful to know the names of other single women who were there. The sheriff should begin gathering those names promptly. Soon enough people will become forgetful. I'll mention that to him first thing."

"Good thought. I wonder if there were any confrontations last night between Masters and someone else over a girl."

"I'll mention that to the sheriff, too." The county attorney squared himself around and leaned his elbows on the desk. "There's always the possibility, I suppose, that the note was a ruse. Suppose someone killed that man for another reason and wanted to lead us astray."

"What could that reason be?"

"Have no idea. It's just a thought."

Spence started to rise but then sat back. "The sheriff will bring the bayonet and the note to your office when he gets back to Harlo."

"Good. I'll need to discuss the notion of a chain of custody with Lester. That will be something new to him. And if this matter results in a trial, I don't want any technical problems."

Spence hesitated, then asked, "What about fingerprints? Maybe some will show on the weapon."

"The sheriff in Lewistown is supposed to have a deputy who can dust for prints. We can call him for help if the need arises. But even if prints are found, they won't do us any good until we have some others to compare. I can't go around the county asking every big burly man for a fingerprint sample, hoping to get lucky."

"No. But if you get some other leads, the prints might be the thing that results in a conviction."

"Have you figured out how the killer persuaded Arnold Masters to lie still on the boardwalk and wait for that bayonet to be rammed through his middle?" When Spence didn't respond, he continued. "It seems to me that Arnold must have been killed somewhere else, hauled to the boardwalk and dumped."

"Why would anyone do that?"

Davidson rose from his chair. "Who knows?" Near the door he grasped Spence's hand again. "Well, I'll go over to Doc Scanlan's office and take a gander at the body after Lester Graves gets here and before Doc starts his work. Don't know what good it will do for me to look, but I'll do it. Maybe Doc can tell us something of importance after he finishes. Let's hope so."

As he jogged down the courthouse steps, Spence thought, "We've got to get word to Masters' family. I hope Merci knows where to send the wire."

6 Spence's law office was on the ground floor of a two-story building located on west side of Central Avenue. On the window facing the street were large black letters trimmed in gold that read, "Spencer L. Bruce, Attorney At Law." Entry was to an open reception area with chairs for waiting clients and a desk for Helen, his secretary. A short hallway led to a larger room in the rear that served as a conference room. His private office was on one side of the hallway.

After an early noonday meal at Mother's Cafe, the young lawyer, back in his office and deep in thought, tapped his index finger on the desk as he pondered. Arnold Masters arrived in Two Dot with Merci, both of them having traveled on the train from California. Masters first stayed at the Bruce Ranch while waiting for the freight car to arrive with the disassembled Jenny. Then, after two days, he'd become uncomfortable as a guest, worried about taking up the time of the Bruce family. He moved to a room at the Hopkins Hotel in Two Dot to be closer to his work when the aircraft arrived, ten days later.

Arnold was outgoing, friendly, full of humor, and patient with Merci's demands while they were assembling the Jenny. Hard to believe that anyone would want him dead. Spence's mind turned to circumstances of the murder. Most certainly, the killer was someone from the local community, especially if Merci was the object of that person's obsession. With Merci's cooperation, it should be possible to narrow the number to a very few. It would probably be wise to have a family discussion about the possibilities before the sheriff or county attorney arranged to interview her. Tonight, perhaps. For now, he had legal work to do. Spence grasped the rough draft of a business contract that his secretary had typed. He needed to make corrections so she could put it in final form. He'd drive to the ranch for supper.

The phone rang. Spence lifted the receiver from the phone hanging on the wall. The operator said, "Your father's on the phone, Spence. I'll connect you." Apparently, the dew that had partially grounded the phone line from the ranch to Two Dot had burned off.

His father's voice came through clearly. "The sheriff will want to interview Merci. She'd like to get it over with. We'll leave for town shortly. Could you arrange for the sheriff to come to your office to visit with her?"

"Of course, Dad. I'm certain he'll do it if he's back in town. He was going to talk with some of the people in Two Dot to try to learn more about Masters' activities. He should be here by midafternoon." Spence quickly added, "The county attorney may want to be here. I'll let them both know."

"We should arrive about two o'clock. Let's talk this over before the sheriff arrives. Will you ask the sheriff and county attorney to meet us at three?"

"Sounds good. I'll call the sheriff's office right now and ask his clerk to let Graves know. And I'll call Davidson, too."

His secretary, Helen, was a recent high school graduate. She stepped from the reception area to the door of his private office to announce, "The judge will be in town from White Sulphur Springs today, and you have a hearing to prove the Harrington will. It's scheduled for one o'clock, and it's well past noon." She pushed away from the door jamb and announced, "I'm going to get some lunch."

She was right, of course. He had to drive to the Harrington house, gather up Mrs. Harrington, and take her to the courthouse. She was old and moved very slowly. He would be lucky to get her to the courthouse on time. Thank goodness he'd eaten early.

Spence was barely settled in his chair after returning from the court hearing when Helen poked her head in the door again. "There's a woman here to see you. I don't know her name. And she didn't say what her problem is."

"Well, let's see what she wants." He stepped out to the reception area to find a tall, well-dressed young lady standing quietly near the window. He extended his hand. "I'm Spencer Bruce. May I help you?"

Her grip was firm, and her smile was pleasant. "May I speak to you in your office, please?"

He returned the smile, gestured to the door, and held a chair for her. Seated in his own chair, he leaned forward with his elbows on the desk top to ask again, "What can I do to help you, Ma'am?"

The woman glanced over her shoulder at the door that was not fully closed. Spence rose and pushed the door until the latch clicked. Back in his place, he resumed his pose and scrutinized his visitor while he waited for her to speak. The clothing she wore was of the finest quality and in colors that complemented her dark hair and deep brown eyes. She wore a cloche hat of the kind that was becoming more and more popular. She was very nice to look at if not a classic beauty.

The woman inhaled and said, "My name is Eunice Syvertson. I arrived in your town yesterday."

Spence smiled. "I'm pleased to make your acquaintance. And, as I said, I'm Spencer Bruce, and I'm a lawyer. You must have a reason to visit with an attorney or you wouldn't be here in my office."

Miss Syvertson seemed to gather her resolve and straightened in the chair. "I don't have a legal problem. I just need some advice." She paused. "You see, my father was a lawyer, and he helped people in ways other than taking them to court."

"He must have been a good man."

"Indeed he was, but he died much too young."

"I'm sorry." Spence leaned farther forward. "Is his death the matter about which you need advice?"

"No. No, not that. He died some time ago." She pulled her purse closer on her lap. "Your Doctor Scanlan advertised for a nurse, and I may apply for the position." When she spoke next it was in a rush. "I need to know something about him before I apply. My father always told me the lawyers in any town know everything about everybody. So here I am—to ask what you can tell me about Doctor Scanlan."

Spence leaned back in his chair and nodded. "Well, Doc lost the woman who was his nurse not long ago. She ran off and got married. I know he needs help."

"But that's not what I'm asking. What kind of man is he?"

"Doc's a good man, well regarded here in Harlo."

Miss Syvertson dropped her eyes to her hands, fidgeted with her purse again, and then looked up to say, "I worked for a doctor in Missoula. He made a serious mistake with a patient, and the patient died." She paused. "When the patient's husband accosted him about the mistake, he blamed it on me." She looked down at her hands again and murmured. "And I wasn't even there when it happened."

The smile had faded from Spence's face. "So you want to know if Doc Scanlan is the kind who will pull something like that."

She nodded. "Exactly. That's what I need to know. I don't ever want that to happen to me again."

"Miss Syvertson, I've known our doctor since I was a child. He's as honest and straightforward as anyone can be. I suppose he's made some mistakes along the way. Who hasn't? But I'm confident he would never try to dump the blame on another person." After a moment's thought, he added, "And I'm sure anyone else in town would tell you the same thing."

The lady across the desk breathed a sigh. "That's reassuring to hear. It was a long train ride from Missoula, and I'm not anxious to get on the train to go back." She scooted forward in the chair and said, "Assuming the doctor will hire me, I will need a place to live. Is there a rooming house for women in this town?"

"Mrs. Gilfeather has a big house on Mill Hill, and she takes in roomers. She's rather selective, but I believe she would accept you. Shall I call her to ask if she has a room available?" Before Miss Syvertson could respond, he added, "She can be kind of crotchety, sometimes but she's good hearted, none the less."

"Yes, please. Call and tell her I'll be there directly for an interview, if that's what she requires."

Spence placed the call, described the nurse in complimentary terms, and made the arrangements for Miss Syvertson to meet with Mrs. Gilfeather. At the door she extended her hand again, offered her thanks, and smiled the warmest of smiles. "Mr. Bruce, I'm sure we will be seeing one another again."

"It's a small town. And another meeting will be my pleasure."

Back at his desk, Spence thought of Doctor Scanlan's reputation as something of a rake. *Perhaps I should have told her. No. I think it's just town gossip without any basis in fact.* Another thought crowded out anything more of the doctor. *Eunice Syvertson was quite attractive. Perhaps he could invite her to dinner some evening.*

"The man was garroted. That, not the bayonet, is what killed him." The doctor pulled the collar away from the neck of the deceased. He poked with a probe at the dead flesh. "Look here at the discolored area. You can see where the rope encircled his throat."

County Attorney Davidson was determined not to let his squeamish stomach force him to leave the room, but his breathing was shallow and his face was pale

Doctor Scanlan continued. "It appears from those marks that the rope was small in diameter—about like a lariat."

Spence wasn't quite as disturbed as Davidson seemed to be by the doctor's probing. "Wasn't a lariat. Or at least not one made of sisal or hemp. Any kind of grass rope would have left scratches from the bristles. Could have been braided rawhide, I suppose, but I'd bet it was a plain old cotton rope. You know, the kind we sometimes use to tie up bundles or boxes or use for a clothesline." Spence backed away from the corpse as he muttered, "To do this, someone had to sneak up on Masters and catch him from behind."

Doc Scanlan nodded. "Must have—unless there were two of them in on the killing. I suppose one could have held him while the other wrapped the rope around his neck and hauled on the ends."

"Unless he was unconscious first." The county attorney stopped to think. "Maybe the killer whacked him and then did this to him while he was lying on the ground."

The doctor shook his head. "Not likely. I don't see any bruises that appear to have come from a blow. There's dirt and debris on the back of his clothing and some evidence of scratches and scuff marks on the heels of his shoes. Makes me think the killer dragged the body from the place where the garroting took place to where Olive Breen found it."

Davidson crossed his arms as he asked, "Why the bayonet if the man was already dead?"

"Only the killer knows. Perhaps to send a message of some kind." The doctor moved to open the door. "I've got patients to care for right now. I'll do a better job on the body later and give you a written report." Before they could leave, he offered one more comment. "It isn't easy to garrote a man. Whoever did this had to be mighty strong—or so possessed by rage as to have uncommon strength."

T. C., Felicity, and Merci arrived at Spence's office shortly before three o'clock. Merci wore a fawn colored skirt of the latest fashion. It hugged her legs, and was hemmed at the ankles. A darker brown, tailored jacket complemented the skirt. Felicity, however, wore the conservative pre-war attire. The full skirt of her dark colored dress brushed the floor, and a broad brimmed hat covered her head.

The group was barely settled before Helen brought the sheriff and county attorney to the conference room. When they were gathered around the oval-shaped table, Lester Graves leaned forward with his hands on his knees, glanced at the county attorney, and announced, "There wasn't any blood on the boardwalk or under it. That man must've been killed somewhere else and dumped there." His voice had its usual rasping sound, as though he had a bad cold. "I talked to as many of the town folks as I could find, and no one saw or heard any-thing out of the ordinary—once last night's party broke up and the partiers either pulled out of town or went to bed." He leaned back and scratched at his bald spot.

Roger Davidson straightened from his slouch. "I can explain the lack of blood. That man wasn't killed by the bayonet. He was garroted. Doc Scanlan showed the marks to Spence and me."

"Garroted?" T. C.'s voice betrayed his incredulousness.

"That's what Doc said. Someone wrapped a length of something—probably a narrow rope—around his neck and choked him until he died." The county attorney paused briefly. "Took a person with some strength to do it."

Merci felt the tears begin again. "How could anyone do that to Arnold? He was a gentle person. The Arnold I knew would never do anything to offend anybody."

T. C. scowled. "I'm sorry you had to hear this, sweetheart." Turning to Felicity, he said, "Maybe you and Merci should leave for a while. Go to Spence's house. We can call you if you're needed."

Merci dabbed at her eyes with a handkerchief and shook her head. "No, I'll stay. And I'll answer any questions that Mr. Davidson and Sheriff Graves may have. It might help them find the one who's re-sponsible."

"Are you sure you're up to it?"

"Yes, Daddy. I'm sure." Her voice was hoarse, though, as she asked of the sheriff, "What about the bayonet?"

"That bayonet has a broken tip." When none of the others re-sponded, he quickly added, "I asked Lippy Lippincott, the barkeep, about it, and he said it belongs to Nate Hamilton." The sheriff shifted in his chair and leaned his elbows on the table top. "Lippy has some souvenirs hanging in his saloon—things the boys brought home from

France after the war. Kind of a souvenir wall, I guess. I'm sure you've seen it." Graves paused. "Lippy calls that place a club now, but it's still the same old saloon." Then, in his gravelly voice, he continued. "Some of the things hanging on the wall are American—pieces of uniform, a gas mask. Some of them are English. Some French. And some are German." The sheriff glanced from one to the next of those in the room. "Lippy said Nate thought there should be a bayonet among the stuff. He offered the one with the broken tip to be used as one of the wall decorations."

Roger Davidson broke in to say, "The sheriff showed the bayonet to me. The extreme tip of the blade has been broken for some time. It didn't happen when it was jabbed through that man's body. There was rust in the break."

Graves nodded his agreement before continuing his monologue. "I asked around about the things that happened at that party last night." Turning to Merci, he said, "It seems that Nate Hamilton took umbrage when your friend Arnold Masters danced with you. He did a lot of grumbling to those leaning with him against the front wall of the saloon."

"Maybe so." Merci nodded. "But that's just Nate. It doesn't mean a thing."

The sheriff looked at her out of the corner of his eye, "Perhaps. But then Nate really became angry when Masters danced with a woman named Irma Lewellyn too many times." Looking around at the others in the room, he added, "He grabbed Masters by the coat sleeve and hollered at him to leave Irma alone." Graves paused for effect. "I guess Masters just jerked away and laughed at him. Nate doubled up his fists and started to go for Masters, but a couple of the other sports grabbed him and pulled him away."

When the sheriff leaned back to indicate he was finished with his report, Spence asked, "Was that the end of it?"

"Yes. Lippy said that Nate just sat alone out in the back for a while after that."

"Then what?"

"Well, according to Lippy and a few of the other people who were there, Masters and Irma disappeared. No one seemed to know where they ended up, but they disappeared out back of the saloon. No one saw either one of them again that night." Graves took a breath. "I took it from what the barkeep said that most of the gang had left and the party was coming to an end, anyway."

Spence waited, but Graves didn't offer more, so he asked, "What about Nate?"

"Not sure. Lippy thinks he disappeared about the same time as Masters and Irma, but he can't swear to it. None of the others I talked to knew just what time Hamilton left the place. But they all thought it was about the time Irma and Masters went out back."

Sheriff Graves shoved his chair back, crossed his legs, and folded his hands on his belly as though he had no more to offer. The others sat silently for a second while absorbing the things he'd said. At last Spence asked, "How could Lippy know who was coming and going when he was busy tending bar?"

"Don't know. Maybe he was relying on things other people told him."

"Not very reliable information, then."

The sheriff sighed. "Perhaps. I'll find out as fast as I can."

"Where's Nate Hamilton now?

Graves shook his head. "Probably at the Hamilton ranch. I tried to call but their phone's not working. I'll drive up there first thing in the morning to find him." He turned to Merci. "But first I want to hear what you can tell me about last night's party, Ma'am."

Merci shifted around in the chair, looked toward Felicity as though for reassurance. "Well, as I told my parents, it was just a lot of people having fun. There was a piano and an accordion making music and we were dancing in the street. I danced with Arnold a couple of times. But I danced with some others, too. I even danced with Nate more than once. As I said, we were just having fun." She paused for a moment in thought. "Arnold was dancing with Irma when I left. But Irma had danced with lots of guys. I saw her dancing with Lyndon Morgan once."

The county attorney asked, "Did you see the quarrel between Hamilton and Masters?"

"No. But I think old Lippy may have been exaggerating about Nate. He's more bark than bite. Whenever I happened to spot him he was just like the rest of us—having a good time."

T. C. Bruce frowned as he said, "I don't know Irma Lewellyn." Turning to Merci he asked, "Who is she?"

"She waits table at the cafe in Two Dot. Irma's about my age. She's a big girl. Nice looking and friendly."

Spence nodded and added, "Her folks had a homestead north of Two Dot, but they dried out and gave it up. I think they went back to the Midwest where they came from. Irma had married Luke Lewellyn by that time and went with him to Livingston where he had a job."

The sheriff said, "Luke is a worthless drunk."

Spence said, "I guess Irma decided the same thing because she divorced him and came back here and got the job at the restaurant. I think she rents a room with Mrs. Porter, the woman with the little house over by the Two Dot School."

Roger Davidson leaned his elbows on the table, looked from one to the other of the group, and finally focused on Merci. "I've thought the note found on Masters' body referred to you, Miss Bruce. Now it appears the note may have referred to Irma Lewellyn." He leaned back again in the chair. "If that's the case, it may have been Nate was saying 'SHE'S MINE' about Mrs. Lewellyn." To the group in general he asked, "Could Nate Hamilton be our killer?"

Merci shook her head. "No, Mr. Davidson. Nate's got a temper, but he really isn't a bad person. He couldn't choke a man to death the way you've described it." She looked down at her hands and frowned in thought. Then she shook her head even more vigorously. "He just couldn't." She turned to the sheriff. "Who else did Lippy say might have been angry at Arnold?"

"No one."

"But Lippy wasn't out on the street much of the time. A lot could have happened that he didn't know about."

"I suppose." Sheriff Graves scratched at his head. "What about you? Did you see anything that might help us find the killer?"

"No, Sheriff. Like I said, I spent most of my time dancing and visiting. I didn't pay much attention to what others were doing."

Graves pushed away from the table and stood. "Well, it's getting too late in the day to drive to the Hamilton ranch, but tomorrow I'll talk to Nate. He seems like the one most likely to have done the deed. I'll visit with Irma Lewellyn, too. And try to learn more from Lippy and some of the others who were at the party." He looked down at Merci. "You'll be around won't you, Miss Bruce? We may need to talk again."

"Yes, of course. I'll be at the ranch. I hope to fly on the nice days and may take the Jenny to Lewistown for some barnstorming. You know—do some stunts—sell some rides. But Dad and Spence will always know where I am."

T. C.'s head jerked up. "I know you want to continue to fly that blasted machine, but who will help you? Arnold Masters was the one who pulled the propeller to start the motor, wasn't he? He's gone!"

"I've been thinking about it. I can show Lyndon how it's done—

Lyndon Morgan. He can do it at the ranch. I'll have to figure out a way to handle it when I'm not at the ranch."

The distress felt by Felicity at the thought of her daughter risking her life by flying to places far away showed on her face. She put her arm across the back of Merci's chair, but she remained silent about her feelings. She and Merci would discuss such things later.

The sheriff stood and scratched at his head once more as though the scratching might help him think. After looking once again at Merci, he said, "If we're done here, I'll be on my way. Somebody's dog chewed up Mrs. Swallow's cat, and she's on the fight. I have to go see about it." He turned toward the door, stopped, and said over his shoulder, "Dead cats are important stuff. Know what I mean?" Graves slammed his hat on his head and was gone.

The county attorney wasn't finished. "Miss Bruce, what other young women were at the party?"

"There were several besides Irma and me. Barbara Pennington was there. You know; her dad works for the Wilsons on their ranch up near Martinsdale. I don't know how she got to the party. Maybe she rode the train down and planned to spend the night with the Richards. She and Sue Richards are friends. Sue was at the party too."

"Who else?"

"Let's see. Evelyn somebody. I don't know her last name. Someone said her folks have a homestead northwest of town." Merci pondered. "There were two other young women that I didn't know. And three or four older women were there, some married, some not. They were just like the rest—dancing and enjoying themselves."

"Did any of the men seem to be particularly interested in any one of the women? A woman who might have danced with Arnold Masters one time too many?"

"I don't know, Mr. Davidson. The music was great, so like everyone else, I was just too busy having a good time to worry about such things."

Davidson stood and smiled at Merci. "I know this has been hard for you. I appreciate your willingness to cooperate." He shifted his stance. "If you think of any other women who were there, please let me know their names. The sheriff will be gathering the names of the men." With a nod to the others, who were also on their feet, he ambled out the door.

As he held the coat for his mother, Spence looked across her shoulder at Merci. "Do you know how to contact Arnold's family? They need to be told what happened."

"I believe his parents live in Oregon." Merci thought. "I guess the best thing is to send a telegram to the manager of the flying field and ask him."

"If you'll write his name and location on this tablet for me, I'll send the wire."

Tears welled up again in Merci's eyes. "His family will blame it all on me."

8

The next day it rained. T. C. reminded Merci that she should expect it. June was the rainy month in Montana. Frustrated by the weather that kept her from flying, Merci paced the floor. At last she turned to her mother and asked, "Where's Dad?"

"Off with the men somewhere."

"Do you think he'd mind if I took the Runabout and drove to Two Dot? I could bring back the mail."

"The mail can wait—unless there's some other reason you want to go."

"There is, Mom." Merci hesitated. "I think I'll talk to Irma Lewellyn. Maybe she can tell me something that will lead to the one who killed Arnold."

"The sheriff will talk to her, I'm sure."

"But he's the sheriff, and he's a man. I'll bet she'd talk more freely to me than to him."

"It can't hurt to talk to her, I guess. Your father won't mind if you use the car. Be careful. The road will be muddy. Just don't get stuck."

Ford Motor Company produced a variety of automobiles. Among them was a high-wheeled, two-seated Model T called a Runabout. It had a fold-down windshield and a fold-down top. Today, both the windshield and top were in place to provide shelter from the rain. Merci set the spark and cranked the motor. She climbed behind the steering wheel and splashed her way the five miles over the muddy dirt road to town.

Olive Breen's café was in a low, frame building across from the hardware store. A counter with stools in front ran along one side. The rest of the room was occupied by tables with chairs pushed next to them. The kitchen was in the back. At ten o'clock in the morning the place was empty of customers.

Irma sat on one of the stools, smoking a cigarette, and reading a dime novel when Merci walked in the door. She stubbed out the cigarette and stepped around behind the counter where she dropped the book onto the low shelf. When Merci slid onto to a stool she asked, "What'll you have?"

"Just coffee."

Merci watched as the woman pulled a mug off a shelf, wander to the kitchen, and return with the mug full of the black liquid. Irma was a tall woman, about twenty years of age, hair the rust color of barley straw. Her body was large, with broad muscular shoulders, but it was rounded in the all the right places. Her eyes were blue and bright. Most people would call her good looking, perhaps even beautiful. Today, she wore an ink-colored dress with a soiled apron tied about her waist.

After a moment's hesitation Irma took sip from a cup that had been resting on the back counter. Still standing, she shook her head once and said, "It's too bad about your friend. He seemed like a nice guy."

"He was more than that." Merci, hands around the mug, asked, "Tell me what you remember about the party the other night?"

Irma looked across the counter out of the corner of her eye. "What do I remember?"

"I just wonder what happened. What happened at that party so that Arnold Masters ended up dead?"

Irma slid her coffee mug onto the counter and crossed her arms. "Someone stuck him with a bayonet is what I heard."

"But why? Something must have happened—something that made somebody so angry that he killed Arnold."

"It seems plain enough, doesn't it? Whoever did it thought Arnold was getting too close to you." Irma's lip turned up in a sly grin. "Who you been sneaking around with that's got a temper?"

Merci's back stiffened. "I don't sneak around, Irma. And whoever made that placard may have been referring to you—not me."

Irma barked a laugh. "Men don't kill for a homestead girl who lived in a shack with a dirt floor—one that's had a bad marriage and a divorce to boot. Now you—you're different. Your daddy has that big ranch and lots of money. You've flown an airplane." She pronounced it 'air-e-o-plane'. "Men think your kind is something special. Maybe something so special it was worth killing for—if his chances with you looked to be in trouble."

Merci shook her head with vigor. "I've never given any man the impression that I was seriously interested in him." She crossed her arms on the countertop and looked across at the tall woman on the other side. "You danced a lot with Arnold that night. Who would be angry because of that? Who has his eye on you?"

"Who's interested in me?" Irma snickered. "The ranch hands, that's who. And the railroad gandy dancers. Any man who sees a single woman with no prospects and thinks he can get her into bed. That's who's interested in Irma. Even old Lippy. He thinks I may be desperate enough to marry him." She snorted. "But a nice man who could provide me with money and a home? Ain't none. Those guys are all looking at you and other proper girls whose folks have cash in the bank."

"But you and Arnold did dance a lot. Did he keep asking you or did you ask him?"

Irma frowned. "Look, he was a great dancer—the best I've ever met. And he was fun. And he treated me like I was special." She paused for a moment. "So we danced. What difference does it make who asked who?"

"None, I guess. It's just that it seemed out of character for him."

Irma leaned against the back counter. "Maybe you don't know it, but he stopped in here one evening when he first got to town. He ordered a piece of pie and we got to talking. After that when he had time he'd stop in and we'd talk—just talk. He's the first man I've ever met who seemed interested in more than my body." A slight smile touched her lips. "And then at that party we danced. And he held me close. And I begin to think of something more." The smile disappeared and she shrugged. "Foolish me. Even if he hadn't been killed, nothing would have come of it. He couldn't ever be serious about someone with my background."

Merci stared at her. Then she dropped her eyes to her hands and then up again at Irma. "I'm sorry. It never occurred to me that his death would affect you, too." When Irma didn't respond, she asked, "Don't you think we should do whatever we can to find the one who did it?"

"That's the sheriff's job, ain't it?"

"Yes. But maybe we can help." Merci took a breath. "Tell me everything you remember about that night. Who was there? What happened that was out of the ordinary?"

Irma's turn to take a deep breath. "Okay. Who was there. Most of the men were ranch hands. There were a couple of single homesteaders that haven't starved out yet. Nate Hamilton was there. So was his neighbor up the creek—Sam Hopkins. You know Sam. When he got out of high school his folks sent him to college back east somewhere. You can bet he never asked Irma to dance." She thought for a trice. "Hugh Baxter. You know, the homely-faced forty-year-old guy with the ranch up on Daisy Dean Creek. He was there. He's always around whenever there are women to ogle." Irma frowned. "There were girls there beside you and me, but I don't remember who they all were. I know Lucy was there. She works for Mrs. Hopkins. And the daughter of the railroad section foreman. What's her name?"

"Mildred."

"Yes, Mildred was there, trying to catch Nate Hamilton's eye."

Merci remembered the things that Lippy had told the sheriff. "I've heard that Nate got mad at Arnold for dancing with you too much."

"Yes, Nate hollered at Arnold. But, you know Nate. He's got a temper, and when he's drinking he doesn't think straight. But he's really harmless. I doubt that he would have done anything more than holler." She laughed. "Not long after he hollered at Arnold he was laughing and was doing rope tricks—trying to impress Mildred."

"What else do you remember?"

"Well, Nate got that bayonet off the wall and was bragging about how he took it off a German soldier." She snickered again. "I'll bet that German was dead first and Nate just found it."

Merci drained the last of the cold coffee. "Well, none of that tells us who's responsible for Arnold's death, does it?" She stood, dropped twenty-five cents on the counter. "If you think of anything that's different, please share it with me." She smiled. "Apparently, we both thought a lot of Arnold." She stopped at the door and looked out at the rain. It would be a fast run to the car in order to stay dry.

Just as she reached for the doorknob, Irma spoke again. "One more thing. Late, after you'd left, I saw a tall, good-looking man grab Arnold by the arm and say something to him. Arnold just stared at him and shook his head. He pulled away from the guy and walked around to the back of the saloon. I suppose he was going to get another drink of Lippy's booze."

Merci turned in surprise. "Who was it? Who grabbed Arnold? Maybe he was someone angry at Arnold—angry enough to kill him."

"I'd never seen him before, and I didn't see him again that night." Irma chortled. "But, nah, I don't think he was about to kill anyone. He was too good looking, and he was wearing a jacket that said he had money. I'd've asked him to dance but he got away."

"Did he talk to anyone else?"

"I don't know for sure, but I don't think so. He disappeared too quick."

Merci turned back to the door. "I think I'll go see Lippy. Maybe he knows who that man might be."

Irma laughed. "If you really think the note on that cardboard was about me, you should give thought to Lyndon Morgan. He hangs out here whenever he can get away from his mother and from your dad's ranch. He seems to come in here just to watch me. Never says much. Seldom spends a dime. Maybe he's the one who was mad because Arnold and I danced. Maybe he killed Arnold."

"That's crazy. Lyndon couldn't kill anyone. He doesn't have that much gumption."

"Who knows?" She chuckled again. "And while you're looking for someone who might have killed Arnold because of me, don't forget old Lippy. He thinks if he can keep others away long enough, I'll marry him—marry him to have a better place to live or for some other reason. And he has a mean streak about him."

"A mean streak?'

"You bet." Irma eyed Merci for a moment. "You aren't around here all the time like I am. So you haven't seen him beat on someone with that sawed-off pick handle. You know, some drunk who upchucks on the floor. Or tries to start a fight. Or just a drunk who doesn't look right to Lippy. He whaps that drunk alongside the head. And if he gets him on the floor and he's really mad, he works him over with that club some more."

"I didn't know that."

"There's lots about life that you don't know, Missy. Now get out of here before old Olive Breen catches me talking instead of working."

The door was locked at Lippy's saloon, so Merci trudged through the rain back to her car. She'd talk to Lippy Lippencott some other time. Once inside the auto and out of the weather, she thought for a time about the things Irma had said. Nate Hamilton could have been angry because Arnold danced too often with Irma. Lippy might have worried that Arnold would steal Irma away to California. Lyndon apparently had feelings for Irma. Yet it didn't seem that any of them could have been angry enough about Irma's friendship with Arnold do anything so rash. Still, as she started the car, Merci felt it was most likely that the words "SHE'S MINE" referred to Irma and not her. She drove south on the main street of Two Dot with a feeling of relief.

9

The next morning dawned bright and clear. Merci was out of bed at five o'clock and barely touched the breakfast her father cooked and placed before her. Today, she and her Jenny would take to the air from the ranch landing field for the first time. She explained to T. C. that she needed to get Arnold out of her mind—at least for a brief time.

Merci, her father, and Lyndon Morgan rode out to the aircraft hangar in the Model T truck and then struggled to push the Jenny out into the open. Merci fairly bounced in her walk as she strolled around the machine checking to ensure that nothing had been damaged since she left it in the hangar. All the while, T. C. stood to the side and tried to conceal his concern.

At the front of the Jenny, she positioned the propeller. With her hands on her hips and speaking in a stern voice, she gave Lyndon a simple admonition. "Watch." Merci grasped the heavy propeller blade, threw her right leg up and across and then dropped it quickly down and backward while at the same time pulling downward on the prop. Her action moved her body around and away from the place where the propeller would be turning when it was running. After repositioning the propeller, she stepped back and motioned for Lyndon to give it a try. Lyndon was tall—over six feet tall—plain of face, muscular, and accustomed to hard work. He easily pulled the prop through the partial turn that would be required start the motor. Merci emphasized the need to move back and away at the end of the pull. After he completed the maneuver a second time, the aviatrix nodded her approval and placed her hand on Lyndon's shoulder. In her most earnest voice she said, "Now remember. When you finish the pull, get back out of the way! Don't let the prop grab you when the engine catches."

Lyndon, excited about his chance to be involved, grinned and bobbed his head up and down. "You bet! I won't let it get me."

Merci patted his shoulder and climbed into the cockpit. Once seated, she checked the movement of the controls. Then she gave a wave and a grin in the direction of her father.

T. C. had been looking at the trees along the creek and the hills to the west, all of which seemed ready to grab the Jenny out of the air. Now he smiled a wan smile and gave a small wave in return to Merci's grin. The thought of his daughter in flight made his stomach cramp.

Merci tripped the ignition switch and pumped the throttle a couple of times. Then she straightened to peer over the windscreen at Lyndon. She smiled at his eager face and gave a twirl in the air with her finger as a signal for him to pull the prop. The young man threw his leg high and dropped it through with vigor and then staggered quickly away to the side. The motor coughed once and then began to run smoothly. Merci gave Lyndon two thumbs up. One more look over her shoulder at her father, another quick wave of her hand, and it was time to go.

The flat pasture that she had chosen as her airfield sloped very gradually from west to east. Absent any other consideration, she would always take off to the east in order to take advantage of the downhill run. But the prevailing winds blew from the west. The movement of the wind over the wings would generally offset any advantage the downhill run might provide.

Merci craned her neck to look at the windsock affixed to the top of the flat-roofed hangar. A very slight breeze blew from the west. She eased the throttle forward and taxied slowly to the extreme eastern end of the pasture and turned the machine around to the west. She paused for only an eye blink, willing away the sense of trepidation that plagued her today as it had before her first takeoff near Two Dot. Then Merci leaned forward and pushed the throttle all the way to the stop. The OX5 engine coughed before catching and roaring to full power. As with the initial flight, the machine seemed to gain speed very slowly. Merci urged it along by body motion and with a mumbled, "Come on. Come on." Just as before, the Jenny eventually gained flying speed and lifted from the ground. Merci relaxed and dropped the nose slightly to increase the airspeed. Then she banked the aircraft gently to the right in order to pass through a low place between two hills. She continued to climb as she circled once over the ranch buildings and turned eastward toward Harlowton. Time to show off her toy to the folks at the county seat, sixteen miles to the east.

The air was smooth as Merci followed the railroad tracks alongside the Musselshell River as it meandered down the valley. In a few minutes' time she was over Harlowton, situated on the bluff overlooking the river. Merci laughed out loud at the sight of people streaming out of doorways to crane their necks and gawk upward at the strange machine. It was only the third time that an airplane had visited the central Montana community.

She made two complete circles over town waving from time to time at the figures below. Then she turned the Jenny back toward the west for a return to the ranch. As she straightened from the turn, the motor began to cough and sputter. Merci did as she had been trained to do and as she had done before. She worked the throttle to try to get the engine running smoothly again, while searching below for a place to land. A half mile north of town, near the cemetery, was the stretch of open, level ground that she needed. She spotted it just as the motor stopped completely.

The aviatrix silently thanked her lucky stars that she had gained nearly eight hundred feet of altitude in her flight from the ranch. She dropped the nose of the plane, now moving quietly through the air without noise from the engine, in order to maintain flying speed. A one-hundred-eighty-degree turn allowed her to lose altitude and line up for a forced landing.

Merci held the machine in a glide over a low hill at the east end of the open field. She quickly realized she needed to lose even more altitude to avoid overshooting the landing area. The aviatrix crossed the controls—ailerons opposed to the rudder—causing the aircraft to side slip. As the machine neared the ground Merci abandoned the slip to straighten the machine for the landing. The Jenny bounced hard once and bounced again before coasting to a stop. Merci didn't move. She sat for a minute in relief, her hands sweaty in the gloves. At last, she puffed out her cheeks and blew out a huge sigh. "Made it!" She'd survived her first Montana forced landing. More would surely come and no matter how many more there were, each would be nerve racking. Such landings were all too common for the pilot of a Curtis Jenny. The OX5 engine was notable for its lack of reliability.

But what now? First, find out what caused the loss of power, get the problem fixed, then find someone to crank the engine. She climbed out of the cockpit onto the lower wing, pulled her gloves from her hands, and held them in the one that rested against her hip. A glance toward town disclosed a string of automobiles racing over the hill in her direction—the driver of each auto wanting to be the first to learn if she had crashed. Merci recognized the elderly man who drove in through the open gate and pulled his car to a halt about twenty feet from where she was standing. The owner of the Graves Hotel clambered out of the driver's side of the Model T. He tipped his hat, and she greeted him with a smile. When his passenger arose from the other side of the car and grinned at her over its top, Merci's own smile vanished. Her greeting to him was a cold, silent stare.

That fellow, who moved forward to stand with his hand on the fender of the auto, appeared to be in his late twenties. He stood more than six feet tall, broad shouldered, muscular, and with uncommonly good looks that were emphasized by a square jaw. He might have been a movie star. The man waited only a second before saying, "In case you've forgotten, I'm Chris Cape." Straight, white teeth showed through the smile. "And you still are, I believe, Miss Merci Bruce." His voice was melodious—and it was a voice Merci remembered all too well.

She dropped off the wing and then remained immobile beside the aircraft, hands clenched at her side. Finally, she shook her head one time and asked in a tone that was so flat as to approach a hiss, "Chris, what are you doing here?"

"Why, I'm here because you're here. Why else?"

Merci focused a steely glare on the tall man. "If that's the reason, you'd better get yourself back to California."

Cape's smile grew wider. "It seems to me you can use my help right now. After all, I'm a mechanic—just the same as Arnold Masters. I can figure out what caused your engine to fail. And once that's done, I can crank the prop so you can get in the air again." He took a step forward. "And I'm also a pilot, as you must surely remember, so maybe we can fly together."

Anger colored the tone of Merci's voice. Her posture—rigidly erect with both fists now on hips—emphasized it. "I don't need your help." Turning to the owner of the hotel, she growled, "Please, sir, take

Mr. Cape back where you found him. He isn't welcome here."

The old fellow, surprised by the vehemence with which she spoke, backed away, tipped his hat, and said, "Why, yes, Miss Bruce. As you wish. I'll surely do that." He opened the door to his auto and turned to look expectantly at his passenger.

Chris Cape said without looking at the man, "I'll be staying to help the lady with her flying machine." He swiveled his head to add, "But thank you, sir, for the ride from town." The big smile flashed again. "If necessary, I'll walk back. But I hope Miss Bruce will let me fly with her to her family's ranch."

"You're not flying with me, Chris. All that ended in California."

The elderly man cast a confused look from one to the other. Finally, he jerked his thumb in the direction of this erstwhile passenger as he asked Merci, "Can I stay if he doesn't want to go? I'm as curious about your airplane as all these other people." Merci glanced around to find several more autos discharging onlookers.

She smiled a wan smile at the hotel owner. "Stay if you want. Join the crowd. But please don't get in the way." With another fierce glare at Cape, she jumped back up on the lower wing of the airplane, reached into the front cockpit to retrieve a small footstool from behind the seat. Back on the ground, she placed the stool next to the left side of the motor, stepped up on it and unfastened the hooks that held one side of cowling in place. It was a long stretch for her to swing the metal sheet high enough so it overbalanced and fell to rest on top of the engine compartment. As she stood on her tiptoes to reach for the distributor to loosen the cap, she felt a tug to her jacket sleeve.

Tall Chris Cape grinned up at her as she wobbled on the perch. "I can do that much more easily than you. And I'll know what I'm looking for. After all, you've seen me demonstrate my mechanical skills many times." The grin vanished and a sincere look took its place. "Please forget your anger for a few minutes, Merci, and let me help."

"I've already told you, I don't need your help." She stabbed her hand toward the distributor and, in doing so, ran her arm along a protruding metal edge. Merci jerked the arm back and stared at a slash that extended along the back of her hand to the cuff of her jacket. A rivulet of red welled from the wound. She shook the hand and then grimaced as blood splattered across Cape's jacket. "Damn!"

He pulled a handkerchief from a pocket and handed it to the young woman. A frown had replaced any semblance of a smile. "Use that to stop the bleeding. And get down from that stool and allow me do the fixing." It was spoken like an order.

Merci grabbed the cloth and pressed it to the wound. "Still trying to tell me what to do, aren't you?" She dropped off the stool. "That's only one of the reasons that I asked Arnold Masters to come to Montana instead of you." She brushed at him with her arm. "Get out of my way. I need to see if anyone has something to use for a bandage." She turned toward the gathered throng and found her brother pushing people out of his way as he hurried from his Roadster.

Spence's first words to his sister were, "Are you all right?" Then, seeing the blood seeping through the handkerchief, he asked, "What happened?" Before she could answer, he reached toward her. "Come on. Let me get you to Doc Scanlan." He turned and tugged at the Merci's arm as though to drag her away.

"I'll be fine. Just find somebody who has some material for a bandage and help me wrap this up."

The hotel owner produced a clean cloth from somewhere in his automobile. Spence gently removed the handkerchief and used it to wipe at the blood that was smeared over the wrist area. It was clear that the bleeding hadn't stopped and the cut appeared to be deep enough to require a stitch or two. He made wraps around the wrist after splitting the cloth end in two and tied the newly created ends securely together. Only then did he put his arm around Merci's shoulder, smile down at her, and ask, "Will that do for the moment?"

She examined the bandage and then returned the smile. "That will do fine, thank you." Merci turned again to the Jenny. "I still need to get this thing running."

"Ah, come on, Sis. That cut still needs Doc Scanlan's attention. I'll take you in to his office and bring you back after he's patched you up."

Merci was still showing her reluctance when Chris Cape, who had been leaning casually against the aircraft, stepped forward, stuck out his hand. "Let me introduce myself. I'm Chris Cape, one of the instructors who gave your sister flying lessons." When Spence didn't respond, he dropped the hand, but maintained the smile as he spoke. "At times when we all gathered in the office at the airfield—students and instructors alike—Merci would tell us about your family ranch and about the town named Two Dot. Then she began to talk of shipping the Jenny to Montana. The idea of flying a Jenny at this altitude and in this state began to intrigue me." Cape paused, smile still in place waiting for Spence to comment. When no comment was forthcoming, he continued, "So I decided to travel to Montana and see Two Dot for myself." A serious look replaced the smile. "It's probable that Merci will want to do some barnstorming, and I hope she'll let me fly with her when she does. It would be easier, and probably safer, with two pilots rather than one."

Merci pushed between them and barked, "Chris Cape, why in the world would I even think of flying with you? You had your chance."

An apologetic look crossed his face. "I know. I was wrong. I behaved badly, and I'm here to apologize and to ask for a chance to spend time with you, both in the air and otherwise.

Spence looked from one to the other. "When did you arrive here, Mr. Cape?"

"Call me Chris, please." The smile returned. "I arrived in this town a couple of days ago on the train and was able to rent a car—a Model T—from the dealer here. I drove to Two Dot and rented a room at the Hopkins Hotel in Two Dot. The next day I drove around your valley for a time and even asked for directions to the Bruce Ranch. But it didn't seem proper to just appear at the door to your parents' home without some kind of introduction, so I didn't take the road they said led in that direction." The smile remained. "Didn't get much sleep night before last, though. There was some kind of celebration going on and the noise in the street outside the hotel was mighty loud." Cape's eyebrows gave him a look of inquiry as though asking Spence if the explanation for his presence was adequate.

Spence stood quietly for a long moment, before he spoke in a serious tone. "You may not be aware that a murder was committed in Two Dot the night you just mentioned. If you flew with Merci, you probably knew Arnold Masters. Someone drove a bayonet clean through him and left his body on the boardwalk. Merci was fond of Arnold. As I'm sure you can understand, she's been terribly upset."

Cape frowned. "Of course, I knew Arnold. We were all at the same airfield." His eyes shifted to Merci and back to Spence. "And I heard about his death." His shoulders slumped, and he looked past Spence into the distance for a moment. At last, he returned his gaze to the lawyer. "He was a really nice fellow. It's hard to think of him dead."

"Well, I heard you say you're a mechanic. Will you see if you can figure out why the Jenny's engine stopped running while I take my sister to the doctor?"

"I'll do that." Turning to Merci, he said, "Go. I'll see what I can do about the motor and watch the airplane till you get back. It would be wise to have someone here so the spectators can look at the Jenny but not climb all over it."

Merci raised her hand to see that blood was seeping through the crude bandage. Her response was directed at her brother. "All right. I'll go with you, Spence." Scowling again at Cape, she growled, "We'll be back soon. Then you can get yourself back where you came from."

Merci held her injured arm against her abdomen for protection as Spence maneuvered the auto over the rutted track made muddy by the rains of the day before. At last, she glanced at him. "You're wondering who he is, aren't you?"

"Mr. Cape? Yes, and I'm also wondering why he's here." Spence, in turn, looked at her out of the corner of his eye. "And most of all I wonder about your reaction to his arrival. It certainly doesn't appear that you two are on friendly terms."

Merci's eyes remained on the road and she didn't respond for a long while. Then she heaved a sigh, turned to look at Spence, and began to talk. "There were lots of young men at that airfield. I was the only young woman. You can imagine the kind of attention I got. I was asked every day to go to dinner, to go to a dance, to go to a motion picture show, to go sailing, to do something that the man doing the asking thought might appeal to me." She moved her wounded arm seeking more comfort. "But not Chris Cape. He was friendly enough, but for a long time he showed no interest in me beyond that of instructor and student."

"So, what happened?"

"Well, as you saw, he is really good looking. And he can be very charming. And he drove a fast, expensive car." Merci looked across at her brother. "And—he never asked me for a date." She took a breath. "So one day I asked him."

Spence took his eyes off the road to look directly at her. "What was his response?"

"I asked him to go to dinner at the Shore View—a nice restaurant just north of Los Angeles that sits on a bluff overlooking the ocean. I was kind of surprised when he said he would enjoy having dinner with me. I dressed myself up to look my best, and Chris complimented me on my appearance when he appeared at my door that evening.

The dinner was excellent—and, of course, he insisted on paying for it. And he proved to be a great conversationalist." She paused in thought. "I suppose I thought he was a great conversationalist because he spent the entire dinner either asking questions about my life or giving me compliments about something or other. I talked about myself and he listened."

"Sounds like a nice person."

"Doesn't it, though?" Merci shifted the sore hand again. "After dinner he suggested we go dancing at one of those places where you pay a cover and then dance to a live band—dance as long as you want." A smile played at her lips. "He was a smooth dancer—so good that some of the single women who frequent such places tried to cut in. He refused, of course, but always in a very gentlemanly way."

"Then what happened?"

"He drove me back to the house in which I had my room, walked me to the door, shook my hand, and said goodbye. He didn't even try to kiss me."

"Did you want him to?"

Merci glanced across at Spence. "I don't know. Maybe I wanted him to try just so I could refuse. Or maybe I really wanted to kiss him. After all, I'd had a good time. He was charming, and he drove a fancy car." She turned her head to look directly at Spence. "He was a flight instructor, and at that time of my life, flight instructors were kind of like gods." She shifted her gaze to her injured arm. "Anyway, I was upset that he didn't try and decided he must have found me to be boring company."

Spence pulled the auto to a stop in front of the doctor's office and said, "That doesn't seem to be enough reason for you to display the dislike that was so evident a few minutes ago."

Merci used her good arm to open the car door. "Oh, you're right about that. But there's more—lot's more. I'll tell you after Doc gets done patching me up."

When they entered the doctor's office they were met by Eunice Syvertson, dressed now in the white uniform of a nurse. Spence raised his eyebrows. "Well, Doc didn't waste time in putting you to work."

"He hardly gave me time to change clothes." She smiled a gracious smile. "And thank you ever so much for your help. Mrs. Gilfeather and I had a nice visit. She's given me a pleasant room. And the doctor is just as you described him."

Spence turned from Eunice to introduce Merci. The nurse took one look at the bloody bandage. "Come with me. That needs immediate attention." With a gesture, she ushered them into one of the doctor's two examination rooms.

Merci gently removed her jacket. Miss Syvertson carefully peeled the cloth from the injured hand and poured water over the gash to clear the blood away. After patting the excess water from the area around the wound, she handed Merci some bandage material to press against the cut until the doctor could see her.

Doctor Scanlan was in the door before the nurse stopped talking. He was in his sixties, short, stout, and with a bald pate and a small mustache. He'd cared for Merci since she was a child. He pulled a stool next to her and lifted the bloody cloth to peer at the wound. Then he leaned back to look up at her with a gentle smile. "Did a good job of it this time, didn't you? That cut's deep and in a place where your skin moves when your wrist moves. It'll have to be stitched or it'll never heal right."

Spence frowned. "That's going to hurt."

The doctor looked from Spence to his sister and back. "I can inject it with an anesthetic, but the injections will hurt almost as much as the stitching."

"No injections, doctor. Just sew it up." Merci poked the hand in his direction. "I'll grit my teeth."

Doctor Scanlan patted her on the knee. "You were tough even when you were tiny. I sewed you up once before, remember?

"I sure do. I'd fallen out of the tree in front of the house onto a toy I'd left there and really cut my leg." A smile touched Merci's lips.

"I yelled like a demon all the while you were doing the stitching." The smile broadened. "You were very patient."

Doctor Scanlan returned the smile. "If I remember correctly it healed without leaving much of a scar."

"I'd show you, but the scar is on my thigh and I'd have to take off these jodhpurs."

"Isn't necessary." The doctor gathered suture material, a long thin, curved needle, and a small pair of pinchers onto a bench near at hand. He cleansed the wound with alcohol and threaded the needle. With another smile, he said to his patient, "All right. Now's the time to close your eyes and grit your teeth."

Merci lay her arm on the bench and said, "I'll do my best not to yell too loud." She talked tough but her face was white.

"If you need to holler, go to it. It won't bother me." He worked quickly and with precision. Merci mashed her teeth together. It took all her will power to refrain from uttering a groan. In less than a minute, several stitches, carefully tied, closed the long cut. The doctor wrapped a bandage tightly around her hand and wrist with an anchor around her thumb. Adhesive tape held the material in place. The old physician leaned back and said, "Young lady, be careful with the arm. Try not to flex your wrist. And come back in eight days so I can look at it and take the stitches out."

Before Merci could respond, Spence said, "Doc, her airplane is north of town. Is it safe for her to fly back to the ranch?"

Merci voice approached a screech. "Damn it, Spence, I can fly. You don't need to ask."

The doctor patted her on the knee once again. "You can fly, child, if you take care not to injure the arm some more." He started to rise from the stool. "Will someone be flying with you, just in case?"

"No, doctor. I'm flying by myself." In a more calm voice, she added, "It's all right. I'll be careful."

Doctor Scanlan rose to his feet and put his hand on Spence's arm. "She has her own mind, doesn't she?" With a chuckle he hurried away.

Miss Syvertson smiled at Spence again and wished Merci well. Spence grasped the nurse's hand. "I'm the one to thank you for being so kind to my sister." Then he added, "Maybe I can buy you a sundae sometime. They make good ones at Andy's Corner."

"That's a nice thought, Sir. Perhaps you can."

Back in the auto, he turned to face Merci and said, "Now, tell me the rest about Mr. Cape."

Merci's eyebrows were raised as she said, "First, you tell me what's going on with that nurse?"

"Nothing's going on. She's new in town and asked me for some advice. Now tell me the rest of the Cape story."

It was evident to Spencer that the arm was giving her pain by the way she cuddled it to her stomach. And there was no smile when she answered. "After we had dinner and danced on the night I told you about, Chris was polite but distant—for at least a week. Then one day we flew together. After we landed and were walking back to the office he stopped, turned to grasp my shoulders, and said, 'I'd like to take you to dinner again. I'll pick you up at seven.' And he walked away without another word."

"What's so bad about that?"

Merci pursed her lips for a moment, looking straight ahead. "What's so bad is that he didn't ask—he told me." She turned again to face Spence. "But I said OK. I was glad he was interested. And I had a good time—just as I had on the first date."

"Wasn't that the important thing?"

"It should have been." She shifted her injured arm. "Anyway, after that he did it again—simply told me what we would do and when he'd pick me up. And we did fun things together. I'd never been on a sailboat. His family has a huge one, and we sailed all the way to Catalina Island and back. We drove to San Diego to an aquarium. And we motored up in the mountains for a picnic on the shore of a beautiful lake."

"Sounds like he was really good to you."

"Oh, he was good to me, but always, it seemed, on his terms. We went where he wanted, when he wanted. He never asked me for a date. He just so much as told me to be ready each time."

Spence finally pushed the starter button and got the auto engine running, but left it idling in neutral as he asked, "You said you were disappointed when he didn't try to kiss you on the first date. Am I right to assume a romantic relationship began?"

Merci looked away, and Spence could see a slight blush cross her cheeks. She turned back to face her brother. "It did, Spence. And I thought I was in love." She looked away and then back again, the blush gone. "He talked about visiting Montana and meeting my family." She gave her head a shake. "In fact, I began to assume he would propose and we would get married."

"But he didn't propose?"

"No, he didn't propose." She scowled at the remembrance. "One evening when he didn't say he would pick me up, a group of us went to a motion picture. I was the only girl in the group. Just of bunch of fellow aviators together. Arnold was one of them." She shifted her arm with a groan that was barely audible. "The motion picture theatre was dark when we went in. After a while my eyes became accustomed to the gloom. There—two rows down—was Chris Cape with his arm around another woman."

Spence didn't know how to respond, so he just looked at her with raised eyebrows.

"That's right. All I could think was 'What the hell is going on?' But then the anger set in. I almost charged down there and confronted them."

"But you didn't."

"No, I just got up and left." After another head shake, she added, "The next day Chris told me—that's right, told me—that we were going to the same motion picture that evening." Her chin was up in a defiant pose. "And I told *him* where to go!"

"Was that the end of it between you? Not so for him, it seems, or he wouldn't be here."

"No, that wasn't the end of it." First Merci gritted her teeth as she moved the arm. Then she grinned at the brother. "Spence, you've never seen a man behave the way he did for a few days. Chris was at his most charming—always at my side, always being gracious, always asking for dates."

"Did you accept?"

"No, I sure didn't. I was cold as a woman can be. And after a while he just seemed to give up."

"But that still wasn't the end of it?"

"Nope. When I decided to ship the Jenny to Two Dot, everyone at the field knew about it. I didn't try to keep it a secret. Chris came to me right away and asked if he could travel to Montana with me to help reassemble the plane. I'd already asked Arnold Masters, and Arnold had agreed. So I told Chris, 'No dice.'"

"How did he take it?"

This time Merci's head shook from side to side several times. "Not good. Not good at all. He became extremely angry and he—ranted." She paused. "Chris yelled that I needed him, that I'd be sorry if I didn't let him accompany me, and a lot more that I can't remember. It was kind of scary. But after a few minutes he calmed down and apologized. I didn't change my mind, though. And I was glad I had already asked Arnold so I had an excuse."

"But now Chris Cape is here; not here, but out at the field north of town, watching your airplane." Spence put the car in gear and started up the street. "And he seems to be over his rant and anxious to patch things up with you." He shifted gears to increase the speed and added, "He may even have the engine fixed by the time we get back.

"He'll have it fixed, all right. Those OX5 engines run rough or stop when dust or moisture gets in the distributor and fouls the points. I'm certain that's all that's wrong this time. Chris will have it all cleaned up, and he'll be ready to pull the prop."

Spence looked at Merci's pasty face. "Look Sis, you're still favoring the arm. It's obvious that you're hurting like the devil. Let Cape fly with you to the ranch. Better to be safe." He waited a second for her response, then added, "I'll drive out there later and bring him back to town so he's out of your hair."

Merci looked down as she moved her arm and grimaced. "It does hurt like the thunder." After a long pause, she said, "I guess you're right. He is here and he can fly. So, all right, he can ride with me. But you have to get him away from home as soon as you can. I don't want him hanging around."

Spence stopped the car close to the Jenny. Merci was careful not to bump the arm as she stepped out. Chris Cape reacted with a big smile when she told him he could have the front cockpit. "But" she said, "I'll do the flying."

Spence touched her shoulder. "Call me when you're safely home, please, so I can stop worrying."

"Of course, I will."

The engine caught on Cape's first pull, and he quickly climbed into the front cockpit. She wasted no time in taxiing to the east, turning the plane to the west, pouring power to the motor, and taking to the air. Through gritted teeth she growled to herself, "I'll fly directly to the ranch, land the Jenny, and be done with Chris Cape."

10 T. C., directing a couple of men in the butchering of a dry heifer, heard the growl of the motor and looked eastward to see the Jenny approach for a landing. He called for Lyndon Morgan and together they clambered into the Model T truck to head for the landing field.

Merci killed the engine to the airplane in front of the hangar. She was careful to grasp the side of the cockpit with her left hand when climbing onto the wing. And she held her right arm against her side when she dropped to the ground. Her first words to her father were, "I need to lie down. Please take me to the house." She gestured toward Chris Cape with her good hand. "Lyndon and Chris can put the Jenny away."

T. C., looking first at the bandaged arm and then at the pasty white of his daughter's face, turned to Lyndon to say, "Do as she says." Without so much as a word to Cape, he led Merci to the truck and helped her into the seat. Turning again to Lyndon, he said, "You'll have to walk back to the buildings."

As the truck pulled away, Lyndon glanced once at Cape and then turned away. Cape gestured with a hand. "Let's get this machine put away. Then I guess we'll do some walking."

The men kept their distance, Lyndon striding rapidly three paces ahead of Cape, during the walk to the buildings. Neither spoke.

T. C. met the two men when they trudged into the barnyard. He hurried to introduce himself to Cape and to apologize for the rude manner in which he left them at the flying field. Lyndon turned abruptly away, head down, and hurried off to the barn.

T. C. led Cape to the house and introduced him to Felicity. Merci had given her parents a brief account of her flight. She also told them that Cape was a man she'd known in California—nothing more—before retiring to her room. T. C. and Felicity exchanged pleasantries with their unexpected guest, until the conversation died for want of more to say. At that point Cape surprised them. "It's a nice day. I think I'll just walk on down the road to Two Dot. Enjoy the beautiful country you have here."

T. C. hesitated. "I can take you to Two Dot. Or Spence is to be here this evening, and he'll give you a ride back to town."

"I know. He told me. And give him my thanks. But the idea of the walk really appeals to me, so I'll just be on my way." He grasped T. C.'s hand, nodded in Felicity's direction saying, "Ma'am," and strode out the door.

With Chris Cape out of sight, T. C. turned to Felicity to ask, "What do you think is going on between that man and our daughter?"

"She said that nothing was 'going on.'"

"I wonder."

As Chris Cape strolled along the road to Two Dot he grinned. "Merci Bruce will come around soon enough. Masters is out of the way."

Spence arrived in the late afternoon. With apologies to both his parents he explained that he must return to Harlowton immediately. The judge had appointed him to represent an elderly woman in an emergency hearing—a hearing to be held at nine o'clock the next morning. "Her children are attempting to have her declared incompetent." Spence shook his head. "I think they are just after her money. She's supposed to have a decent amount deposited in the bank. I need to spend time with the woman and review the incompetency statutes." Then he asked about the Californian.

T. C. said, "He only stayed a few minutes and then walked off to town,"

Spence nodded. "Good. Merci didn't want him here." Still standing, he turned the conversation to the sheriff's visit, ending with the possibility that Nate Hamilton might be charged with the killing.

Felicity listened with interest. "I surely hope not. That would about ruin his mother."

T. C. nodded. "And Amos, too. They both dote on their son."

"Well, we'll just have to wait. It seems to me that it's a stretch for Davidson to file charges against Nate with the little that he has for evidence of guilt." Turning to leave, he said over his shoulder, "Perhaps I'll see that man Cape again in Harlo."

Merci remained in her room until late afternoon, not knowing the Californian had long since left the ranch.

Spence found Sheriff Graves in his waiting room visiting with Helen, and He ushered him to his private office. When seated, the law officer dropped his hat on the floor, leaned forward with his elbows on his knees. "I guess I should tell you what I've learned since we visited last." When Spence simply waited to hear more, he continued, "Irma Lewellyn said the reason she disappeared with Masters during the party was to get him away from the crowd because he was about to be sick. He'd had too much of Lippy's hooch. She led him out by the creek behind the hotel and watched him upchuck. When she was sure he was all right, she left him there."

"Did she mention anyone else who might've seen them? Like Nate Hamilton? I think you said he disappeared at about the same time?"

"Didn't say and I didn't think to ask." Graves waited for another question. When none came, he leaned back and said, "She did tell me that Nate had been showing off earlier in the evening. He had a cotton rope and put on a twirling demonstration. You know, spinning a rope in a circle. He's been known to do that before, especially when he thinks he can play the cowboy and impress some girl."

Spence leaned forward. "What became of the rope?"

"Mrs. Lewellyn didn't know." The sheriff shifted in the chair. "She also told me that the bayonet got handed around a lot that night. Some of the boys who'd been in the army began to tell stories and used the bayonet to demonstrate. She seemed to think the ones doing the telling were the ones who never got to the trenches. Some others—men who actually did some fighting—were disgusted with the braggarts. She didn't seem to be much impressed by the stories, either. Anyway, she saw the bayonet and said it was the one with the broken tip." Graves smiled. "I gather her real interest was in dancing—dancing with lots of the fellows."

Spence shifted so he was sitting sideways, elbow on the desk top, looking to his left at the lawman. "Looks kind of bad for Nate, doesn't it? His rope and his bayonet. And his show of anger because Masters danced too often with Mrs. Lewellyn."

"I caught up with Lyndon Morgan last evening at the Morgan place. He confirmed most of what Irma said. And he told me that he was certain that Nate had both the bayonet and the rope out back of the saloon."

"What does Nate have to say?"

"Haven't been out to the Hamilton place yet. I'm on my way as soon as I get done here."

"I suppose you reported all this to the county attorney."

"Just came from there." Graves reached down for his hat and shoved it onto his head. Then he rose from the chair to say, "This is just a courtesy call. Please tell all of this to your family – especially your sister."

Spence stood and walked around the desk. "I'll call the ranch later today and I'll tell them." He took the sheriff's hand. "Thanks, Lester. You took extra time to stop here. I appreciate it, and so will Merci and my parents."

Graves paused at the door to say over his shoulder, "Roger Davidson is thinking about filing murder charges against Nate—unless Nate has an alibi." He slowly shook his head. "Nate's dad, old Amos, will be mad as hell. He doesn't think Nate can do anything wrong."

11

Merci's arm was still painful two days later. To pass the time, she rode into Harlo with her mother in the Packard Town Car. While Felicity shopped and visited friends, Merci, clothed in a woman's proper dress, went to Spence's office. Once seated, she asked, "Have you been able to locate Arnold's family to let them know about his death?"

"I sent a wire to the operator of the California flying field the day we found his body and asked for an address for his family. I've received no reply so far."

As they were speaking Sheriff Graves wandered in. He gave a courtesy nod to Merci, threw his hat to the floor, and dropped into the other chair across the desk from Spence. Without preamble, he began, "Got a telegram from Masters' father. The operator of the flying field must have sent him a wire. Anyway, he said he would leave from Portland on the first train and arrive here tomorrow. Wants to be sure justice is done. Whatever that means."

Merci choked and swallowed hard at the thought of the burial of her friend. She took a moment to control her emotions before asking, "What did he say about funeral services and burial?"

"Not a word."

Spence offered, "He's lost his son. May not be thinking clearly. And probably wants to be sure that the killer is found and prosecuted."

Graves nodded. The law officer shifted in the chair seeking more comfort. "I drove out to the Hamilton Ranch yesterday morning. Young Nate Hamilton got mad as the dickens when I tried to talk to him about Masters' killing. He did a lot of yelling. Said he didn't have anything to do with the bayonet or anything else. He wasn't very co-operative and wouldn't answer questions. Nate maintained he left the dance early and drove home alone." The sheriff drummed his fingers on the arm of the chair. "The man doesn't have an alibi."

Spence asked, "Did he admit to having the rope and doing the rope tricks?"

"Didn't admit it or deny either one. Wouldn't talk much about what happened that night."

Merci muttered, "That's sounds like Nate."

Spence rubbed a hand at the back of his neck. "What's the county attorney going to do? Charge Nate?"

"You should ask him, I guess. But he seems reluctant. Isn't certain there's enough evidence. He wants to find something that ties Nate directly to the murder."

Spence nodded. "That's understandable."

The sheriff reached for his hat, stood and leaned to stretch his back. "Amos Hamilton will be in to see you. He's not as hot headed as his son. The old man knows Nate has a problem, and he wants some legal advice."

Amos arrived shortly after Spence and Merci returned from the mid-day meal at Mother's Cafe. He was about ten years older than T. C. Bruce and was one of about a dozen men who conducted extensive cattle operations in the upper Musselshell Valley. Merci had known him since childhood. The difference between the Hamiltons—father and son—had been a matter of interest to Merci for a long time. Where

Nate was tall and brawny, Amos was short and slender. Where his son was bombastic and quick-to-anger, Amos was quiet, even-tempered, and quick to smile. Nate liked to play the big time cattleman, wore fancy boots, and a large western hat. Amos' clothes were those of a working man, and his hat showed all the signs of wear. That was his garb when Helen ushered him into Spence's office.

Amos half bowed to Merci and shook Spence's hand. Then, like all the other men who came to Spence for advice, he dropped his hat on the floor and took a chair. They exchanged the usual pleasantries. Finally, the expression on Amos face shifted to one of extreme concern. "Nate swears he didn't have anything to do with the killing of that man. But from what the sheriff said, the boy's in real trouble." He took a deep breath. "I told him we needed to hire a lawyer right away and suggested we get one of the hot-shots from Helena."

Merci rose from her chair, still cradling her wounded arm, and said, "This is a conversation that I shouldn't be hearing." Turning to her brother she said, "Thanks for the meal." Returning her gaze to Amos, she smiled. "It's nice to see you again Mr. Hamilton."

Amos turned to look up at her. "You needn't leave. Please stay. I haven't anything to say to Spence that you can't hear." Merci hesitated before easing back to her seat. Amos offered her a homely smile before turning again to Spence. "Nate wouldn't hear of hiring a Helena lawyer. He said he's known you since you were kids together and if he had to have a lawyer, it was going to be you."

"Amos, if Nate didn't having anything to do with the death of Arnold Masters that should be evident soon enough. You may not have anything to worry about."

"But I am worried." The old rancher leaned forward for emphasis. "The things the sheriff said made it sound like it's a certainty that Nate will be charged with a crime. We need to be prepared. That means putting some lawyer to work as soon as possible—to work doing the things that will show that Nate's innocent. And it means getting that lawyer hired and at the task right away."

Spence folded his hands together and laid them on the desk. "Amos, your first instincts are correct. There's a possibility that Nate may be charged. That being the case, he needs a lawyer. And he needs a lawyer with more experience than I have. Please ask him to come into my office so we can have a chat. I'll make him understand."

"He'll show up in about an hour." Amos paused, "He doesn't know I'm here. He doesn't want me telling him what to do. Says he's twenty-six years old and can take care of himself. But I felt I should share my feeling with you before he arrives." The older man puffed out a sigh and turned to Merci. "I don't mean to ignore you, Miss Bruce, and I hope you'll forgive me for barging in here while you were visiting with your brother."

"Please call me Merci, Mr. Hamilton. After all, you've known me since I was a child."

Amos smiled. "I have at that, haven't I?"

"And, for what it's worth. I don't believe that your son had anything to do with Arnold's death. That kind of vicious act just isn't something Nate could do."

"That's what his mother and I believe. But it's comforting to hear you say so."

Spence spoke without a smile. "I agree with Merci. Nate just isn't the killing kind." His face reflected the gravity the situation deserved. "I'll give him the names of a couple of good criminal defense attorneys in Helena and a couple in Butte. He can pick any one he wants."

Amos heaved a long sigh. "That's mighty generous of you."

He reached for his hat and climbed stiffly to his feet. "I feel lots better already." He turned his hat around by the brim as he gave a pained look at Spence. "Nate has a temper, and he's done some foolish things. Maybe he knows more about that party than he's telling me. But he's my son, Spence, and I want to protect him—no matter the cost."

"Understood."

After Amos Hamilton was out the door, Merci was on her feet. "He's right about Nate's temper. But it's all bluster. He gets over it as fast as he gets angry. It's been true since we were children." She turned away, then stopped. "Mom will be waiting for me so I'll get out of here and let you get on with your legal business." Still cradling her arm she paused at the door. "The sheriff is probably doing all he thinks is necessary to learn who is Arnold's killer. But I intend to talk to Irma Lewellyn again. I'm going to ask some questions of the barkeeper, too and some of the others that were on the street that evening. They may tell me things they won't tell the sheriff." Merci's face was grim. "I have more at stake than the sheriff, Spence. I brought Arnold to Two Dot."

Nate Hamilton arrived, as his father said he would, about an hour later. Spence noted again what a striking figure he presented—tall with a trim but muscular build. He was handsome in a rugged way with craggy cheekbones, thick black brows hovering over clear blue eyes, a stubby nose, and wide lips. The man's jaw jutted out in a way that gave him an aggressive look, even at times of repose.

He began speaking even before Spence could acknowledge his presence. "God damn it, man, I didn't kill anybody. And I don't like the insinuation that I did." With that he dropped the hat on the floor and himself into a chair.

Spence put his elbows on the desk. "No one has said that you killed Arnold Masters. But there seems to be a lot of things to make Sheriff Graves wonder—things you did the night Masters died."

Nate leaned forward and reached wide to place his hands flat on

Spence's desktop—a gesture of aggression to match his appearance. "I'm told he had a bayonet sticking in him and it had a broken tip. That's my bayonet, but so what? It was right out there for anyone— anybody at that party—to take and use."

Spence nodded slowly. "Did you show off a piece of soft rope that evening?"

"I sure did. I used it to impress the girls. I've done it a hundred times. What's wrong with that?"

Instead of responding to the question, Spence asked, "Where is it?"

Hamilton leaned abruptly back in the chair. "It's at the ranch hanging in the saddle shed along with a bunch of other ropes. Hell, Spence this is cow country. Everyone has rope."

Spence decided it was time to take charge. He leaned forward with his arms on the desk. "Here's the thing, Nate. You were angry at Arnold and tried to go after him. You'd taken your bayonet off Lippy's wall and were displaying it. You also had a cotton rope of the kind that might have been used to strangle Masters. And you disappeared from the scene about the same time he did." He paused for effect. "It doesn't look good, and you may as well face it."

Nate Hamilton leaned back and his eyes widened as though he finally understood that the whole thing wasn't a joke. Then his aggressive posture reappeared. "So I left the party at the same time as Masters did. Again, so what? That man's body wasn't on the walk in front of Lippy's at midnight, about the time I left. The killer had to drag it there after everyone was gone and the street was deserted. I was at the ranch and in my bed by then."

"Do you have anyone who can testify to that?"

Nate shook his head vigorously. "Hell, no. I sleep alone."

"Your folks hear you come in?"

"Probably not. My room is at the other end of the house from where they sleep."

Spence leaned way back and clasped his hands behind his head. "Nothing may come of your activities that night. Graves may focus on someone else as the killer. But you need to be prepared to defend yourself properly. That means hiring a good criminal lawyer right away. I'll give you the names of a couple in Butte and a couple in Helena. Either one you choose can get here easily on the train."

Hamilton seemed to slowly slump in the chair as though in final recognition that his situation was serious. "I'm not going to hire some shyster from Butte. You and I've known each other since our Two Dot school days. You always were the smartest one around. If I have to have a lawyer, you're the one I want."

Spence smiled. "That's a nice compliment. But I haven't had the kind of experience it would take to properly defend you if you're charged with murder. The risk is too great for you to take a chance on me."

Nate's eyebrows scrunched together. "You mean you refuse to do it?"

Spence shook his head. "It isn't that I refuse to do it. It's just that you shouldn't ask me to do it."

The aggressive posture returned. "Well, I'm asking you to be my lawyer. Will you do it? Answer me—yes or no."

Spence shook his head again, thought a moment, then leaned forward again. "All right. Here's how we'll handle it. Until an actual charge is filed—and I hope it doesn't happen—I'll do what I can. But should you be charged, we'll decide if a better attorney than I am should be brought in. I could act as his co-counsel in that event. Then you wouldn't be left alone with a stranger. How does that sound?"

"Just as long as I can rely on you to be in my corner. I just don't trust anyone else to make sure they don't railroad me."

"All right. We'll do it that way." Spence stood and walked Nate to the door. "When you see your Dad, ask him to stop by. I think I should ask him whether or not he heard you come home that night. He may find it easier to give answers to me than give them to you."

"You're probably right. The old man and I don't always see things the same way."

Amos was back in Spence's office in fifteen minutes. He must have been waiting at one of the saloons or at a cafe. "Nate told me you agreed to represent him. That right?"

"At least until a better lawyer is needed."

"Thank God! I was afraid you'd say no."

Spence smiled at the old man. "Well, I didn't. But here's the thing, Amos. This is going to take a lot of my time so I need a retainer."

A frown crossed the rancher's face. "Retainer? Hell, Spence, I've always been good for my bills. You know that."

"I do know that. But I need a retainer just the same. It's the way lawyers do business."

"How much?"

When Spence told him, Amos Hamilton whistled. "That's quite a chunk."

Spence agreed. "It is." He paused to let the man ponder. "The way it works is this. I charge the time I spend on Nate's matter against the retainer. If it runs out, I'll need another advance." Spence paused again as Amos stared. "The amount I just asked for is only a fraction of the amount a really good criminal lawyer will demand up front. My hourly fee is small in comparison to the one that some city lawyer will charge." He paused again. "And if Nate is really charged with murder, he will need that good lawyer." Spence waited for the old rancher to comment.

When Amos just sat slumped in the chair with a distraught look on his face, Spence ended by saying, "Now you have some idea of what the cost will be if your son is charged with a serious crime."

Amos grunted, "Jesus!" Then he blew out a sigh. "Well, all right. But I need a few days to get that much money together. Is that all right?"

Spence leaned forward again, arms on the desk. "Relax." His face softened. "You don't need to give me a retainer, Amos. I just told you I'd need one so you'd understand how lawyers work and realize how much all of this could cost. I know that you are good for your debts." He smiled. "I'll just send a bill once a month as this goes along. But, Amos, a big town lawyer is going to ask for lots of money up front, and he won't go to work until he has it in hand."

12

Felicity asked her daughter about the man who arrived at the ranch in the Jenny. Merci gave a short version of the same tale she'd related to Spence. Her mother accepted the explanation. She'd get the whole story and all the details as time passed. She always did.

Merci continued to suffer from the pain to her hand and arm. Three days after the injury, she was in the house, curled up in an easy chair, and cuddling the arm to her middle. Her rest was interrupted by a sharp knock on the back door. It was a surprise to find Nate Hamilton standing on the back stoop, hat in hand, horse tied to the back fence. When Merci didn't speak for a moment, Nate waited, then broadened his smiled. "May I come in?"

Merci recovered, smiled, and offered a small hand wave of invitation. "Of course, Nate. I didn't mean to be rude. It's just that I wasn't expecting you."

Nate moved two steps into the kitchen. "I was checking cattle in our west pasture. It isn't far from here so I decided to ride on over. We've all heard about your injured arm." He suddenly seemed embarrassed, turned his hat around by the brim, and shuffled his feet. "I just wonder if there's anything I can do to help."

Merci looked down at the bandaged arm and back up at Nate. "The arm is painful, but it will heal in time." She smiled again. "No,

Nate. There's nothing you can do to make it better. I'll just have to be careful for a while." Then her good manners asserted themselves. "But it's awfully nice of you to ride all the way over here to show your concern. Mom's at the cook house. Dad's out with the men somewhere, moving heifers." She backed farther into the room. "But come on in. I'll make some coffee, and there're cookies in the jar."

Nate moved back, concerned that he'd committed a social error. He hadn't given any notice of the visit. Neither Merci nor her parents had a chance to prepare. Embarrassment showed on his face. "Coffee and cookies sound good. But I need to get back and finish checking the cattle." With a quick step he was outside before Merci could respond. He placed his hat on his head and looked back through the kitchen door. "I should have called before I came." Shuffling of his feet, he added, "It's just that I like you, Merc. I can't help but worry."

"Nate, you're a good friend to worry. But I'll be fine after a few days. "

Nate turned away while saying over his shoulder, "I certainly hope so." He loosed the horse, stepped into the saddle, and looked down at the young woman to add, "But I'll still worry."

Merci watched until he was through the entrance gate. "He really is a thoughtful person. And he isn't always the impetuous, quick to anger individual that so many believe him to be." Her eyes followed him on down the road. "Yes. He is kind. Nate wouldn't deliberately hurt anyone. And I really am fond of him."

13

On the morning of the fifth day, the pain had subsided so Merci walked the one-eighth mile to the hangar just to look at her airplane. The following morning dawned clear and still. Her arm was still painful, but this was a day to fly the Jenny.

After fibbing to her mother by saying that the arm felt fine, she asked her father if she could take Lyndon Morgan away from his other work. T. C. agreed after expressing his concern about her injury. It wasn't difficult to get Lyndon to go to the landing field with her. Together they dragged the Jenny from the hangar with Merci using only one arm. She helped Lyndon pump gasoline from a barrel into a five-gallon can equipped with a spigot. The barrel was one of three placed behind the hangar for ready access. She then directed the ranch hand to climb a short ladder and pour the fuel through a funnel into the plane's gas tank. The bottom of the funnel was covered by a chamois skin to filter the gasoline. Dirty gasoline caused emergency landings.

Lyndon made three trips up and down the ladder before the Jenny was fully fueled. Merci donned her flying helmet and pulled the jacket over her sore arm with great care. At last, she jumped up on the lower wing and started to climb into the cockpit. On an impulse, she called to Lyndon, preparing to pull the prop. "After the motor's running, get in the front cockpit and put on this helmet. I'll give you a ride." With that she tossed a spare helmet and goggles in his direction. A grin as wide as his cheeks would allow lit Lyndon's face. He heaved on the propeller with a vengeance. The motor roared, and Lyndon raced around the wings, pulling the helmet on his head as he ran. Merci waited until he was safely seated before beginning a short taxi to the east end of the field. After checking to assure that all the controls worked freely, she pushed the throttle to the stop. Once again the ungainly machine began the slow process of gathering speed. When the aircraft cleared the hills to the west, Merci let out a war whoop. It felt that good to be in the air again. Lyndon looked back at her, still grinning.

Southward up the valley of Little Elk Creek toward the craggy peaks of the Crazy Mountains flew the Jenny, climbing all the while. Four miles south they passed the place where her grandfather, T. C.'s father, had his homestead. Having at last gained enough altitude, Merci banked left to pass over the low saddle between Two Dot Butte and Coffin Butte. In the near distance she could see Porcupine Butte and far beyond loomed the bulking range of the Beartooth Mountains. They soon were over Big Elk Creek, which flowed from the Crazy Mountains northward to Two Dot. Merci chose a course that generally followed the creek, but banked the plane to one side or the other so both she and Lyndon could look down on various ranches along the way—the Mathers Ranch, the Hopkins Ranch. Four miles south of Two Dot they passed over the sprawling conglomeration of buildings that was headquarters of the Hamilton Ranch. Merci thought of Nate, the arrogance he sometime displayed, and the difficulties it might bring him.

After passing over Two Dot, Merci turned to the west again and began a slow descent. As they approached the Morgan Homestead Lyndon peered intently over the side of the cockpit. Merci flew a long circle and was pleased to see Mrs. Morgan step from the house to wave.

Her passenger was waving frantically at his mother below. The grin was still glued on his face.

But the throb in her arm was becoming too much to ignore. She widened the turn to align the aircraft for a landing. Just as before, there was a lot of waving from those in the barnyard below as the plane passed over the Bruce Ranch compound. Merci congratulated herself when the Jenny touched down with only one small bounce. Damn, she was a good airplane pilot!

Later, in her room, she reflected on the flight. Maybe it wasn't wise to take Lyndon Morgan for the plane ride. It really emphasized the difference in their circumstances. The Morgans, like too many others, came to the valley expecting to find fertile land and a temperate climate, both of which would lead to the establishment of a successful farm. Hiram Morgan chose as his homestead a quarter-section of government land that had been open range before he arrived—land upon which the Bruce family had long pastured cattle free of cost. Soon enough, he found that the soil was not deep and black like that in the Midwest. It was thin, rocky, and in some places, alkaline. Nonetheless, the first years, 1914 through 1917, were reasonably good. Rain was plentiful and grain prices were favorable. The Morgan family built a house that was more substantial than the shack that was the norm on many homesteads. They had arrived with the resources needed to purchase horses and machinery for farming and to build the barn and outbuildings such an operation required.

Lyndon, then in his teens, worked with his father to dig the well, to dig the pit that became the root cellar, and to build a fence along the one side of the claim next to the Bruce property. T. C. Bruce, as was the custom, took on the task of providing the fence along the other side.

Not long after the Morgans' arrival, Hiram's wife, short and spare with graying hair, walked the mile and a half along the roadway to the

Bruce Ranch where she introduced herself as Sophia. It was her purpose to assure Felicity that the Morgan's wanted to be good neighbors. Felicity took note of the sturdy shoes on her new neighbor's feet—good for walking—that were in contrast to the carefully chosen dress, cape and hat. She found the neighbor to be a cultured woman and took pleasure in their conversation. When they next met in the store in Two Dot, she invited Sophia to join her for tea at the cafe across the street. The homesteader's wife proved to be both educated and personable. The two women shared conversation whenever they met in passing.

The road west from Two Dot ran past the Morgan Homestead. On a town trip, several days after the women made their acquaintance, Felicity noticed that there was no large pile of firewood near the Morgan house. And the Morgan's first winter in Montana would arrive all too soon. What would they use for fuel during the bitter cold to come? The nearest growth of timber that was not owned by one or another of the established ranchers was in the distant mountains. That evening she suggested to her husband that a couple of their ranch hands could cut up a wagon load of the cottonwood trees that had died along Little Elk Creek. The wood should be hauled to the Morgan homestead.

T. C.'s response was, "We can't provide for every homesteader who seems to need help. There are too many of them. And too many of them need help."

Felicity listened to her husband and then said in her quiet voice, "They're neighbors, Thad."

The wood was delivered later that week.

Sophia walked the mile and a half again, this time to thank Felicity for the Bruce family generosity. Felicity, genial as always, provided tea and conversation. When Sophia left for home she was carrying a cut of beef. Handing it to her, Felicity simply said, "In this warm weather it will spoil before we get it used."

The Morgans, like the other homesteaders, had reasonably good crops for the first years. Then came 1918—the year when spring arrived but rain did not. The acreage that Hiram had worked so hard to plow and plant dried to hard crusted dirt. The new growth of grain shriveled to nothing. And the winds came, day after day. The soil, made loose by the plowing and the harrowing, blew eastward in dusty clouds.

The following year was worse. The little rain that fell barely wet the ground and the wind dried it immediately. Then winter arrived with below-zero temperatures.

Day after day the bitter wind blew—from the west, then from the northeast, and from the west again. When spring arrived in 1920 the other three families who had settled on the section of land near the Bruce Ranch were gone. One after the other they had disappeared from the acreage upon which they had labored so hard to improve. Some left most of their belongings behind. Soon Bruce cattle were grazing once again on the little grass that remained on the three abandoned homestead sites.

But the Morgans stayed. Lyndon walked to the Bruce Ranch and asked for a job. T. C. hired him instantly. Hiram, like his wife, was an educated man. He sought and got a part-time job as a clerk in the bank at Two Dot—the bank of which T. C. Bruce was president. And Sophia Morgan strove mightily to keep the dirt from seeping into her house through its every crack and cranny.

Upon T. C.'s advice and with his support, Hiram Morgan was now a candidate for the job of county assessor. His opponent was another dried out, but well liked homesteader from the Judith Gap region, north of Harlowton. If Hiram was elected, the family would again have a reliable income. When not at work at the bank or doing his best to save what could be saved at the homestead, he traveled the county in their Model T—an auto purchased when the crops were good—soliciting votes wherever he could find them. T. C. helped. When he found himself in the company of one of his acquaintances T. C. would often end the conversation by saying, "Give Hiram a vote. He's a good man, and he'll do the county right."

Felicity helped in another way. At least once a week she asked one of the ranch hands to hitch up the team to her buggy—she was reluctant to take the car—and traveled to the Morgan house for a visit with Sophia. On each trip she carried food. And each time she had a reason, other than charity, for the trip and the food: meat would spoil, too many eggs to use before they went bad, more buttermilk than the men could drink. Sophia understood what was going on and reacted as required. She accepted the offerings quietly and with genuine thanks.

So Hiram Morgan campaigned. Lyndon rode a horse, furnished by his employer, back and forth from the homestead to work at the Bruce Ranch each day. Sophia Morgan spent much of her time praying that her husband would be elected in the fall.

Reflecting on all of this in her room, Merci cradled her injured arm and wondered if she'd been wrong to take Lyndon with her in the Jenny. She didn't think of herself and her family as wealthy. Her parents had just been there for a long time and had worked hard for what they now had. But, she wondered, did Lyndon hate it that they had so much and the Morgans had so little? How could she know his thinking when he seldom showed any emotion—except to grin any time that she appeared?

Lyndon, milking his mother's cow in the evening, also reflected on the Jenny and the one who flew it. Merci was, he thought, the loveliest woman in the world. Could she ever see him as someone other than a ranch hand? He could always hope, now that the man she'd dragged here from California was dead and gone.

14

Two more days passed and Spence heard nothing about the killing of Merci's mechanic. Then a morning came when the county attorney was on the phone. "I just had Arnold Masters' father in my office. Not a nice man. He's headed your way. Thought I should warn you."

A short man wearing an expensive suit, a bowler hat, and a savage frown brushed by Helen and barged into Spence's office. He planted himself in front of the desk, hands on hips, and growled, "You're her brother, aren't you?"

Spence accepted that as a statement rather than a question. He stood, crossed his arms, and said in a calm voice, "Merci Bruce is my sister, Sir, if that's what you're asking." Then he added in the same quiet manner, "You might exercise the courtesy of introducing yourself."

The angry man leaned forward with his fists on the desktop. "I'm Warren Masters and Arnold is—was—my son. Your sister lured him to this godforsaken country and got him killed." He leaned farther toward Spence, the scowl deepened, and the voice raised a notch. "Now I've just learned that you've agreed to defend the bastard who killed him. And it's easy to see that your county attorney doesn't have either the brains or the moxie to prosecute a goat." The voice became more shrill. "By God, I won't have it. I'm going straight to Helena to the attorney general of this miserable state. Before I'm finished, there'll be a lawyer doing the prosecuting who'll make a monkey out of you."

Spence prided himself in his ability to control his temper. This raving maniac, however, pushed him too far. He, too, leaned his hands on the desk top so his face was only two feet from that of Warren Masters. He didn't shout. His voice dropped to a chill whisper. "Mr. Masters, no one lured your son to Montana. He came of his own volition. As far as the prosecution of criminals is concerned, Roger Davidson has demonstrated his ability to do so many times." When Spence leaned another inch forward, Masters pulled back. "I've agreed to represent a man who may or may not be charged with a crime." His voice was close to a hiss. "Frankly, sir, what I do is none of your damn business."

Arnold Masters' father straightened, anger contorting his face. "We'll see about that. Before I'm done, I'll tear this town apart. And, by God, I'll destroy you, your sister, and your whole damn family!" He whirled, kicked the door open, and stormed from the building.

Helen peeked in the door, eyes wide. "What was that all about?"

Spence, after struggling to get his emotions under control, was finally able to grin. "We've had angry people in here before, but that guy may have broken the record for mad."

Later that day, Spence learned that Arnold Masters' body was put on the train. After his encounter with Warren Masters he didn't ask where it went.

Merci woke in the middle of the night. It seemed no one was doing anything to show that someone besides Nate Hamilton killed Arnold Masters. She'd put off the visit to the barkeep. The next morning would be the time.

Shortly after breakfast, she led Lucky from the barn. Lyndon had saddled the piebald sorrel gelding purchased by T. C especially for her. She smiled and a waved to her mother as she and Lucky passed the house. Felicity smiled, pleased that her daughter was dressed in a long divided skirt instead of trousers—even if she was riding astride instead of sidesaddle.

Leonard Lippencott was about forty years of age. He was of medium height with a muscular build. His complexion was dark, and his facial features were round and regular. The man's head was bald but for a monk's fringe of hair circling above each ear. He considered himself to be handsome. He had arrived in Two Dot about four years earlier and bought the saloon from old Wallace Linton. He reputedly paid cash.

As Merci rode her horse the four miles through the meadows from the ranch to the town she thought about ways to approach the barkeep—how to get him to willingly discuss the night of the party. At last, she decided to just be what she was—a young woman wanting to know what happened to her friend.

The time to catch the bar owner was early in the morning before any of the usual customers arrived for an eye-opener. Merci pulled Lucky to a stop at the hitching rack in front of the saloon. Through the open door she could see dust boil up in a cloud where Lippy was using a large push broom to clear the floor in the gloomy front room. Merci stood in the doorway until the barkeep looked up. At the sight of her, he stopped his sweeping and leaned on the broom handle.

"Help you, Miss?"

"Yes, Mr. Lippencott, if you will. I'd like to visit about things that happened the night Arnold Masters was killed."

Lippencott dropped his eyes to the floor and gave the broom another push. "Told the sheriff everything." Leaning on the broom handle again, he looked her way. "Ain't got nothing more to tell."

Merci stepped through the door. "Please, Mr. Lippencott. Arnold was my friend. I can't help but wonder what happened that night to get him killed."

"You were here. You probably know more than I do. I was busy tending to my business. I didn't pay much mind to the things outside."

She took another step into the room. "The sheriff said you saw Nate Hamilton try to take a poke at Arnold."

Lippy shifted the broom handle to the other hand and seemed to relax. "Nah. I never saw that. But the whole bunch was talking about it. They all said Nate was red in the face and hollering. Using a lot of words I ain't going to repeat for you." He paused. "A couple of the Haymaker Ranch boys dragged Nate away. I was told it wasn't hard for them to do. Like Nate really didn't want to fight."

Merci smiled. "No, Mr. Lippencott, Nate isn't a fighter."

"Well, I guess Nate went around back and acted like he was sulking. After a while he was gone. I didn't see him no more that night."

"If you were out back, did you see Irma Lewellyn lead Arnold over to the creek where he upchucked?"

Lippy grabbed the broom with both hands and gave it one angry jab at the floor. "Ever since you brought him here, your *friend* has spent time with Irma at the café. Maybe at her place for all I know. She began to get ideas that he would take her with him when he went back to California." Another jab with the broom emphasized his anger. "That wasn't going to happen, and I told her so. That dude had money, and he wasn't going to waste serious time with a girl from a dried-out homestead—one who'd been married and divorced. He was just playing her."

Merci was quiet for a long moment. "But did you see them over by the creek that night?"

"Didn't see 'em. Was busy. Wasn't looking."

"Who else was out back by the creek that night?"

"Missy, there were lots of men. That's where they go to take care of business when they've been drinking." A look crossed Lippy's face and he added, "Drinking soda and near-beer is what they'd been doing."

"Anyone of them could have choked Arnold when he was really drunk. Right?"

"Maybe. But like I told the sheriff, Nate Hamilton was the only one with that cotton rope hanging over his shoulder just before he disappeared."

Merci concluded she'd get nothing more from Lippencott, so she thanked him for his time and strolled away from the saloon. Farther down the street and past the small house next door, she turned to walk between it and the hotel and then on toward the creek. Time to take a look at the place where Arnold must have met his death. Wiping away a tear, Merci wondered if she'd ever stop shedding them at the thought of her lost friend.

Alkali Creek wasn't much of a stream. Only a small flow of water followed its meandering path behind and about one hundred fifty feet west of the Main Street buildings. Privies stood behind most of the buildings, each some distance from the creek.

A few cottonwood trees grew along the stream bank upstream from the general store. From there downstream past the barbershop, the saloon, and the hotel willow brush lined the stream. The brush was sparse directly behind Lippy's place. In back of the hotel, however, the brush grew thick and gathered in large clusters that were interspersed with open areas. Merci found the grass and weeds behind the buildings trampled flat from foot traffic. Apparently, men who drank in the saloon used the area for a latrine most any night.

She followed the stream to where the brush was the thickest. This must have been the place where Irma took Arnold to upchuck. It was also most likely the place where he met his death. Who killed him? And how did his body then get to the boardwalk? She pondered those questions as she and Lucky made their way back to the ranch.

15 Three days later in midafternoon, the county attorney was on the phone. "Thought you should know, Spence, about government at its best. I've just been told that a deputy attorney general will handle the prosecution in the Masters matter—if there is a prosecution. I'm out. Apparently, Warren Masters went to the state's attorney general and the AG agreed to assign one of his deputies to the task. Masters probably greased some palms to get it done. Anyway, our illustrious county commissioners have just appointed that guy a special deputy county attorney. They did it without even asking me."

"Well, I'll be damned!"

"The one you'll be dealing with, if you represent Nate Hamilton and if Nate is charged, is Garth Swain. I've worked with him in the past. Good lawyer."

"Have you talked to him?"

"Not yet. He's to be in town tomorrow."

Spence thought for a second, then asked, "Does the sheriff know about this? He's the one who'll be most affected. He's used to answering to you. Now, he'll have a new boss, so to speak."

Davidson chuckled. "Lester wouldn't like hearing you say he needs a boss." Serious again, he added, "The commissioners told him at the same time they told me. I'm not sure he realizes that it may mean a change in the way he goes about investigating Masters' killing."

Spence ended the conversation by saying, "I guess he'll find out tomorrow." With the phone on the hook, he sat back and pondered the situation. After a few moments of quiet thought he muttered, "Time to find out about the Masters family from Merci." He was soon out the door, driving westward into the afternoon sun.

The Bruce Ranch buildings lay east and in the shelter of tall cottonwood trees that grew along Little Elk Creek. A large frame house dominated the view as seen from the roadway leading to the buildings. Barns and corrals were near the creek. To the north and behind the house were a shop, a chicken coop, a cookhouse, and a bunkhouse. All of the buildings except the house were of log construction.

The house, two stories in height, was painted light silver gray with trim of darker gray. A broad porch ran across the front. Two large windows stood on each side of a wide front door. Spence always enjoyed a sense of homecoming when he followed the dirt track into the barnyard. Two dogs ran out to yap at the tires of his automobile as he pulled through the entry gate. They followed along, barking as they went, and only gave up when he stopped near the stoop that guarded the rear entry to the house. T. C. greeted him at the door with a handshake and a pat on the shoulder. "This visit is a surprise. But you're right on time, Son. Felicity and Merci prepared a rib roast, and they're about to call us to the table to enjoy it."

"Sounds great. I did bring my appetite. And I'm sure the food will be as tasty as always."

In the confines of the stoop, T. C. gestured with his thumb. "Hang your hat on the peg and we'll join the ladies." Then he stopped and turned. "Anything you might want to tell me while we're alone?"

"No, Dad. I need to talk to Merci. And both you and Mom will want to hear it, too."

"Let's get to dinner, then."

The aroma of cooking food filled the large kitchen. Felicity turned from the glowing coal range while holding a large spoon in one hand and a hot pad in the other.

Perspiration dampened her brow. She was short, just over five feet tall. Her husband liked to describe her as "pleasingly plump." The warm smile that always seemed to grace her round face now beamed at her son. Spence put his arm around her waist and murmured. "Hi, Mom. What's cooking that smells so good? Beside the roast."

"You'll know soon enough." She pulled away and waved the spoon in his direction. "Now get out of here so we can finish," she said, with a widening smile.

Spence turned to Merci. She was holding silverware to be placed on a table that was located at the far end of the room. His smile disappeared and his voice was somber as he stepped to her side, pulled her close, and asked, "How're you doing, Sis?"

She leaned into him for a moment before pushing away to scatter the silverware next to plates. Spence noticed she still favored the injured arm. He pointed at it, "Still painful, I can tell."

Keeping her eye on her work she muttered, "The arm's OK." She stopped, shook her head, and looked directly at him. "But, like I told Mom, I'm not okay about Arnold. How could I be all right when he's dead? Not only dead, but murdered by someone? And maybe murdered because of me." She dabbed at an eye with her sleeve. "He was a friend, Spence, a good friend, especially when I was alone in Los Angeles. He was fun to be around, and I could always use him for an excuse when some boring sport bothered me for a date. I just told whoever it was that I had a date with Arnold,and he confirmed it, if necessary."

"Like you did after you were finished with Chris Cape?'

"Exactly."

Felicity raised her head to cast sharp a look at her children. "What's this about Chris Cape?"

Merci smiled. "Nothing, Mom. Can we discuss it later?"

Her mother stared at her for a brief moment. "Of course. But be sure that we do."

Spence didn't help by asking, "Did you and Arnold date at all?"

"We never dated in the way that you mean. We were at parties together but always with other people." She wiped with her sleeve again. "He was just a really good friend, that's all." She sniffed. "I don't know why this is all pouring out now. Most of the time I'm okay. But once in a while it just gets to me that Arnold's gone."

The family gathered around the oblong table situated away from the heat of the stove. The little conversation during the meal consisted of Spence asking T. C. about water in the creek, whether it was sufficient to complete the June irrigation and about the preparations for haying. T. C. responded with brief and quiet answers. His final remark about conditions on the ranch brought that discussion to an end. "The drought continues."

Spence finished devouring a piece of apple pie drowned in thick cream before he pushed back from the table and turned to Merci. The change in his tone indicated his question had a purpose. "Tell me about Arnold Masters' family."

"Why do you ask?"

"Just tell me what you know."

Merci brushed at crumbs clinging to remnants of the bandage on her arm. "His home was in Portland. Arnold said his grandfather made a lot of money in the lumber business. I understand that his father diversified the business and made the money grow." She shifted to face Spence. "Most of the men at the flying field had money—money enough so they didn't have to earn a living. She looked away again "Arnold didn't talk much about his family life. I got the impression his father thought he should be at home, working in the family business. Why do you ask?"

Spence pushed his chair farther away from the table and crossed his legs. "Warren Masters, Arnold's father, was in Harlo a couple of days ago. He barged into my office raving that you'd lured his son to Montana and then gotten him killed. He'd already talked to the county attorney and decided Roger wasn't vicious enough to prosecute his son's killer. Apparently, he'd heard enough to conclude that Nate Hamilton really is the one responsible." Spence looked from one to the other of his family. "From Harlo, he went to Helena and somehow talked the attorney general into assigning one of his deputies to prosecute Arnold Masters' killer. Our illustrious county commissioners have already appointed the guy as a special deputy county attorney."

T. C. asked, "You mean Roger Davidson is out?"

"He sure is. And I think he's relieved. It wouldn't be any fun to prosecute a local boy for murder."

T. C. asked, "So is this new man focused on Nate as the killer?"

"Seems to be the case."

"What does Lester Graves think of this?'

"Haven't talked to Lester. But I know he isn't convinced that Nate did it. It should make for an interesting conversation between Lester and Garth Swain, the new deputy county attorney."

Felicity leaned to pat Spence on the arm. "Let them sort it out. I'm glad you're not mixed up in it.

"But I am, Mom. Nate asked me to defend him if he's charged. I told him he needed a better lawyer than I am, but he was insistent. So I said I'd look after his interest until he's charged…if he ever is." Spence turned to his father. "I asked Amos Hamilton for a retainer. He almost choked at the amount. Then I told him a really good lawyer will charge a whole lot more. I think Amos got the message about what it will cost if Nate's charged. I'll try to persuade Nate to hire a good criminal defense attorney from Butte or Helena to take the case if the need arises. Amos understands that this is a serious matter, but I'm not sure Nate really grasps the kind of problem that's facing him."

Merci mumbled. "That can be Nate's problem. Too much talk and not enough think."

Felicity turned from daughter to son. She seldom frowned, but now a frown crinkled her brow. "If they actually charge Nate with murder, you won't have to defend him, will you? He'll get someone else?"

"That's what I told both Nate and Amos. I'm sure Nate will realize the need and agree to a change."

Concern was also evident on T. C.'s face. "Amos had to buy hay the last two years. The hay came from Dakota, was terribly expensive, and was nothing but slough grass and tumbleweeds. There's talk that far too many of his cows died during the last hard winter. Paying an expensive lawyer may be difficult."

Spence nodded in agreement. "That may be so, but if his son faces a murder charge, Amos will just have to find the money somehow." He turned to Merci. "Have you heard anything more from Chris Cape?"

Her face wrinkled in disgust, Merci answered, "No, not a word, thank goodness." Then she asked, "Have you seen him? He must be in Harlo...unless he had the good sense to return to California."

"Haven't seen him and haven't heard a word about him."

Merci frowned. "Good riddance."

Spence paused. "Then again, he may not have appeared here at the ranch again only because of the rain. There haven't been any days you could fly, have there?"

"Just one. And the rain's frustrating. It's been nothing but windy showers. Never enough moisture to do much for the grass and grain." She looked down at her injured arm. "And the Jenny just sits. That machine is meant to be in the air." Resignation sounded in her voice. "But I shouldn't fly much anyway until this cut heals some more."

T. C. had been listening quietly. Now, he interjected himself into the conversation. "I'll talk to Paul Toohey, our state senator, about the attorney general taking over legal matters in Wheatland County."

Spence rose from the table. "Good idea, Dad. Let me know what you learn." From behind her chair, he hugged Felicity. "Thanks for another good dinner, Mom. I have to get back to town. My law practice continues to grow, and I've some contracts to prepare. Must keep the clients happy."

16

Sheriff Graves growled, "This is what I got." The document he handed to Spence was a warrant for the arrest of one Nathaniel Hamilton for the crimes of murder in the first degree, kidnapping, and mutilation of a corpse. As Spence was reading, the sheriff continued his growl. "I'm supposed to go to the Hamilton place right now, arrest Nate, and put him in the jail until the judge gets here next Tuesday. Thought you should know about it."

Spence stood with his feet spread. "When did you get this?"

"Just before I called you on the phone. That man Garth Swain walked in, handed it to me, told me to arrest Nate, and walked out."

"Where's Swain now?"

"Don't know." Graves shook his head in disgust. "But he had an automobile so he may have lit out again for Helena."

"Have you told the county attorney about this?"

"I sure did. He told me to serve the warrant and arrest Nate."

Spence handed the warrant back to the sheriff. "Roger's right, of course. You haven't any choice but to find Nate and bring him in."

Graves struggled from the chair. "I guess I'd better be on my way." His face twisted to show his displeasure. "God, I hate to arrest that young man. Amos really helped me when I ran for sheriff. This will nearly kill him—and his wife."

"There's no fun in this for anyone in our community, but you've got to do your duty." Spence spoke quietly as the sheriff turned to the door. "Let me know when you have Nate in jail. I'll need to visit with him right away."

Back at his office, Spence scratched his head as he pondered which of the criminal defense attorneys in Butte and Helena he should recommend to Nate Hamilton.

Before any decision could be made, T. C. interrupted his musings. Like all the others who entered that private office, his father dropped a hat on the floor before dragging a chair away from the front of Spence's desk and slowly settling into it. "Senator Toohey did some nosing around when he was in Helena the last couple of days. It seems that Arnold Masters' father is a bigwig out in Oregon. While he was in our capital city he spent the night at the governor's mansion, of all places. He said the attorney general almost curtsied when Masters showed up at his office. The man seems to have a lot of political clout."

Spence stared at his father for a minute. "What else did the good senator have to say about Masters?"

"He said the man genuinely believes the locals here in Harlowton won't try to bring his son's killer to justice. And he's determined to do something about it. That's the reason for the special prosecutor."

"Well, the special prosecutor has been busy. Lester Graves just left for the Hamilton Ranch to arrest Nate and jail him." Spence remembered his father's training in the law. "Nate is charged with murder in the first degree, kidnapping, and the mutilation of a corpse."

T. C. frowned. "Why not just the murder charge?"

"Don't know, Dad." Spence took a deep breath. "Now I'm in it whether I want to be or not. I'll have to try to persuade the judge, when he's next in town, to allow Nate to post bail in a reasonable amount. And I'll bet this man Swain will resist the motion with a massive brief, dozens of affidavits, and a vigorous argument."

"Judge Crawford knows Amos Hamilton and must know that Nate has lived in this community all his life. The judge should agree that the young man isn't a flight risk."

"But the charges are so serious he may not feel comfortable granting bail." Spence frowned and rubbed his jaw. "We'll find out soon enough, I guess."

T. C. retrieved his hat and stood to leave. He appeared on the verge of telling Spence something, seemed to change his mind, and then changed it again. "Merci's arm is feeling better. She told me she's planning to fly to Lewistown tomorrow morning to do some barnstorming. I guess she's planning to circle over the town a couple of times to stir up the populace and then sell some rides. Your mother is dead set against it, and I don't much like it either, but you know your sister. Her mind's made up." The older man looked down at his hand, brushing at a spec of dirt on his hat. Eyes back on his son, he said, "I'm not going to tell Merci about Nate's situation right away. Might as well let her enjoy flying that airplane for another day or two."

Spence winced at the thought of his sister traveling in the Jenny to a place sixty miles away. "I just hope she's careful, Dad."

17 It was a typical end-of-June morning. The morning skies were clear. The air was cool and still—perfect for a flight to Lewistown. Merci took to the sky at five o'clock and pointed the Jenny toward the Judith Gap—that wide, open expanse between the Little Belt Mountains to the west and the Big Snowy Mountains to the east. North of the Gap, she winged her way over the green grain fields of the Judith Basin. More rain here than where I live, she thought.

Lewistown rested in the shallow valley created by Big Spring Creek—with the creek and town nestled in the broad basin formed by the Snowy Mountains to the south and the Judith and Moccasin Mountains to the north.

Merci circled above the community three times, long enough to attract the attention of every living soul able to step out of doors. Turning west toward the flatland overlooking the valley, she began her descent toward an expanse of pasture grass that lay among field upon field of grain, some the bright green of spring wheat and barley and some the yellow color of early ripening winter wheat. A glance at the scene below showed people streaming up the hill and on toward the field where she would land. Most were in automobiles, but some were on foot and a couple were riding horseback. A wide smile blossomed on Merci's face. She wouldn't have trouble selling rides.

On the ground, the aviatrix taxied the Jenny slowly toward a gate in the fence that was closest to the road and cut the motor. She peeled off the flying helmet and stood in the cockpit, prepared to wave at the arriving onlookers. It was a shock when she recognized Chris Cape as the first of them to step from a car. Merci gave up the idea of a wave to the curious. She crossed her arms and glared as Cape sauntered to the Jenny. He rested one hand on the fuselage while saluting with the other. "I was certain you'd arrive here sooner or later. And I've been waiting." His smile was as bright and engaging as she remembered it from California.

"Chris, you're supposed to be back where you came from." The tone of her voice exhibited more exasperation than anger. Merci turned her back to him, pulled off her gloves—the one on the injured arm larger than the other—and began to unbutton her flying jacket.

His voice when he spoke again was light and playful. "Couldn't leave. I've got to be here to serve as your pitchman—help you sell rides. And crank the prop every time you want to take to the air."

Merci spun around, grasped the side of the cockpit with her good hand, and leaned over the edge of it to growl, "Listen Chris Cape, I don't need a pitchman or anything else from you. Now get the hell out of here, and go back where you belong."

Cape shook his head slowly as his smile broadened. "My, my! Such language." He shoved himself away from the Jenny and turned to face the throng that clustered along the fence. More were arriving every minute. Smiling, he raised his arms, palms of his hands outward, to quiet the crowd. "Folks, you may have seen airplanes and aviators before. But I'll bet you've never seen an airplane flown by a lady. And you'll never again see one flown by a lady as lovely as Miss Merci Bruce." He half turned and waved a hand to where Merci still stood in the cockpit. "There she is, folks. Montana's first lady of the air."

Merci looked back at all the eyes now fixed upon her and realized they expected some response. She formed her own smile and reached high to wave with both arms from side to side. The wave drew a smattering of applause from the crowd.

Cape wasn't done. "That charming damsel will be selling airplane rides in about an hour. First, I've got to take her into town for refreshment and relaxation. It's stressful work flying an airplane all the way to Lewistown from the Bruce Ranch near Two Dot." Chris turned to an elderly man, dressed as a farmer, who had strolled from a house on the other side of the pasture. "Is this your property, sir?"

The fellow, standing with legs wide apart and hands tucked into the front of his bib overalls, stared at him for a second before nodding his head. "Yup. Name's Abe. And this field is mine."

"Abe, do you mind if Miss Bruce uses it to give rides to folks for a day or two?"

The old boy scratched at the stubble of a beard as he pondered. "Give me a ride if I say it's okay?"

"I'm sure she will." Turning to Merci still standing in the cockpit he asked, "How about it? Fair exchange? A ride for use of this man's landing field?"

What could she say? Directing her attention to the farmer, she turned on the charm. "Of course, sir. Would you like to be first to go?"

Abe scratched some more, then smiled a toothless grin. "Got to think about it."

Chris jumped in to say, "Miss Bruce needs someone to watch over this airplane for an hour or so while she's in town. She needs assurance that no harm comes to it. I'm sure you can understand that. How about if you stand guard—keep anybody from clambering around on it while she's gone. People are welcome to look, but nobody can touch."

The older man surveyed the crowd before nodding his head again.

"Guess I can do that."

Cape slapped him on the shoulder. "Thank you, Abe. Miss Bruce really appreciates your help. And you can have the first ride."

The old fellow repeated, "Got to think about that."

Merci needed to get to a restroom. The only privy in sight was next to the farmer's house. It was some distance away, ramshackle in appearance, and leaning sharply to the north. Like it or not, she needed the ride to town that Chris was proposing. She climbed out of the cockpit, jumped lightly to the ground, and waved to the crowd.

For some reason, this activity brought cheers, hoots, and hollers from the throng. She smiled her widest smile and waved once more. Turning to Cape she said, "All right, you offered a ride to town, so let's get going."

She clambered into the open Model T while Chris cranked the motor. Seated beside her, he turned to ask, "How's the arm?"

"Arm's healing. Now let's go."

The lady's room at the Fergus Hotel was clean and tidy. Comfortable once again, Merci entered the dining room and slipped into a chair across the table from her one-time California companion. "I hate to say thank you, but I must." She grinned. "So, thank you." The grin widened. "That old fellow's privy sure didn't look inviting, but I'd have been forced to use it if you hadn't rescued me."

Chris returned the smile. "It'll be hot soon, so I ordered some lemonade. And a couple of doughnuts. I hope that's satisfactory."

"Sounds just right."

"No need to thank me. Remember, I've done some flying, too, so I know about the need for such things as a rest stop.

A waitress set two tall glasses before them, each filled to the brim with cold liquid. She slid a plate of doughnuts across the tabletop and flashed a fetching smile at Chris, "Anything else I can get you, Hon?"

Chris favored her in return with the white-toothed smile Merci had once thought so winsome. "That'll be all, Ma'am. Thank you."

Once the woman was out of earshot, Merci giggled, "She just found you, and already she's smitten. Better take her dancing tonight."

"I'd do that but I plan to be at the Bruce Ranch." Merci jerked her head upward with her chin jutting out—about to speak. Cape rushed to finish. "Look, lady, you no longer have Arnold Masters to help with the Jenny. I'm here in Montana, and I can do all the things he would have done. And I promise I won't be a bother otherwise." When Merci just stared at him, he rambled on. "When we get back to your ranch, I'll catch a ride to Two Dot. Or I'll walk again if necessary. I can take a room at the hotel and rent a car. When you feel the urge to fly, I'll drive to the ranch and be at your service. Other than that, I'll stay away." He waited for Merci to respond. When she just stared, he asked, "That doesn't sound so bad, does it?"

Merci waited for a long second to answer. "What about the car you have here?'

"It's rented. I'll return it before we leave."

Merci moved to stand, seemed to change her mind, and dropped again into the chair. She placed her forearms on the table, hands clasped together, as she leaned toward Cape. Resolve colored her voice when she spoke. "Listen, Chris, you and I have nothing in common but the ability to fly an airplane. If you can keep that in mind and not get any other ideas about our relationship, I'll let you return with me to the ranch." With the chin still jutting out, she almost snarled. "And then get yourself to town." After that outburst she relaxed a bit. "I do need someone to replace Arnold. But only if you can do it on my terms. Understand?"

"Your terms aren't what I had in mind, but how can I argue?" He stuck his hand out. "Deal? Shake on it?"

Merci waited a moment, then shook his hand. "Deal!"

At the door to the hotel, Chris grasped her upper arm. "You're going to need fuel if you give very many rides. The garage where I rented the car also sells gasoline. Let's stop there and ask them to bring a barrel of gas to the field. And, since I'm leaving with you, I'll ask them to bring the car back when they return to town."

Merci didn't hesitate. "I will need fuel. Let's do it."

The crowd had thinned some by the time they arrived back at the pasture. Many people were bored by the lack of activity. The farmer remained as they had left him, standing with his hands stuck in his overalls, directly between the crowd and the aircraft. Merci was pulling on her flying helmet as she thanked him for protecting the machine. She asked, "So, Abe, are you ready to fly?"

"Been thinking about it. I'll let someone else try it first." He strolled to the fence and leaned against a post, content to watch.

Chris raised his arms to attract the attention of those in the crowd—as though that were needed. His voice was clear but not loud. "All right, ladies and gentlemen. Miss Bruce is rested, refreshed, and ready to take one of you for a trip over the beautiful city of Lewistown. Who will be the first to go?"

A middle-age man in a business suit with the look of a banker asked, "How much is it going to cost?"

Chris smiled. "Ten dollars a ride. Best deal you'll ever get."

A boy about ten years old had been hiding behind the man in the suit. The boy slipped around to look up and ask, "Can I go, Dad?"

The father rested his hand on the boy's head as he asked Chris, "Does that woman know what she's doing?"

Chris turned slightly toward Merci and whispered. "Grab the chance to give that boy a ride. Embarrass the others because a child was brave enough to go first. Then they'll all want to go." Turning back to the banker, he said, "She flew in here, didn't she?" Then he added, "Listen, I've flown with her many times. She can handle that airplane as good as any man and better than most." Then he pointed at the boy and said, "Let the little tyke show the rest of these folks how it's done."

The banker thought for a full minute before looking down at his son to ask, "Are you sure you want to get in that airplane?"

"Yes, I do, Dad." The boy bounced up and down as he added, "I really want to fly, you know, like a bird."

The banker pursed his lips, shuffled his feet, and then directed his attention to Merci. "Are you certain it's safe? Charlie's my only son."

She grabbed the spare flying helmet, put it onto the boy's head, and grinned at the banker. "I promise to bring him back safe and sound." Merci waved to Chris to boost Charlie up on the lower wing and then help him into the cockpit. Cape decided the boy wasn't dressed warmly enough so he wrapped his own jacket around the child's small body. The helmet was too big to fit snuggly on Charlie's head. Chris tightened the elastic on a pair of goggles and slipped them tightly over the helmet to hold everything in place. With all of that finished he checked to be certain the child was seated comfortably in the cockpit. Cape patted the boy's shoulder before dropping from the wing to the ground.

He strode around to the front of the plane and grasped the propeller, ready to start the motor. At Merci's signal he pulled mightily on the prop. The engine coughed once and roared into life. She leaned forward to check her passenger. The boy grinned back at her. Merci waved to the banker and then pushed the throttle forward to taxi to the east end of the field. After a short take-off run, she was in the air with the first paid passenger of her flying career.

Chris had them lined up ready to go when she returned to the ground and taxied to a stop. He helped Charlie out of the cockpit and onto the wing. Charlie shed the helmet and jacket, jumped to the ground, and rushed to where his father was standing. "Dad! Dad! It was great! We were as high as the birds. I could see everywhere! I even saw our house. It sure looked small." He stopped to look upward at his father. "You better take a ride."

The father just shook his head. "Not today, son."

The child's enthusiasm helped to pump up the crowd even more. From then on till two o'clock in the afternoon one passenger climbed in the Jenny as soon as another climbed out. Each trip consisted of a long circle over the countryside on the outskirts of Lewistown and then a second pass directly over town so the passenger could peer downward at his residence.

Merci climbed from the machine after the two o'clock flight, stretched, pulled the helmet from her head, and ran her fingers through her hair. Then she turned to Chris. "The air's heating up and beginning to get bumpy. Time to call it quits and head back to the ranch."

"We'll disappoint some people, but you're right about the bad air. No need to have one of these nice people get airsick in the cockpit." Turning to face those waiting a turn, Chris announced, "It's time for us to return to Two Dot. Miss Bruce will be back another day to take the rest of you for a tour over the city." He paused, then added, "Don't forget to hurry out here to Abe's field next time she arrives." Turning to Merci he gestured toward a Model T truck with a tank in its box and said, "They're here with the gas and the tank has a hand pump. Time to fuel the Jenny. Got a chamois skin for a filter?"

"Of course." Merci put up a hand to stop him as he started for the truck. "One last thing before we leave." She strode over to the farmer, still leaning patiently against a fence post. "How about it, Abe? Want the last ride?"

"Nope. Too expensive."

Merci tousled her hair again, damp from the heat, and then said,

"That wasn't our agreement. We use your field, you get a free ride."

The old fellow thought for a moment, then pulled his hands from the front of his overalls and said, "Yup. That was the deal."

"Well, let's go then." She led him to the Jenny. "What's your last name, sir? I feel foolish calling you Abe."

"Name's Abe Sobolik. Prefer to have you call me Abe."

"All right. Climb up on the wing, Abe, and over into the cockpit." When he was seated, helmet in place, she asked, "That your house over there?"

"Yup. That's mine. The Missus is standing there in the doorway."

"I'll be sure you get a good look at the house from the air, and you can wave at your wife."

Heat thermals jostled the aircraft as Merci made the circle over the town. She made a larger circle to give Abe a good look at his farm. His wife still stood in the doorway with her hand shielding her eyes as she peered at the Jenny. A sharp upward thermal was followed by a quick drop. Merci began to worry that her passenger might get sick. She banked the machine around tightly for the landing approach and bounced the Jenny onto the ground once again. Abe clambered to the ground, grinning a huge toothless grin. "By God, that was all right!" The old man walked a few feet toward the house, then said over his shoulder, "You can use the field again if you give me another ride."

18

Merci was reliving the trip to Lewistown. "It sure was fun to watch the dirt farmers and city folks gape at a lady in a flying machine—one who wears jodhpurs." She told her parents as she sat in a kitchen chair in a pose that emphasized her attire.

T. C. grumbled, "It's risky enough that you want to fly around near home where things are familiar. You know that the idea of you performing stunts somewhere far from here doesn't sit well with me."

Felicity added, "And I don't like to have you wearing pants, even where everyone knows you." She frowned. "I just hope our neighbors will at least understand that a ruffled dress isn't appropriate in an airplane."

Deep lines furrowed Merci's brow. "Mom! Dad! I know you were upset when I wrote from California that I was taking flying lessons."

Felicity spoke before Merci could continue. "Of course, we were upset. You asked to go to California to visit your cousin. How were we to know that you'd involve yourself in something as reckless as flying an airplane? Such a notion never occurred to us."

"I know you were upset, Mom," Merci repeated. "But when I mentioned bringing a Jenny to Montana, you could have told me to forget it. Instead, you sent the money to purchase the plane and ship it to

Two Dot." She walked around behind her parents. Leaning over the back of their chairs, she gave a hug, first to one and then to the other. "I love you both so very much. You've been better to me than any child deserves, but, please, I'm all grown up now. I have the Jenny, and I hope to do more than fly it around the ranch. I intend to show the world what a modern woman can do."

T. C.'s. smile was wan. "Neither of us has any intention of keeping you from living your life. It's just that flying is dangerous, so we worry." The smile died. "That's part of our job, I guess." T. C. straightened his back and asked, "Tell us more about this man Chris Cape. How did he just happen to be in Lewistown? And then fly back with you?"

"Apparently, I spoke of barnstorming before I left California. I guess I mentioned selling rides at Lewistown. It's the closest town of any size. Chris must have remembered." She looked from father to mother. "All I know is that he was there when I landed the Jenny and helped while I gave rides to passengers."

"Then you brought him here."

"Yes. And thank you, Daddy, for telling Lyndon to take him in to Two Dot. I know that interrupted the things that Lyndon would have been doing."

Felicity focused intently on her daughter. "If he's going to help you with your airplane, he should stay in this house as our guest. Not at the Hopkins Hotel in Two Dot or the Graves Hotel in Harlowton. After all, Arnold Masters was treated as a guest for a couple of days before he decided it was more convenient to stay in town to work on the airplane."

"Mom, it's different with Chris. I invited Arnold. Chris invited himself. He can help with the Jenny, but I don't want him around me at any other time."

Now Felicity knew there was more going on with Mr. Cape than Merci was telling her.

T. C stood to focus a serious look on his daughter. "They have Nate Hamilton in jail. He's charged with the murder of Arnold Masters."

Merci's head jerked around. "What? Nate in jail? Charged with murder? That's ridiculous."

"Perhaps, but it's true. We didn't tell you sooner. Didn't want your flight spoiled by the news."

"Flight spoiled? If I'd known Nate was in jail there wouldn't have been a flight." She took three steps toward the stairs, then looked over her shoulder. "He'll need me. I'll visit him, right now!"

The Wheatland County Jail, standing by itself one hundred yards east of the courthouse, was a square concrete structure not much larger in size than Merci's bedroom. A barrier of metal rods, an inch and a half in circumference, separated the tiny entryway from the single cell. The lock on the cell door required a key that was huge and unwieldy. One tiny barred window at the back of the cell provided a small amount of light during the day. There was nothing to provide light once the sun went down. An odor of stale sweat and grime constantly permeated the gloom. An even more odoriferous privy was located behind the jail.

Nate Hamilton rose from the bunk and grasped the bars of the cell door when Merci walked into the tiny entry area. "God, it good to see you, Merc. No one's been here except Spence and my old man. Sitting all alone in this place is more than I can stand." His grip on the bars was so tight that his knuckles were white. The look on his face was one she had never seen before. "Spence's got to get me out of here, Merc! I'll go crazy if they keep me here another night. I don't even have a newspaper to read." His voice rose and he gave the cell door a shake. "What the hell's going on anyway? Old Lester Graves wouldn't tell me anything." He rattled the door once again, then, in seeming resignation, dropped his hands to his sides and shook his head. He added in more quiet tones. "I was going to invite him to go to hell when he came to the ranch to arrest me, but my old man made me go with him. Then he just brought me here and locked me in without saying how long I'd be here or anything else."

Merci waited until she was certain Nate was finished. "I'm sure you've been told that a special prosecutor has been appointed. He's a deputy attorney general named Garth Swain. Spence says neither Sheriff Graves nor Roger Davidson have much to say about any of this. Swain's in charge."

Nate grabbed a bar. A frown deepened the lines on his craggy brow as anger showed again. "How did that happen?"

Merci leaning closer, kept her voice gentle and level. "Arnold Masters' father is some kind of political powerhouse, and he pulled some strings in Helena to get it done." She gripped a bar next to the one in Nate's big fist. "Spence has prepared the papers asking the judge to release you on bail. But, the judge's judicial district covers three counties: Wheatland, Meagher, and Broadwater. He lives in White Sulphur Springs and we're told he's in Townsend today. It's Friday so the judge won't be here until Monday. You're in here that long...at least." Merci stood back an inch as even more anger spread over Nate's face. "And you might as well understand that the judge may not grant bail. Spence says that if he refuses to do so, you'll be here until the trial. "

The anger disappeared. Nate slumped onto the bunk. He sat with his head down, elbows on his knees. "I'm not sure I can handle that, Merci. This place is hell. I'm used to lots of room. I may go crazy if I have to stay here very long." The sentence ended with a rough head shake. Merci, at a loss for a way to console him, let the silence run. At last, he looked up at her. "Merc, I appreciate your coming here today more than you can ever know. It makes me realize I'd better do what I should have done a long time ago—apologize to you for my behavior the night you told me to take a hike." He paused. "You remember how it was after of us boys came back from the war. I assumed that you had feelings for me and that we'd be married when I got home." A wry smile appeared. "You let me know in no uncertain terms that it wasn't going to happen then—or ever."

Merci frowned as she stepped away from the cell bars. "Nate, you're behavior that night was as bad as it could be. Your language was inexcusable." Then the frown went away. "But that was almost two years ago. I've forgotten it, and so should you."

"The problem, Merc, is that my feelings haven't changed. When I heard you were coming back from California I thought we might spend some time together. But it seemed that mechanic had the inside track." Nate kept his eyes on the floor. "Then your mechanic was gone." He looked up at his visitor. "I know it sounds foolish, but my first thought when I heard about it was that I might have a chance after all." He grimaced. "Now this." Nate waved one hand and then dropped his arms between his knees. "Now, I'm a jailbird."

Merci straightened her back and placed her fists on her hips. "Forget about all of that. It's not what's important right now." She looked squarely at him. "What I'll do, Nate, is try to find out who really killed Arnold. I'm as certain as night and day that you didn't do it." She turned to leave, then looked over her shoulder to say, "I'll bring the Montana Standard and some other things for you to read before I leave town." After a pause, she added, "And some coffee and a piece of pie from Mother's Café."

19 The courtroom on the top floor of the courthouse was long but narrow. The judge's bench and the witness stand took up most of the front part of the room leaving only a narrow walkway between them and the side walls. The morning sun shining through the windows at the far end of the room created streaks of light in which tiny specks of dust appeared to float.

Judge D. D. Crawford was glowering from the bench. Spence had learned from experience that the man glowered easily and often. Now, the judge pointed with the handle of his gavel at Garth Swain. "All right, Mr. Swain, I've heard your reasons why this man should be held in jail until trial." Turning to point the gavel at Spence, he growled, "And I've heard your argument, Mr. Bruce, with the reasons why your client should be released without bail into the custody of his father." He turned his attention back to Swain as he said, "I'm doing neither. The accused, Nathaniel Hamilton, is to be released on bail, and bail is set at three thousand dollars." He turned his attention to Spence. "Mr. Bruce, make certain that your client understands that he's to stay out of trouble and that he must appear at all court hearings." The judge banged the gavel, rose to his feet, and growled again, "Court's adjourned."

Spence sprang to his feet and stood until the judge had cleared the room. Then he looked down at his client still seated in a chair next to him. Nate was unmoving and seemed to be in a daze. After a couple of seconds, he recovered, struggled to his feet, and asked, "Do I have to go back to that jail?"

Spence turned to see the sheriff striding forward from the rear of the courtroom. Lester Graves spoke to Spence, not Nate. "I'll take him back to the jail until the bond's posted." Grasping the young man's arm he added, "I hope it's soon." He tugged at his prisoner. "C'mon, Son, let's get you out of here." Nate cast a resigned look at his father, who stood nearby, as he was led away.

Garth Swain was middle age, small, wiry, good-looking, but with a serious demeanor. He was dressed in an expensive suit. He waited until Nate was out of sight, then stepped across the room, hand outstretched. "I didn't get a chance to introduce myself before we began." He grasped Spence's hand lightly then released it quickly. "I guess we'll be facing each other in a trial—unless your client wants to plead it out."

Spence looked the man squarely in the eye. "First, I don't think Nate Hamilton will plead guilty to any crime he didn't commit. Second, if there is a trial, Nate will probably have a lawyer who's had more trial experience than I."

Swain's eyebrows went up. "He's bringing in someone else? Who would that be?"

"I've recommended that he retain an experienced criminal defense attorney. He hasn't done that yet."

The special prosecuting attorney reached for his valise. "Well, I'm prepared to deal with any lawyer who shows up. Your man's guilty. The evidence we produce will make it clear." With briefcase in hand he strode out the door. Spence noted that he had never smiled once during the conversation.

Amos Hamilton was waiting on the courthouse boardwalk, agony twisting his face. He looked both ways to see if anyone but Spence was listening, then moaned, "God, Spence! Three thousand for bail, I can't get that much money up." Spence thought Amos might cry. "I'm next to broke. That's the size of it. These last three tough years have about ruined me." The old man slumped down next to his wife who was seated on a bench beside the wall of the building. "Nate will just have to stay in jail."

Beatrice Hamilton, a heavy woman, whose lined face was somber at the best of times, now showed pure anguish. She put her hand on her husband's arm as she looked at Spence. Her voice trembled. "We'll get the money somehow. And we'll get whatever money you need to take care of our son." A tear glistened in the corner of her eye. "Nothing is more important."

Amos patted her hand and then struggled to his feet. "Of course, nothing's more important." He offered his wife a hand as she rose from the bench. "I'll talk to that fellow at the bank in Two Dot this afternoon. God, I hope he'll lend me the money."

Mrs. Hamilton didn't follow her husband as he turned away. She stood fast with her eyes focused on Spence. "Our son can't kill anything. He won't go hunting because he can't stand to kill a deer. He won't even step on a spider. Amos is always complaining because Nate will help dress out a beef, but doesn't want to be there when the killing is done. We don't know why he's the way he is. But we both know our son can't kill a single thing. And he certainly didn't kill your sister's friend."

The bond was posted. As father and son walked away from the jail, Nate was so relieved to be away from the place that he was close to giddy. Without thought about how it might sound, he suggested a beer before leaving for the ranch. His father's cold stare would have frozen boiling water. "There'll be no beer. And further than that, you ain't go-

ing near to town, either Two Dot or Harlo, until the start of the trial…
or until the charges are dismissed."

Merci learned that Mrs. Hamilton had ridden the train to Butte where
she sold heirloom jewelry in order to raise the three hundred dollars
for the bondsman. One day up, one day in Butte, one day back. Merci
marveled at the fierceness of mother love. She vowed once again to do
whatever she could to find Arnold's real killer, beginning with another
chat with Irma Lewellyn.

The mail arrived in Two Dot on the morning train and was deposited in mail boxes at the general store at about eleven o'clock. Many
of the town and ranch folk gathered at that time to pick up their mail.
Merci met Irma as the waitress walked out the post office door, a newspaper and an envelope in hand. Irma nodded a hello and turned to
stride down the dusty, dirty street toward the café. Merci hurried to
walk alongside, saying, "Let's visit some more about the party."

"What's to visit about?"

"You didn't tell me you helped Arnold Masters when he upchucked
out behind the saloon."

"It didn't seem important."

"Who else was back there at the same time?"

Irma smirked. "You may not want to know."

Merci gritted her teeth for control. "I do want to know. Who else
was out there?"

"Nate Hamilton was the only one that I saw. He was standing next
to the creek side emptying his bladder." Irma raised her eyebrows.
"Isn't that what they call it in polite society?"

Merci ignored the sarcasm. "Did Nate leave when you did?"

"No. Nate and Arnold were back there together when I left. And I
never saw either one of them again that night."

"What time did all of this take place?"

"It was late. That's all I know." Irma stopped and turned toward Merci. "Look, everybody knows what you're trying to do. You're trying to show that someone other than Nate killed Arnold. I don't know why. Maybe you and Nate are more than chums from school days. But that has nothing to do with me." She turned to continue her amble down the street. "Don't bother me with your questions again."

20

Two days later Amos shuffled into Spence's office, threw down his hat, and dropped into a chair. "There ain't any more money, Spence. We can't pay some high-priced lawyer to go to court for Nate." He slumped with his elbows on his knees, head down, eyes to the floor. "And we can't even pay you any more than we already have."

At last, he raised his head, a look of anguish contorting his face. "God, Spence, I hate to be in this position, but will you continue to look after our son for us, please? Even if we can't pay?" His voice choked as he added, "I don't know what else to do—but just beg."

The unexpected confession and plea jarred Spence. He had assumed that Amos and Beatrice Hamilton could somehow raise the money for an experienced criminal attorney to represent their son. He pushed his chair back from the desk as though instinctively distancing himself from a responsibility too great for his ability. He received no solace from a look at Amos' face. A tear traced down from the old man's eye to follow a deep crease, along his cheek and finally drop to the floor.

"What about Harry Ward down the street? He's had more courtroom experience than I have."

"Spence, Harry's all bluster and no substance. Everyone in town knows that. He's just as likely to cave in and tell Nate to plead guilty so he wouldn't have to face a trial. And he ain't going to work for nothing. You're the one we want and need."

"Amos, you're asking me to do something I may not be good enough to do. I've never been involved in a serious criminal case. If I mess it up, Nate will go to jail—or worse."

The old rancher wiped at his eye with a knurled hand. "Spence. All of us—Nate, Beatrice, and I—would rather have you as the lawyer than some sport from Butte that we've never heard of." He leaned forward. "You do it and we'll take whatever the outcome might be." Then he slumped back again. "But please, Spence, take care of our boy."

Spence's mind was racing. What could he do? After only a moment he realized he needed to discuss the matter with his father. He offered the older man a smile that he hoped was a reassuring. "Amos, let me talk to Dad about this."

Mr. Hamilton's face brightened. "Of course. I can understand why you'd want to do that." He nodded as he continued, "And I'll feel better if you talk to your dad about Nate's problem. He'll give you good advice." His face was fierce with determination. "But don't ask him to front the money so we can hire another lawyer. He's helped me out in the past. That's more than enough."

After Amos Hamilton shuffled out the door, Spence rose from his chair and began to pace the short distance from the back of his office to the front while he thought about his father.

T. C. Bruce had been educated as a lawyer, but chose to make his life as a cattle rancher. He didn't follow the law as a profession. He had no regrets about the decision and loved the close-to-nature life that a rancher was able to live. And he'd been remarkably successful in that endeavor. But he still kept shelves of law books in the room he called his office. Once when Spence was twelve years old, he heard T. C. and another rancher talking about something called a "herd district."

Later that evening he asked T. C. what a herd district was. The older man started to explain, but then he remembered Spence's penchant for reading. So instead of just answering the question directly, T. C. took the boy to the office and pulled a book from the shelf. He thumbed through it, found the right page, and handed the book to Spence, saying, "You can learn a lot from these volumes." And he left the boy alone to read.

Read he did and then would often discuss the meaning of the Montana statutes with his father. His curiosity about the law and the evening conversations with his father eventually guided him to the law school at the university in Missoula.

Upon graduation and admission to the bar, Spence had a decision to make. He could put his education to work and practice law, or he could do as his father had done—make his life on the ranch. T. C. was healthy and active. He didn't need Spence. So Spence set up shop in Harlowton and practiced his profession for about a year. Then, three years ago in 1917, the United States entered the war in Europe. Like many young men of his age, Spence was anxious to do his part in the war effort and enlisted in the army. The mind-numbing slaughter of human beings during battles in France removed any notion from his mind that war was romantic.

He was fortunate enough to return to Montana without permanent injury to body or spirit. In the year since his return, he'd reestablished his practice. A considerable number of the local farmers and ranchers, as well as town folk, sought his legal assistance. Spence realized that many of those who came to him did so only because they, like Amos Hamilton, respected his parents.

Spence had tried only one felony case and lost—not because he'd made any legal or tactical mistakes, but because his client was clearly guilty of butchering a neighbor's cow. He knew and understood the fundamental elements of a criminal defense. What he lacked was the savvy, the shrewdness, the cunning, the quickness of wit, that a lawyer could only acquire from long hours spent jousting in the courtroom. The lack of those attributes could result in Nate's conviction if Spence was his lawyer.

He surely needed to seek the counsel of his father. And he also needed to hear the thoughts of his sister. Spence grabbed his hat, told Helen he would be gone for the rest of the day, and pointed his auto toward the Bruce Ranch.

Spence, Merci, and their father and mother sat in chairs facing one another across the kitchen table. After listening to his son's recital of the conversation with Amos Hamilton, T. C. frowned, brushed his hand over his graying hair, and looked off into the distance for a long moment. When he returned his gaze to Spence, he said, "As you know, Amos is much older than I am. He was one of the early ones into the valley when the range was open. He worked hard, gathered together a lot of cattle, and did pretty well until other ranchers began to build fences so they could keep their cattle at home. That closed off the open range in the upper Musselshell Valley to all the early ranchers, including Amos. Then he was late in his efforts to acquire deeded land, so he had to scramble to buy tracts from the railroad and from others who had proved up on homesteads and were willing to sell. The Hamilton Ranch, as you know it, was acquired at significant cost. These last few years of drought and low livestock prices have really been tough on him financially. I can certainly understand why he can't borrow money to hire an experienced criminal defense attorney."

T. C. paused in the monologue, shifted in his chair, and heaved a sigh. "Amos's situation is sad in a way." He leaned forward, placing his elbows on the table. The tone of his voice, when he continued, carried earnestness not evident before. "All that doesn't address the problem facing young Nate. Nate may be guilty, or he may not be guilty. But he needs a lawyer to assure that he gets the benefit of our justice system. If Amos can't hire anyone but you and if you can't—or won't—represent Nate, our neighbor's son could find himself in court without any attorney. If that happens he'll be convicted whether he's guilty or not."

Spence finally interrupted. "But, Dad, having me as his lawyer is almost as bad as having no lawyer at all."

"You said *almost* as bad, son. You admit that having you as his lawyer would be better than no lawyer at all. That may be the best that Nate can hope for."

"That's an awful slender reed for anyone to lean on. All I can think about is the possibility that I might miss something that could save him—a motion that should be made, an objection that should be raised, a question that should be asked. Or that I might do something in court that was just plain stupid, something that could lead to his conviction."

Felicity broke into the conversation. "Spencer, I believe you are underestimating your ability. You certainly know the law. You reason well. And your thinking is quick and clear, even in difficult circumstances."

Before Spence could speak, T. C. smiled at his wife and nodded his agreement. "She's right, Son. Amos hasn't done as well financially as we all would like. But he's still an old and valued friend. He's asked you to care for his son. Now I'm asking you to do it—for me if not for Nate—because Amos's friendship is important to me."

"Will you help me, Dad, when I need it? By letting me to share my thoughts with you? By reviewing any motions I prepare? And reading through instructions for the jury? By making suggestions for questions that I might ask of witnesses at the trial itself if it gets that far?

"Of course. I'll help anyway that I can. So will your mother. And so will Merci." T. C. paused and then continued rather quickly, "I think lawyers too often focus on the law that governs a case and focus too little on the facts."

Spence nodded. "In this case that could be true. The facts, as we know them, have me puzzled. The ones that Swain seems to be relying on for conviction are only three. First, Nate was angry because Arnold danced too often with Merci—or the Lewellyn woman—and nearly attacked him. Second, the bayonet found in the body is Nate's and he showed it off during the party. Third, Nate used a rope to entertain the ladies. It may have been the kind used for the strangulation. Those three things alone hardly seem adequate to convince a jury that Nate is a killer." Spence looked closely at this father. "Do you agree?"

"I agree. But he may have found something that we don't know about. Perhaps someone who can provide testimony that will buttress those facts." T. C. leaned toward his son. "If you decide to help Nate, I suggest that you interview every potential witness. Don't rely on the sheriff or anyone else to provide you with the evidence you need. "

Merci spoke for the first time, addressing her father. "I can help with the interviews. That will save time for Spence. I'll begin by trying to find everyone who was there on the street that night and listen to what they have to say." She cast a look at her brother. "Can I do that, Spence?"

"Of course, you can, Merc. Any person you interview may be one that I won't need to bother with. That will relieve me to do other things that Nate's defense will require. If you learn something that will help Nate, you and I can talk to that person together. It will help a lot."

T. C. leaned across the table and patted his son's hand. "One more thing. If you need an expert witness for any reason, we'll help with the cost."

Spence stood. "Your advice is good, as always. And thanks for the offer. If I need an expert, I'll let you know." He touched his father's arm. "Thanks for listening to me pour out my worries."

T. C. also rose from the chair and put his hand on his son's shoulder. "Amos can't pay you for your time and effort. But your mother and I will make certain that you're compensated for your time."

Spence shook his head. "That isn't necessary. You've provided for me in every way since my earliest childhood."

His father smiled. "We'll do it because I've asked you to take on a task that you might have chosen to avoid." His arm was around Spence's shoulder as they turned to the door. "You'll do fine, Son. Felicity and I—and Merci, too—will be proud of you for helping Nate and Amos, no matter the outcome.

21

The day's heat was beginning to bleed away when Spence locked the door to his office late that afternoon and began a leisurely stroll to the Graves Hotel. Near the street corner he almost collided with Eunice Syvertson as she stepped from the doorway of the dry goods store. Each of them hastily stepped back—she gasping in surprise while holding her hand to her breast—he fumbling to tip his hat. After an embarrassed moment, Spence smiled, "Why good evening, Miss Syvertson. Please forgive me. I should be more careful where I walk."

"No need for an apology, Mr. Bruce. I was the one who should have been more careful. I'm afraid my mind was still on a small child—one who was injured today."

"Not seriously, I hope."

"Seriously. The Chestnut girl. You probably know the family. The neighbor's dog bit her face and removed a large piece of skin from her nose and lip."

"How horrible!"

Miss Syvertson shook her head as her eyes dropped to the ground. "They brought her to the office right away and had the good sense to bring the piece of skin along with her." She twisted her hands together as she looked back at Spence. "The poor child was screaming in agony. The doctor had me scrub the skin the best I could, and then he sewed it all back in place. But it doesn't seem likely that it will heal together again." Miss Syvertson heaved a long sigh. "If it doesn't, the child will go through life terribly disfigured."

"Well, let's pray for the best outcome. It seems too often that praying is all we can do."

"Do you pray, sir?" The question was asked as though she thought it unlikely.

Spence smiled his response. "I think we all pray on occasion, especially when our human efforts appear to be inadequate." Then impulse took over. "Miss Syvertson, I'm on my way to supper at the Graves Hotel. Would you be so kind as to join me?" Before she could answer, he began his apology. "It was impertinent of me to ask." He paused in embarrassment. "An explanation, if not an excuse, is that a meal alone just isn't very appealing."

She offered a warm smile at his embarrassment and put her arm through his. "Nor does a lonely meal appeal to me. Of course, I'll join you at the Graves Hotel. The only time I dined there both the atmosphere and the food were enjoyable." They turned to continue the trek to the hotel as she said, "Please call me Eunice. And I'll call you Spencer—unless you object."

"I won't object. Why should we be so formal?"

They shared small talk until the food was served and then ate in silence. With the eating at an end and the table cleared, Spence leaned slightly forward, folded hands on the table. "You've been here a few days. How do you like our town?"

"It's nice and quiet. The people are friendly." She smiled as she leaned forward to mimic his pose. "People like you. I really appreciate the things you did for me when I first arrived."

"I didn't do much." Spence turned slightly sideways and put one elbow on the table. "What do you think of our doctor, if I may ask?"

"You may ask. I've been impressed by his ability. The skill he showed today while stitching that poor child's face was incredible. And he has a wonderful way of dealing with his patients."

"How does he treat you?"

The smile brightened. "He's really good to me. He includes me in his discussions with the patients. He takes time to explain the reason for the treatments he prescribes. He couldn't treat me better."

Spence returned her smile. "That's nice to hear. Maybe you'll stay with us. Doc needs you here. And so do the rest of us."

"You needn't worry about that. This town has made me comfortable."

Spence pushed his chair away from the table. "I'm sure there are things you have to do, and I'm keeping you from them."

Eunice nodded and stood. "There is always something to do. Laundry, if nothing else."

"May I walk you home?"

"Yes, you may. And I'll thank you for the meal and the conversation as we walk. This evening has been delightful."

The June rains, infrequent and sparse as they had been, came to an end, as they nearly always do near the end of the month. After that, came hot days with strong, gusty winds. The Jenny remained in the hangar. The third morning of July had been clear and quiet. Assuming the next day would be the same, Merci thought of asking Lyndon to pull the prop, but decided, instead, to send word to Chris Cape to come to the ranch early the next morning, ready to fly. They'd wow the folks at the various Fourth of July celebrations with a flyover.

The summer air was cool and still when the Jenny left the ground at ten o'clock. They flew west over Martinsdale where they could see the beginnings of a small parade forming at the south end of the main street. Merci banked the plane to the south and then northward again. She pointed the nose downward for a shallow dive over town. People poured out of doorways and joined those preparing for the parade to wave arms and hats at the aviators. Merci made one more pass over the burg, as she and Chris waved back to the throng below.

Leaving Martinsdale behind, Merci put her machine into a slow climbing turn to the northeast. The crowd in Judith Gap was gathering around a fireworks stand and patriotic display. Merci flew low over the town so she and Cape could wave to those on the streets below. Those in the crowd responded with their own waves and shouts.

Hedgesville offered much of the same. A small crowd was listening to a speaker, standing on a small platform. A large U. S. flag draped from a pole beside it. The man on the platform halted his speech to join the others in the waving at the passing flyers.

They flew on southwestward to Harlowton. The parade in the county seat was just beginning its march down Central Avenue, from the courthouse at the street's upper end to the railroad depot at the bottom of the hill. Two men on horseback carried flags and led the way. Other riders followed. Behind them, an open auto carried the king and queen of the celebration. Autos of various manufacture followed the royalty. The high school band strutted along.

At the baseball field in the park, the groundskeepers were preparing the field for the annual holiday game—Harlowton versus Two Dot. The Two Dot nine won the last match and the Harlo team vowed to avenge the loss. Some of the Harlo players stood to the side of the field, waiting to get in some pre-game practice.

Merci made one pass over town to attract attention and then made the second pass much lower. She waggled the wings of the Jenny as she approached the front of the parade. The flag bearers halted. Their horses, frightened by the sudden noise, skittered about and tried to run. The king and queen stood up in the back of the open auto to join in the waving. All the others along the parade route followed suit.

Looking down from above, Merci saw a number of folks dashing to their automobiles and heading for the field to the north, apparently thinking she would land as she had once before. She hated to disappoint them, but she had to get back to the ranch. The whole Bruce family planned to attend the ball game in Harlo.

Back at the ranch, Chris and Merci shoved the Jenny back into it hangar. When the gates were closed, she turned to Cape with her feet spread and her hands on her hips, a picture of defiance. Time to get him to talk about the night of the party. "What haven't you told me about the happenings the night Arnold was killed? I understand you were there, and I've been told you talked with Arnold."

Cape backed away. "I can't talk now, Merc. I've got to get back to Harlo." He grabbed the crank to the Model T and gave it a turn. With the motor running, he yelled, "Perhaps we can get together after the ball game."

Merci watched the auto speed away and wondered why the man was in such a hurry—and why he refused to answer her questions.

Before the three members of the Bruce family climbed into the auto, T. C. looked at his daughter with a devious grin. "The Harlo boys don't know it, but Two Dot has a new pitcher who can really throw a fireball."

Merci asked, "Who's the pitcher?"

"That new Baptist preacher who came to town a couple of weeks ago. He's from Kentucky."

"The man who held services in the Community Church in Two Dot last Sunday?"

"That's the one."

"How'd you find out he could pitch?"

"I was visiting with him at the post office. He told me he'd played ball for his hometown team and could pitch some. I took Lyndon to Two Dot to test the man's ability. As you know, Lyndon's the catcher for the Two Dot team. Well, we watched that preacher throw and knew right away that we'd made a find."

T. C. had invited the Morgans—Hiram, Sophia, and Lyndon—to join them on the ride into Harlowton. The seven-passenger Packard touring car carried all of them in comfort. They stopped at Mother's Café for a noon repast before going down the hill to the park.

The baseball diamond was laid out on level land with a tall back-stop, and bleachers behind the home plate. A low fence enclosed the outfield.

The Bruce entourage found autos parked, facing inward along both the first and third base side of the diamond. T. C. located an open spot for the touring car about midway down the third base line. Lyndon was out of the car in a flash and running across the field to join the other members of the Two Dot team.

T. C. hoisted some folding chairs from the trunk attached to the rear of the Packard. He and Hiram helped their wives to the ground and around to the chairs. Each of the men then perched on a front fender of the auto—feet on the bumper. Good place to watch the action. The fellow leaning against the auto parked next to them, turned to T. C. to shake hands and grin. "We'll beat your Two Dot boys this time, T. C."

The rancher returned the merchant's smile. "What makes you think so, Milt?"

"We've got a ringer—a new guy who can cover more of the outfield than I've ever seen before. And he can hit a ton."

"Who is this guy?"

The grin widened. "You'll see soon enough."

Merci listened to the conversation between the men while leaning against the car's radiator. She hadn't seen a game for a while and there always seemed to be some changes. She was surprised to see Nate Hamilton in a uniform, tossing a ball back and forth with another young man in a Two Dot uniform.

The remark to her father reflected her chagrin. "I thought Amos told Nate he couldn't come to town until the trial."

"He's our power hitter. I called Amos and asked him to give Nate a reprieve for this day only."

Merci shook her head. She didn't think it was a good idea for Nate, an accused killer, to be playing. How would potential jurors react? Would they be offended to think he took his situation so lightly as to engage in frivolous activity?"

Spencer had asked Eunice to join him and his family at the game. She agreed after expressing some reluctance about meeting Spencer's family, but when they arrived, Felicity and T.C. greeted her warmly and quickly put her mind at ease. Merci moved close to hold out her arm, the sleeve of her blouse pulled away from the site of her injury. "The gash you and Doc repaired healed completely."

Eunice ran her fingers along the thin white line. "Doctor Scanlan always takes so much care when he's stitching that there's seldom a scar." Before more could be said the bustle of the crowd drew their attention to the ball field. The action was about to begin.

The home team always batted last. Merci watched with interest as the Harlo squad ran out to take up their fielding positions. She gave a start to see Chris Cape among them, heading for center field. So this was the reason he hurried away from the ranch. Merci couldn't help but wonder what stunt the Californian would pull next.

The hardware owner—thirty years old, small, and wiry—was first at the plate for Two Dot. A burly section worker batted second. Both went down swinging. Nate was the cleanup man. On the first pitch he flied out to deep center. Cape moved gracefully to easily snag the ball.

As the Two Dot team took to the field, T. C. grinned across at Milt, still standing by the next car. "Well, that was quick. But now watch the pitcher. He's our ringer. We call him Kentuck." It was a moniker, Merci assumed, that the man preferred.

Kentuck didn't fail them. The speed at which he fired the ball seemed to baffle the men at the plate. First inning, three up and three down.

The game rolled along through seven scoreless innings. Both Nate Hamilton and Chris Cape managed to connect several times with the ball, but neither reached first base. Their hits were either high flies or grounders for easy outs. In the top of the eighth, Nate swatted a fly that dropped into shallow right between the Chris and the right fielder. In his attempt to retrieve the ball, the other man interfered with Cape's effort to do the same. Cape finally corralled the ball in time to see Nate already past second base and on his way to third. His throw was mighty and accurate. A sliding Nate Hamilton reached third base in a cloud of dust at the instant the ball hit the third baseman's glove. Prone on the ground and with his hand resting on the base, Nate looked triumphantly upward at the umpire. But the umpire squatting close at hand, jerked his thumb over his shoulder, and hollered, "Out!"

Nate was on his feet in a flash, anger on his face and in his voice. He yelled a curse at the umpire and had both hands up about to shove him in the chest when one of his teammates got between them.

The ruckus would have ended right then had Chris Cape not strolled up. He stopped in front of the rancher to stand with his legs spread, open hand on one hip, and the gloved hand on the other with a smirk on his face. "What's the matter, country boy? Can't take it when things don't go your way?"

Nate threw the punch from his waist toward Cape's jaw. The Californian moved backward and blocked Nate's fist with the gloved hand. The sound that came from Chris's mouth wasn't so much a laugh as it was a snigger. "You can't throw a punch any better than you play ball." Turning, the Californian shot a last remark over his shoulder. "I know you didn't kill Arnold Masters. You aren't man enough."

It was all that several teammates could do to drag Nate away. Spence ran across the field, grabbed Nate by the arm, and snarled, "You damn fool! The jury that decides whether you're guilty or not will come from this crowd. And now they've just seen what a temper you have. It'll serve you right if you're convicted!" He gave Nate a shove and walked away. Nate was red in the face and breathing hard when Amos arrived. One word to his son and Nate's participation in the game came to an end.

Merci, watching it all, shook her head as she said to herself, "Nate, Nate. You just can't seem to help yourself."

The game resumed. Chris Cape homered in the bottom of the ninth inning to win the game for Harlo.

Milt gave T. C. a friendly punch on the arm. "I told you our new guy would win it for us. Have you met him?"

"Yes, I've met him." T. C., sober faced, nodded. "You're right. He sure can play ball."

23 Merci paused to consider the work worn horses hitched to the farm wagon in front of the post office. Inside she found Susan Richards pulling letters from a mail box. Susan was the daughter of a homesteader, one of the few still hanging on. Her dress was clean but showed the effect of many washings. She had a petite figure and an attractive countenance. Merci remembered that Susan had not wanted for dance partners the night of Arnold's death. With the Bruce Ranch mail in hand and back out of doors, Merci touched the other woman's arm lightly. "Pardon me. Can we chat for a minute?"

Susan turned from the wagon to look Merci up and down. When she answered, her face was without expression. "You're Merci Bruce. What do want with me?"

"Just a few questions—if I may."

"Look, Miss Bruce, everyone knows that you're trying to find out something that will help keep Nate Hamilton out of prison—or maybe the hangman's noose. But I can't help you." The driving reins had been tied to the wagon brake. She gathered them in her hands, put a foot on the hub of a wheel to climb up onto the seat. Settled at last, she looked down at Merci. "Maybe what they're saying is right—that you're so in love with Nate that you'll help him even though he murdered your mechanic."

Merci was so completely taken aback by that last remark that, for a moment, she couldn't respond. But she recovered in time to put a hand on the wagon box and bark, "Wait a minute!"

"I don't have time to wait a minute. So leave me alone."

Merci stepped back and placed her fists on her hips. "Well, maybe you'd rather my brother secure a subpoena compelling you to testify about things that happened the night Arnold was killed."

"What do you mean?"

"He can get an order from the judge compelling you to appear in court and tell all that you remember about that night."

Susan Richards blinked, thought a second, then seemed to relax. "All right, all right. What do you want to know?"

This time Merci smiled as she spoke. "Look, I don't want to cause any problems for you. But Arnold's dead. Nate's charged with murder. Maybe he did it, but I don't believe so. Maybe you're certain Nate is the killer. If you're not certain, why not help me?"

Susan heaved a sigh. "I don't know who killed your mechanic. Frankly, I don't much care. I have my own problems." She straightened. "But ask your questions. I'll do my best to answer them."

"First of all, did you hear Nate hollering at Arnold, accusing him of dancing too often with Irma Lewellyn?"

"Of course, I did. Everyone who was on the street heard him. He yelled something like, 'Irma doesn't need some no-good, fancy dude from California. Stay away from her.'"

"Did he do anything beside yell?"

"He stopped yelling and started for Masters as though he wanted to punch him."

"What happened?"

"A couple of other guys grabbed Nate and dragged him away."

"Did Nate try to resist their efforts?"

Susan laughed. "Are you kidding? No, he didn't resist. We all know that Nate's nothing but bluff. He really didn't want to fight. He was just being his usual self, trying to impress the girls."

"I've been told he went out behind Lippy's place and sulked after that."

"If he did, it couldn't have been for long. The guys were keeping me busy dancing, and I was having lots of fun—so I didn't pay much attention to Nate. But pretty soon he was out there in the middle of the street, spinning that rope, doing his tricks."

"For how long?"

"Not long. A couple of songs later, he asked me to dance."

"Did you dance with him?"

Susan laughed. "Why not? He's a good-looking man—for all his faults. And he lives on a large ranch. Who knows, maybe he'd decide on me, not you." Her laugh continued as she drove the team of skinny horses up the street and on toward her home.

24

Three days of rain—not real rain, just intermittent showers—were enough to keep the Jenny on the ground. Not a single day was fit to fly. When the clouds cleared away the next evening, Merci cranked the two short rings on the telephone that roused the Two Dot storekeeper. Stef Steiner answered with a grumbling, "Mercantile."

"Mr. Steiner, do you know if Chris Cape is staying at the Two Dot Hotel."

"Who?"

"Chris Cape. Tall. Well dressed. Good-looking."

"Never seen him."

"Will you ring Harlo then, please? I'll try the Graves Hotel."

Connected at last, Merci asked Gladys, the operator on shift during the evening, to ring the hotel. Finally, she asked the clerk if Chris was registered. Told that he was, Merci said, "Please give him this message: flying at six o'clock in the morning."

The clerk repeated the message, then added, "I'll tell him as soon as he comes by for his room key."

Merci placed the receiver onto the telephone hook. Chris could pull the prop first thing tomorrow. And she'd press him harder about the night Arnold met his death.

The next morning, Chris Cape parked a Model T coupe next to the hangar just as Merci arrived on foot from the ranch house. "Great day to fly, Merc!"

"It is, Chris. So let's get the machine out of the hangar and into the air." Together they pushed and pulled the Jenny outside and away from the structure. As they were donning warm jackets and flying helmets, Merci reminded Chris, "You pull the prop. And remember, you ride in the front cockpit and you're just a passenger. Don't even think of touching the controls."

"Let's be brave. I'll fly, and we'll pull a loop."

"At this altitude? You're crazy." She stepped up onto the bottom wing. "Just pull the prop and then get in." She pulled the earflaps down. "They're moving cows and calves from the north side of the Two Dot Butte to the basin on the south. It's rough country so it's difficult for the riders to know if they've found all the cattle they plan to move. We're going to fly over the pasture and make sure none are left behind."

"That should be interesting." Chris grabbed the prop, then peered around the motor at Merci to add, "But someday we have to try a loop."

"Not a chance."

Once in the air, Merci held the Jenny in a steady climb until she had enough elevation to pass safely over the upper reaches of the north-side pasture. The ranch crew began gathering the cattle shortly after dawn in order to have the animals moving before the sun pushed the temperature upward to summertime levels. With the heat came flies. When the flies hit, the animals scattered in their desperate effort to get to the shade of the trees. The trees gave some relief from the torment the insects inflicted. It was nearly impossible for the cowboys to control them.

But, the morning was cool. Looking down, Merci could tell that the riders had most of the cattle gathered and moving slowly toward the west and south. A couple of the horseback riders waved hats as the Jenny passed overhead. A short distance to the east, hidden in trees lining a tiny stream, Merci spotted a group of about ten cows with their calves. The riders had missed them in the gather. She would report the strays to her father who would have riders after them the next day.

Merci made two more passes over the pasture without seeing any other cattle that were missed. The purpose of the flight was successfully completed, but the air remained quiet and smooth. She increased the power from the motor and eased back on the stick to begin a climb for a long swing to the west along the base of the Crazy Mountains and over the town of Martinsdale. Past that burg, a turn to the north took Merci, Chris, and the Jenny to the foothills of the Little Belt Mountains and finally eastward to the mouth of Haymaker Canyon. She made one more turn, this time westward one hundred eighty degrees to begin the descent for the landing at the ranch. As the flight path straightened, she felt a shake of the stick and looked forward to see that Chris had his hand beside his head giving it a wave. The shake of the stick and hand gesture were the universal request that she release control of the aircraft. Her anger boiled. Not a chance that she would let him do the flying! She gripped the stick firmly to dampen his next attempt to shake it. Chris seemed to get the message, raised both hands so she could see them, and turned his head partially around to offer her a grin. He got no grin in return.

Once again on the ground, Merci shouted at the man. "You listen, Chris Cape! The Jenny is mine. I'll do the flying. You can ride along—nothing more. Is that clear?"

"Pulling a loop still seems like fun to me. I thought if you were unsure of how to do it, I'd show you."

"I know you've flown fighter planes—French Spad and an English Nieuport. So what? Those planes are intended for acrobatic flight. A

Jenny is a training plane. There's a difference."

Cape stood with his arms wide, hands facing up. "I looped a Jenny over the field at Los Angeles. All you have to do is climb about three thousand feet, put the nose down to gain speed, drag the stick back to climb up and over onto you're back, and then dive down again."

"At Los Angeles you were starting at sea level. Here you'd be starting at five thousand feet. To get high enough for the loop at this altitude, you'd have to climb to eight or nine thousand feet. The Jenny would never make it."

Cape's eyebrows lifted. "How will you know unless you try?"

Merci whirled away in disgust while saying, "The Jenny's mine, Chris. I'll do as I like. You can fly with me so long as you understand that fact and accept it." She stopped a few feet away, then turned back. "Now, tell me what you were doing in Two Dot the night Arnold lost his life."

"Nothing to tell, Merc. I was only there for a short time, and I was just an observer."

"Were you out behind the saloon at all?"

"Never was. As I told you and your brother, I was in my room in the hotel and heard all the noise. So I ambled down to see what was going on. Once there, I just stood away from the crowd and watched the dancing." The smile returned. "You sure seemed to be having fun."

"What I was doing isn't the question. Did you see anything that would help in finding the real killer?"

"Nope. Sorry. Can't help." He waved once, cranked his car, and was gone.

Merci pursed her lips in thought. Chris Cape wasn't telling her everything he knew about Arnold Masters' death. And he didn't even offer her a ride back to the ranch house. He remained the same self-centered man she'd known in California.

Spence hadn't seen the sheriff for several days so he smiled as the man approached on the sidewalk. "Good to see you again, Lester. You've been a stranger."

Graves lifted his hat and wiped his brow. "That man is cold, Spence."

"What man?"

"That man, Garth Swain. He never smiles. He never says a casual word. He's all business."

"Has Swain been in town?'

"Oh, yes. He comes and goes, asking questions and giving orders."

"What kind of orders?"

The sheriff shook his head. "Well, for one thing, he told me I can't talk to you."

Spence raised his eyebrows in astonishment. "Can't talk to me? Why not, for goodness sake?"

"Well, I can talk to you like this. But I can't tell you anything about the investigation into the murder of Arnold Masters."

"What is there to tell me?'

"Can't say, Spence. But it ain't looking good for Nate Hamilton." The sheriff nodded a farewell and walked on down the street.

Spence remained rooted where the sheriff left him. What the devil could they have found to use in their case against Nate?

Two days later he learned some of it. He'd driven to the ranch for a visit. Lyndon Morgan saw him pull into the barnyard and hurried to catch him before he reached the house. "Got a minute, Spence?" Lyndon glanced over his shoulder as though what he had to say was a secret.

"Of course. What's on your mind?"

Lyndon looked again at the house as though checking to be sure that no one would catch him. "The sheriff and that lawyer came to the homestead one evening and asked me a lot of questions."

Spence raised his eyebrows. "What kind of questions?"

"They wanted to know what I could tell them about the night when Merci's friend was killed."

"What did you have to say?"

"Spence, that lawyer scares me. He told me I couldn't tell you anything that I said to them." After taking a breath, Lyndon blurted, "I think he scares the sheriff, too."

"Lyndon, he can't keep you from telling me things you know about the murder." Spence waited a moment, then asked, "What did you tell them that they don't want me to know?"

"Will I get in trouble if I talk to you? That guy made it sound as though the sheriff would put me in jail if I did."

"Neither Garth Swain nor the sheriff can do anything to you for talking to me. If they try, just let me know. I'll deal with it." He paused for Lyndon to absorb his assurance. "Now, what did you tell them?"

Lyndon waited a long minute, then took a deep breath, and began. "I stayed at that party until nearly everyone else had left. I don't know why I stayed that long. Maybe because Irma said she'd dance with me again, and I was waiting for that chance. Anyway, I'd been having a good time, and I guess I just didn't want it to end." He paused and Spence waited for him to continue. "But it seemed that Arnold was dancing with Irma every time they started playing a new piece. So I never got to dance with her again." He paused again. "Merci'd gone home, but Arnold was still there."

Spence leaned back against the car with his arms folded. Lyndon shifted from foot to foot. Spence prompted him. "You said you were one of the last to leave."

"I was. And right before I left I went out back to relieve myself. Down the creek toward the depot I saw Arnold Masters and Nate Hamilton. I couldn't hear what they were saying, but Nate had his fist doubled up and was shaking it at Masters. He must have been really angry from the way he was behaving."

"What happened then?"

Lyndon dropped his head and scuffed a toe. "Irma was back there, too. She saw what was going on and ran to get between them. She was pushing Nate in the chest to try to move him away, but he just kept trying to get to Masters."

"Did Nate finally give it up?"

Lyndon hesitated, then looked up again at Spence. "I don't know. That's when I headed cross country for the homestead. I didn't have a ride so I had to walk."

Spence paused in thought before he asked, "You told all of this to Mr. Swain and the sheriff?'

"Yes. They asked and I told them."

"What else did you tell them that might relate to the killing?"

"Nothing, Spence. I swear." Lyndon straightened his back as he asked, "Am I in trouble for telling all of this to you?"

"No, you're not. And, as I said, if either Mr. Swain or the sheriff tries to give you grief, just tell them to talk to me."

Lyndon turned toward the barn before saying, "Thanks, Spence. I feel better now."

26 The Bruce family gathered around the kitchen table while Spence related the things Lyndon Morgan had told the sheriff. T. C. was first to respond. "That dude from Helena can't keep witnesses from talking to you!"

"Legally, no. But he can scare witnesses so they won't talk to me."

Merci frowned as she spoke. "Spence, forget Lyndon. What real evidence do they have that Nate is the one who killed Arnold?"

"Let's see. They have the bayonet that belongs to him. They have him spinning a rope of the kind that might have been used for the murder. They have a report that Nate tried to 'get at' Arnold when he was dancing with Irma Lewellyn." He waited for an instant before adding, "And now they have Lyndon saying the two had another confrontation late that night and that Irma tried to stop it."

T. C. spoke. "Lyndon's testimony directly contradicts Nate's statement that he left town and went directly home much earlier in the evening. It's bad for Nate." He twisted his face into a grimace. "That and his temper display at the ball game aren't going to help him with the jury."

Merci leaned forward with her elbows on the table. "But who's the real killer? Let's go through the possibilities." She lifted a finger. "There's Lippy. He seems to think he can get Irma to marry him if he keeps all the other men away long enough. Who else can you suggest?"

Spence shook his head. "You've got me. There doesn't seem to be anyone else."

T. C. shook his head. "I can't think of anyone either."

Irritation showed on Merci's face. "Listen, Nate isn't the one. I know him. He couldn't do such a thing. So the real murderer is still out there, feeling safe and secure." She leaned forward for emphasis. "Come on, think."

Felicity spoke quietly. "May I suggest someone to investigate?"

Spence turned to her. "Who's that, Mom?"

"Irma Lewellyn. It seems she was out behind the bar late that night. Arnold had visited with her at the café and then danced with her frequently at the party. She may have gotten the impression his interest went beyond visits and dancing—perhaps marriage."

"You think that when he was drunk he may have told her she was just someone to pass the time? And when he did so, she lost her temper and throttled him?" Spence was intrigued by the suggestion.

Felicity continued. "She's a big, strong woman, Spencer. And she's accustomed to hard work. Irma surely had the strength to wrap a rope round his neck and choke him to death."

"But why the note pinned to the body by the bayonet?"Merci asked.

"To point everyone in the wrong direction."

T. C. leaned back in the chair. "But what can be offered as evidence that Irma did it?" When that question left the others without a response, he said, "There's another possibility." Turning to Merci he said, "Irma told you she saw Chris Cape in Two Dot that night. Isn't that correct?"

"Yes. That's what she said."

"Well, it's obvious to Felicity and me that he has a greater interest in you than just a chance to fly an airplane. He could fly in California or at any other place he might choose. He seems to be hanging around here, not doing much of anything, just waiting for a chance to spend time with you."

Merci frowned. "You think he was jealous of Arnold and killed him?

Spence stared into space for a moment, considering the possibility. "Could be. He sure didn't express much regret when Arnold's death was mentioned."

Merci shook her head. "You're right about a lack of regret. And Chris has a huge ego. But it's really hard for me to think of him killing someone."

Her brother rubbed at his cheek. "We need to find out more about his activities since he arrived in Montana."

Felicity spoke again, but with apparent reluctance. "What about Lyndon?" Turning to Merci, she said, "He worships you. That's evident in his behavior whenever you're around."

"Lyndon kill Arnold? Mom, you're really trying too hard."

T. C. chimed in. "Lyndon was late for work the morning after the party. He said their milk cow got out and he had to hunt her down." After a moment, he added, "Could it be that he'd had too much of Lippy's booze, got drunk, and then did something he wouldn't do under any other circumstance—like kill a man."

Merci shook her head. "I just can't believe Lyndon would have the gumption to do such a thing."

Spence broke in. "If he's the killer, it doesn't seem likely that he'd tell the sheriff he was out back of Lippy's place late that night. He'd want to hide that information."

T. C. leaned back and looked at Spence. "There's always the possibility that Nate Hamilton really is the murderer. Have you considered that?"

"Of course, Dad. But even if he's the killer, it's my job to defend him. That's why I was glad to learn what the sheriff and Swain heard from Lyndon. I have to structure Nate's defense in a way that will minimize the damage any witness may create." He shook his head. "That will be difficult unless we can point to some other person as the actual murderer. And have some evidence to support that theory."

Merci pushed the chair away from the table and came to her feet. "Listen! I'm sure Nate is innocent. Don't ask me how I know. I just know." She looked at T. C. "And I'm almost as certain that Chris Cape isn't the one who killed Arnold Masters." Turning to Felicity, she said, "Mom, can you really believe that Lyndon Morgan would kill someone? You know how he behaves. He doesn't even show much initiative in the ranch work. Lyndon always waits for Dad to tell him what to do, or he follows along and does whatever the other men are doing." She pulled the chair back and sat again. "The one who killed Arnold has to be Lippy Lippencott. He's got his eye on Irma Lewellyn. Arnold had been spending time with her at the café. And he danced with her a lot that night. Irma told me Lippy has a temper and isn't reluctant to beat on people with a pick handle." Merci took a breath. "We need to concentrate on Lippy. We need to learn more about him and about his doings late the might Arnold died."

The others remained silent for a full minute. Then T. C. said, "What you say makes sense. I'll see what I can learn about Lippy's background —where he came from and what he did before he arrived in Two Dot."

"Great, Dad!" Merci exclaimed. "And I'll talk to others who were at the party and try to find out what that man did after most everyone was gone. I haven't thought to do that till now."

Spence grinned at his sister. "You're taking charge, Sis?"

"You bet I am. I'm not going to let 'em hang Nate."

"Anything you learn will be a help. And it will leave time for me to prepare for the trial, along with the other things my clients demand."

Felicity put her hand on Spence's arm. "Remember, the person responsible for Arnold Masters' death may be someone we haven't even mentioned."

"You're absolutely right, Mom. I do have to keep that in mind."

T. C. shoved his chair to the side and turned to speak to his son. "What about a trial date?'

"The judge hasn't set one yet. He usually tries to avoid trials during the summer months. The courtroom gets too hot. But he's to be here Tuesday. Perhaps he'll decide then."

27

And decide the judge did.

Spence was the first to arrive at the courtroom on the second floor courthouse. He dropped his file on the counsel table, stood with his hands in his pockets, and scanned the courtroom. It was long and narrow with a large window at the rear and two narrow ones on west side—to the judge's right. Hard narrow benches that could seat about forty spectators filled the area behind the bar. A low wooden fence with a swinging gate—the bar—separated the spectators from the lawyers, their clients, the jurors, and the court personal. The judge's bench was elevated on a wooden platform, and the jury box was on the judge's left. The witness stand was next to the bench between the judge and the jury. A table for the court reporter was located in front and to the judge's right of the witness stand. Two long tables for counsel faced the bench. The national flag and the state flag stood in a corner just before the bar.

This was where the fate of Nate Hamilton would be decided. Soon enough, it would be Spence's responsibility to save his client from prison or, to consider the worst, the hangman's noose. He closed his eyes, inhaled sharply, and dropped into a chair.

Nate followed Amos into the room and walked forward to sit beside Spence at the counsel table. Amos took a seat behind them and next to Merci. Garth Swain ignored them all as he strode to his place at the far end of the other table. Four old men with nothing better to do entered the room to sit quietly toward the rear, just there to observe. The clerk and the court reporter soon took their places. All of them rose to their feet as Judge Crawford burst through door and stomped to the bench. The judge turned to the clerk for the file and scanned it briefly as though to refresh his recollection of the reason they all were there. He looked from one to the other of the men standing before him and said, "Please be seated." Once they had all assumed their places, he flipped the corner of the file once with a fingernail as he growled, "We're here today to set a date for trial in the matter of State of Montana vs. Nathaniel Hamilton." Looking toward Swain he asked, "Is that correct, Sir?"

Swain rose from his chair and stood with his hands clasped at his belt line. Without expression he said, "That's correct, Your Honor. And we request an expedited trial date."

Judge Crawford turned to Spence. "And you, Mr. Bruce? What say you?"

Spence was caught unprepared. It had never occurred to him that Swain would want an early trial date. It took him a moment to gather his thoughts. But at last he said, "We're still pursuing our investigation of the events that occurred the night Arnold Masters was killed, Your Honor. For that reason we ask that the trial not be scheduled for at least two months." Then he added, "A trial in the fall when this room is not so insufferably hot would be better."

The judge scowled at him. "I'll decide about the temperature of my courtroom, Mr. Bruce. You needn't worry your mind about it." Spence kept himself from flinching at the rebuke. Before he could say anything more, the judge continued. "It's my belief that a person charged with murder in the first degree is entitled to have the matter decided promptly. If he's found to be innocent, he can then get on with his life. So, too, the victim's family members. They need to have the matter resolved as quickly as is reasonably possible." He looked at Swain again. "Today is July fifteenth. I've reviewed my calendar and find I have free time beginning on Tuesday, August twenty-fifth. Would that date work for you, Mr. Swain?"

"Indeed it would, Your Honor, although we'd prefer a date even sooner."

Turning to Spence he asked, "And you, Mr. Bruce? Can you fit that date into your heavy trial schedule?"

Spence didn't appreciate the sarcasm, but replied in a calm voice. "As I said, our investigation isn't complete and we would prefer a later trial date. If August twenty-fifth is the date you set, Your Honor, we will, of course, be here."

"Good! Be sure that you are here and that you are prepared." His voice lost some of its harshness. "That's settled." The judge turned in his chair. "There being nothing further, court's adjourned." Judge Crawford banged his gavel and rushed from the courtroom.

Spence was left standing with Nate at his side as Swain strode purposefully past, without so much as a glance in his direction. He reached for the file on the table just as Nate grabbed his arm. There was a deep frown on his Nate's face and worry in his voice. "That judge has it in for me."

Spence was still wondering why the judge seemed so anxious to bring the matter to trial. Was it possible that the judge and Swain had discussed the matter without his presence? He turned to Nate to say, "Judge Crawford is known to be crotchety. It's just his manner. I'm sure he will be fair in all his rulings." He put his hand gently on Nate's shoulder. "Remember, it will be the jury—not the judge—that will render the verdict."

Nate persisted. "You said you needed time to get ready. Will you be able to do that—get ready? The date he set is less than six weeks away."

Spence weighed his answer. He couldn't let his client know how worried he was about that very thing. "We'll be ready, Nate." He dropped his hand from the man's shoulder and turned toward the back of the room. "To be sure, I need to get back to my office."

Spence had forgotten that Amos Hamilton was in the room to hear the things the judge had said and to listen to his conversation with Nate. The old man rose from bench behind the bar and stepped into the aisle in front of Spence. "I agree with Nate. That old judge worries me."

"Amos, we're stuck with him, and there's nothing we can do about it—unless he does something to clearly show that he's prejudiced— something to demonstrate that he will try to prevent Nate from getting a fair trial." He shook his head. "That isn't going to happen."

"Can we get a decent jury, Spence? One that won't let that judge railroad Nate?'

"I'm sure any jury in this county will be fair, Amos."

"God, Spence, I hope so."

Merci and T. C., who had just arrived in town, were waiting on the street when Spence walked out of the courthouse. T. C. motioned with his hand. "Let's walk to your office. We need to talk."

With Spence behind his desk and the others in client chairs, T. C. leaned forward with his hands on his knees. "Wallace Linton, the man who sold Lippy Lippencott the saloon, told me that Lippy came from a small county seat town in Kansas. I sent a wire to the district attorney down there. He was quick to respond with a wire of his own. It seems Lippy was suspected of a killing in that town, but there wasn't enough proof to prosecute."

Merci sat bolt upright. "A killing?"

"That's right. A killing."

Spence asked, "What else have you learned?"

"A wire from the president of the bank in that town said Lippy may have gotten a chunk of cash in the robbery that ended in the killing. But no one is sure."

Merci reared back and slapped her thighs with her hands. "Like I told you, Lippy has to be the killer."

"Perhaps," Spence said, "but how do we prove it, Sis? He's not going to confess."

28 Once again, several days of wet bluster that one could hardly call rain, accompanied by lightening, thunder, and gusty winds kept the Jenny grounded. Merci paced the large kitchen in frustration while wondering how to gather evidence that Lippy was the real killer. Spence was right, of course; he wouldn't confess. She tried to think through a list of those who could have stayed around to the very end of the party—someone who might have seen Lippy throttle Arnold. No one came immediately to mind.

Perhaps Irma could provide more information. Merci reached to a hook in the back hall for a light jacket. Better get to town and talk to the waitress again. As she shrugged into the jacket, Chris Cape came to mind. Evidently, he'd been hanging around the fringes of the party late the night Arnold was murdered. The thought of her friend's fate still brought a lump in her throat. She swallowed once, dabbed at an eye, and muttered, "Got to find out what Chris knows."

Midday mealtime was past, and the last of Olive Breen's customers drifted out the door as Merci arrived. With the heavy cooking, baking, and serving finished for a couple of hours, Olive plodded up the street toward her home, leaving Irma to watch the now empty café. The heavy scent of the noonday fare greeted Merci when she opened the door.

Irma's displeasure was immediately evident. Before Merci could say a word, the waitress spat, "I told you I wasn't going to talk to you anymore about the death of your boyfriend."

"First of all, he wasn't my boyfriend. And how do you know that I came here to talk about his death?"

"That's why you're here, isn't it?" The words came as an accusation.

"I admit it. That's why I'm here."

"It ain't going to do you any good." Irma crossed her arms. "I'm through answering questions from you. I'm also through answering questions from that creepy lawyer that the sheriff brought in here."

Merci slid onto a seat beside the counter. "Mind telling me the things you told Garth Swain and the sheriff?"

"None of your business." Irma turned toward the kitchen. "Just leave."

"Did you tell them that you got between Nate Hamilton and Arnold Masters way late on the night Arnold died?"

Irma turned back. "He didn't die, Honey. He was murdered." She leaned toward Merci with her hands on the edge of the counter. "Yes, I told them. And I also told them how Lippy came tearing out there to yell at me. 'Get yourself away from both of them jokers!' he barked. 'I've told you that before!'"

"What happened then?"

"Both Nate and Arnold wandered away somewhere. Lippy kept yelling at me to get the hell out of there—to get to my room where I belonged. Nearly everyone had left, and the music had stopped so I did as Lippy said. I went to my room."

"Because the party was over or because Lippy told you to?"

Irma waited a moment to answer. "Both I guess. Lippy scares me, and he was really on the fight that night."

"On the fight enough to go after Arnold for spending time with you?"

Irma looked back at Merci out of the corner of her eye, her arms crossed over her chest. "God, I don't know. I just don't know. I've asked myself that question a thousand times." She turned, stared out the window for an instant, then turned back to Merci. "I've seen enough of Lippy Lippencott to believe he's capable of killing when he's in a rage."

"Irma, that lawyer—Garth Swain—has charged Nate with murder. Right now, he's gathering all the evidence he can to prove his case. If there's any chance at all that Lippy is the real killer, we need to find evidence to show that there's at least the possibility that Lippy's the one." Merci waited, then added, "Help me."

"Damn it, Merci. I don't know anything else."

"Who might be able to help?"

Irma hesitated. At last she took a breath and said, "Well, maybe the tall, good-looking guy who's been flying that airplane with you. I didn't see him, but I've heard he was still hanging around on the fringes of the party late that night."

Merci's eyebrows went up. "Who told you that?"

"I can't remember. It was a couple of days after the party, there was a big gang here for the noonday meal. As I passed by their table, I heard someone say a tall stranger stayed at the edge of the crowd and didn't take part in any of the fun. I don't remember who was talking."

Merci mumbled, "I've got to find out who that was."

Irma raised her eyebrows. "Why don't you just ask Chris Cape?"

Merci was on her feet. There was determination in her voice when she said, "I'll do just that!"

The first time Spence met Eunice Syvertson as she walked purposely toward Mother's Café, he had pretended it was an accident. He had tipped his hat and asked if she would join for the noonday meal. The meal finished, he walked her to the doctor's door, and asked, "Would you join me for lunch tomorrow?" She had accepted with a smile. He soon gave up any pretense, and their mid-day visit became routine.

Today their talk, while they ate, was of the summer festivities that took place in the larger towns in the upper Musselshell Valley: Harlowton, Two Dot, Martinsdale, Judith Gap, and Hedgesville. Spence mentioned that some of the ranchers had agreed to provide wild horses for a riding contest in Two Dot to be held the coming week-end.

"Sounds exciting. I've never seen a one . Tell me about it."

"The local cowpunchers try to ride horses that have a propensity to buck. Each one wants to put on the best show. The town merchants usually give a small money prize to the winner. They decide the winner by the cheers of the crowd."

"Are there rules?"

"Not really. But if a rider hangs on to the saddle horn, he gets heckled and booed. The best riders wave their hats and yell to the crowd. Spurring the horse is good. And, of course, how hard the horse bucks makes a difference." Spence smiled at his companion. "There's always a big pot-luck feed beforehand. Would you like to go?"

"Why, yes, I'd like to go, if the doctor will let me."

"It's my guess that Doc Scanlan will be there. Some of those cowpokes drink too much before they ride. Those that do often wind up the ground, and some of them get hurt. Doc patches up their bruises." He grinned. "And he enjoys the sociability of the affair. He gets to spend time with a lot of his friends in casual conversation, with no mention of their aches and pains."

"When you asked if I'd like to go, was that an invitation?'

"It was. This will give you an opportunity to become better acquainted with my parents—and they with you. They've been asking when that might happen."

Miss Syvertson inhaled. "Oh, my!"

29

The hot days of summer with thunder storms that brought dangerous winds but little rain continued to keep the Jenny in its hangar. Then a day arrived when the air was clear and quiet. Merci sent word to Chris Cape to get himself to the ranch early the next morning, ready to fly. They'd wow those at the riding contest with a fly-over.

The air was cool and still when the Jenny left the ground at ten o'clock. With Cape in the front cockpit, Merci banked the plane to the south, and began a climb that would take them over the Two Dot Butte. She spied a string of cattle ambling their way toward a spring for a drink of water after the morning graze. Must have climbed through the rimrocks and up onto the top of the butte from the basin to the south. Her dad would want to get riders up here to put them back where they belong.

As they approached Two Dot the aviators saw automobiles parked, side by side, in a large circle, each facing toward the middle. The enclosure thus created was where the bronc riders would perform. In an open space away from the autos, long tables were set in rows and women were already scattering utensils for the potluck meal to be served to the gathered throng.

In every direction, cars could be seen raising dust in their trek to

Two Dot. Families in buggies traveled slowly. Individuals on horseback and some simply walking were plodding their way into town.

Bucking horses from the GL Ranch, the Mathers Ranch, the Hopkins Ranch, the Haymaker spread, and other ranches from the Upper Musselshell Valley were already encircled in a rope corral across the street to the north. The rough-stock riders had begun their drinking and bragging on the street in front of Lippy's establishment.

Merci was still high in the air for the first flyover. It was intended to attract the attention of the crowd below. She circled around to descend for a low pass directly over the people on the ground. There were the usual waves of arms as the Jenny roared over the heads of those below. Merci and Cape waved in return.

One more time around and she began the trip four miles back to the ranch. Chris looked back over his shoulder with a grin and raised a hand above the cockpit to wave a circle with his finger. There he was again, wanting to pull a loop with Merci's aircraft. The young woman gritted her teeth and gave him her own gesture: a vigorous thumbs down. In her anger she just wanted to get the machine back on the ground, get down the road to Two Dot, get rid of Cape, and join the others in the fun.

But first, straighten out Chris Cape. He was out of the cockpit and standing on the ground when she stepped from the cockpit onto the bottom wing. She jerked her helmet from her head and glared at him. "Listen, you. There isn't going to be any loop-the-loop stuff with this Jenny. Don't mention it again." She paused for effect, then snarled, "If you do mention it again you're not flying with me anymore. Got that?"

Cape showed his shining grin and raised both hands with the palms facing out. "OK. OK. I've got it." He grasped her elbow as she moved toward the edge of the wing. "I promise, Merc, I'll be good from now on."

She jerked her arm away and jumped lightly to the ground. "See that you do." Shedding the flight jacket, she said, "Let's get the Jenny back in the hangar. Then you can give me a ride to Two Dot. I saw the Packard going down the road. Dad and Mom are already on their way to the celebration."

"First, you threaten me. Then you tell me I'm a taxi driver. What's a man to do?"

"Whatever a woman tells him to do."

With the airplane safely back under the hangar roof, Merci grabbed the door to Cape's car, and barked, "Get in and drive." Then she stopped and stepped back to stare at the Model T coupe. "This isn't the car you've been driving."

"Nope. I rented the other one. This, I bought."

"What will you do with it when you go back to California?"

"Who says I'm going back?"

"Stay here in Montana? Not a chance."

Cape opened the car door for her. "We'll see, Merc. We'll see."

Spence parked his Hudson, dashed around to open the door for Eunice, and handed her to the ground. She snuggled her arm through his as they began the tour through the crowd to find his parents. When T. C. saw them approaching, he doffed his hat and smiled a greeting. "Miss Syvertson! How nice to see you again."

Felicity, close behind, grasped Eunice's upper arms lightly with both hands. "We're awfully glad that you've joined us. It's nice to have you for company."

Eunice almost blushed at the compliment. "Well, Spencer asked, and I accepted, so here we are." She glanced around. "But where's Merci? I thought she'd be with you."

T. C answered, "Our daughter should arrive soon. She insisted on flying her airplane over the crowd this morning. We saw her winging her way back to the ranch a short time ago. She's catching a ride in to Two Dot with that fellow who flies with her—Chris Cape." He changed the subject by pointing toward the long tables. "The potluck feed will begin before the riding contests."

Felicity also pointed. "The food we brought is on the tables and ready. I'd better get myself over there to help the other women with the serving."

The nurse asked, "What can I do? I don't want to be the only woman who isn't working."

Felicity touched Eunice's elbow. "Relax. Your task is to lead these men to the tables and see that they get fed. They're helpless when left to themselves, you know." Even though her contribution to the food supply was in its place, she felt it might need a final touch in order meet the standard set by the most fastidious of the women.

That's when Merci came charging through the crowd with Chris Cape ambling along behind. "I was afraid we missed the food." She hugged her father and turned to Eunice. "I haven't seen you since the ball game." She added with a grin, "But we've kept track of your doings. I hear that Spence has made certain you don't forget the Bruces. Has he become a real pest?'

"Not a pest. He and I have just enjoyed some meals together in the middle of our working days."

Spencer turned to Cape. "Please meet Eunice Syvertson. Miss Syvertson is Doctor Scanlan's nurse."

Cape touched the brim of the western hat he'd taken to wearing and dropped his head in a sort of a bow. "Miss Syvertson and I have already met. How nice to see you again, Ma'am."

Eunice's voice was chilly when she nodded. "Indeed, Sir." Turning to T. C., she asked, "Isn't it time for us to be joining the food line, Mr.

Bruce? It would be a shame to miss the riding contests because we hadn't finished eating."

"There's time. But we'll do as you say." Jutting his elbow toward her, he added, "Come with me." She placed her hand on his arm and smiled over her shoulder at Spence as though to say, "He's your father. What else can I do?"

Merci grabbed T. C.'s other arm. "Don't forget me." T. C. as good as strutted while parading the two attractive young ladies through the crowd. That left Spence standing alone with Cape. Spence hesitated, then said, "You're welcome to join us at the food line—unless you have other plans."

"No other plans. And, yes, I'd like to spend time with your family. Merci never let's me forget how special she thinks you are."

The young men, plates filled, followed T. C. and the ladies to the rear of the Packard. Folding chairs for the ladies and a blanket on the ground for the men provided the eating place. Several mugs and a large cream can filled with lemonade were nearby. Conversation was sparse until all were finished and the plates and mugs were shoved aside. Eunice turned again to T. C. "When does the riding begin?"

T. C. stood to point. "They're bringing out the first horse right now. Let's move around to the front of the car so we have a good view."

She nodded and asked, "How are the animals chosen for the contest?"

"Most ranches have a horse or two that likes to buck. Those are the ones we'll be seeing today."

"How are the riders selected?"

"Any cowpuncher can put his name in the hat. The names of the horses are in another hat. The name of a rider is drawn and then the name of a horse is drawn. The rider tries his luck with the horse."

"Are there any favorites?"

"Among the riders? I'd say so. Some are favored because they're riding skills are well known, some just because they're likable."

Merci chimed in. "Many of the people are here to watch a horse called Tom's Sorrel."

Eunice cast a questioning look at T. C., so he explained. "Tom's Sorrel is from the GL Ranch. He's an interesting animal. No one has managed to ride him, although several tried. Every one of them ended up flat on the ground. Tom Purdue is the GL Ranch foreman. For some unknown reason, Tom tried getting on him one day while he was standing in the barn. The sorrel didn't buck in the barn and, believe it or not, he behaved peacefully after he was ridden out into the open. That's the way Purdue has used him ever since. He gets on the horse in the barn and then goes out the door to join the other riders for the day's work."

"If he can now be ridden, why would the crowd be anxious to see him?'

"Because he'll still buck if anyone tries to mount him in the open."

"Who will try to ride him today?"

Spence spoke from his place on the blanket. "I haven't heard, but I'll see if I can find out." He climbed to his feet. "There's usually some bets made on the various horses and riders. There are certain to be bets on Tom's Sorrel. Those who bet against him will demand large odds."

It wasn't long before Spence came striding back. T. C. was first ask, "Who drew the sorrel?"

"Nate Hamilton." That bit of information ended the conversation. None of the others noticed the smirk that crossed Chris Cape's face.

The men hoisted the chairs around to the front of, but slightly between, the fenders of the Packard and the autos next to it. A safe place for the women to sit while watching the contest. Across the open space the rough-stock riders were gathered. A bottle was passed from one rider to another. Spence checked to see if Nate Hamilton was among those sharing the liquor. He wasn't there. He finally located Nate standing with his parents near their automobile. Evidently, he understood the problem he'd created for himself with the ruckus at the baseball game. He seemed intent on staying sober and out of trouble.

Soon enough a cowboy, mounted on a stout gelding, dragged the first of the bucking horses into the enclosure—about three hundred feet in diameter—created by the automobiles. Near the center he stopped and pulled the head of the lead animal as near to his leg as possible. Then he took tight turns with the halter rope around the horn of his saddle. Thus snubbed up, the bucking horse couldn't do much but stand and roll his eyes. Two other cowboys were close at hand to make certain that the animal remained quiet. The contestant lifted his saddle from the ground and heaved it onto the animal's back. With a jerk of the latigo he pulled the cinch tightly into place.

The rider stepped back to survey his work, decided it was satisfactory, and turned to wave once at the crowd. He reached for a stirrup and stepped lightly onto the back of the horse. The fellow who led the horse into the arena quickly loosened the halter rope from his saddle horn and handed it across to the contestant. Then he jerked his own animal to the side and out of the way.

Action began immediately. The horse dived his head downward and then made one great leap upward and forward, immediately throwing the rider off balance. The next jump came before the rider could recover. The jump was sharply to the right. The cowboy lost a stirrup and began to reach with his free hand for the saddle horn. Then he seemed to remember the razzing he'd get if he grabbed the horn. The horse threw his head to the left and followed with a high leaping twist in that direction. The maneuver sent the rider sailing loose from the saddle and down into the dirt where he landed squarely on his shoulder. For a moment he appeared to be stunned, but recovered to scramble hurriedly to his feet. He squinted around until he located his hat a few feet away. He picked it up and waved it once to the crowd. The crowd reacted with shouts; some were shouts of condolences and some jeers for his failure to complete the ride. With his head hanging, the fallen rider trudged back to join the other contestants. Those hard men of the range greeted him with joshing comments and slaps to his arms and back, all of which he took with a show of good humor.

And so it went. One after the other, nine horses were led into the arena to be met by a cowhand with a saddle. The performance of each animal varied in its effort to throw the rider. And the performances of the riders varied in their attempts to remain astride the animal. Some managed to complete the ride and also put on a show by fanning the horse with their hats and using their spurs to rake the animal from shoulder to flank.

One tall, lanky cowhand from the Haymaker Ranch was matched to the tenth horse—an ugly-headed, roan mare. The mare proved to be a showy performer, rising high in the air with each leap. With each leap she shifted direction from side to side, dropping a shoulder at each turn. Spence explained to Eunice that the riders called that maneuver a "fence row." Hard to ride. But ride is what the Haymaker hand did. He waved his huge dusty hat over the lowered head of the animal and spurred in long strokes along the animal's sides. As the horse bucked past the gathering of rough-stock riders, he turned his head to shout, "How d'ya like her, boys?" His friends whooped and hollered and the whoops and hollers were accompanied by shouts and yells from the crowd. At last, the mare seemed to concede defeat. The gyrations turned to a lope and then to a trot. The rider pulled on the halter rope to bring the animal to a halt and stepped gracefully to ground. That's when the noise from the gathered throng arose to its highest.

T. C. turned to Eunice to say, "That cow dog just won the money."

Spence countered, "Maybe not. We still haven't seen Nate Hamilton and Tom's Sorrel."

Merci stood, stretched, and shook her head. "Nate's a pretty good horseman but not as good as he thinks he is. He'll never ride the sorrel. I just hope he doesn't do anything foolish—anything like his behavior at the ball game."

Felicity, who generally remained silent, spoke in a soft voice. "I hope he wins. Nathaniel needs something good in his life right now."

A small girl, on foot and showing a big grin, led Tom's Sorrel into the arena. The animal, appearing as docile as any child's pony, shuffled along behind. Near the center of the clearing the child stopped, dug into her pocket, and pulled out a handful of oats. When she reached out with her small hand, oats in the palm, the sorrel stepped up to softly nuzzle the oats into his mouth. To the onlookers it appeared that he was exhibiting great care not to bite her.

There had been noise and stirring among those who watched when Tom's Sorrel made his appearance. And there had always been yelps and shouts of encouragement when any of the previous riders dragged a saddle out to the middle of the arena for the ride. Not this time. A strange silence greeted Nate. Everyone at the site knew he'd been charged with murder. Those of the ranch community simply didn't know how to treat him.

Spence noted all of this and mumbled, "If that's the attitude of Nate's neighbors, we're not likely to get a sympathetic jury."

Merci also took note and said to herself, "We absolutely must find proof that Lippy is the killer—somehow."

The sorrel stood placidly as Nate hoisted the saddle over his back. He even turned his head as though to watch the rider in his task. Nate, from years of habit with horses, gave the animal's jaw a pat. Saddle in place, the cowboy turned to the child. She handed him the halter rope and then scampered across the enclosure to the place where her father, Tom Purdue, was waiting.

Nate stood for a moment, offered a small wave to his father. Then he turned to nod at Merci. He stood next to Tom's Sorrel for a long moment in thoughtful preparation for the ride. Pull the halter rope back toward the saddle horn as tight as possible. He couldn't let this animal jerk away as he swung into the saddle. One more look at the sorrel's head and he grabbed the left-hand stirrup to turn it for his boot. Left foot up and right leg over, he jammed his right foot quickly into the off-stirrup.

The sorrel remained completely relaxed, standing with one hind hoof resting on its toe. He seemed to ignore the weight that was now on his back. Nate waited two breaths for the horse to move. Then he kicked at the sorrel's rib once gently with a spur.

If a horse could snarl, the sorrel might have done so. All four feet were off the ground in an instant—upward in a twisting leap. His hooves barely returned to earth before he was up on his hind legs, standing at such an erect angle that it appeared certain he would topple over backward. Nate leaned far ahead over the saddle horn to avoid injury if that should happen. But the sorrel didn't topple. He dived forward, hind legs kicking high behind.

Nate was hanging tough. He managed to maintain his seat through the horse's opening gambits. For a few seconds the gyrations of the horse seemed to become repetitious. They were nothing more dramatic than those any horse might perform while trying to shed a rider.

Nate had been cautious. No hat waving. No unnecessary spurring. But as the sorrel bucked his way across the arena, the rider seemed to gain confidence in his ability to complete the ride. Needing to put on a show he reached forward with a leg to spur his mount in the shoulder.

The spur never touched horseflesh. Tom's Sorrel was airborne. In mid-leap he somehow swapped ends. The horse that had been traveling west was suddenly traveling east. Nate didn't make the transition. He continued to travel westward, flying as far out and away from the horse as his hold on the halter rope would allow. When the slack disappeared from the rope, Nate was jerked horizontal and slammed into the ground, face down.

The sorrel, having disposed of another cowhand, stopped, stockstill, and looked back at the fallen rider. It seemed to the observers that the horse was taking time to admire his handiwork.

Nate didn't roll over. He didn't even move. He just lay with the left side of his face pressed against the ground. Amos Hamilton started across the arena toward his son as fast as his old legs could carry him. Doctor Scanlan was not far behind. But Merci and Eunice moved the fastest and reached the fallen rider just as he groaned and tried to struggle to his knees. With a yelp of pain he fell back while grasping at his shoulder.

Something wasn't right. Merci reached to help, only to have Eunice grab at her arm. "Don't move him. Let the doctor do it."

Doctor Scanlan dropped to one knee, rolled Nate over, and pushed him to the ground—flat on his back. The doctor ran his hand over the shoulder that Nate was trying to reach. He probed gently—only to have Nate yelp again. Looking up at Eunice he ordered, "Hold him." Spotting Spence who was standing nearby, he added, "You help her."

Eunice lifted her skirt to kneel in the dirt and pressed down on the fallen rider's other shoulder. Spence straddled the man's legs. Doc Scanlan mumbled, "This will hurt." Before Nate could respond, the doctor grabbed the arm at the elbow. While pressing firmly at the shoulder, he gave the arm a jerking twist. Nate howled in his agony, but the twisting motion did as was intended and returned the dislocated shoulder to its correct position. For a minute Nate lay still, sweating, and breathing hard. But then he began to notice relief from the pain. After another minute he jacked himself into a sitting position. Finally, with help from Doc Scanlan and Spence, he struggled to his feet.

There was a patter of polite clapping from some of the crowd. Nothing like that given to the other riders who had fallen to the earth. Nate was still the man accused of a heinous crime.

Amos reached for his son, "Come on, Nate, get over to the car and rest."

The doctor stopped them. "Make a sling from a towel and keep your arm in it for at least four days. Then stop at my office so I can check it again."

Amos was the one to respond. "We'll see to it. And thanks, Doc, for the help. I owe you."

Across the arena, Tom Purdue had pulled Nate's saddle from the sorrel and dragged it to the Hamilton truck. The horse was last seen with the small girl leading him away toward the livery stable.

Spence stopped the roadster in front of the rooming house. Eunice looked across at him. "The riding contest was worth seeing." After an eyeblink, she added, "I hope young Mr. Hamilton recovers properly."

"He will. Nate's been hurt before."

"Your parents are nice people. It was kind of them to make me comfortable."

"And it's kind of you to say so." Spence climbed out of the car and hurried around to hold the door for her as she made her exit. When she stepped to the ground he put his hand on her arm. "You've met Chris Cape before?"

"Spencer, he's been around town a lot. One day he nodded to me as I passed him going to the doctor's office. The next day he tipped his hat and said hello. The next day he asked me to dinner."

"And you said, 'yes?'"

She nodded and looked away from Spence toward the distant mountains. "We went to the Graves Hotel." Looking back at Spence, Eunice paused. "The food was good as it always seems to be. But, Spencer, all the man did was talk about himself and all the things he's done and all the things he's going to do. I wasn't impressed."

Spence was surprised that a feeling of relief crept over him. He hadn't realized how much this woman now meant to him. Without thinking, he blurted, "I'm glad."

Eunice smiled as his face started to turn red. Then her smile disappeared. "You should know the things he said about Arnold Masters."

"Like what?"

Eunice thought a moment. "Mr. Cape made it clear that his family had lots of money. He indicated that Arnold Masters' family also had money, but not in the same amounts as the Capes. And it sounded like the Masters got theirs recently—not old money like the Capes."

"So Chris Cape liked to brag about his family?"

"That's only part of it." She looked up at her companion with a serious face. "Mr. Cape talked like he was the best airplane pilot and airplane mechanic in the world. He said he'd flown all the best of the pursuit planes of the war. Some of the names were a Spad, a Fokker, and a Sop-something." She smiled a shy smile "I may not have pronounced those correctly."

"The last one a Sopwith Camel?"

"I think so."

"But what does that have to do with Arnold Masters?"

"He made it plain that Masters had never flown anything but a Jenny. He said that Masters couldn't be trusted as a mechanic."

"So?"

Eunice was serious again. "The implication was that your sister was a fool to bring Arnold Masters to Montana instead of him." She reached for Spence's arm. "In a peculiar way, he seemed obsessed with Merci."

Spence turned sharply to stare at his companion. "How do you mean, obsessed?"

"Like she's a prize to be captured and he intends to do the capturing, and that he thought that Arnold Masters was trying to cut him out with your sister." Eunice dropped her hand from Spence's arm and turned again to look into the distance. "He seemed pleased that Arnold was dead—or 'out of the way' as he put it. And he said Nate Hamilton would be convicted of murder and either hanged or sent to prison forever." She shook her head. "Then Mr. Cape said the only other man who had eyes for Merci was one of your father's ranch hands." She thought for a moment. "I believe he said the man's name is Lyndon." She turned to face Spencer. "He said Lyndon was foolish to even think of himself in the same league as Chris Cape when it came to women."

Spence smiled. "He didn't impress you with that remark?"

"No he didn't." Her face was somber. "In a sense, it was frightening to listen to him. He was just too cocksure of himself, and he acted as though he would get his way no matter what."

Spence touched her arm. "Thank you for telling me all of this. I think we should take a closer look at Mr. Cape's activities since he came to our town. Maybe he knows more about the death of Arnold Masters than he's told us."

30

The Runabout rattled along the Big Elk Road to the Mathers Ranch, ten miles southward from Two Dot. As Merci twisted the steering wheel this way and that to avoid the worst of the bumps and holes, she contemplated how best to learn about the beating that Nate Hamilton reportedly gave to a horse. From what the sheriff had told Spence, the beating had been severe enough for Mrs. Mathers to report it. Turning onto the driveway to the Mathers house, she decided to just ask what happened.

Harley Mathers came to the door, hat on his head. He greeted Merci cordially and stepped back to invite her into the hallway and beyond to the living room. "Mrs. Mathers is visiting Mrs. Pierce up the creek so I can't offer you anything but some coffee left over from breakfast."

Merci, seated in a comfortable armchair, smiled and said, "No need for coffee or anything else, Mr. Mathers. I'm fine, Sir."

Mathers removed his hat, hooked it over his knee after taking an identical chair near at hand. He leaned toward his guest. "It's a pleasure to see you, Merci, as always. What brings you to our house this day?"

She straightened her skirt, then folded her hands and let them rest easily in her lap. She smiled. "As you know, Nate Hamilton is accused of murdering Arnold Masters."

"Everyone in the valley knows that."

"And you must know that Nate asked my brother, Spencer, to defend him."

"We all know that, too."

Now she leaned toward her host. "Spence has heard that Nate beat a horse during one of your brandings so badly that Mrs. Mathers reported the incident to the sheriff."

Harley Mathers leaned back with a look of chagrin. "Oh, that." Then he leaned forward again. "My wife has a tender heart and can't stand anything she sees as abuse of an animal. She drove one of my good hands away a month ago because he kicked a dog out of the way. Didn't kick hard, didn't hurt the dog, but she saw it. I wasn't here at the time, but I guess she gave it to him good." He shook his head. "When I got home the fellow was waiting by the gate and told me he was leaving. Said he didn't want to be a problem."

Merci listened, figuring he'd get to Nate soon enough.

Mathers straightened. "Well, enough of that. About Nate. He'd been dragging calves to the branding fire that day. The horse he was riding got the rope under his tail. As you can guess, the old pony took a jump or two and loosened Nate up a bit in the saddle. Kind of embarrassed Nate. He thinks of himself as an expert horseman, you know."

Merci smiled. "At least he did until he tried Tom's Sorrel."

Harley chuckled. "You're right about that." He turned sober again. "Anyway, Nate used the end of his catch rope to whip the animal down his front legs a couple of times. It wasn't anything unusual at all. Lots of riders treat a horse worse than that." The man ran his hands along the arms of the chair while looking at the floor. After a moment he raised his eyes. "But Mildred saw it and got real upset. She demanded that I tell Nate to get off the place right then. Well, I couldn't do that, of course. The Hamiltons are good neighbors, and Amos is a good friend.

And we hadn't finished the branding." Harley ran his fingers through his graying hair. With a wan smile he said, "Both Nate and I were in trouble that day."

"So, if you were asked to testify, you would say that Nate didn't really abuse a horse the way Mrs. Mathers told the sheriff?"

The man's head jerked. "If Mildred was to take the witness stand and say Nate abused that horse, I sure as hell wouldn't come along later and say it wasn't true. No way am I going to do that, Merci. She's the most important thing in the world to me. You must understand that."

"But if it was the sheriff who told what Mrs. Mathers said to him, could you tell exactly what happened—that the horse bucked, that all Nate did was whip him twice with the rope end—nothing more. And then let the jury decide if it was abuse?"

"I guess I could do that."

Merci pushed on the chair arms as she got to her feet. "I surely don't want to put you in a difficult position, Mr. Mathers. From what Spence says, it probably won't come to that." She extended her hand. "You have things to do. Thanks for visiting with me."

He walked her to the door and then to the Runabout where he turned the crank to start the car. Then he held the door. "I hope it goes well for Nate. He's a good young man. It's just that sometimes he doesn't use the best judgment."

As Merci steered the auto back down the road, she mused, "I hope most of the folks in this community feel the same way."

Her next stop was at the Hopkins Ranch, halfway between the Mathers Ranch and the Hamilton Ranch. The Hopkins house was much larger and more elaborate than most. Sam Hopkins had inherited money from an uncle, and Mrs. Hopkins liked to spend it. She had a concrete sidewalk leading to the kitchen door so the men wouldn't track dirt into the house at meal time.

When Merci knocked on that door, Lucy Simpson opened it. The chubby young woman's sole job was to help Mrs. Hopkins. Her employer referred to her as the maid. Another woman did the cooking.

In a small room off the kitchen, Lucy gestured toward a straight chair and took another. "Mrs. Hopkins is feeling poorly. Is there some way that I can help you?"

"It's you I wanted to see. You were at the dance in Two Dot the night Arnold Masters was murdered, weren't you?"

"You were there. You know I was."

"Of course. You know that Nate Hamilton is accused of killing Arnold Masters. I don't believe Nate did it. I've wondered if you saw or heard anything that might help my brother defend Nate."

The maid was shaking her head before Merci stopped speaking. "I've already told the sheriff and that other man that I didn't see nothing and I didn't hear nothing. And besides, I left long before you did. One of the section hands gave me a ride back here to the ranch."

"Did you see Nate Hamilton try to attack Arnold Masters while Arnold was dancing with Irma Lewellyn?"

Grim faced, she repeated, "Didn't see nothing. Didn't hear nothing." She stood. "I ain't got nothing more to say to you." She was up and heading for the door. "I've got work to do, Miss Bruce. Ask someone else your questions."

As Merci walked to the auto, she thought, "Not much help for either side."

Her next stop was the Hamilton Ranch. She felt a need to check on Nate.

Beatrice Hamilton, faced creased by worry, met her at the door. In response to Merci's inquiry, she said. "Yes, Nate's here. His father told him not to try to work till the arm's healed. Please come in." After she had Merci settled in the parlor, she called up the stairway, "Nathaniel,

Merci Bruce is here to see you."

Mrs. Hamilton didn't follow when Nate shuffled into the parlor. He wore a disheveled look—clothes were wrinkled and hair uncombed. His arm was in the dishtowel sling but his face broke into a smile at the sight of his neighbor. "Hi, Merc. Nice of you to come by." He glanced down at his clothing. "Forgive my appearance. I know I don't look my best."

"Don't worry about it, Nate. I was up at the Mathers Ranch and thought I'd stop and see how you're doing."

Nate wiggled the fingers of the injured arm and reached for his shoulder with the other hand. "It hurts a little if I move my arm around. I don't think I need this sling, though. But mother insists that I keep using it until I see Doc Scanlan." He looked out the window. "I'd rather be outside. There's work to do."

"You remember what we were always told as children? Do as your parents say, like it or not."

"And I guess I will." Nate finally dropped into a chair. "Merc, what's happening? No one tells me anything. How's Spence coming with his preparation for the trial? It isn't far away."

"Well, he tells me there's a lot to do. I don't understand it all, but there's legal research, motions to prepare and briefs to write. It all takes time." She paused. "I've been trying to help. Garth Swain has subpoenaed a bunch of people he may call as witnesses. I've talked with many of them, and I'm trying to get to the rest as fast as I can. Spence says we need to know what each one will say."

"Any of them going to say something that will hurt me?"

She shook her head once. "That's the thing of it. Nothing that we've heard really ties you to Arnold's death. It all seems to be speculation. But Spence keeps saying Swain must have something more that we don't know about."

"What could it be?"

"I just don't know. We keep hoping to find out before too long."

Nate frowned. "I hear that Arnold Masters' father has been in town. What's he up to?"

"Yes. He and Swain have been closeted in the house Swain rented for an office. I imagine Warren Masters is trying to give Swain orders, and I'll bet Swain isn't taking it very well."

Nate was quiet for a second, then his expression changed. "Merc, when you visited me in the jail, I said some things that maybe I shouldn't have."

Merci stiffened. "Like what?"

He hesitated. "I told you about my feelings for you." He hurried to add, "I'm afraid I embarrassed you, and I'm sorry for that."

Merci straightened in the chair. "Nate, don't bring that up again. You and I have been friends since childhood. I hope we'll always be friends." She slapped the arm of the chair. "What's important right now is to make sure the jury understands you didn't kill anyone. That clear?"

"It's clear. And I won't mention the other again."

Merci mused on her way back home. Harley Mathers will help if Swain tries to make something of the horse incident. Lucy Simpson won't be of any use to either side. And Nate? Nate will always be Nate—for good or bad.

Irma's shift ended at four o'clock. He was standing by his auto when she walked out the door. Off came his hat. "Good evening, Miss Lewellyn."

She cast a scrutinizing eye at the man, then crossed her arms. "Mr. Cape, why are you here?"

"It's a nice afternoon and I'm going to drive out north and look at the flatlands where all the homesteads are located." He hesitated, then added, "Or were located."

"So?"

"I hope you'll ride with me and show me around."

Irma frowned and took a deep breath. "Do I have a choice?"

He flashed a white-toothed smile. "No, you don't. But let's enjoy a drive. Maybe we could travel up to Martinsdale for some supper later in the day."

Irma had heard it all before. No man ever made such an offer with good intentions. There was always the other thing. She looked him up and down as she considered it all. At last she thought, why not? He's nice to look at, the car's new, he has money, and I don't have anything better to do. Maybe this one really is a gentleman. Then came a black thought, he was right. She didn't have a choice. So she asked with a smile, "May I go to my place and change clothes?"

He opened the passenger door of the Model T. "Let me drive you to your room."

3 1 The prospect of the trial for Nate Hamilton consumed much, but not all, of the time and energy of the members of the Bruce family. The ranch work continued as though there was no such thing as a trial for a neighbor. A large crew labored each day, mowing, raking, and stacking hay along the length of Little Elk Creek. From time to time it was necessary to move cattle from one pasture to another. On those days the haying ceased and most of the ranch hands mounted horses early in the morning and rode till late in the day. T. C. spent his time supervising the hay harvesting. And when it came time to move cattle, he was on a horse with the rest.

Hiram Morgan had survived the primary election and was now spending as much time campaigning as his position at the Two Dot Bank would allow. On occasion T. C. walked the streets of Martinsdale or Hedgesville with him, lending support. Hiram always expressed his extreme appreciation.

Irma Lewellyn had found Chris Cape to be a gentleman indeed, if somewhat demanding. About two times a week he would stop at the café to tell her he would pick her up at her room. It was never an invitation. Cape always provided something pleasant to entertain her. They drove to Big Timber and on south to a hot springs where they took to the waters. During a trip to Lewistown they dined at the Fergus Hotel.

The atmosphere and the cuisine were new and exciting for Irma. And when, at last, he invited her to spend the night with him in the house he'd rented north of the river between Harlo and Two Dot, away from prying eyes, she didn't say no.

At five o'clock the county attorney looked up to see Spence standing in the doorway. He jerked a thumb toward the chair in front of his desk and said, "Sit. Let me finish this sentence." Roger Davidson scribbled some more on a yellow pad and then dropped the pen. He leaned back with his hands clasped behind his head. "To what do I owe the honor of this visit, Mr. Bruce?"

"Just over to the clerk's office. Thought I'd say hello."

"Say hello and then ask if I know what's going on with the Hamilton matter, right?"

"You've got me. That's why I'm here." Spence dragged a chair away from the desk and dropped onto it. "What's that man Swain up to?"

Davidson shook his head. "Can't help you much, Spence. Swain has cut me out completely."

"Really? I thought you'd at least sit with him to pick the jury."

"He hasn't said a word to me since the first introduction. Swain's holed up in a house that he's rented over on Mill Hill. I'm told he has a secretary set up there—brought her from Helena—and uses one big room for an office and a smaller one for the secretary." Davidson dropped his arms to the desktop and leaned on his elbows. "It's great for old Mrs. Barnes who lives next door. She cooks meals for them and delivers the food to the house three times a day."

"You must learn things from the sheriff."

"Poor old Lester is scared to death of Swain. He does exactly as he's told. And he's been told not to say a word to anyone about their investigation or about anything else related to the Hamilton trial."

"Not even to the county attorney?"

"Especially the county attorney. Apparently, Swain thinks you and I are friends, and that I can't be trusted."

That remark brought a smile to Spence's face. "Well, if you don't know facts, what rumors do you hear?"

The county attorney leaned back and folded his hands across his stomach. "Let's see. Swain and Graves are trying to question every person who was at Two Dot the night Arnold Masters was killed. And they're trying to find anybody who can offer any testimony about Nate Hamilton that may be harmful to him."

"Like what?'

"One example. A kid Nate beat up and then harassed when they were both in the Two Dot School."

"Must be Little Homer Dirks! That happened." Spence shook his head. "Hardly admissible. Too remote in time, if nothing else."

"Probably not. But he may try to sneak it in."

Spence leaned forward, elbows on his knees, his hands folded. "Roger, have they found anyone or anything that can really tie Nate to the killing?"

"Not that I've heard." Davidson shook his head. "But, as I said, I'm not someone that either Garth Swain or Lester Graves confides in."

"What about the jury pool? What are people saying?"

"I hear the same things you hear. Nate Hamilton has a reputation as a blowhard and something of a bully. So there are those in this town who just assume he's guilty." He thought for a moment. "Most of the folks in the community know your sister. They also know that she doesn't believe Nate had anything to do with Masters' death. Merci is well liked, and that's a plus for Nate." Davidson smiled warmly. "Your whole family is well regarded. It will help with the jurors just to have you representing the defendant."

"Nice to hear you say that, but it's hardly true."

"Well, Spence, you know how it is with any jury. When they get in the jury room anything can happen."

"Too true. And that scares the hell out of me. I can't help but worry that I won't be up to the task—and Nate will pay the price for my lack of experience.

Davidson shook his head. "No different than any other lawyer." Spence stood, so the county attorney rose from his chair and stepped round the desk. "Look, friend, you know the law, and you're good on your feet. You'll try this case properly and get as good result as is possible. Whether Nate Hamilton is acquitted or convicted will depend on the facts." He patted Spence on the shoulder. "So, just do the best you know how. And don't put too much of a burden on yourself. That won't do either you or your client any good."

Late that afternoon when Chris Cape stopped his auto on the street in Two Dot, Lippy Lippencott rushed from the front door of his establishment with the pick handle in hand. He was already talking when the tall man stepped from the car. There was menace in his voice. "Stay away from her, you hear? Irma Lewellyn doesn't need you any more than she needed Masters, that other California dude." He pointed the pick handle upward at Cape's face and his voice became a growl. "Don't forget what happened to him!"

A small grin appeared on Cape's face as he snatched the pick handle from the barkeep's hand with speed Lippy could not have anticipated. One glance at the weapon and he tossed it away as though it was of no importance. The smile was on his face but not in his voice when he spoke. "Mr. Lippencott, never make a threat unless you're able to carry it out. And, Sir, you are no match for me." The smile disappeared. "Never again address me in such a manner. If you do, you will pay the price." The semblance of a smile returned. "Mrs. Lewellyn is an attractive lady. She enjoys my company, and I enjoy hers. We will continue to see one another." He paused. "Understand?"

Lippincott's face was red, and his breathing labored. "He poked a finger at Cape's chest as he looked up at the taller man's face. "Smart guy, huh? Listen, I've dealt with smart guys before. I'm warning you one more time. Don't mess with Irma!" Then, he swiveled and marched back to the door of his business, leaving the pick handle lying in the street.

32

Nate sat on one side of the conference table. Spence and Merci were across from him. "What person, beside little Homer, can accuse you of a beating?

"No one. Damn it, Spence, I'm not a bully, and I never was." He swiped at a cheek with the back of his hand. "Homer Dirks was just such a little sissy. And he made fun of me that day—called me a dummy because I couldn't spell a word in class. I wouldn't have cared except that he spelled it right. That was—what? Twenty years ago? What difference can it make now?"

Merci spoke up. "Nate, they have your life under a microscope." She leaned forward with a frown. "Now who, beside little Homer, might appear at your trial and say bad things about you?"

"God, Merc. I don't know. There may be lots of people I've offended somehow. How am I to know who they are or what they might say?" Nate turned to Spence. "I'll bet even you've said something once or twice that offended someone. That kind of thing just happens."

Spence nodded. "True." Then, he asked, "What about the time you beat a horse at Mathers' branding and made Mrs. Mathers so angry she reported you to the sheriff?"

Nate bristled. "The damn horse tried to dump me while I was dragging calves to the fire. I just whipped him once with the end of my rope. Didn't hurt the horse. And he behaved after that."

"Will others who saw it say the same thing?"

"Well, they should. But how do I know what anyone will say?" Petulance found its way into his voice. "It seems to me that everyone is after old Nate."

Merci jumped in. "Not so. You have lots of the ranch folks who know you and don't believe you should have been charged. They're worried that the real killer might get away."

Nate relaxed. "That's nice to hear, Merc." He took a big breath. "It makes me feel better."

Spence waved a hand. Time to get back to the important things. "Think back to the night Arnold Masters was killed. Name the ones who can place you with Masters after most of the others had left."

Nate shuffled his feet under the table and squirmed in the chair. Turning to speak first to Merci, he said, "You know about Lyndon Morgan. I guess he told the sheriff he was there, although I don't remember seeing him." He turned back to Spence. "Irma Lewellyn was there. She'll say that she thought Masters and I were about to have it out. We weren't, but she'll say we were. She got between me and Masters and yelled cuss words at both of us. That's when I decided to leave." He paused in thought. "Lippy, the barkeep, was there, of course. I heard him hollering at Irma as I walked away." Nate thought for a moment. "I just can't think of anyone else." He turned again to Merci, "My car was out on the street, and I just got in it and left. There may have been some people still in front of Lippy's place as I drove away, but I didn't pay any attention to them if they were."

Spence leaned across the table. "Nate, it would really make a difference if we could locate someone who saw you leave. That person could then confirm that Masters was still alive when you left Two Dot."

Merci, too, leaned forward for emphasis. "Think, Nate, think. Your whole life is on the line."

"God, Merc, I know." Nate pushed back his chair and stood. "I've been trying to remember things that happened that night, and I'll continue doing it. I'll tell you if I think of anything else. Believe me, I understand that I need lots of help." With a shake of his head, he looked at Spence and added, "And I know you need better information than you have right now in order to save my bacon."

Spence followed Nate to his feet. "That's true." He walked Nate to the door. "We need to go over the jury list. Could you and your parents come in to my office day after tomorrow? Merci and our parents will be here, too. Together we should be able to decide which of the potential jurors may have some reason to dislike you."

Merci chimed in. "And those who may be inclined to give a sympathetic ear to your side of the story."

Nate nodded. "I'll bring the folks." He pushed his big hat on his head. Grasping Spence's hand he said, "Thanks, friend, for taking on this chore. I know it isn't easy for you." Turning to Merci, he said, "And thank you, Merc, for standing by me. It means more to me than I can ever explain."

When Nate was out the door, Spence and Merci returned to their seats. Merci said, "I bumped into Roger Catton on the street yesterday. You know who I mean. He ran the Stockman Bar before Prohibition came along."

"Yes. He's got the meat market now."

"I asked him if he remembered any time Nate was in the bar and got into fights. Or if Nate ever caused a problem by badgering someone else."

"And?"

"To my surprise, he said he never had a problem with Nate." She grinned. "Then it got better. He told that a ranch hand from the Melville area started jawing at Nate one night. Nate just ignored him. The guy finally challenged Nate to step into the alley and have it out." The grin got wider. "This is where it gets good. Catton said Nate just sat there on the bar stool for a minute, staring at the guy. Then, he said, 'You're pretty brave when you're drunk. Maybe not so brave when you're sober. I'll be here at seven o'clock tomorrow night and if you still want to try me, we'll do it out back. But for now, just get the hell out of my way.' And Nate pushed by him and left the saloon."

"That's good."

"It gets even better. Nate was there the next evening—just like he said. But the guy from Melville never showed."

Spence's smile reflected Merci's grin. "So, if Garth Swain is successful in getting Little Homer on the stand to say Nate is a vicious bully, we use Catton and his story to show that Nate walks away from confrontations. And it didn't happen twenty years ago."

"You've got it!"

"Good work, Merci. Maybe I'll have to hire you as my private investigator."

Merci stood and turned to the door. "Not a chance. I'm going to spend my time in the air. I've already let Chris Cape know that we're flying to Lewistown tomorrow morning to sell some more rides."

"You know how that worries Mom."

"Yes, it does some. But she understands that I enjoy it." At Spence's look, she added, "I know. I'm still a spoiled kid."

Irma was standing on the street corner when Merci climbed out of her auto in front of the general store. The waitress put out a hand. "I told you Lippy Lippencott was mean and crazy."

"So?"

"He threatened to beat the hell out of your friend, Chris Cape."

Merci cocked her head. "First of all, from what I hear, Chris Cape is now your friend. But what do you mean Lippy threatened Chris?"

"The other day Lippy caught Cape on the street corner. He had his pick handle in his hand and threatened to use it on Cape if he didn't stay away from some girl."

"That girl would be you, I assume."

Irma smiled a sly smile. "Yes. And you're right. Chris and I have been spending time together. But Lippy must still think I'll come around and settle for him some day."

The smile turned warm. "Chris Cape treats me in a way I've never been treated before—like a real lady. Why wouldn't I spend time with him?"

Merci's first inclination was to say that was typical of the man's behavior until he got tired of the game. The mention of the threat was of more importance, however. "How did Chris respond to the threat?"

"I understand he jerked Lippy's club from his hand and threatened him right back."

"Then what?"

"Nothing more. Lippy growled some more before stomping off to his saloon."

Merci's eyes were wide as she asked, "Do you know what this means?" She paused. "It's evidence that Lippy was the one who printed 'SHE'S MINE' on the cardboard that was on Arnold's body."

Now Irma's smile was more of a leer. "You figured that out, huh?" She turned to walk away. "Your brother will want to know, won't he?"

33 A trip to Lewistown to sell rides was part of the plan. Questioning Chris Cape was the other part. He arrived on time, showing the same white-toothed smile. The morning was cool, and the air was clear. Chris cranked the prop and climbed into the front cockpit. Merci taxied slowly to the end of the pasture and turned the Jenny to the westward for the take-off. The OX5 engine roared to full power and the aircraft slowly gained the speed needed to become airborne. When the machine was about two hundred feet off the ground and beyond the western edge of the level field, the motor began to cough, run rough and lose power. Merci pumped the throttle, but the engine failed to respond. Directly in front of them were hills, the tops of which were higher than the aircraft. A low swale lay slightly to Merci's right and between the tallest of the hills. She began a shallow turn in the direction of the lower ground, still furiously working the throttle. The motor continued to cough and sputter while delivering just enough power to maintain their altitude. They'd never get over the hills. She just hoped they'd be able to creep through the shallow swale. As the aircraft approached the low area it was clear they'd never make it.

In the forward cockpit, Cape stretched upward in the cockpit as the plane appeared certain to strike the ground. He dropped his head and crossed his arms over his face seeking protection from the wreck that was sure to come. Merci kept pumping the throttle and muttering, "Come on! Come on!"

A moment before a crash was inevitable, the motor roared to life. The extra power lifted the aircraft about ten feet, just enough to clear the lowest point. In an instant they were beyond the hills and over the open river valley that lay beyond.

Cape looked back at Merci, wide eyed. He just shook his head in evident wonder. Merci heaved a sigh of relief. Even though the motor seemed to be running properly it was better to get back on the ground. She flew in a wide circle to line up for a landing on the flat they'd just left and Merci brought the Jenny smoothly back to earth. With the aircraft stopped before the hangar, she killed the engine. She and Cape sat in the cockpits for a brief moment reflecting on the near disaster.

Cape moved first. He clambered to the ground and began the process of opening the canopies to get at the engine. Merci climbed slowly over the side of the cockpit and onto the lower wing. Hands on hips, she snapped, "That could happen when you try to pull a loop—lose power just when it's needed most." She jumped lightly to the ground. "Go ahead. Figure out what's wrong with the engine. But we're done flying on this day." Merci stomped ten steps before turning. "When you're finished, we're going to have serious chat."

"Serious chat? What about?"

"For one thing, Lippy Lippencott threatened you because you were spending too much time with Irma Lewellyn. Why haven't you told me about it? That information will help Spence defend Nate Hamilton."

Cape's face showed confusion. "Lippencott threaten me? Never happened. Where'd you get that notion?"

"Irma told me. She said it happened a few days ago."

He shook his head. "I've never even spoken to that man. And he's never spoken to me."

"So Irma's lying? Is that it?"

"Don't know, Merci. All I know is that it never happened."

Merci stood, hands on hands hips, as she thought about it. Slowly her temper came to a boil. "Listen, Chris. I've thought you'd help me find out who really killed Arnold Masters. But it's plain that you have no inclination to do so." She stepped one step closer to him. "You were there the night Arnold was killed, watching from the sidelines. What did you see that will help the sheriff identify the real killer?" She bunched her fists, still on her hips. "Every time I've asked, you've avoided answering that question."

Cape turned to face her squarely, his brow crunched in a frown. "Why do you keep insisting I saw something that others didn't? I was just a guy who was in a hotel room and was bothered by the noise you and the others were making. Once outside, I was nothing but a by-stander. Any one of those people who were hollering, dancing, and drinking knows more about the happenings on the street than I do." The frown deepened. "It seems you're accusing me of trying to hide evidence." There was anger in his voice. "I don't like that kind of accusation." He dropped the engine cowling back in place, wiped his hands on his trousers, and walked to his auto. "I have nothing more to say to you." Once in the Ford with the motor running, he yelled, "Fix your own blasted Jenny."

So she did. Bad spark plug.

34

T. C., Felicity, and Merci waited while Spence ushered the Hamilton family through the front door of his office building and out onto the street. The whole group had spent a couple of hours discussing the people who would comprise the jury pool. Amos Hamilton was concerned about one. The man was a homesteader from whom he had bought some oats—only to find that the grain was damp and had soured in the bin. Amos complained and asked for his money back, but the homesteader refused. The homesteader had bad mouthed Amos as a person who tried to back out of a deal—or so Amos had heard. Spence made a note on a pad.

Nate mentioned a railroader from Harlo who might be angry because Nate spent time with a waitress at the Beanery. The guy thought he owned her. Even those two seemed unlikely to be aggravated enough at Nate or his parents to vote to convict if the evidence didn't warrant a conviction. But Spence made another note.

The members of the Bruce family were alone again and seated around the conference table, Spence asked, "Where are we?"

Merci spoke first. "As far as we can tell, there isn't anyone or anything that ties Nate directly to Arnold's death. All they appear to have is the rope, the bayonet, and the statements of Irma, Lippy, and Lyndon that Nate and Arnold were in an argument late that night." She straightened in the chair. "And we have Irma who can tell that Lippy Lippencott threatened Chris Cape because he was spending time with Irma."

"She didn't hear it, Sis. If it happened she just heard it from someone else—probably from Cape. That's hearsay—not admissible. You said Cape denied it and would probably do so in court if he's subpoenaed to testify."

Merci shook her head. "That doesn't seem fair."

"Perhaps not, but it's the rule."

Felicity, who seldom spoke during these discussions, spoke now. "Nate told a lie. First, he told the sheriff that he left the party long before the killing took place. Then, he admitted to us that it wasn't the truth. The lie will be plain to the jurors when they hear the sheriff tell his story and then hear Mr. Lippencott and Mrs. Lewellyn tell theirs."

"And the jurors won't like it" Merci said, scowling. "And most of them will have seen the demonstration of Nate's temper at the baseball game on the Fourth. That won't help."

T. C. turned in his chair to more directly face Spence. "Will you put Nate on the witness stand to tell his version of things?"

"I have to. How else can we get that information in front of the jury?"

"Are you worried about how he'll handle himself on cross examination?"

Spence frowned. "Of course. That's the biggest worry. No matter how good his behavior's been lately, Nate has a temper. If Garth Swain can badger him into displaying that temper in court, it would really hurt."

Felicity asked, "Spencer, what witnesses beside Nathaniel do you have?"

"That's our problem in a nutshell, Mom. Garth Swain will parade a bunch of folks to the stand and let each one talk as long as the judge will allow. He'll try to make it appear there's more to his case than there really is." He shook his head. "We don't have anyone but Nate."

Merci said, "We have Roger Catton, the backup, to show Nate doesn't hunt for fights or even quarrels."

"I'd rather not use that testimony unless we have to. It opens the door for Swain to introduce character evidence that may be detrimental to Nate. Nate may have punched or threatened someone we've never heard about."

Merci's patience with the discussion was at an end. "I'll keep asking." She grabbed her purse from the floor. "Something that will clear Nate completely may come up yet." Turning to the door, she said, "I'll start right now."

T. C. rose from the chair to wrap an arm around her shoulder. "Ask away, child. But be careful."

She flashed the grin. "I'm always careful, Dad." She was out the door and gone.

Felicity stood to join her husband near the door. Spence, rising from his chair, raised his hand to stop them. "Dad, sometime soon, will you take a look at the jury instructions? And the verdict forms? I'll have them ready tomorrow."

"I'd be glad to, but I'm a rancher not a lawyer. It's been years since I looked at those kinds of documents."

"Nonetheless, you might think of something I've forgotten."

T. C. reached for the door handle. Spence inhaled, and spoke in a rush. "What I really want you to do is sit with me at the trial—be my co-counsel."

T. C. stopped, turned back, and cocked his head to one side. After a long moment of thought, he seemed to say more to himself than to the others, "Well, I've maintained my license to practice law all these years." He straightened his back as a bemused smile crossed his face. "Yes. I guess I could to that." The smile disappeared. "But I won't be much help."

"If nothing else, you can keep Nate under control so he isn't bothering me while I'm trying to listen to the prosecution witnesses."

T. C., put out his hand. "We'll be a team?"

Spence grasped the hand. "We'll be a team."

35

Merci walked north on Main Street, mind on the need to find a helpful witness. Sheriff Graves, coming from the other direction, doffed his hat and cast a furtive look around. "Miss Bruce, can we visit a bit?"

"Of course, Sheriff. And please call me Merci. No need to be so formal."

The sheriff grinned. "Nice of you to say that." He scanned the area again, leaned slightly toward Merci, and spoke in a low voice. "No matter what that man Swain says, I don't believe Nate Hamilton killed your friend. But I've asked about every man who was there that night, trying to find someone to say he saw Nate leave. I ain't had no luck. The only one who came close was Sam Hopkins. He told me that Nate was out front of Lippy's, looking toward his car about the time the party began to break up." The sheriff scratched at his hairline. "Not much help."

"Well, it's something. I'll tell Spence."

"Please do. But for God sake don't tell him it came from me. Swain's given me hell for even asking questions of anyone other that the ones he's picked."

"I'll be careful, Sheriff. I don't want to cause trouble for you."

Sheriff Graves looked around, again. No one was close by, so he said in a quiet voice, "I hear that you've talked to some of the women who were there. Any of them tell you something that will help Nate?"

"No, Sheriff. My luck hasn't even been as good as yours."

"I've learned one thing that might be important. Lippy Lippencott seems to think he owns Irma Lewellyn. And he's threatened more than one young man who spent too much time with her. And everyone in Two Dot knows that your friend Arnold passed the time at Olive's café while he was waiting for your airplane to arrive on the train."

"Did Lippy ever do any more than threaten?"

"Not that I can find out."

"If he did, I wish we could learn when and where."

The law officer glanced behind him. Two ladies were strolling in their direction. He ended the conversation by saying hurriedly, "Well, I'll keep trying. And I hope you will, too."

"You bet. I'm like you. I've known Nate since we were children. He just isn't the kind of person to commit such a crime."

The sheriff gone, Merci mumbled to herself, "Didn't tell him about Lippy threatening Chris. No need to let Garth Swain know about it."

Between them, Merci and Spence had questioned most of the people who'd been served with Garth Swain's subpoenas. Now she made the rounds again. It seemed that Cape had been busy. He and Irma were seen together, once in the dining room of the Fergus Hotel in Lewistown, once at the hot springs south of Big Timber.

She went to the house Chris had rented between Two Dot and Harlowton, but his auto was missing and no one responded to her knock on the door. She even tried to call him on the phone. No luck. Cape didn't have a phone. The man must be purposely avoiding her.

When Merci walked through the door of Olive Breen's café, Irma immediately ducked into the kitchen and refused to say a word. At the saloon Lippy Lippencott just yelled at her to "Get out."

For all her effort, she still hadn't gotten any more information to help Spence. She may as well have been flying.

None of them slept soundly the night before the trial began. Merci, lying in her bed under the eaves of the big ranch house, thought of Nate Hamilton. Nate was facing the possibility of life in prison—perhaps execution. She thought of how he must feel at this moment. For all his faults, she really was fond of her longtime friend. He was basically good-hearted—just seemed somewhat at a loss in life. Since their childhood he'd always had a difficult time in his relationships with others. To compensate, he'd bluff and brag and behave in ways that caused even more difficulty for himself.

In her effort to assist Spence, she'd talked to every person she thought might have helpful information. The information she'd gathered pointed only to Lippencott as the possible murderer. That information, however, was so nebulous it was all but worthless. But it seemed to be all they had. What if it wasn't enough?

The whole mess was her fault. If she'd never gone to California and brought the Jenny to the Bruce Ranch, none if this would have happened. God! What if Nate was convicted? What would her life be if Nate Hamilton were no longer a ranch neighbor, near at hand, always wanting to look after her?

In the large bedroom on the ground floor of the ranch house, T. C. shifted in the bed once again in his effort to relax and fall asleep. He'd spent an hour re-living the one time he'd been in court as a lawyer. Years ago—just out of law school—he had represented a man accused of murder, gotten an acquittal, and then learned the man actually committed the crime. Could that happen again?

Felicity rubbed his shoulders and whispered, "Are you worried about Spence, Dear? If so, don't. He'll do as he has always done—the best he can."

Her husband turned over onto his back and pulled her close. "I know he will. But tonight I wish I'd never asked him to take on the defense of our neighbor. What will it do to our son if Nate's convicted?"

"No sense in worrying yourself about that in the middle of the night."

T. C. gave her another squeeze. "Easy to say." After a deep sigh, "The truth, Felicity, is that I'm more worried about myself than I am about Spence. I'm a rancher, not a lawyer. What if I do something stupid? Something that destroys Spence's efforts and Nate is convicted?"

She brushed her hand gently along his cheek. "That won't happen, so forget it." She gave the cheek a pat. "Just go to sleep now so you'll be fresh and ready in the morning."

Spence had once confessed to a fondness for pumpkin pie. At seven o'clock that the evening, Eunice appeared at his door carrying such a pie, small and freshly baked. They sat across from one another at a round table in Spence's tiny kitchen to share the dessert. Eunice made small talk. She explained that the landlady had permitted her to make the pie and bake it in the boarding house stove. She spoke of happenings at the doctor's office. She told of the rumor that the federals were about to raid several of the moonshine sites near the Crazy Mountains. Spence nodded at each remark and responded in monosyllables when a response was required. Eunice seemed aware of the turmoil he was suffering in these last hours before the trial began. She was striving to give him comfort.

At last Spence pushed the plate to one side, turned his chair to rest an arm on the tabletop, and looked across at her with a smile. "Bringing the pie—just being here with me right now—is appreciated more than you can know. I'm sorry I'm not very talkative. My mind is stuck on the question—what if I'm not up to the task, and Nate Hamilton is convicted?"

Eunice placed her hand over his on the tabletop. "It's the evidence that will either convict your client or not. You've prepared as best you can. You'll handle your responsibility as Nate's lawyer to the best of your ability because that's the kind of person you are. You can do no more than that, Spencer, and no one can ask for more than that."

"Still, what if I miss something? Fail to ask a critical question? Fail to make a timely objection? Fail to make a proper argument to the jury? Fail at any of the many things a lawyer must do and—because I failed—Nate is convicted? How will I live with myself?"

"Spencer, you won't do any of those things." She rose from the chair. "Now let me wash the dishes, and then I'm leaving so you can get some sleep."

She washed; he dried and put the dishes in the cupboards. At the door, she put her arms around his neck and stood on her tiptoes to give him a soft kiss. "You are a special man, Spencer Bruce. Each night I thank God I came to this small town." She pushed back, turned, and said over her shoulder, "Now get that rest. And remember I'll say a prayer for you—and for Nate Hamilton."

Spence spoke without thinking. "Eunice, I hate to have you leave."

She turned to face him. "And I hate to leave." Her smile tripped his heart. "But, we must think of the community. It wouldn't look good if the defense attorney spent the night with a woman not his wife, would it?"

"No, of course not." After only a second, he added, "I shouldn't have said such a thing. Your reputation is too important."

"Yours more than mine. Good night, Mr. Bruce. Get the rest you need."

Spence stared at the door after she was gone. Over time he'd begun to wish Eunice would look at him in a romantic way. She had never given him much hope that it would happen, but now, he was left with new and strange feelings for her that were intermingled with the persistent agony of his legal burden. After a moment, he muttered, "God, I wish she'd stayed with me this night."

He stumbled off to bed and tried to sleep. But the hours passed and sleep didn't come. Too soon the morning light led him from his bed to face the day—to do his best to save Nate Hamilton from a life in prison—or from something worse.

And Nate Hamilton didn't even try to sleep. He tried to read a dime novel but couldn't follow the words. He paced the floor. He tried to think of the good things of his life. None of it worked to ease his mind. He was simply terrified of the possibility of life in the prison at Deer Lodge. His body shuddered at the thought of the hangman's noose. At last, near dawn, he collapsed on the bed to sleep fitfully for an hour. Then he was up to face the day—and his time before the court.

The late August day was hot, and the room was stuffy. Judge D. D. Crawford climbed to the bench and glanced around the courtroom, his eyes finally falling on Garth Swain. Then he turned to scan the other counsel table. At first the presence of T. C standing next to Spence didn't seem to register. Then he did a double take. "Mr. Bruce, strange to see you in my court."

Spence responded. "Your Honor, I move the court for an order adding Thaddeus C. Bruce, Jr. as an attorney for the defendant."

"Objection, Your Honor. " Garth Swain's voice was calm but frosty. "The prosecution has received no notice that additional counsel would represent the defendant."

The judge raised his hand, palm out, to stop anything more from Swain. His eyes, however, were on T. C. "Mr. Bruce, I seem to remember that you attended law school many years ago. But apparently you haven't practiced for a long time—if ever."

"It's true, Your Honor, that I've not been practicing law of late. But over the years I've maintained my license in good standing with the State of Montana. I've continued my membership in the Montana Bar Association. And, Your Honor, I've checked with the Clerk of the Supreme Court to learn if there is any reason I cannot participate in this trial. There is none."

"And what do you see as your role in this proceeding?"

"My son, Spencer Bruce, will conduct most of the examination of defense witnesses. I may take part in some of the cross examination of the prosecution witnesses." T. C. paused, "And I may participate in argument to the court, should any such arise."

Swain spoke again but more forcefully than before. "My objection remains. No notice and opportunity to prepare."

Spence responded. "No notice for addition of counsel is required, Your Honor. We've reviewed both the statutes and the case law, Sir, to be certain."

The judge turned to Swain, "Do you claim the law is contrary, Mr. Swain?"

"Justice and equity require that opposing counsel be given notice of any significant matter, and—of more importance—given the opportunity to prepare and respond."

The judge appeared to be annoyed. "How are you or your case harmed by the addition of Mr. Bruce?"

"How can I know? I could only answer that question if I had an opportunity to investigate."

Judge Crawford shook his head. "If at any time during this trial you honestly believe that the participation of the elder Mr. Bruce is detrimental to your case you may renew your objection." He looked hard at Swain. "For now, I must wonder if you are just offering argument to show that you intend to contest everything done by the defense whether it is reasonable or not." After a long pause, he said, "I hope that isn't the case, Sir." He turned to Spence. "The order is granted." A hint of a smile crossed the old jurist's face. "Now, how are we to address you? Just saying Mr. Bruce will bring both of you to your feet." The smile broadened. "How about Mr. Bruce, the younger and Mr. Bruce, the elder? Will that offend either of you?"

They spoke in unison, "No, Your Honor, it won't," and they settled into their chairs.

Felicity, seated in the middle of the audience section, was proud of the appearance of her men. Both were clothed in dark suits—one black, one blue—purchased from and tailored by a Chinese clothier in Butte. The fancy lawyer from Helena held nothing over her men when it came to dress.

Beatrice Hamilton made certain that Nate, too, was dressed in a conservative business suit. No high-heeled boots, no big western white hat. He was seated between Spencer and T. C. The two lawyers had explained—forcefully—to Nate that he should appear calm and avoid exaggerated facial expressions no matter what the testimony. They emphasized that he should look directly at the jurors when they entered and left the courtroom. Finally, they made it clear that the lawyers would be concentrating on the courtroom proceedings. He was directed to refrain from interrupting their concentration by whispered questions or comments. Spence gave him a tablet and pencil with which to make notes that they could discuss during court recesses.

Amos and Beatrice were seated in the first row of the spectators' section directly behind their son. Merci was perched on the front edge of the bench in the same row, directly behind Spence. Spence wanted her close. She'd been his investigator and he might need her help.

Warren Masters, the father of Arnold Masters, was on the other side of the aisle, seated behind Garth Swain. His face seemed a constant contorted scowl. The man had arrived in Harlowton two days before the day the trial was to begin and had taken a room at the Star Hotel. Merci had approached him on the street to offer condolences on the loss of his son. He'd simply glared at her for ten seconds before turning to walk away. She wondered how he could be the father of happy-go-lucky Arnold Masters.

The rest of the benches in the audience section of the room were filled with the curious from the community—those with nothing to do and those who could take time from their ordinary tasks. The lawyers' opening statements were expected to be good theatre.

It didn't take long to pick a jury. Garth Swain, dressed in an expensive and perfectly tailored gray suit, extensively questioned each prospective juror. Spence's questions were perfunctory. Neither Spence nor T. C. could perceive a particular pattern in Swain's use of his preemptory challenges, but assumed he had a reason to eliminate those prospective jurors that he struck. In the end, the jury was comprised of two railroad workers, three businessmen from the town of Harlowton, one railroad worker from Two Dot, two homesteaders, and four ranchers. The two alternates were a teacher and a bank clerk. Spence or his father had some acquaintance with every juror. Both felt confident that each would do his best to listen to the evidence and make a decision based only on that evidence.

The twelve jurors and the two alternates, were sworn. Judge Crawford looked at the large clock that hung on the side wall of the courtroom and turned to the newly chosen members of the jury. "It's coming up on noon. The court will be in recess until one thirty. You are free to go for dinner, but be sure to be back here by that time. The prosecution will make its opening statement when we reconvene." Banging his gavel, he barked, "Court's in recess."

The judge stood to leave the bench. Swain stopped him. "I wish to make a motion, Your Honor, out of the hearing of the jury."

Judge D. D. Crawford scowled as he settled back into his chair. "Very well." He continued to scowl and twiddled his fingers until the last juror had absented the room. "All right," he growled. "Let's hear your motion, Sir."

"I move the court for an order excluding each person from the courtroom who has been subpoenaed to appear at this trial until each has concluded his or her testimony."

"Your reason, Sir?"

"The reason, Your Honor, is to prevent any witness from attempting to conform his or her testimony to that of another who has already testified."

The judge considered the request. "Your response, Mr. Bruce?"

Spence spoke. "No objection."

Crawford smiled. "No objection. I like that." He banged the gavel again. "So ordered. And court's now finally in recess."

When the court was once again in session, the prosecutor stood before the podium and spoke in crisp, flint-like tones. "Members of the jury, we are here today because a young man of great promise—Arnold Masters—was brutally murdered in this county on June the ninth of this year. It is the responsibility of the State of Montana to provide proof to you—proof beyond a reasonable doubt—that the defendant, Nathanial Wilson Hamilton, is the person who committed not one, but three horrible crimes—murder in the first degree, kidnapping, and mutilation of a corpse. I intend to fulfill my responsibility to the state, and to you, by presenting that proof.

"The proof will be in the form of evidence. That evidence will come from the testimony of witnesses. It will also be in the concrete form of the devices used to end the life of Arnold Masters and mutilate his body—devices owned and displayed by the defendant—the man seated over there next to his lawyers."

Swain stretched his arm straight from his shoulder in an exaggerated pose to point at Nate. Spence cast a quick glance at his client to catch his reaction. Nate maintained a calm demeanor in the face of the gesture. He returned the attorney's stare.

Swain shifted his attention again to the jurors. "You will hear the sheriff of Wheatland County speak of his investigation of the circumstances surrounding the murder." Swain then went on to set forth in detail the things the sheriff would say. They included verbal recitations of purported conversations the sheriff had with Nate Hamilton. He spoke to the jurors of the words that the sheriff would attribute to others who claimed to have heard threatening statements made by the defendant. Then Swain said, "And the sheriff will describe the devices used by the defendant to kill and then mutilate the body of Arnold Masters. You will see those devices."

Swain paused for an instant, apparently to allow the jurors to assimilate the information he'd given them. With a glance down at the notes on the face of the podium, he continued. "Doctor Scanlan of this community will tell of his examination of the body of Arnold Masters. You will learn that Masters was garroted. A rope was wrapped around his neck and used to throttle the life out of him. You will also learn that a bayonet was the thrust through his body after death. A note on cardboard was pinned to the body. The note read in crude printing, 'She's mine.'" After another pause for effect, he continued. "And you will hear from Mr. Lippencott, the proprietor of a café in the town of Two Dot." Again Swain recited the words that he believed Lippencott would speak as a witness about a confrontation between the defendant and Arnold Masters behind his establishment—a confrontation that was escalating toward violence until he intervened.

The suave attorney continued, "You will listen to Mrs. Irma Lewellyn. She will confirm the testimony of Mr. Lippencott about that encounter. Christopher Cape will also confirm that testimony."

Merci almost leaped from her seat. Cape had never admitted to seeing or hearing anything related to the death of Arnold. As soon as she could catch him, she'd learn what that was all about. And since he'd been subpoenaed by Swain he must remain in town or at least near at hand. Good God! How could she have ever had any romantic feelings for that man?

Garth Swain stepped to one side of the podium. The smallest appearance of a smile touched his lips. "The defense may try to show that others had reason to want Mr. Arnold Masters dead. Don't let that fool you. Only Nathanial Wilson Hamilton—seated there at the defendant's table—had the means, the motive, and the opportunity to commit this atrocious murder." He paused for several seconds. "After hearing the evidence, I'm certain you will do your duty as citizens of Wheatland County and bring in a verdict of guilty of murder in the first degree and guilty of the other charges as well." The man began a turn away from the podium, then swiveled back to face the jurors and added, "Thank you for your kind attention."

The judge looked up at the large clock that hung on the wall of the courtroom and then turned to the jury. "We'll take a fifteen-minute break. The bailiff will show you to the jury room." He took a moment to look at each juror. "When we reconvene you will hear the opening statement of Mr. Bruce." He looked toward Spence and T. C. with a scowl as he added, "One of the Misters Bruce. Which one?"

Spence rose slowly to say, "That will be me, Your Honor."

The judge nodded to acknowledge that information, then turned again to the jurors. "You are admonished not to discuss the things that have transpired here in the courtroom—or anything else about this case—among yourselves or with anyone else until I tell you that you may do so. Do you all understand?" After several of the men nodded their heads, he said, "All right. Don't forget it." He banged the gavel. "Court's in recess."

It was difficult to get through the crowd at the entry to the courtroom. Everyone wanted a word with Nate or Spence or T. C. At last, they huddled with Nate in a cubbyhole in the courthouse basement.

Spence, standing next to the door, muttered, "That opening was good—effective." His concern about matching Swain's performance was evident in his demeanor.

T. C. looked at his son as he leaned on the small table that took up most of the space in the small room. "He made a mistake, in my estimation, when he told the jurors the words each of his witnesses would say. Now, he'll have a problem if one or more of them fails to follow the script. I still think your plan is right, Son. Just give them the minimum of information so you aren't boxed in. And tell them about Nate—the homely things." Turning to their client, he added, "They need to know who you really are and what you're really like. And they need to hear it right up front."

Nate's face was pale. Listening to the prosecutor tell the world that he was a murderer made him realize his situation in a way he hadn't fully grasped. He might be convicted and executed. When he tried to speak, his voice was a choke. The accused man cast a pleading look at Spence. "I have no one else to depend on, so do what you think is best."

Spence's smile was intended to give some solace to his client. "Dad's right. I'll keep it simple."

T. C. added, "And don't attempt to be Garth Swain. You are Spencer Bruce. Every juror knows you as Spencer Bruce. Just be yourself."

"I'll try." Spence turned to the door. Time to get back to the courtroom. Time to begin his defense of a person accused of murder.

The judge returned to the bench, surveyed the room to assure that all the players were present, and muttered, "Court's in session." With a nod to Spence, he said, "You may begin, Sir."

The young lawyer stood, glanced once at his father, then nodded in the direction of the bench. "Thank you, Your Honor." He almost took a deep breath but halted in time. Spence stepped around the end of the counsel table and walked slowly to the podium, buttoning his suit coat as he went. He rested his hands on the wooden stand and took a moment to look from one juror to another.

When he spoke, his tone was moderate, and his demeanor was pleasant. "This is a small community. Many of you know Nate Hamilton and have known him since his childhood. And you must know that this is the first time in his life that Nate is accused of serious wrong-doing. But he's now accused of murdering another human being, killing a man in a gruesome manner." He stopped to slowly scan the jury. "Because the law requires it, and because the charge is so serious, the state must prove that Nate actually committed the crime." He stopped for a second. "That proof must be beyond a reasonable doubt. The judge will give you an instruction that emphasizes that requirement. It is the most important obligation that the state must fulfill. It is one that you must keep in your minds as you listen to the testimony—all of the testimony—throughout the entirety of this trial." Spence moved to the side of the podium while resting one hand on its surface. "Mr. Swain has recited statements you can expect to hear from witnesses during this trial. Please listen carefully to each of those witnesses when he or she testifies. Do not rely on the prosecutor's representations as to what that testimony will be. It is the witness on the stand who will provide you with the correct information—correct information as that witness swears it to be."

Spence stepped closer to the railing that separated the jurors' seats from the well of the room. "Mr. Swain told you that a particular piece of rope may have been used to garrote the victim, Arnold Masters. Through a witness, Mr. Swain may bring before you a short piece of cotton rope and have you believe it is the one that was used to kill the victim. You will, I know, demand proof that the rope you see is—for certain—the one used to commit the crime. Not implications. Proof.

Mr. Swain has implied that the rope belonged to Nate Hamilton. Maybe, maybe not. Nate readily admits to owning rope. So do lots of other people in this community. Probably some of you do. The state must prove that Nate possessed that particular piece of rope—the one that is brought to you as the murder device. And the state must also prove that particular piece of rope actually did the killing. Proof—not speculation. And the state must prove that Mr. Hamilton was the one who used it for that purpose." He shifted his stance. "Absolute, concrete proof of each of these contentions is required."

Spence moved away from the railing. "And you heard from Mr. Swain about a bayonet. The bayonet is unique because it has a broken tip. Nate Hamilton served with distinction in the army during the worst of the trench warfare in France. He brought the bayonet home with him. It's been on display at Mr. Lippencott's establishment ever since. The fact that the bayonet belongs to Nate proves nothing. It certainly isn't proof that he—Nate Hamilton—used it to pin a note to the body of the victim, Arnold Masters. Proof is required. Listen carefully to learn if any such proof is offered."

Spence stepped back to the podium. "The sheriff's investigation into this matter was focused on Nate as the killer right from the beginning. Had that not been the case, a more thorough investigation might have identified the actual killer. There are others who had the opportunity to commit the crime. The prosecution will ask you to believe that the note pinned to the dead body was meant to show that Nate Hamilton killed Arnold Masters because Masters was spending too much time with Merci Bruce, or, perhaps, spending too much time with Irma Lewellyn. Others who had the opportunity to commit the crime may have also disliked the time that Masters spent with someone." He paused again. "Speculation about a motive for Nate is not proof that he is a murderer."

"Folks, Nate Hamilton will take the witness stand, and he will tell you that he did not kill Mr. Masters. He's not obligated to testify. He's not obligated to present any evidence at all. The presumption of innocence shines on him. You mustn't forget it! He doesn't have to prove he didn't commit murder. The state must prove he did commit the murder—and that proof must be beyond a reasonable doubt." Spence stood quietly for a long ten seconds to let the jurors reflect on that statement. "Nate wants you to know the truth. So he'll take that witness stand, tell his story, and allow you to judge his truthfulness." The young lawyer rested both hands on the podium as he looked from one juror to another. "As he speaks you will have the opportunity to gage his sincerity."

He pushed back from the podium and paused again before continuing. "You will listen to Nate Hamilton—a man who's lived his life among you—and be able give consideration to his testimony. And you will be able to give consideration to the testimony of others. Then you can determine for yourselves which of those who give testimony deserve credence. Later, in the jury room, you must decide whether or not the State of Montana has fully fulfilled its obligation. That obligation—don't ever forget—is to prove that the one the state has accused of killing Arnold Masters is the one actually guilty of the crime—and of most importance, that the proof they offer must convince you beyond a reasonable doubt. If at that time there is doubt in your mind, you must return a not-guilty verdict. That is your duty. It is your obligation to Nate Hamilton. Finally, it is your obligation to the rest of us in this community."

Spence stepped to the side of the podium, and faced the jurors squarely. "I'm sure you will fulfill your obligation by finding Nate Hamilton innocent of the crimes of which he is accused." With a slow nod of his head, he added, "Thank you for listening to me so attentively and patiently."

As Spence walked slowly to his chair, the judge looked at the clock and then turned to the jury. "It's nearly noon. We'll be in recess until one thirty so you all have a chance to get some dinner. Remember my admonition to refrain from discussing anything about this matter among yourselves." He leaned to his left toward the jury box. "Now an additional admonition. Don't discuss anything about this trial with anyone at all—not your friend, not your neighbor, not your wife." He scowled as he asked, "Is that fully understood?' After watching all the bobbing heads in the jury box, he continued. "If anyone tries to talk to you about this trial, turn that person away by telling him that you're not allowed to speak about it or listen to anything said about it. If that person persists, let me know who it is. I'll see that he wishes he hadn't done so." Glaring at the jurors, he asked, "Understood?" When all the heads bobbed again, he ended by banging his gavel. "Court's in recess until one thirty when Mr. Swain will introduce his first witness."

The day was hot. The Bruce and Hamilton families trekked four blocks down the west side of Central Avenue past the auto dealer, the mortuary, and a gas station. They crossed a street and walked by a grocery store and the doctor's office. Across the next street was another grocer, the cobbler shop, what had been a saloon but was now called a dance hall, and, on the corner, the soda fountain. Across the street was another former saloon, now vacant, the butcher shop, and the building that housed Spence's office on the ground floor. *Spencer C. Bruce, Attorney at law* was painted on the window. The building also housed the abstract shop on the second floor. Near the end of the last block they passed the pharmacy and a dry goods store. At the Graves Hotel, across the next street, the men headed for the restroom. The women gathered in the private room already set for a meal by the hotel staff. Spence had rented the room as a place away from the distractions of his office where he could work and meet with witnesses.

As they picked at the food, each of the others assured Spence that his opening was effectively presented and convincing. He wasn't as sure as the rest seemed to be. He tried to eat but could hardly swallow. All too soon it was time for him to return to the courthouse to joust some more, with Nate's life at stake.

37

Court was again in session. Merci focused her attention on the prosecutor. As was his habit, he had the thumb of his left hand under his chin with index finger extended along his jaw. His left elbow rested on his right arm crossed along his chest. Such was his posture as he began the examination of the first witness.

Olive Breen was that witness. She told of finding the body and alerting the storekeeper. The two men who helped the sheriff load the body into the back of the sheriff's vehicle came next. Spence decided that cross-examination of any of them would be a waste.

After a break, the doctor took the stand. He spoke of his examination of Arnold Masters' body and of his conclusions as to the cause of death. Spence looked across at his father. T. C. shook his head.

Sheriff Lester Graves was next. He lumbered to the front of the courtroom and took the oath. Perspiration showed on his brow as he climbed into the witness chair. It was the man's first time to give sworn testimony, and his discomfort was evident.

"State your name and occupation for the court record, please." Thus, in that frigid voice, Garth Swain began the meat of the case for the prosecution.

"My name is Lester Graves, and I'm the sheriff of Wheatland County, Montana."

"What person was recently found murdered in your county?"

Sheriff Graves shifted in his seat and said, "You must mean that man, Arnold Masters."

"Of course, Sir. That's who we're here about, isn't it?' Before Graves could respond, Swain asked, "Where was the dead body of Arnold Masters found?"

"Old Olive Breen found him lying on the boardwalk in Two Dot on the morning of June 9, 1920." The sheriff leaned forward in the witness chair and grasped each arm rest tightly. Merci suppressed a grin at the sheriff's careful way of speaking. He had been thoroughly coached.

Through questions to the sheriff, the prosecutor laid it out for the jury—how the body was dressed and how it was delivered to Doctor Scanlan's office. The jury listened to the sheriff tell of his efforts to find witnesses who could shed light on the events that occurred in Two Dot on the night of Masters' death. They heard about the bayonet found in the body of Arnold Masters.

Swain hoisted a bayonet from beside the clerk's table and turned to the jury. He held the bayonet in both hands long enough for each juror to have a good look. Then he handed it to Graves. "Is this the bayonet to which you refer?"

The sheriff turned the weapon to look at the tip. "That's it. It has a broken tip."

"Offer State's exhibit number one, Your Honor."

Judge Crawford's eyes shifted to Spence. "Objection?"

"No, Your Honor."

"It's admitted."

Next, the jurors were told of the rope found on the ground next to the creek behind Lippy Lippencott's emporium.

"Who found the piece of rope?"

"Mr. Lippencott. And he gave it to me."

The prosecutor lifted a short piece of cotton rope and handed it to the sheriff. "Do you recognize this, Sir?"

"I do. It's the rope that Lippy gave me."

"Offer State's Two."

Spence spoke quickly. "No objection."

Swain retrieved a piece of pasteboard from the clerk's table. "Do you recognize this, Sir?"

"I surely do. I'm not likely to forget. It's was pinned to the body of the dead man by the bayonet."

"And was the printing on it at that time, Sir?"

"Yup. It sure was."

"Please read what the printing says."

"It says 'SHE'S MINE.'"

Swain turned to the judge. "Offer State's Exhibit Number Three."

Spence half rose from his chair. "No objection, Your Honor."

Judge Crawford mumbled, "State's Three is admitted."

Finally Swain asked, "Did you talk to the defendant, Nathaniel Hamilton, about those events?"

"I did."

"Did he tell you the time that he left the party that took place in Two Dot the night that Arnold Masters was murdered?"

Spence rose from his chair. "Objection, Your Honor, hearsay!"

Swain spoke as though being patient with an unknowing child. "Not so. Statement against interest. Clearly admissible."

The judge's look toward Spence showed less patience. "Indeed it is. Objection overruled." He addressed the sheriff. "You may answer the question, Sir."

Sheriff Graves shifted in the chair, again. He was becoming more relaxed. "Yes Sir. I asked him what time he left and he told me he left early—before the party was really over."

"Did you later learn that statement was false? Did evidence later materialize to show that the defendant was seen at the party much later in the evening? Long after the time he told you he'd left town?"

"Yes, Sir. Lippy Lippencott told me Nate was out behind his cafe after most of the folks had left."

This time, Spence spoke with more force. "Objection! Multiple questions! Hearsay! there is no statement against interest."

The judge's frown was directed toward the prosecutor. "The objection is sustained. And, Mr. Swain, you just demonstrated that you know the rules of evidence. Follow them from now on, Sir."

Swain didn't change expressions. "Of course, Your Honor." He turned his attention to Graves. "Who else did you learn was out behind Mr. Lippencott's café late that night?"

"Well, there was Irma Lewellyn. And then the fellow from California who's been flying that airplane with Merci Bruce."

"You mean Christopher Cape?"

"Yeah. That's who I mean."

"Did any others speak of the defendant's actions that night?"

"Yes! Lots did. They said they saw Nate try to get at Masters once."

Spence was on his feet. "Objection, Your Honor. Hearsay."

Swain frowned. "The statement will be confirmed."

Spence whirled to face the prosecutor. "Still hearsay."

The Judge scowled at Spence. "You made your objection, Mr. Bruce. Don't argue with opposing counsel." Turning to Swain he said, "I've warned you, Sir. Do not entice hearsay again." Then he admonished the sheriff by saying, "Sheriff Graves, do not try to tell the jury what others might have said to you. That's not permitted."

Graves' face fell at the criticism. "Sorry, Your Honor. I didn't know."

"Now you do. The objection is sustained." To Swain, he said, "Next question?"

The prosecutor paused a moment, then stepped back. "Nothing more from the sheriff."

Judge Crawford nodded at Spence. "You may cross, Sir."

Spence swallowed hard. Here we go. He glanced once at his father and then offered a small smile at his client. He stepped around the end of the counsel table where he stopped to face the witness. The sheriff seemed to relax at the sight of a familiar person before him. Then he stiffened with the realization that Spence wasn't his ally and would almost certainly try to make him look bad. Once again he gripped the arms of the witness chair until his knuckles were white.

"One question, Sheriff. You've testified about witness statements. Other than those statements, did you, in all of your investigation of the death of Arnold Masters, find any evidence that Nathaniel Hamilton was responsible for the Masters' death?"

The sheriff blinked. Then he sat for an instant with a blank face. He rubbed the side of his head. After a long moment the blank face changed to one with an appearance of surprise. He stared at Spence for a second, then turned to the jury to say, "Why no. I guess I didn't. Nothing at all."

"I have no more questions for the sheriff, Your Honor." He kept his face neutral as he passed before the jury on his way back to his chair. Then he smiled as his father gave him the tiniest nod of approval.

The judge looked at Swain. "Redirect, Sir?"

Swain seemed to hesitate, then stood. "No, Your Honor. None."

The judge turned to the jurors. "The end of the day is at hand. We'll recess until nine o'clock tomorrow morning. The admonition still applies. Don't discuss any of this among yourselves. And don't discuss the matters that you've heard in this courtroom with anyone else, including your wives—especially your wives." Banging his gavel once, he growled, "Court's in recess."

Once again the Bruce and Hamilton families gathered at the Graves Hotel. There was agreement among them that Garth Swain hadn't done much to show that Nate was the murderer. The Hamiltons felt that the one question Spence put to the sheriff was a perfect way to end the day. The burden of hearing their son described—over and over again—as a killer had left Amos and Beatrice exhausted. After each of them and Nate thanked Spence and T. C. for their efforts, they walked from the hotel and left for their ranch. The Bruce family opted for Mother's Café. It seemed unlikely that they'd be bothered by the curious in that establishment, especially since they could get a table near the back that was somewhat sheltered by a movable screen.

Spence fidgeted for a bit before he mustered his nerve to ask if he might invite Eunice to join them. He was pleased and relieved to see his mother break into a warm smile at the suggestion. Leaving them to garner the table at the café, he hurried to the boarding house. The first thing he said to Eunice was, "I never should have said what I said last evening. Suggesting you stay the night. Will you accept my apology?"

Eunice, her demeanor pleasant as always, peered upward at him. "No need to apologize, Spencer. And I'm flattered to be asked to join you and your family for a meal, especially today when you must have much to discuss with them." She tucked her arm in his and walked close to him as they trekked back to the eating place.

The men remained lost in their thoughts. Felicity visited quietly with Eunice about her work for the doctor. Merci fumed. Chris Cape must have told Garth Swain something that he hadn't admitted to her. Now she had no idea where to find him. Swain must have told him to hide out until his testimony was needed. If she did find him, she would no longer allow Cape to avoid answering her questions as he had in the past. And, he'd never, ever fly in the Jenny again.

38

Judge Crawford slumped into his high-backed chair and slowly surveyed the room to assure that all of the actors were once again in place. He turned to the prosecutor and said, "Mr. Swain, call your next witness."

Swain glanced down at some notes. Then, with a slight turn in the direction of the courtroom door, the prosecutor said, "The state calls Leonard Lippencott." The sheriff's only deputy, standing at the rear of courtroom, pushed the door open to call, "Lippencott!"

The man known to everyone in Wheatland County as "Lippy" strode purposely up the aisle and into the well of the courtroom. He stopped before the clerk with his hand in the air. It was obvious to T. C. that the man had been in a courtroom before.

"Please state your name and address, Sir." Swain again assumed the pose that Merci had come to expect—hand to face with thumb under chin and finger along his jaw. His voice remained crisp and icy.

Lippy's voice was like a sharp bark. "Leonard Lippencott. Two Dot, Montana."

The prosecutor walked around the counsel table to place both hands on the podium. "What business do you operate in Two Dot?"

"I operate a café. I serve food—coffee, tea, soft drinks. Some near beer."

"Was your business open on the night of June ninth of this year?"

"It was."

Swain thought for only a second, before asking, "Was business good that night?'

Lippy was stone faced as he answered. "Yes, it was. A party got going. The boys hauled my old piano out the front door and someone began to play dance tunes. Some other dude had an accordion. Pretty soon there were people dancing in the street. Lots of people."

"Was Nathaniel Hamilton among them?"

Lippy looked across the open space at Nate and then back at the prosecutor. "Yep. He was there."

"Was there anything about the defendant's behavior that night that sticks in your memory?'

"Several things."

"Please tell us one of them."

Lippy looked again at Nate, then back at Swain. "Well, he grabbed that bayonet from the wall and waved it around while telling about how he took it from a German soldier. He called the soldier a 'Kraut.' He was trying to impress the girls."

"Any girl in particular?"

Spence was on his feet. "Objection. Calls for speculation."

Before the judge could rule, the barkeep tilted his head to the side and peered around the head of the prosecutor at Merci. "Maybe Merci Bruce."

The judge spoke sharply. "Mr. Lippencott, when there's an objection, wait until I rule before you speak."

Lippy peered upward at the judge to say with a nod. "Yes, sir. I will."

Garth Swain glanced at Spence with a hint of a smirk. Then he strode to the clerk's table and reached below to retrieve the bayonet. He handed it to Lippy. "Is this the device of which you speak, Sir?"

"It is. That's Nate's bayonet. Or at least he always claimed it as his."

Swain returned the weapon to the floor beneath the clerk's table before turning again to the witness. "What other activities of the defendant that night did you observe?'

"Later he had a piece of rope and was doing rope tricks. Showing off some more."

The prosecutor collected the piece of cotton rope that had previously been introduced into evidence. He handed it to Lippy and asked, "Is this the rope you just mentioned?"

The barkeeper moved the rope around in his hands, squinting at it. At last, he looked up at Swain and said, "It sure looks like it."

"You're not certain?"

"Rope's rope."

The prosecutor acknowledged the remark with a nod before he handed the rope to the clerk. "Mr. Lippencott, did you see the defendant later in the evening?"

"I did."

"Where and under what conditions did you see him?"

"He and that man, Arnold Masters, were out back, not behind my place but farther down the creek behind the hotel. They were close to that big bunch of brush. And they were in a shouting match. It looked like it was about to get rough, so I started in that direction with my pick handle in my hand. I got there just in time to grab Hamilton's arm as he tried to take a punch at Masters."

"What did the defendant do then?"

"Well, I got in between them and let them see the pick handle and the fight went out of both of 'em."

"Then what happened?"

Lippy squirmed in the chair. "Masters walked off even farther down the creek. Hamilton went back up toward my building and out to the street—out of sight. I assumed at the time that he was going to his auto."

Swain stepped one step closer to the witness stand. "Mr. Lippencott, was the defendant the aggressor in the confrontation he had with Arnold Masters?"

"It appeared like he was."

"You said that the defendant and Masters were in a shouting match. Did you hear what the defendant said?"

"I heard him say something like 'Keep the hell away from her.'" ,

It was T. C. who barked, "Objection! Hearsay."

Swain maintained his composure. "Once again, it's a statement against interest. Admissible under the rules."

The judge didn't hesitate. "Yes. The objection is overruled."

T. C. accepted the ruling with a nod in the direction of the judge.

"Nate Hamilton was angry at Masters and was intent on doing him harm, wasn't he?"

"Objection. Leading." T. C.'s voice was muted but sharp. "Calls for a conclusion. Has no basis in the evidence."

Before the judge could rule, Swain said, "I withdraw the question." He scanned the jury, then added, "No further questions for this witness, Your Honor."

Judge Crawford looked toward the defendant's counsel table. "Mr. Bruce —the elder Mr. Bruce—am I correct in assuming you will handle the cross-examination of Mr. Lippencott?"

T. C. stood. "You are, Your Honor."

"How long do you think that will take, Sir?'

"It will take some time. There's a lot of ground to cover."

The judge displayed a hint of a smile. "I thought so." He looked at the clock. "It's close to noon." Turning to the jurors, he said, "We'll be in recess until one thirty. Don't be late in getting back to the courthouse. And remember the admonition. You are not to talk to anyone about things that you heard today." The gavel hit the desk top. "Court's in recess."

Spence and the others gathered in their room at the Graves Hotel. They picked at the food that was delivered from the kitchen, all the while making small talk and refraining from mentioning the events of the morning. All of them suffered the agonies that bedevil those who are caught in the turmoil of a trial.

Some of the food was eaten. Most of it was merely pushed around on the plates. Eventually, when the dishes were removed by the waitress, Spence turned to his client. "Let's start with you, Nate. Tell us your reaction to the events so far."

Nate furrowed his brow. "I don't think the sheriff did much to hurt me." He looked at T. C. "But some of the things Lippy had to say were bad." He turned his eyes to Merci. "Merc, I never said anything like 'Keep the hell away from her' that night." I don't even know why I was back there with Masters." Nate turned to his mother. "I'd just had too much to drink." He winced at the admission.

Spence held up a hand. "What you may have said behind the hotel isn't the most important thing we heard." He turned to Felicity. "Mom, what are your observations?"

"Mr. Lippencott wasn't telling all he knows."

"What makes you think so?"

"I can just sense it. He isn't trustworthy."

Mrs. Hamilton nodded her head vigorously. "I agree. That man is a liar. He knows something that would help Nathaniel." Looking to Spence, she asked, "Can you make him tell what it is?"

T. C. answered. "I'm the one who will ask questions of him and I'll try. But don't expect him to suddenly become helpful." He turned to

Spence. "You're the lead lawyer here. Tell us, Son, what do you think of the evidence so far?"

Spence leaned forward and put his elbows on the table. "So far the testimony hasn't really hurt Nate very much. Swain messed up when he tried to claim the rope someone found behind Lippy's place was the one that Nate was using to perform tricks." Spence dropped his hands flat on the table surface and faced Nate. "Lippy Lippencott's testimony didn't do anything to tie you to the killing. The most it showed, if the jury believes him, is that you and Arnold Masters had an argument, nothing more."

Nate took a breath and asked, "What will happen this afternoon? And tomorrow? Will it be worse?"

"Almost certainly." Spence thought for a second. "Swain will call others who were there that night. They'll be asked to tell the jury what they saw or heard. We don't know what any of them will say for sure, but none of it will be good." With a smile at his client, he added, "Dad will cross-examine Lippy the first thing. He may get the barkeep to cough up some helpful things. But don't get your hopes up."

Amos Hamilton raised his hand in a tentative manner, as though asking permission to speak. "How long will this go on?"

T. C. responded to the question. "Until it's over, Amos. Until it's over."

39 T. C. and Spence had discussed the way to handle
Lippy Lippencott's sale of alcohol out of the back of
his business. Prior to the trial, Swain secured an order from the court prohibiting them from asking him
about it directly. He'd argued successfully that such
questioning would put the man in the position of having to admit to such sales—and by doing so also admit to a breach of
the federal law with the penalties that admission could bring—or deny
that such sales took place and risk being charged with perjury. Faced
with the judge's order, they decided T. C. should not raise the matter
in a question. Perhaps it would come up in an answer from a witness.

The air was hot when they trekked back up the street to the courthouse at one fifteen. T. C. felt the perspiration running down from his
arm pits as he stood to cross-examine Leonard Lippencott.

"You understand that you are still under oath, don't you, Sir?'

Lippy had his head slightly turned so that he was looking at T. C.
from the corner of his eye. His concern about the questions to come
was evident, but he responded to the first one amicably enough. "Yes,
I know that."

T. C. turned to the clerk. "May I have the rope that's been marked
as an exhibit, please?" With the rope in hand, he lifted it by the hon-
da end so that the remainder dropped down toward the floor. It was

about six feet long. "Mr. Lippencott, you can't say with certainty that this piece of rope is the one that Nate Hamilton was twirling that night, can you?'

Lippy pursed his lips. "No, Mr. Bruce, I can't."

"In fact, Sir, the rope that Nate was using to entertain his friends that night was much longer. Right?"

"I don't know about that."

"Well, if a rope is to be twirled, it must be long enough to make a large loop. Am I right?"

"It would seem so."

Handing the rope to Lippy, T. C. asked, "Can you make such a loop with that, Sir?"

Lippy looked down at the rope, stretched it out by grasping it at either end, looked some more, and then returned his attention to T. C. "Nope. It isn't long enough."

"You don't even know if that piece of rope is the one that someone used to garrote Arnold Masters, do you?"

"I guess not."

"There is a lot of rope like that in the community, isn't there?"

"Sure is."

T. C. took the rope from Lippy and returned it to the clerk. Facing the witness again, he said, "Mr. Lippencott, you told the jury about a party on the night that Arnold Masters was killed. There was dancing in the street. Isn't that right?'

"Yes. That's right."

"Isn't it true, Sir, that many of those doing the partying and the dancing were inebriated?"

Lippy stiffened and gritted his teeth till the muscles in his jaw appeared to vibrate. After a glance toward the prosecutor, he said, "I wouldn't know whether any of them were inebriated or not."

"If, after a while, some witness climbs up there where you are and says he or she was drinking that night, will you deny it?"

The barkeep looked again at Swain who remained stone faced. After that he turned to cast a quick glance toward the jury. Finally, he returned his gaze to T. C. and answered, "No, Sir. I wouldn't try to deny it. There could have been people there that had jugs of moonshine they were willing to share with others. How am I to know?"

Merci, watching the jurors, saw knowing smiles on the faces of several of them.

T. C. sensed he'd gotten what he wanted regarding the barkeep's business. It was probable that every juror knew Lippy still pedaled booze—regardless of Prohibition. He stepped back to the counsel table to glance down at some notes, then turned again to face the witness. "You've testified that you saw Nate Hamilton and Arnold Masters together out behind your establishment late the night of the murder. And you said they were engaged in what you called in a shouting match. That implies both men were shouting doesn't it, Sir?'

Lippy seemed to relax at a question that didn't have to do with the nature of his business. "If you say so."

"That doesn't answer the question. Were both men shouting?"

"Yeah. They were both going at it."

T. C. moved away from the table to stand in front of the witness. "You also testified that Nate Hamilton tried to take a punch at Masters but you stopped him. Tell us, Sir, exactly what Nate was doing to make you think he was 'trying to take a punch'—to use your words."

Lippy began again to show signs of temper. "He had his fist clenched and he was leaning toward Masters like he was getting ready to swing."

T. C. raised his eyebrows. "That's all?"

Lippy growled. "That's enough."

T. C. crossed his arms. "Mr. Lippencott, there was another person back there at the time that you said the two men were arguing, wasn't there?"

Lippy shifted uneasily and hesitated. "Well, yes, there was."

"Who was that person, Sir?"

The man frowned and glanced toward Swain. Finding no help there, he turned to again face T. C. When he spoke his tone had changed and his voice was soft. "Irma Lewellyn was there when I first saw them two going at it."

"Mrs. Lewellyn was between them, trying to push them apart, wasn't she?"

Lippy's aggressive manner returned as he answered. "She may have been. But when I got to them, she moved back out of the way quick enough."

"Isn't it true that Masters had been drinking and got sick to his stomach? And isn't it also true that Irma Lewellyn had been holding his arm while he upchucked?

"Objection. Multiple questions."

T. C. spoke before the judge could rule. "Mr. Swain's right. Let me try again." Turning again to the witness. "Masters was sick and Mrs. Lewellyn was helping him. Isn't that right, Sir?"

"I don't know anything about that."

"And then Nate Hamilton came along and the argument began. Right?"

"I didn't see it begin."

"You've said you heard Nate say something like 'Stay away from her.' That reference, if your assumption of its content is correct, was probably a reference to Mrs. Lewellyn. Isn't that right?"

Lippy stared at his questioner before growling, "He meant your daughter."

"You can't know that, can you, Sir?"

The barkeep leaned back in the chair and crossed his arms. "I just know it."

"Come on, Mr. Lippencott. Irma Lewellyn was there. The logical conclusion was that the words Nate Hamilton spoke, if he actually spoke them, referred to Mrs. Lewellyn. Correct?"

Lippy wasn't about to budge. He merely mumbled, "Maybe."

T. C. shook his head once slightly at Lippy's refusal to answer the question. "After the two men went their way, you yelled at Irma Lewellyn to stay away from both of them and get back to her room, didn't you?"

Lippy's face gave him away. It was apparent that he wondered how the lawyer knew that. The man took a breath. "I told her it was late and she should get back to her room and get some sleep."

T. C. stepped one step closer to the witness stand. "You're enamored of Mrs. Lewellyn, aren't you, Sir?"

"What do you mean?"

"You hope she will marry you. Isn't that right?"

Now the Lippy was really nervous. He looked at Swain to see only the man's wooden face. He turned to glance upward at the judge. No help there. Then, during the time he was looking around, he seemed to find an answer that would do. "She's a nice-looking lady, and she's had tough luck. I can give her a good home."

T. C. waited a few seconds before asking the next question. "You were infuriated because Arnold Masters had spent time at Mrs. Breen's café. And because that time was spent visiting with Irma Lewellyn, weren't you?"

Lippencott turned again to the judge as though hoping for help. Judge Crawford merely said, "Answer the question, Sir."

The barkeep turned back to face T. C. and barked, "What's between me and Irma ain't none of your business."

T. C.'s response was quick and sharp. "It's the business of this court, Sir. Do as the judge just said, and answer the question."

Lippy sat for what seemed a long time. Then he turned to speak to the jurors. His voice was harsh. "That dude, Masters, was trying to make time with Irma. He hung around Olive's café whenever he wasn't working on that damned airplane. And he danced with her too many times the night of the big party." He stopped speaking as though in thought, then continued in a softened voice. "I was afraid that Irma would start to believe the man had a serious interest in her. But he was just playing with her. One day he'd be gone—without a word to her—and then she'd be hurt again. Irma had married a bummer and had to divorce him. That one hurt was enough."

"So, Mr. Lippencott, it is true that you are enamored of Irma Lewellyn, isn't it?'

Lippy turned from the jury to look at the lawyer. "I don't know what 'enamored' means. But I like her and I can provide for her—if she'll let me."

"And you will make sure no other man comes along and upsets your plan. Right?"

"What do you mean?"

T. C. spread his suit coat, clenched his fists on his hips, and moved one step toward the witness. "You killed Arnold Masters, didn't you, Sir?" He paused. "You did it to keep him away from Irma Lewellyn."

Swain leapt to his feet. "Your Honor! That's outrageous!"

Leonard Lippencott didn't hear. He lunged forward in the chair and appeared about to attack his questioner. Then, half on his feet, he shouted, "You bastard! I didn't kill anyone. You're just trying to pin the murder on someone beside that guy who's stuck on your daughter."

The judge reacted by banging his gavel, but Lippy wouldn't be stopped. He stood up straight and put out an arm to point at Nate. "There's the man who did the killing." Turning again to the jury, he almost yelled, "Don't let this shyster fool you. I didn't kill anyone."

Judge Crawford banged the gavel until Lippy finally stopped his shouting and collapsed backward in the witness chair, seemingly spent by his outburst. Dead silence ruled the courtroom. Then, with Lippy seated once again and silent, the judge turned the gavel and used its handle to point at the witness. "I'll have none of that kind of language in this courtroom, Sir. And from now on you are to answer the questions asked of you and nothing more. No more outbursts. Is that clear?"

Lippy was still breathing hard. Without looking at the judge, he said in a small voice, "Yes. I understand."

T. C. hadn't been sure what Lippy's reaction would be to the accusation, but the outburst left him nonplused. He wasn't sure what to do next. He turned to the counsel table to scan some notes. He peeked from the corner of his eye at Spence who silently mouthed, "Enough."

Nate was so stunned by the barkeep's outburst and accusation that he sat with unblinking eyes, his face a complete blank.

T. C. continued shuffling the notes as though deciding on another question. At length he looked once toward the jurors, gave a vigorous nod of his head, turned to the judge to say, "I have no more questions of Mr. Lippencott."

Judge Crawford inhaled and blew out a long breath. He seemed relieved that no more intemperate behavior from that witness would disrupt his courtroom. Swiveling in his chair, he said to the jury, "We've gone a long time. It's time for a fifteen-minute break. Remember the admonition." With the bang of the gavel, he said, "Court's in recess."

Merci watched Garth Swain as he stood by his chair. For the first time, she saw anger on his face. At the sight of his icy demeanor slightly fractured, she had to stifle a giggle.

Spence and his trial team gathered around the small table in the tiny room in the courthouse basement. T. C. stood while shaking his head as he spoke. "I went too far. I'm afraid my accusation that Lippy killed Arnold may have angered the jurors."

Merci, standing near her father, looked up at him to say, "I don't agree. First, you made him look like a possible liar. The jury saw how angry he can get. And you showed the jury that he had a good reason to commit murder. All of that will surely make each one of the jurors think carefully about the man and what he could do." She grinned a wide grin. "And it sure was nice, Dad, to watch that man Swain lose his composure."

Spence, already seated, stretched his legs away from his chair. Leaning back, he clasped his hands behind his head. "Merci's right, Dad. You planted the seed in their minds. That seed—Lippy did it—will remain there, no matter what Garth Swain does."

Felicity smiled and reached a hand toward her husband. "I was proud of you, Dear. You made that man appear to be what he is—a liar and a crook." T. C. responded by grasping her hand. The face he turned to her bore a warm smile of thanks.

Beatrice Hamilton, still standing, patted her son's shoulder but spoke to T. C. "Felicity's right. I'm glad you treated that man the way you did." Her face scowled into wrinkles. "He's the one who committed the crime. I'm certain of it."

Nate, slumped in another chair, eyes on the floor, appeared to be in a daze when Spence turned to him to ask, "What are your thoughts?"

The young rancher blinked and suddenly seemed to remember where he was. He looked around the room and then asked, "What? Sorry. I guess I wasn't listening."

"What are your thoughts about the things Lippy said?"

Nate dropped his hands and rubbed them together. Finally,

he looked at Spence to say, "I really don't know. I hope he didn't say enough to convince those folks that I did it."

"We'll all hold that thought." Spence brought the conversation to a halt. "Time to get back upstairs. Soon enough we'll learn what Mr. Swain will do next."

As they started up the aisle, a local businessman seated at one bench grabbed at Nate's arm and asked, "Are you the one who did the killing, Kid?"

Nate seemed about to answer, but Merci gave him a push and murmured, "Move along and keep quiet. Don't say a word." He gave a small shrug as though irritated by the push but continued on to the counsel table without speaking. T. C., following them, gave Merci a nod of approval.

Judge Crawford barged through the door and gave the room his usual sweeping look. "Let the record show that the jury, the defendant, and the attorneys are in place, and the witness is on the stand." He lowered himself into his chair, turned to Swain, and said, "Redirect, Sir?'

The prosecutor hissed, "I certainly do, Your Honor." He strode around the end of his table to stand directly before Lippy. For once his hand wasn't alongside his jaw in a relaxed manner. "Mr. Lippencott, you didn't kill Arnold Masters, did you?"

Lippy had gotten his feelings under control. His voice was calm when he said, "No, Sir, I did not."

"Have you spoken the truth through all of your testimony?"

"I have."

Swain looked once at T. C. with an expression that conveyed either anger or contempt. He turned to the jurors to hold a defiant pose for an eyeblink. Finally, he faced the judge to say, "That's all, Your Honor."

"Recross?"

T. C. remained seated and composed. "No, Sir."

The judge shifted to gain more comfort. "All right, call your next witness, Mr. Swain."

Three young men, ranch workers all, paraded to the stand in turn to tell of seeing Nate Hamilton showing off his bayonet and of watching him perform rope spinning tricks to impress the girls. Only one said he saw Nate move aggressively toward Masters on the street while Masters was dancing with Irma. He didn't hear any threatening words but added that someone had dragged Nate away before anything could happen.

As each ended the direct testimony, the judge asked, "Cross, Mr. Bruce?"

To each inquiry, Spence responded, "No, Your Honor."

When the last of them had descended from the stand and wandered down the aisle to leave the room, Swain announced with some flourish, "The state calls Irma Lewellyn."

40

Irma was clothed in an expensive dress of the latest style. Her hair, recently coifed, was covered by a cloche hat of a matching color. A very modest touch of make-up completed the picture. All of it emphasized what an attractive woman she was. The eyes of every juror carefully followed her progress from the courtroom door to the place where she stopped before the judge's bench.

Merci realized someone had spent money to assure that Irma's courtroom appearance was proper. Was it Swain? Or was it Warren Masters? Or maybe Chris Cape? She couldn't help but wonder.

The young woman's nervousness was evident. The jurist's smile was kindly. He, too, enjoyed having someone so pleasant of appearance in his court. "The clerk will help you take the oath."

Irma raised her hand as directed. After listening to the clerk, she uttered the required, "I do." The judge pointed to the witness stand with an open palm. Her movements were prim as she settled into the chair and tucked the skirt around her legs. That done, she crossed her arms and waited.

Swain waited, too. Was it to allow her to collect herself? Or was it to allow time for the interest of the jurors to build? Maybe both, Spence decided.

The prosecutor stood some distance from the witness. The smile he presented was one he apparently intended as friendly. "Madam, please tell the jury your name and where you live."

"My name is Irma Lewellyn. I live in a rented room in Two Dot."

"Mrs. Lewellyn, where do you work?"

"I'm a waitress in Olive Breen's café."

"Is that also in Two Dot?"

"Yes, it is."

"Do you know the defendant, Nathaniel Hamilton?"

Irma looked beyond the prosecutor toward Nate. "Yes, of course. He lives on a ranch south of Two Dot and is often in town. When he's there at mealtime, he comes into the café for something to eat."

"And did you know Arnold Masters, the man who was killed in Two Dot?"

Irma clasped her hands in her lap and looked down. After a second, she raised her eyes. "Yes. He came into the café once in a while."

"How often did you see Masters in Breen's café?"

Irma frowned and looked into the distance. "I don't know how often he was in the café. Maybe once or twice a day, when he wasn't working on that airplane." The last was offered tentatively—as though she wondered if the answer was what the prosecutor wanted.

"Mrs. Lewellyn, did the defendant ever demonstrate any romantic interest in you?"

Irma blinked as though the question was unexpected. She looked across at Nate and then turned back to Swain to say, "You mean Nate?"

"Yes, that's who I mean. The man sitting over there." He pointed with a thumb.

"Well, he took me to a dance at the Olaf school house once." A hint of a frown. "That was before my marriage, of course."

An appearance of irritation flitted across the prosecutor's face. Evidently, that wasn't the answer he wanted. "Beyond that one instance, did the defendant ever give you reason to believe he was seriously interested in you in a romantic way?"

Irma's head began to shake before he'd finished. "No, not likely." She paused and then added quickly. "Merci Bruce is the only one he's been interested in—ever since we were in school."

"What did you mean when you said 'interested in'?"

"Well, when she was a freshman in high school, Nate just seemed to follow her around—tried to be near her whenever he could. Then, when she was an upperclassmen he would ask her for dates. You know, go to the movie, go to Andy's Corner for a Coke, that kind of thing."

"How did Miss Bruce respond to the defendant's invitations?"

"Merci could have a date with any boy she wanted. Most of the time she just seemed to ignore Nate."

"How did the defendant react to the rebuff? Did he show anger?"

She shook her head vigorously. "Not that I ever saw. He just kept on trying to get Merci to pay attention to him."

"You say he never showed anger?"

Irma blinked as though remembering something she was supposed to say. "Well. There was the one time." She turned toward the jurors, then quickly back to Swain. "We were all standing on the sidewalk in front of Andy's. Ansell Lomas was a big guy—played on the football team. He made a smart remark to Merci—really kind of an insult. Nate lost his temper. He doubled up his fists, stepped right up to Ansell, and told him to 'get the hell out of here.' Ansell backed away quick and did as Nate told him to. Nate smiled at Ansell's back. That was when he asked Merci if she'd go up the street with him to Simpkins Soda Fountain—the other place us kids went for a treat. She gave him a little smile as she said, 'No thanks, Nate. I'll stay here with the girls.'"

"What did the defendant do then?"

Irma glanced at Nate. "His anger seemed to return and he doubled up his fists again. But then he just took off up the street by himself." She looked at Nate again. "I heard Nate use some more cuss words as he walked away."

"When he doubled up his fists did Nathaniel Hamilton appear to threaten Miss Bruce? Is that what you're saying?"

Irma thought for a moment, then said, "Oh, no! He didn't threaten her. He just seemed really mad."

Swain nodded as though in satisfaction. It was the best he was going to get from the witness about Nate's past temper outbursts. "Let's turn to the night Arnold Masters died. There has been testimony that the defendant tried to attack Masters while you and Masters were dancing. Do you remember that?"

Her head moved from side to side as she spoke. "No. If that happened, I didn't see it." She paused. "The music was good. They were playing all the newest tunes—Paul Whitman's 'Whispering' was one of them. Like I said, we were just dancing and having fun."

"Did you dance with Masters more than once that night?"

"Oh, yes! We danced several times." More remembrance and then, "I also danced with Nate a couple of times. And some of the other young men who were there. It was just one big party."

Merci smiled to herself as she watched Swain's small frown. The prosecutor must have spent a lot of time with Irma to prepare her to testify. Evidently, she wasn't following the script.

Swain stepped back toward his counsel table, then turned again. "We've heard that Masters became sick and you tried to help him. How did that come about?"

"Well, he'd had quite a bit to drink, just like some of the others, and it started to get to him. The crowd was beginning to thin out. Some of the folks were leaving. Arnold and I had been dancing when he just stopped and said, 'I have to get out of here.' He walked off toward the rear of the saloon." She looked toward the jury. "I could tell what his problem was, so I followed along."

Swain was quick to take a step forward and ask, "There isn't any saloon in Two Dot, is there Mrs. Lewellyn?"

A wisp of a smile that crossed her face. "No, I guess not. Lippy— Mr. Lippencott—calls his place a café ever since Prohibition began."

"Back to Arnold Masters. You said you followed him. Why did you do that?"

"Arnold was a nice man, and he'd been kind to me since he came to town. I wanted to help him if I could. So, as I said, I followed him."

"Where did Masters lead you?"

"There's a kind of an alley between the Lippy's place and that little house next door. Arnold went along that alley and over to the creek that runs behind the buildings on the west side of Main Street. He turned toward the depot and walked some more until he was behind the hotel where there's some thick willow brush along the creek bank. He stopped near the brush. That's were he got sick to his stomach."

"What did you do?"

"There wasn't much I could do. After he finished, I gave him a handkerchief to wipe his face."

"Did anyone else appear upon the scene?"

"Yes. About that time, Nate Hamilton saw us and came trotting to where we were standing."

"What happened then?"

Irma peered across at Nate, then glanced quickly at the jury before she focused again on the prosecutor. "Well, Nate said something about Arnold and that airplane. I didn't hear just what it was that he said."

"Didn't the defendant tell Masters to stay away from Miss Merci Bruce?"

"I didn't understand him to say that—although he could have. He was yelling a lot, and he'd had a lot to drink so it was hard to understand just what was bothering him."

"What happened after that?"

"Arnold just laughed."

"And then?"

"It seemed that the laugh made Nate mad because he used some swear words on Arnold."

"Did he do anything else to show his anger?"

"Not that I saw. Mr. Lippencott came busting in between them about that time and everything kind of stopped."

"What did Mr. Lippencott do?"

"Well, he got between the two men and pushed them apart. Then he waved that sawed-off pick handle he uses to keep the peace in his saloon." She stopped, inhaled sharply, and turned to the jurors. "I meant to say his café."

Smiles touched the faces of some of the jurors.

Returning her attention to Swain she finished answering the question. "Lippy told them both to clear out."

"Did they? Clear out?'

Irma nodded. "They sure did. Nate headed back up toward the saloon. Arnold staggered off down the creek toward the depot."

Swain stepped back. "What did you do?"

She looked out into the audience section where Lippy was sitting. His face bore a fierce scowl. She glanced down at her hands before looking up again at the lawyer. "Lippy—Mr. Lippencott—waved that pick handle at me and told me to get myself back to my room." She turned to the jury. "He was plumb mad, and he really scared me. So I got out of there as fast as I could."

The prosecutor frowned and asked, "Did you, at any time, see Mr. Lippencott harm Arnold Masters in any manner?"

"No. That's the only time I ever saw them together. Lippy didn't do anything then but get Nate away from Arnold and send them both on their way."

Swain stood for a couple of seconds and then said, "One last question, Mrs. Lewellyn. Did the defendant have a rope with him at the time you've described?'

"You mean back behind the hotel?"

"That's where."

She pondered in thought. After an instant her eyebrows went up as though in surprise at the remembrance. "Why, yes, I think he did. It seems to me that he had it draped loosely around his one shoulder and under the other arm."

Swain stared hard at Irma. Spence could tell that wasn't the answer the prosecutor wanted. Too late to change the answer now. The prosecutor showed the slightest frown, began to walk to his chair, stopped, and looked up at the judge. "No more questions for this witness."

Judge D. D. Crawford leaned back in his chair for a second. He appeared to be relieved to have reached the end of the day. He turned to the jury. "We'll recess until nine thirty tomorrow morning. Please be on time. And remember my admonition not to discuss this trial with anyone." He raised the gavel, but stopped with his hand in mid-air. "Mrs. Lewellyn, be certain to be here on time in the morning. You will take the witness stand again, and you will still be under oath." He looked at the defense table, then back at Irma. "Mr. Bruce—one of the Bruces—will ask questions of you tomorrow." The gavel came down with a bang. "Court's in recess."

41

The courtroom emptied out onto the sidewalk. The heat that had been so intense at noon had dissipated. Dark thunderheads were climbing in the west. Merci was about to begin the trek down the street with her family when Irma hurried out of the courthouse door. She grabbed Merci by the arm and dragged her around the corner. Merci waved to the others to go along without her.

Irma pulled Merci close to speak. "Merci, I don't know what to do." She looked around with skittish eyes. "I'm getting out of town just as soon as I'm done with this trial. I thought today would be the end of my part. Now the judge says I have to come back tomorrow." Her eyes flitted around at those nearby. She dropped her hand from Merci's arm but moved even closer. "Lippy came to my room last night and said he'd kill me if I said anything in court that might make the jury believe he murdered your friend." Her eyes were wide. "He meant it, Merc. I'm scared to death of that guy."

"He threatened you?" Merci grabbed Irma by the arms. "Let's go right now and tell the sheriff."

It appeared that Irma might cry. "No! I'm not going to do that. Old man Graves will just go to Swain. Swain will just tell Graves to forget it. That lawyer scares the sheriff as much as he scares me. And either Swain or the sheriff might tell Lippy what I told you." She reached again for Merci's arm and her voice became a confidential whisper. "I'm meeting a friend in a few minutes. He and I'll get out of sight. I'm not going back to Two Dot tonight, and I'll be getting out of town sometime tomorrow—unless Lippy somehow finds me." Again, she scanned her surroundings. "Listen, Merc, I only told you all of this because it seems to me that your brother should know what Lippy's like."

Irma seemed to ponder, looking down at the sidewalk. She seemed to make a decision and looked up. "There's more, Merci." She checked yet again to be certain no one could hear. "As I was hurrying to get to my room that night—you know the night it all happened—after Lippy got between Arnold and Nate? I heard Lippy—down by the creek— yelling at Arnold again."

"What was he saying?"

"He followed Arnold down the creek and hollered, 'If I catch you anywhere near Irma Lewellyn again, I'll kill you!'"

The revelation left Merci wide eyed in surprise. "You've got to tell all of this to Spence and my Dad."

Irma drew away. "No! They'll want me to tell about it in court." She pulled her hand away from Merci and wrapped her arms tightly around her chest. "I can't do it. I just can't, Merc." A tear coursed down her cheek. "You don't know Lippy like I do. The man's crazy."

"Why won't you tell Spence? You told me."

Irma wiped at the tear with the back of her hand. "I don't know. I guess I just had to tell someone." A shudder shook her body. "Try to understand." She wiped another tear. "There is one thing though. Lippy's scared of your father. Lippy believes he can whip anybody with that ax handle. But your dad's a lot smarter than Lippy, and Lippy knows it. He's afraid of what your dad might do to him if they ever get crosswise."

Merci thought about that for a minute, then returned to the fear that seemed to have Irma in its grip. "Where will you go?"

Irma's impatience showed. "That's none of your business. I'll be in court in the morning because the judge said I have to. Then I'm gone, and you'll never see me again."

Now it was Merci's turn to grab her companion by the arm. "Come on. You've got to tell Spence about this. You can't just let it go. It might mean the difference between a conviction for Nate or an acquittal." She pulled on Irma's arm, but the other woman jerked away. Merci stood for a moment, then yelled after the departing waitress, "You know that I have to tell all of that to Spence and my Dad, don't you?" Irma didn't look back as she strode across Central Avenue in the direction of the Weber Hotel where a Model T coupe was parked. It took Merci only a second to understand. Chris Cape.

She rushed to the hotel room to find her parents, Spence, and the Hamiltons seated at a table with a glass of ice tea before each of them. Without saying a word to any of them she used her head to signal Spence to join her back in the hallway.

Once there, Spence scowled and asked, "What's so secretive that the others can't hear it?"

Merci grabbed his upper arms with both of her hands. Holding on fiercely, she told him all the things that Irma Lewellyn had poured out. Spence's eyes widened when he heard of Lippy's threat to kill Arnold. "Dad has to hear all of this."

"Irma's afraid of talking in court about the things you've just heard. She's really scared of old Lippy."

"Can't help it. I've got to ask her about all of it tomorrow while she's under oath."

"I understand that." She pursed her lips and then seemed to relax. "Well, I guess Chris Cape will get her out of town before Lippy can do anything to harm her."

"Cape? What's he got to do with it?"

"He and Irma have been seen together a lot lately. I guess he's showing her a good time."

"Well! That's interesting." He stared off to the end of the hall. "I need to give that information some thought. We may be able to use it."

They joined the others in the room to find a waiter bringing another pitcher of the ice tea. Nate turned a questioning look at Spence. The lawyer dropped into a chair and lifted a glass. "Let me cool down for a moment. Then we'll discuss today's happenings."

While Spence was running the things he'd just heard through his mind, he looked from one to another of the small group. The members of the Hamilton family waited in silence. Amos looked like he'd been whipped. Nate might as well have been shell-shocked during the war. He remained slumped in the chair. Mrs. Hamilton's face showed what seemed to be a perpetual scowl, but she put her hand on her son's arm in an attempt to give him some comfort.

T. C. maintained a pleasant demeanor and tried to carry on the trivial conversations that generally accompany any time spent with others. None-the-less, he was suffering the emotions that bedevil all lawyers during the course of a trial.

For Spence, however, thoughts of Irma's revelations overwhelmed any others.

Only Merci seemed upbeat. She chattered with her mother and tried to comfort the Hamiltons. Then she looked across the table at Nate. "Cheer up. They still haven't produced any evidence to connect you to the crime."

Nate wasn't mollified. "Old Lippy did his best to make me look bad,"

"True. But all his testimony showed was that you were out behind the saloon at the same time as Arnold."

"Irma Lewellyn didn't help me, either."

That was when Spence pushed his glass to the side, turned his chair, and stretched his legs. "Irma's testimony is what we need to talk about. She had more to offer—lots more—but Swain either didn't know about it or didn't want to ask." He turned to his sister. "You tell it."

Merci directed her remarks to Nate. "Irma said that after Lippy got between you and Arnold, he didn't go back to the saloon. Instead he followed Arnold on down the creek. The barkeep caught up with Arnold and yelled at him to stay away from Irma or he'd kill him."

Nate jerked his head up. "He said that?"

"Irma said he did. And she seemed sure he meant it."

Nate straightened in a way that he hadn't done since the beginning of the trial. A look of relief spread across his face. "Well, I'll be damned! Maybe he's the one who did it—killed Masters."

Nate's mother scowled at her son's use of profanity, but Nate didn't see it. Shifting his eyes quickly to Spence, he asked, "Can you prove that? Prove that Lippy really killed Masters?"

"No. I can't prove that. But Irma's testimony, if she'll tell the court the things she told Merci, will surely raise a lot of questions in the minds of the jurors." He looked out of the corner of his eye at Merci. "Tell them the rest."

"You mean about Lippy threatening Irma?"

"That's what I mean."

Merci moved her eyes from Nate to Amos and then on to Beatrice. "According to Irma, that man told her if she said one thing at the trial that might hurt him—anything to make it appear that he was involved in the murder—he'd kill her." She stopped, then added. "That was a few days ago. I guess he came to her room after he found out that Swain would make her tell all she knows about the happenings the night of the party."

Mrs. Hamilton looked to Merci and then across to Spence. "Those threats should be enough to make the jury understand that Lippy was the one who murdered Merci's friend—not my son. Not Nathaniel."

T. C. reached toward her, hand flat on the table. "It will certainly help, Beatrice. But I don't believe it's enough to convince the jury that Lippy's the killer." When Amos appeared about to speak, T. C. raised the hand, palm out. "It appears that Irma's rightfully frightened by the threat, even though I don't think Lippy will try to do harm to her. Too much of a risk." He glanced at his watch, pushed away from the table, and rose to his feet. "Right now we should eat and then get some rest. Tomorrow should be an interesting day."

The Hamiltons declined to eat, stood, and made their goodbyes. They would drive back to the ranch for the night. The others had just resumed their chairs and were perusing the menu when Eunice appeared at the door. Spence had invited her to join them for the evening meal. Now, he wondered if her presence would be welcome by the others. He was much relieved to watch Merci step around the table to give the nurse a warm smile. She grasped Eunice's hands in both or her own. Felicity went farther. She pulled the taller woman close for a gentle hug and whispered, "Thank you for coming. And thank you for being helpful to our son."

Having settled into his chair and recited the words with which he began each day of the trial, Judge Crawford turned to Irma. "I see you're in the witness chair where you belong. You understand, don't you, that you are still under oath?"

She looked up at him, sober faced. "Yes, Your Honor. I understand."

"Very good." He shifted his eyes to the defendant's counsel table. "You may begin, Mr. Bruce." Then he waited to see which of them stood. With Spence rising to his feet, the judge added, "It appears that the younger Mr. Bruce will ask the questions."

"I will, Your Honor." He walked slowly around the end of the counsel table to stand for a moment with his hands clasped. His smile was intended to give encouragement to the witness. Spence wasn't sure that Irma would testify honestly about Lippy's threats. Her fear of the bartender might overcome any inclination to be truthful.

"Mrs. Lewellyn, you told us yesterday about the incident when Arnold Masters and Nate Hamilton were together late at night behind the hotel. You then told us that Mr. Lippencott ordered you to return to your room. Is that correct?"

"Yes. It is."

"As you were leaving to do as Mr. Lippencott directed, did you hear anything more from anyone out there behind the hotel?"

Irma frowned, dropped her eyes to her hands. It was a long two seconds before she answered. "Yes. I did."

Spence, too, waited. Let the jury wonder what would be the answer. "What did you hear?"

"I heard Mr. Lippencott yell at Arnold Masters that he'd better stay away from me or he'd kill him."

T. C., seated at the counsel table, turned to look at Garth Swain. The man seemed on the verge of objecting but then relaxed against the back of his chair, thumb under his chin, finger along his cheek.

Spence gave the jurors time to reflect on that revelation. "Have you ever heard Mr. Lippencott make such a threat at any other time?"

Now Swain was on his feet, still calm of demeanor, with a stolid expression. "Objection. Goes beyond the scope of direct examination."

Spence did a quarter turn so he could address both Swain and the judge. "Not so, Your Honor. Mr. Swain asked questions of this witness about things she saw Mr. Lippencott do and things she heard him say. We have the right to pursue other things he said and did that night." A half smile appeared. "And the defense has the right to bring to the attention of the jury other possibilities regarding the killing of Arnold Masters."

"Your Honor, there's nothing before this court to indicate that anyone other than the defendant committed the crime." Swain's voice remained cold and crisp. "Those questions and the answers—whatever they may be—are nothing but a scurrilous attempt to confuse the jury. They should be disallowed, and the jury should be directed to ignore them."

Judge Crawford's impatience was evident when he leaned forward over the bench. "First of all, Mr. Swain, I'll decide what should be done in this courtroom, not you." The judge spent five seconds just staring at the prosecutor. Then he returned to a more leisurely posture. "Now, as to your objection, it is overruled. Mr. Bruce is correct. You opened the door during your direct examination of Mrs. Lewellyn." He turned to Spence and said in his normal, voice, "You may proceed, Sir."

The prosecutor gave a small wave of his hand as though the ruling was of no consequence. After dropping into the chair he assumed his casual position.

Spence faced Irma. "Do you remember the question?"

Irma looked out into the courtroom where Lippy was sitting. His arms were crossed in a defiant manner, and his eyes showed an angry glare. For a moment she seemed to hesitate. Then a look of determination crossed her face and she shifted again to Spence. Her voice carried a hint of vehemence, "Yes, I remember." She turned to face the jurors. "And to answer the question, I sure have heard such a threat. A few days ago—I think it was last Thursday—that man" She jerked her chin in Lippy's direction. "stopped me on the street in Two Dot. He grabbed my arm, is what he did. And he pulled me toward him and growled, 'If you say anything at Nate Hamilton's trial that hurts me, I'll kill you!'"

Spence gave the jurors an eyeblink of time to consider her statement before he said, "Irma"—then, with an open-faced look, "May I call you Irma?'

"You always do when you come into Olive Breen's café. Why not here?"

With a nod of his head and a quick smile, he said, "Of course." With a more sober countenance, he asked, "Had Mr. Lippencott ever threatened you before?"

"He never threatened to kill me before. But he's made it plain that I'm to do what he wants or else." She sent a defiant look in Lippy's direction. "One time I watched him beat the hell out of a drunk in front of his saloon with that pick handle." She paused and glance upward toward the judge. "He scares me to death, so most of the time I've just tried to stay away from him except when I'm working. I can't keep him out of the café."

Spence, standing half turned toward the jury, cast a quick glance over his shoulder at Lippy. The jurors, watching him turn, followed with their eyes. Lippy's anger was readily apparent by his posture and the glower. Spence let the moment hang before slowly returning to face Irma again. "Are you afraid of what Mr. Lippencott might try to do to you because of the things you've said here in court today?"

Swain was on his feet. "Objection." The word was spoken in the same icy voice that Swain had used since the trial began. "That question has absolutely nothing to do with the issue before the court. And it's inflammatory, Your Honor." After a quiet second he added, "Mr. Bruce should be sanctioned."

Spence turned back toward the defendant's counsel table saying over his shoulder, "I withdraw the question, Your Honor. And I have no more questions for Mrs. Lewellyn."

Judge Crawford, elbows on the bench, turned to the prosecutor. "Re-cross, Mr. Swain?"

He stood slowly. "Just one, Your Honor." He walked at a leisurely pace to stand directly before Irma Lewellyn. "You said you are afraid of Mr. Lippencott. Are you also afraid of Mr. Bruce? Is that the reason you just told the jurors a series of lies?" Before she could inhale to reply, he asked, "Or did he promise you money for your testimony?"

Spence began speaking before he was out of the chair. "Objection! It's bad enough that Mr. Swain accuses this young woman of committing a crime, but to accuse me of a crime is indefensible."

The judge's face began to show anger as the import of Swain's question settled upon him. The anger deepened as Spence made his objection. He leaned forward to speak, but Swain, hands clasped at his waist as he faced the jury, spoke first. "I accused no one of a crime. I merely asked a question." Turning to face the judge's glare, he said, "But I'll withdraw that question, Your Honor. And I have no other questions to ask Mrs. Lewellyn." He faced the jury and then briefly locked eyes with Spence. As he did so, the slightest smirk crossed his lips.

At that moment Spence understood. Swain had evidence about which he and his father knew nothing. Lippy's threats would not, in the end, make the slightest difference in the verdict the jury returned.

Judge Crawford, however, wasn't finished. He barked, "Court will be in recess for fifteen minutes. Bailiff, escort the jurors to the jury room." He watched as the fourteen men, twelve jurors and two alternates, disappeared through the door. Then he turned again to the prosecutor. "Mr. Swain!" Swain had reached his place behind the table. At the sound of the voice he remained standing to face the judge. Pointing with the handle of his gavel, Crawford judge snarled, "Never again in my court, Counselor, will you resort to such a tactic, accusing opposing counsel of a crime without any basis in fact. I won't have it."

Swain's response was one word, quietly muttered. "Understood." He dropped into his chair and directed his attention to a folder resting on the table.

The man's insolence left Crawford speechless. At last, he banged the gavel on bench. "As I've already said, court's in recess for fifteen minutes." His anger was still evident as he stormed from the room.

Irma almost jumped from the witness chair and grabbed T. C.'s arm. "Am I finished?"

"Yes, you're finished." He scanned the room to assure that Lippy had left. Then he put a hand on the small of her back as he added, "You did fine." Applying gentle pressure with the hand on her back, he said, "I'll walk you to the door."

Irma pulled away. "Mr. Bruce, your son treated me kindly while

I was on that witness stand. I appreciate it. But no need for any help from you now. I'll be fine." She almost ran from the room.

Merci scooted from the bench and followed Irma to the street. Just as she thought, Chris Cape was waiting in his Model T. Irma jumped in and they sped off out of sight along the street to the east. Merci swore. She'd never been able to find Cape to demand to know what he would say as a witness. Damn the man!

Spence was standing as his father returned to the counsel table. Nate had apparently gone to the restroom so they had a moment alone. Spence said, "Swain has something—some testimony or some other evidence that he believes will clinch a guilty verdict." He asked, "What could it be?"

"From his subpoenas we know he has four witnesses left. One is the fellow you said was called Little Homer when you were children. You said the other one was a different kid from school." T. C. looked around the room to assure they were still alone. "The two remaining are Lyndon Morgan and Chris Cape. We know what Lyndon's going to say. And Merci talked to Cape. Evidently, he won't do anything but confirm that Nate was out back of the saloon that night."

"So, what can Swain have?"

"What makes you so sure he's got something that will crucify Nate?'

"Irma's testimony didn't faze him. And did you see the look he gave me just before the recess?" Spence pulled a hand from his pocket to rub at the back of his neck. "He's got something."

Swain sauntered back past them to his chair where he sat without a glance in their direction. Nate hustled in and the on-lookers again filled the benches. The bailiff gave his cry, "All rise." The cry brought Judge Crawford bursting through the door of his chamber and back to the bench. He scanned the room, made the usual statement for the record that all the principals were in place. Satisfied, he shifted to scowl once more at Swain as he said, "Call your next witness, Sir."

"The state calls Lyndon Morgan."

Lyndon had complained to the prosecutor that he couldn't be away from work for the whole of the trial. After some stalling, Swain had agreed to send word to the young man, telling him when his testimony would be required. The ranch hand received word to appear at the courthouse at midmorning of this day. T. C. offered to arrange a ride into town, an offer Lyndon refused. Instead, he walked to Two Dot and took the morning train to Harlo. As ready as he would ever be, he was standing at the door of the courtroom. He stumbled once on the doorstop as he entered and began the long trek down the aisle to the front of the judge's bench. His face showed either fright or concern as he looked from Spence to T. C. in passing. Once in the witness chair he seemed to shrink, his shoulders rounded, elbows against his sides, hands clenched tightly together in his lap. With a last, seemingly pleading look at Spence, he turned to face the prosecutor.

"Your name and your place of residence, Sir?"

He inhaled and blew out a short breath. "Lyndon Morgan." He shot another quick glance at Spence. "I live on a homestead southwest of Two Dot."

"Who is your employer, Sir?

This time the look was to T. C. "I work for Mr. Bruce—the one sitting over there." He pointed at T. C. and then clenched his hands together again.

"Mr. Morgan, the jury will want to know if the fact that you are employed by one of the defense attorneys will influence your testimony. Will it, Sir?"

Lyndon squirmed. "No!" he said, staring at Swain. "I understand the oath. I know I'll be in trouble if I don't tell the truth today."

Swain nodded slowly, then asked, "Were you among the people who attended a party and dance in Two Dot on June ninth of this year?"

"Is that the day Arnold Masters was killed?"

"It was."

Lyndon wiggled in the chair. He also seemed to relax a little. "Yes. I was in Two Dot that night."

"Did you at any time hear the defendant, Nathaniel Hamilton, threaten to do violence to Mr. Masters?"

Lyndon eyes shifted toward Nate and back to the prosecutor. "Well, he was yelling something out on the street one time when Arnold was dancing with Irma."

"Do you mean Irma Lewellyn?"

"Yes. And then later he was out behind the saloon—well, really behind the hotel—and he yelled at Arnold back there, too."

"Please describe what you saw and heard at that time."

Lyndon hesitated and tried to eye the jury without turning his head. He shifted some more in the chair. When he spoke at last, his voice was almost inaudible. Each juror leaned forward to hear. "I went out back to relieve myself. You know, back in the willows that grow along the creek." That embarrassing admission out of the way, he spoke more loudly. "Nate and Arnold were down the creek a ways. They were face to face. Nate had hold of Arnold by the front of his shirt and was yelling."

"What did he yell?"

"I heard him say, 'Leave Merci alone or I'll kill you.'"

"What happened then?"

"Arnold just laughed so Nate gave him a shove." Lyndon turned to the jury. "Arnold fell down, still laughing. Nate turned and headed back up toward the saloon."

"What did you do?'

"It was really late, and I had to work the next morning, so I just jumped across the creek and started to walk back to the homestead."

Swain waited a couple of seconds, then said, "So, if I can recap your testimony. Hamilton had Masters by the shirt front." Swain reached out to make a fist with his left hand as though grasping a cloth and then dragged the hand toward his chest as though doing the same to a body. "When he had Masters close, he threatened to kill him. And then he pushed Masters to the ground. Is that your testimony?"

Lyndon blinked twice and stiffened. He eyes seemed wild as they swept the room from the jury to Nate and back to Swain. "Oh, yes! One thing I forgot is that Nate had his other fist doubled up when he was doing the yelling."

This time Swain waited a full ten seconds while staring at the witness as though to indicate to Lyndon that the testimony had better be the truth. At last he raised his eyes to the judge to say, "Nothing further from this witness, Your Honor."

Judge Crawford had been leaning with an elbow on the bench. He straightened to ask, "Mr. Bruce—one or the other—will your cross examination take long?"

Spence stood. "I'm not sure how long it will take, Your Honor."

"If that's the case, we'll recess until one thirty. I have another matter that requires my attention for an hour or so." He gave the usual admonition to the jury, banged the gavel, and walked hurriedly through the door to his chamber.

At the hotel Spence followed his father up the stairs from the basement men's room. At the stair top he said, "When Lyndon told me about seeing Nate and Arnold in back of the hotel he didn't say a word about Nate threatening to kill Arnold."

T. C. stopped. "It doesn't matter much. It's merely cumulative. It's the same thing Lippy and Irma have already said."

"Neither one heard that threat."

"That's right. But it's still just a threat. It doesn't really tie Nate to the actual killing. My guess is that right now the jury still sees Lippy as a better bet for the murder."

Outside the door to the room where the food was waiting, Spence stopped. "I don't know how to cross examine Lyndon."

T. C. turned to put a hand on his son's shoulder. "An old lawyer once told me to never cross examine a witness unless I knew I could get something helpful from him. Maybe it would be best to just pass on Lyndon."

Spence thought about that. Then another thought crossed his mind. "Lyndon didn't say anything about either Lippy or Irma being back there when Nate and Arnold were going at it."

"Can't hurt. Maybe the jury will think he tried to hide something. That would help."

Spence blinked and then smiled at his father. "You're right. There's no need to ask Lyndon anything. He won't recant the statement about hearing Nate threaten to kill Arnold. And there was nothing else in his testimony to hurt." He blew out a sigh. "Thanks, Dad. Now I can relax enough to eat."

When both men were at the table, Merci took a bite of the food already on the table, swallowed, and then looked to Spence. "Who will be the next witness?"

Spence dropped his fork onto the plate. "Swain subpoenaed Little Homer, the kid Nate punched when we were children. And one of the others from school but I can't remember which one it was."

Merci frowned. "I've spent a lot of time around Harlo, I haven't seen Homer anywhere. I don't think he's here."

"Swain may've decided those two wouldn't add much to the other testimony. And he probably knew we'd argue anything they could say shouldn't be admitted as being too remote in time."

Merci persisted. "Who else will he call to testify?"

Instead of answering, Spence mused, "It's interesting that he didn't subpoena Mrs. Mathers to tell of Nate beating on the horse."

Nate bristled. "I didn't beat any horse."

Beatrice spoke sharply. "She thought you did, Son."

"It doesn't matter." Spence turned to Merci. "The only witness Swain has left is your friend, Chris Cape."

His sister pushed away from the table and struck a belligerent pose. "Chris Cape isn't my friend. At best, he's an acquaintance." After that outburst, she relaxed a trifle. "I've asked that man what he knows about the things that happened that night. He admitted he was out behind the hotel. And he said he saw Nate and Arnold having an argument. But that's all." Hands on hips, she continued, "And I've tried for the past several days to find him to ask again. He's avoided me." The look of disgust on her face deepened. "He's spending all his time with Irma Lewellyn."

T. C. stared at her in surprise. "Is that so?"

"That's so. And it's no secret around town."

Spence also came to his feet. "That's interesting but not the most important right now." To Nate he said, "If the things Merci's just told us are the only things that Cape will say to the jury—if he's the last witness—your position doesn't look too bad."

43

The judge bustled into the room, hammered once with his gavel, recited the usual introductory remarks, and then turned to Spence. "You may begin your cross examination, Sir."

Spence rose slowly to his feet. "On reflection, Your Honor, I've decided to pass on the cross of Mr. Morgan." He quickly added, "And I apologize if my change of mind has created any problem for the court."

Judge Crawford cast a rare but brief smile at Spence. "Not a bit. I needed the time for the matter that I mentioned." His face sobered as he turned to Swain. "You may call your next witness, Sir."

Swain pushed on the table as he stood, "The state calls Christopher Cape."

Merci turned and there he was, coming through the door. Where in hell did he come from on such short notice, Merci wondered. And where did he leave Irma Lewellyn?

Cape strode up the aisle as though he owned it. He stopped before the clerk who recited the usual "Do you swear to tell the truth, the whole truth and nothing but the truth, so help you God?"

The response, "I do," was given with an apparent sense of both duty and confidence. He moved briskly to settle into the witness chair. Once there, he turned to look from one juror to the next, smiling at each as he did it. At last his attention returned to the prosecutor. Never once did his eyes focus on Nate, Spence, T. C., or Merci.

Swain stepped around the end of the counsel table to stand where he was half facing the jury and half facing the witness. "Please state your name and address, Sir."

"My name is Christopher Lance Cape. My permanent residence is in Los Angeles, California, but I've been staying for some time in a house I've rented just northwest of Harlowton, along a little stream. I believe they call it Mud Creek."

"What brought you to Montana, Sir?'

Cape turned to speak directly to the jurors. "I was one of the flight instructors in California who taught Merci Bruce to fly an airplane. After she purchased a Curtis Jenny and arranged to have it shipped to Montana I thought it would be interesting to travel to this state, see some of the sights, and maybe fly the Jenny with Miss Bruce."

"Were you acquainted with Arnold Masters in California?"

"Oh, yes. We were at the same airfield where Miss Bruce learned to fly. We both met her there."

"What can you tell us about Mr. Masters?"

Cape turned again to the jury with a smile. "Arnold was a pleasant man. He was a good mechanic. Of course, he didn't fly in France during the war as I did. He completed his flight instructor training just as the war ended." The smile broadened. "As I say, he was a nice fellow and, we got along very well."

"Were he and Merci Bruce romantically involved?"

T. C. was on his feet in an instant. "Objection. Calls for speculation. Lacks relevance, in any event."

Swain almost smiled. "I'll rephrase." Turning back to Cape, he asked, "Did you see any evidence that Miss Bruce and Mr. Masters were romantically involved when she was at the airfield in California?"

"Same objection. Lack of relevance. No response to that question can shed light on the matter before the court."

Swain stood for a moment as though exercising patience with a slow student. "Of course it's relevant, Your Honor. It's the state's contention that the defendant murdered Arnold Masters in cold blood because he believed that Masters was an impediment to his desire to capture the heart of Miss Bruce."

Judge Crawford pondered for a second, nodded his head, and mumbled, "I'll allow it." T. C., face impassive, settled again in his chair.

"Do you remember the question, Sir?"

"I do. Merci and Arnold spent a lot of time together. I have no way of knowing what their relationship was for certain. But she brought him to Montana, when she might have asked some other person to make the trip, to assist her in the assembly of her airplane, and to help her with her first flights."

"And who would that other person be?"

"That would be me."

"But she singled out Masters even though he had less flying experience than you?"

"That's correct."

Swain now stepped around the podium to stand directly before the witness. "Mr. Cape, were you in Two Dot on the night that Arnold Masters was killed?"

"I was."

"Did you see anything happen that night that will shed light on the way in which Arnold Masters met his death?"

"I did."

"What did you see, sir?"

"I was staying at the Hopkins Hotel at that time. My room was on the ground floor and in back of the building. There was a lot of noise from a party that was going on. It kept me from sleeping. As the party quieted down, however, I heard some shouting from behind the hotel so I stepped out the back door to find out what was happening. Standing in the shadow of the hotel I saw that man." He pointed a long arm at Nate. "He rushed up behind Arnold Masters, wrapped a piece of rope around his neck, and pulled the rope tight."

Merci's mouth dropped open in astonishment. Cape had never said a word to her about any of it.

Swain leaned forward. "Was there a struggle?"

"Of course. But there really wasn't anything Arnold could do. Hamilton was too strong and too determined."

Spence frowned. T. C. scowled. Nate was white faced in shock.

Swain continued. "Then what happened?"

"Arnold really struggled. He threw his body around and kept trying to pull the rope away from his throat, but at last he just seemed to collapse onto the ground."

"Did the defendant stop then?"

"No." Cape turned to the jury. "He was on his knees, bent over, and twisting the rope to make certain that the man was dead."

Nate began to shake his head from side to side.

"And then?"

"When he was sure he'd finished the job, Hamilton stood, gave the body a kick, threw the rope to one side, and walked calmly away toward the saloon. I thought I'd follow him. So I went back through the hotel and out the front door. Hamilton had reached his car by that time and he drove away. In a hurry, I might add."

Nate grabbed Spence's arm in a frantic grasp. His voice was soft— but loud enough for the jurors to hear. "None of that ever happened." Spence put his hand over Nate's, turned to him, and shook his head. It was a silent admonition to keep quiet.

Swain ignored it all. "Were there any other people around?"

"Not a soul. The street was empty."

"What did you do then?"

Cape turned his attention from the jury to Swain and back again. "I went to the door of the hotel proprietor's rooms to try to wake him. It seemed most important to place a call to the sheriff."

"Were you successful?"

"It took a while to arouse the man. He's quite old, you know, and then additional time to convince him to try to call the sheriff. At last he did so, but apparently there was a problem with the telephone exchange in Harlowton. He didn't get through."

"About what time was that, sir?"

"I believe it was about three o'clock in the morning."

Swain stepped back and leaned an elbow on the podium. "What did you do then?"

"I went back through the hotel and out the back door." He turned to address the jury. "The body was gone."

Merci gritted her teeth as a murmur arose from the spectators. The bastard was playing to the jury—his audience.

The judge rapped his gavel gently to quiet the crowd. T. C. turned an eye to scan the jurors. All of them were leaning forward as though trying to catch each word the witness spoke.

"Then what did you do?"

"I tried again to get the hotel proprietor to call for the sheriff. He refused, saying the telephone exchange here in Harlo was closed for the night."

Swain removed his hand from his chin and dropped his arms to the podium, hands clasped. "Did you try to find the body?"

"I did not. I didn't know where to look."

"When did you find out what happened to Arnold's body?"

Cape shook his head as though to indicate sorrow. "Like everyone else. I found out about it the next morning."

The prosecutor stood for a time with his head down as though in thought. Then he looked up first at Cape and then at the judge. "No more questions of this witness." With a quick turn, he was back at his seat.

Merci's eyes squinted and her entire face was a contorted scowl as she growled to herself, "Chris Cape, you lying son-of-a-bitch. It has to be you who killed Arnold. Now you're trying to hang it on Nate in order to save yourself. "

Spence was stunned by the things Chris Cape had just told the jury—so stunned he wasn't able to think of a way to even begin a cross-examination. He turned to his right to see Nate staring with wide eyes at his accuser. Spence cast a helpless look at his father.

T. C., grim faced, silently mouthed, "I'll handle it." It took Spence a moment to understand. He slumped back in his chair, relieved.

Judge Crawford granted them a reprieve by turning to the jury. "We'll take a fifteen-minute recess. Remember the admonition." And he was gone, with the jurors trailing off to the jury room in his wake.

Nate turned to Spence to say something, but T. C. grabbed him firmly by the arm as he growled, "Outside."

They scrambled out the door onto the sidewalk and around the corner of the building to escape from the spectators who had vacated the building.

"He's lying, Spence. I didn't choke that man. I swear nothing that he said happened that night. All right, I was drunk, and I did cuss out Arnold Masters, but that's all I did." He grabbed the lapel of Spence's suit coat. "I swear, Spence. You've got to believe me. I'm not a murderer." The last came out near to a sob.

Merci joined them. Her boiling anger was evident when she

snarled. "Chris Cape did it, Spence. He killed Arnold Masters in cold blood. That's the reason he told those lies. He's trying to protect himself by blaming Nate." She kicked some dirt. "I'm sure of it."

T. C.'s voice was soft in comparison as he addressed his daughter. "Maybe." Then put his hand on Nate's shoulder. "It's not a question of what any of us believes. It only matters what the jury will believe."

Spence stood, head down. At last he looked up. "Chris Cape told you none of that stuff, did he Merc?"

"Nothing even like it."

Eyes to his father, Spence said, "I agree with Nate and Merci. He's lying. But I have no idea how to cross-examine him in an attempt to undo the damage."

The briefest of smiles crossed T. C.'s lips. "You relax. I'll handle it, Son." He put a hand on the middle Nate's back and give him a gentle shove back toward the door. "Time to get back in there. Can't keep the judge waiting." A faint frown crossed his face. "And, Nate, don't speak. Maintain your composure no matter what you hear."

44

All of the participants were again in their places. They waited…and they waited…and they waited, but Judge Crawford didn't appear. Swain began to fidget with his pen. Then the foot attached to the leg he had crossed over the other began to swing back and forth. Once he seemed ready to stand and knock on door to the judge's chamber but apparently thought better of it.

Nate sat slumped in his chair. Spence glanced at the jurors, from one to the next and then over at his father. T. C. remained erect and still, a look of determination on his face the likes of which Spence had seen only on rare occasions.

Finally, the old judge bustled through the door and scrambled up behind the bench. Still standing, he banged the gavel as he said, "Court's in session." Then he settled more slowly into his chair and allowed his eyes to sweep the room. Turning to the jury, he smiled. "Please forgive the delay. An important matter required my immediate attention." He stared off into the distance for a trice before he looked back at the jury panel to add, "It was something I really had to address." The judge scanned the room. "But now I can see that we're all here as we should be." Looking at the defense table, he said, "You may begin your cross-examination, Mr. Bruce." The judge displayed a flash of surprise when he saw T. C. standing at the counsel table.

The rancher—again a lawyer—had remained on his feet throughout the long wait for the judge. Fully erect, he crossed his arms and stepped around the end of the table and took two paces to stop directly before and near to the witness stand. And there he waited—with his eyes never leaving those of Christopher Cape.

Cape stared back for a fleeting moment. Then he shifted his eyes away and dropped them down to his left hand that rested on the arm of the witness chair. After a second he raised his eyes again with a kind of smirk showing on his face. That's when T. C. asked the first question. "These things that you've described, they happened about three o'clock in the morning. That was your testimony, wasn't it, Sir?"

"Yes. That's correct."

"It was dark at that time wasn't it, Mr. Cape."

Cape looked upward in the direction of a corner of the room as though trying to remember. "Yes, Mr. Bruce, it was pretty dark." Then he quickly added. "No. I remember that there was some moonlight. It wasn't completely dark."

"If it was dark, how could you see so clearly what was happening between Nate Hamilton and Arnold Masters in all the detail that you've described?"

"What do you mean?"

"You've testified that you stepped out of the hotel, saw Nate Hamilton 'rush up behind Arnold Masters and wrap a rope round his neck.' That's right, isn't it?"

"Yes, Sir. That's what I saw."

"In the dark, how could you even tell if you were looking at Hamilton and Masters and not someone else?"

"Well, it wasn't completely dark. And they weren't far from the place where I was standing when it all happened. Maybe half as far as from here to the other end of this room." The witness and all the lawyers watched the jurors' heads swivel to measure the distance—not more than fifty feet to the back of the room. Then Cape completed his answer. "Hamilton was wearing that big hat. It was easy to tell who he was. And I knew Masters well enough to recognize the shape of his body." Cape stopped speaking and sat back in the chair.

T. C. waited, let the witness get comfortable. Then he deliberately unfolded his arms, spread the tails of his suit coat, and placed a hand on each hip. Leaning toward the witness, he asked, "What did you do to help Arnold Masters at that time, Sir?"

The aviator blinked, turned to look toward Swain and then back past T. C. to the jury. Finally, his eyes returned to face his questioner. "I couldn't do anything, Mr. Bruce."

"You've just told the jurors that you were standing close to the place where the altercation occurred—only half the length of this room. Surely, Sir, you could have hurried across that short distance to put a stop to the action you've described—the rush to catch Masters, the wrapping of the rope around the man's neck, and the holding of the rope in place—with Arnold struggling all the while to free himself. That all took some time, did it not?"

Cape blinked his eyes twice and then looked again toward the prosecutor. Swain was stone faced. "There just wasn't enough time."

T. C. turned to gesture for Spence to stand. He stepped to the clerk's table and picked up the piece of rope that had been introduced into evidence as the one used for the murder. Standing once again before the witness, he said, "Let's see how it must have been." Motioning again for Spence to step out into the opening before the counsel tables, he wrapped an end of the rope around each of his hands. Then he moved away from Spence and across to the wall behind the table where the prosecutor was sitting. "You said Nate rushed up behind Arnold and wrapped the rope around his neck." T. C. ran at Spence.

Spence, anticipating what his father was doing, turned his back. T. C. slid the rope over his son's head and dropped it down toward Spence's neck. Spence reacted as anyone would be expected to do and immediately jerked and twisted his body in an effort to reach his attacker. At the same time he raised his hands to grab at the cord in an attempt pull it loose. T. C. braced his feet and tightened the rope just enough to make the demonstration as realistic as possible. Spence's struggling reaction showed clearly that the strangling could not have happened in an instant. T. C. maintained his grip on the ends of the rope. After a full twenty seconds of struggling, Spence sank down to the floor. T. C. followed by dropping to his knees. He continued to hold the ends of the rope for a time that seemed forever. Only at the end of that time did he release one end of the rope and remove it from the neck of his son. Both men climbed back to their feet.

Swain had been on his feet and nearly shouting throughout the demonstration. "Objection! Objection!" Now his voice was more subdued. "I object most strenuously, Your Honor. The jurors must rely only on the testimony of the witness, not on such a contrived performance as we just saw. I ask that the members of the jury be directed to ignore it during their deliberations."

T. C. responded calmly. "Mr. Swain said the jurors should rely on the testimony of the witness. Everything they just saw conforms to that testimony." He replaced the rope at the clerk's table. "May I review that testimony with the witness, Your Honor? The jurors can then judge for themselves if anything about the actions they saw was misleading."

The Judge pondered, chin in hand, before he spoke. "It seemed a permissible demonstration. And yes, Mr. Bruce, ask your questions."

T. C. stepped back in front of Cape. "You testified that Nate Hamilton rushed up behind Masters. And you were watching as he did. It wasn't instantaneous was it, Sir?"

"It didn't take long."

"And, in addition, you testified that Masters struggled. That took a considerable amount of time, didn't it, Sir?"

Cape shrugged. "Mr. Bruce, it took a moment or two."

"A moment or two? Are you asking the jury to believe that it only took a moment or two for Mr. Masters to stop struggling and give up his life?"

"I wasn't keeping time." That remark was directed to the jurors with his face showing a hint of a smile.

T. C. allowed time for the jurors to reflect upon the smile. "Let's make it easy for you. Did the confrontation you've described take less time than the demonstration here in the courtroom?"

"Mr. Bruce, I don't know if it was more or less time."

"You also said that Masters sank to the ground and Hamilton kicked him. Isn't that right, Mr. Cape?"

"Yes. That's what happened."

"Mr. Cape, the jury has just seen how much time it would take for the things that you've described to happen. Do you still maintain there wasn't a chance—not a chance—for you to try to help Arnold Masters?" He paused. "Is it your testimony that you just stood there?" He paused again, longer this time. "Stood there and watched a murder occur without doing anything at all? Nothing to help the victim? Nothing to prevent the killing?"

"Objection. Multiple questions."

But Cape didn't wait. "What could I have done?" It came out as a kind of plea.

Judge Crawford raised a hand, palm toward the witness. "Mr. Cape, when an attorney raises an objection, don't speak until I've ruled." He turned to T. C. "The objection is proper, Sir, and it's sustained."

T. C. ignored the judge—eyes focused on Cape. "Tell me, sir, why couldn't you have run over to them, grabbed Hamilton, and pulled him off Masters?"

Cape jerked his head in Nate's direction. "That's a big man. I couldn't have done much."

T. C.'s arms were crossed again. "Please stand, Sir."

"Why?"

"Because I asked you to do so—Sir."

The witness looked upward over his shoulder at the judge. Crawford merely nodded his assent to the request. So Cape used his hands against the arms of the chair to slowly raise himself to his feet. His posture was erect as he waited.

"You are not a small man yourself, are you, Sir?"

Cape looked again toward Nate. "He's heavier than I am."

T. C. gave one shake of his head, his disgust evident. "Please sit down, Sir." When the aviator was once again in the chair, he asked, "It was your testimony that you tried to get Mr. Albertson, the hotel proprietor, to call the sheriff, wasn't it?'

"Yes. I said that, and I did it."

"And when we bring Mr. Albertson to this courtroom, he'll confirm all that you've said. Is that your testimony?"

Cape hesitated for only an eyeblink. "Yes, I'm certain that he will."

"After you talked to Mr. Albertson, you went out the back door of the hotel again to see that the body was gone. Right?"

"Yes, Mr. Bruce. That's what I did."

"And then what did you do?"

Cape rubbed his left temple before dropping his hand to the chair arm and turning to the jurors. "I went back to bed."

"Just like that, you went to bed. Did you then sleep well, having just witnessed a murder that you might have prevented? A murder about which you did nothing?"

Swain, who seemed to struggle to find a way to interrupt the questioning, was at last on his feet. "Objection! An uncalled for accusation that this witness committed a wrongful act!"

T. C. didn't wait for the judge. "I withdraw the question."

He crossed his arms and stepped back to stand before the counsel table. Then he stood—just stood—while looking intently at Cape. At last the judge felt compelled to ask, "Do you have more questions of this witness, Counselor?"

T. C nodded, his eyes still on the witness. "The things you've told the jury are not exactly true are they, Mr. Cape?"

"What do you mean?"

"You didn't see Nate Hamilton throttle Arnold Masters, did you?"

Cape straightened so he appeared to rise up in the chair. "I surely did. And I described it just the way it happened."

Once more T. C. let time pass without speaking while Cape shifted around in the chair without taking his eyes from his questioner. "You witnessed a murder, Sir. But the murderer was not Nate Hamilton. Isn't that correct, Sir?"

Cape's agitation became evident. "Are you accusing me of lying?"

"The one who throttled Arnold Masters was someone other than Nate Hamilton. That's true, isn't it, Sir?"

"Objection!" Swain raised his voice for the first time. "Mr. Bruce has accused this witness of perjury without a single fact upon which to base the accusation. I move the court for an order directing him to refrain from pursuing this line of questioning—permanently. And for an instruction to the jury directing them to ignore the accusations."

T. C. looked the judge directly in the eye. "The law is clear, Your Honor. Once the prosecution called Mr. Cape as a witness and led him through a tale of seeing a murder, the defense has every right to cross examine him about every aspect of his testimony." He paused. "And if

Mr. Cape didn't commit perjury, he has no reason to be concerned."

Judge Crawford held T. C.'s gaze for a second, then turned to Swain. "Mr. Bruce is correct. The objection is overruled." To Cape he said, "You may answer the question, Sir, if you remember what it was."

T. C. stepped forward. "I'll repeat it. The one who killed Arnold Masters was someone other than Nate Hamilton. You know that to be true, don't you, Sir?"

Cape leaned forward to growl. "I said it was him. And it was him."

T. C.'s silence seemed to fill the room. Every other person in the courtroom took a breath wondering what he would ask next. When he spoke, it was in the softest of voices. "The person that you saw throttle Arnold Masters was not Nate Hamilton, it was Leonard Lippencott, isn't that correct, Mr. Cape?"

There were sudden gasps and muted mutterings among the spectators. Cape's response was a bark that overwhelmed the noise. "No, damn it! It was your client there. The one who was afraid your daughter had a greater romantic interest in Masters than in him!"

T. C.'s face had showed no emotion. Now a faint smile appeared. "Ahh! Now we've gotten to it. How about your romantic interests? You saw Mr. Lippencott commit the crime. It immediately occurred to you to say that Mr. Hamilton did it and eliminate both Masters and Hamilton as rivals for the affections of Miss Merci Bruce. True?"

Another loud response. "Not true!"

"Miss Bruce spurned your advances once in California, didn't she? Then she asked Masters to come to Montana as her mechanic. So you followed her to Montana in the hope she might change her mind. Then you learned that she and Mr. Hamilton were friends—friends since they were in school together. So you thought that Hamilton, as well as Masters, posed a threat to your romantic hopes. Isn't that right, Mr. Cape?"

Swain was out of the chair and around the counsel table to stand directly before the judge. He spoke in a heated manner. "This is outrageous. Not only has this man…" He pointed at T. C. "Not only has he asked multiple questions, he's accused another innocent man of committing a murder. How long will you allow this to continue, Your Honor, before you end it?"

Judge Crawford was not pleased by the outburst and the tone of the prosecutor's voice. "Is that an objection, Mr. Swain? If it is intended as such it should be made in proper form. And you know that, Sir." The Judge, still scowling, swiveled to address T. C. "You did ask multiple questions of the witness, Mr. Bruce. No more of that. Understood?"

T. C.'s face was once again impassive. "Yes, Your Honor. I'll be more careful in the future."

"Very well." The scowl remained. "And you've now accused at least two people of crimes—people other than the one who is on trial. That's enough of it." His eyes remained firmly on T. C. as he added, "Now, you may continue your cross-examination of this witness, but be careful as you do."

T. C. responded in even tones. "One last question for Mr. Cape, Your Honor."

"Very well. Ask it."

T. C. turned again to the witness. "If you insist that you didn't see Mr. Lippencott kill Arnold Masters, Sir, did you do it, instead? Choke the man to death? To protect your interest in Merci Bruce?"

Cape, his face contorted in anger, rose from the witness chair.

The judge's reaction was quick. A wave of his hand sent Cape back to the chair. His voice, when he spoke, was not only loud but stern. "That's three questions, Sir. And you have once again accused the witness of a crime. You were admonished, Mr. Bruce." His scowl deepened. "I'm inclined to punish you, sir. Some time in the county jail might bring you to understand that the orders of the court are to be obeyed. "

Swain was on his feet and speaking even before the judge was finished. "He should be punished. And the jury must be admonished in strongest terms to ignore those accusations, Your Honor."

Judge Crawford didn't even turn to Swain but continued to focus on T. C. At last he said, "I'm going to treat your long years of absence from the courtroom as the reason for your behavior, Mr. Bruce." In tones even more stern, he added, "And I'll say it one more time. Never again ignore the admonitions of this court. Understood?""

T. C.'s face showed a hint of contrition. "Yes, Your Honor, it is understood." After a second, he added, "I have no more questions for Mr. Cape."

The judge wasn't happy. He scowled first at T. C. and then at Swain. He began to speak, then seemed to think better of it. Looking up at the clock on the wall he swiveled to say to the jury, "We'll be in recess for fifteen minutes. Remember the admonition." The gavel banged and he was out of the room.

45 Back around the corner, Nate was all smiles. "You saved me! You made him look like an absolute liar. The jurors will at least have to wonder if Lippy isn't the one who did it."

T. C. wasn't smiling. "I managed to rough him up, Nate. But his original testimony is still out there and in the minds of the jury. During the cross examination he didn't contradict any of that testimony."

Spence put his hand on their client's arm. "Dad's right. And Swain can now ask questions on redirect. He'll try to undo all that Dad accomplished." With that he squeezed his client's shoulder and gave Nate a shove toward the courthouse door. "We'd better get back in there and find out what the prosecutor will do next." With Nate out of the way, he said to his father. "Something's bothering the judge."

"Something other than my behavior?"

Spence grinned. "Well, for a minute there I did think you'd be in the clink." His face turned sober. "No, something even more serious. But I have no idea what it is."

A deep frown furrowed Judge Crawford's face as he climbed to the bench. There was silence in the room as he turned to the prosecutor. "Redirect, Mr. Swain?"

That cold-faced man remained seated and unmoving until the now impatient judge asked, "Mr. Swain. Do you wish to conduct a re-direct examination of Mr. Cape?"

Swain remained mute. Then he nodded his head once and came abruptly to his feet. There he stood, unmoving, behind the counsel table. His eyes never wavered from those of Chris Cape. "Are the things you testified to here today absolutely true, Sir?"

Cape relaxed a little as he answered. "Yes. They are absolutely true."

Swain leaned forward, his fists on the table before him, his eyes still on Cape. "When you told the jury that you saw the defendant willfully and wantonly kill Arnold Masters were you being fully truthful?"

Cape turned to the jury while displaying a look of innocence. "I saw him do it, just the way I told you before."

The prosecutor waited ten seconds before turning to look from one to another of the jurors. At last he faced the judge to say, "Nothing further, Your Honor."

The judge nodded his head in acceptance. Of T. C. he asked, "Re-cross, Mr. Bruce?"

T. C. remained seated to respond. "No, Sir. We're finished with the witness."

Crawford turned again to Swain. "Your next witness, Sir?"

Swain rose, deliberately clasping his hands together at his waist. He ran his eyes across the jury once more. At last he said—with solemnity, "The state rests."

Judge Crawford sighed. He rubbed a hand up and down along his cheek one time before he leaned to his left to say to the jury, "I need to consult with the attorneys for a few minutes so we'll be in recess. It won't be long. The bailiff will call you when we're ready again." Looking at the lawyers, first Swain, then the Bruces, he said, "In my chambers, gentlemen."

The judge's chambers amounted to nothing more than a small room furnished with a battered desk and worn chair. Books, including the Montana Codes and some others that appeared to be ancient, filled wooden shelves that lined the walls. Two straight back wooden chairs stood before the desk and another in the corner. Judge Crawford gestured to the chairs and moved slowly to his own. When all were seated, he seemed lost in thought for a second. At last he placed his arms on the desktop. His troubled appearance foretold his words. "I've received word that my wife has suffered some kind of seizure, and I need to get back home to tend to her." He inhaled and blew out a long breath. "We're at midafternoon on Friday. If I leave now I can be in White Sulphur before dark." He leaned forward, raised his eyebrows as he turned to Spence. "Mr. Bruce, would you object if we recessed for the weekend? You could begin your defense on Monday morning."

Spence's sympathetic instinct immediately took control, and he spoke without thinking of the legal consequence. "Of course not, Your Honor."

Crawford began a nod that stopped when T. C. half stood, hand upraised. "Your Honor, the jurors have just heard Christopher Cape tell them that he saw our client commit murder. If we leave them with those as the last words they hear for a whole weekend, the memory of the words will be firmly impressed on their minds. Irreparable damage may be done to the defendant's case by a delay. The impression of Mr. Cape's words may be impossible to overcome after so much time has passed."

A pained expression took form on the judge's face. "I understand, Sir. But I hope you also understand my situation. I must get back to Meg. She needs me."

Swain leaned forward to say, "Your Honor, you can give an instruction telling the jury not to come to any conclusions about the guilt or innocence of the defendant until all the evidence is in. Such an instruction is common, as you know."

Crawford nodded twice. "That's exactly what I propose to do, of course." Turning back to T. C. he continued, "And I'll put it in the strongest of terms, Mr. Bruce."

T. C. didn't relent. "I appreciate the difficulty of your situation. But our client is facing conviction to a charge of first-degree murder. Your Honor, he's facing the gallows. It's our obligation to do all we can to protect him from that fate. So, Your Honor, I hope you also appreciate our situation." His expression was grim. "We object in the strongest terms to the recess."

The judge straightened, his resolve evident. "My mind is made up. We'll recess now until Monday morning." With a curt nod in the direction of T. C. he almost barked, "If your client is convicted, Sir, perhaps the delay will provide grounds for appeal." He rose and stood erect. "Now, let's get back out there so we can finish and I can be on my way."

"First, may we make a record of our objection, Your Honor?"

"Of course. Please step to the door, and ask court reporter to join us." With the reporter in the room, T. C. voiced his objection. The objection would be reduced to writing and thus preserved should Nate Hamilton be convicted and should there be an appeal of that conviction to the Montana Supreme Court.

Back in the courtroom, Judge Crawford turned sideways in his chair so he was facing directly toward the jurors. When he spoke he leaned forward for emphasis. "We've reached the end of the state's case. Ordinarily, at this time, the defense would begin its presentation. I am, however, going to recess this trial until Monday morning. My reason for doing so is personal. I've received word that my wife has taken seriously ill, and I'll leave immediately for White Sulphur to see to her care." He leaned sideways in the chair and pointed toward the defense table. "The attorneys for the defendant are properly concerned about the long period of time that will elapse before you have an opportunity to hear the witnesses and the other evidence that they present. Mr. Spencer Bruce and Mr. Thaddeus Bruce expect their evidence will counter that presented by Mr. Swain. However, they are especially concerned because the last thing you heard today was the testimony of a man who said that he saw the murder occur." Crawford stopped speaking and took the time to look at the jurors—one at a time and from one to another. "You are strongly admonished not to form an opinion regarding the guilt or innocence of the defendant, Nathaniel Hamilton, until all of the testimony has been heard and all of the evidence presented." He leaned farther forward for emphasis. "You are particularly admonished not to accept today's testimony as being the final word regarding that guilt or innocence. It is not the final word. There is more to come." The judge straightened his back and smiled. "You are all persons of reasonable intelligence. Each of you understands, I'm certain, the importance of your task as jurors and the need to reach the proper verdict during your deliberations. For that reason I'm asking each of you to give me your word that you will do as I ask and not let the things you've heard to this point so influence your thinking as to deny Mr. Hamilton the careful consideration he deserves and must receive." After a pause, he asked, "Will each of you give me your word?"

As expected, there was a general nodding of heads to indicate that each juror would do as he was asked. Spence, listening carefully and watching the men of the jury, wondered if any of them would follow through; if not, Nate might be convicted only because of the sickness of Mrs. Crawford. He hurriedly put the thought from his mind.

Judge Crawford swiveled the chair around to face the room. "Court will be in recess until ten o'clock on Monday morning, August thirty-first." His eyes dropped first to Spence and T. C. and then turned to Swain. "Gentlemen, I assure you that I will be here Monday, and this trial will continue at that time." He looked at the jury. "Remember not only my last request but also the standard admonition that you've received each time we've recessed." The gavel tapped the bench as he rose to a stand and hurried from the room.

The Hamiltons and the Bruces stood on the sidewalk in the hot summer sun. Amos held his hat in his hand as he wiped at his bald head with a handkerchief. "What if the folks on the jury don't do as the judge told them? What if they believe the things that Cape fellow said and they make up their minds?"

Spence answered. "Dad did a dandy job of making Chris Cape look like a liar. I don't think any juror is ready to take what he said as true without hearing Nate's side of things. But who knows, if they make up their minds now, it may be to decide Lippy's the killer."

Merci, standing off to the side, muttered, "I can't believe the Chris Cape that I once liked so much is the same man I heard and watched today. He was lying through his teeth with every word he said."

Felicity stopped the chatter and got them moving. She gave T. C. a push. "It's hot here next to the courthouse. Let's move down to the cafe and get a cold drink. Then we can discuss all of this in more comfort." She and Beatrice Hamilton took the lead. Nate fell beside Merci. T. C. and Spence followed. Amos brought up the rear as they paraded slowly down Central Avenue.

They hadn't moved far before Nate asked, in a voice barely above a whisper as he looked straight ahead, "Merc, am I going to prison?"

She turned her head in his direction and was shocked at what she saw. How could that big man, the one who would brag and bluster and sometimes bully, now have a face like that of a frightened child? How could that muscular body now seem so shrunken? She touched his arm. "Don't think that way, Nate. Spence and Dad are doing all they can for you. And I believe they'll be able to convince the jury that you're innocent"

He still didn't look at her, his voice still small. "Is there any way they can show that your friend Cape really is a liar?"

Merci stopped walking and grabbed his upper arm. "Nate, the only way that can be done is for you to tell your story and make them believe it." She gave the arm a jerk. "And if Chris Cape was ever my friend, he isn't any more."

In a large booth in the rear of Mother's Café, Spence lifted the tall glass of ice tea for a sip. Then he looked across at his client, slumped on the bench. "Here's what we're going to do. First of all, we need to get some rest and collect our thoughts. We've all been under too much of a strain." He looked around at those gathered at the table. "Dad and I need some time to go over our jury instructions once more." Spence pointed. "Nate, you heard all the things that the others have to say. Now, it's your turn. You must tell the jurors everything that happened out behind Lippy's place the night Masters was killed. You must tell them the correct version." He put his hand flat on the table top and pushed it in the direction of his client. "And, Nate, what you say must be believable." He drew his hand back. "So, I want you to go home. Do something to take your mind off this whole mess—something like moving cattle or digging post holes. Then I want you to be in my office at ten o'clock Sunday morning so we can go over your testimony again. And again. And again. Your testimony must be right, and it must be believable." He leaned back, waited a moment, and smiled. "How does that sound?"

"God, Spence, It won't do any good to move cattle. I'll still just be thinking of the things Cape said. How can I think of anything else? He's putting me in prison."

"Do what I suggest anyway." Spence turned to Amos. "Give your son something to do. Keep him busy this afternoon and tomorrow. Have his mind fresh on Sunday."

Beatrice Hamilton looked up to say, "Spencer's right. Let's go home now, Nathaniel. We need some rest after all that's happened the past few days. Our minds are numb." She took one last swallow of tea and pushed herself slowly up and out of the booth. She clutched her large purse as she turned from Spence to T. C. with a somber look on her face. "Thank you both for the things you're doing. None of us can ever repay you." Then she gestured for her husband to slide from the booth, "Come along, Amos. We'll go home, and I'll fix a good meal for both of you."

When the Hamiltons were out the door, T. C. leaned back and heaved a sigh. "You're right, Spence, about the need for rest. I'd forgotten how demanding a day in court can be." Shifting to face his wife, he said, "We'll go home so I can catch up on things there. And you can clean house, as you always do when you're upset." He stood and reached a hand to help Felicity slide along the bench and to her feet. Then he turned to Merci. "Are you ready for home?"

His daughter stood. She sighed, straightened, and then brightened. "Perhaps I can take the Jenny for a flight over the ranch, first thing in the morning. The plane's been sitting too long on the ground. Flying will get my mind off Nate's problem—for at least a short time."

"We still worry about you when you fly." He cast a kindly look. "But I guess you'll do what you want to do." He was all seriousness when he said to his son. "I'm going to talk to the hotel proprietor. We need to know if Chris Cape really tried to call the sheriff the way he testified."

"Good idea. Now that we've heard the testimony of the other side, who else should we question?"

"I'll think about it." T. C. added as he put a hand on Felicity's back as though to move her along. "Maybe we'll get lucky and Albertson will say Cape never talked to him that night."

"We can always hope."

Felicity didn't move. Instead she looked up at Spence to ask, "What about Eunice? Would she join us for dinner tomorrow evening? She's never been to the ranch."

It took Spence a moment to focus on something other than the trial. "It's nice of you to think of her, Mom. I'll ask and let you know."

"Please make certain to tell her I'll be pleased if she comes."

On the sidewalk beside the Packard, Spence faced his father. "Thanks, Dad, for handling Cape's cross-examination. I was at a complete loss." He twisted his face into a picture of self-disgust. "And thanks, too, for raising the objection to the long recess. Now I realize the objection was important. Had you not been there, I would have missed it."

"Well, those things are done and finished. Now we have to be ready to complete our task. I'll be there on Sunday when Nate's in your office. You should take him through his direct examination. Then I'll be Garth Swain and really work him over on cross. We've got to make him understand what's coming. It isn't going to be a pleasant experience for Nate."

"Right." Spence turned and put his arm around his mother's shoulder and gave it a squeeze. "Take Dad home and make him sit and read the papers that he's been missing. That'll do him more good than anything else." With a quizzical look he asked his sister, "Who'll pull the prop for you in the morning? Do you expect Chris Cape to magically arrive?"

Merci's face twisted into a frown. "Chris Cape will never get near that airplane again. I'll get Lyndon to do it." She looked at her father. "That all right, Dad?"

"Perhaps."

The import of that one word hit Merci. Her father didn't want her asking Lyndon. Not after all that had been said at the trial and Lyndon's part in it. She shook her head. "You're right, Dad. I won't bother Lyndon. And I won't fly tomorrow."

Eunice knocked on the door to Spencer's house door that evening at five o'clock. In her hand was a cloth bag. "I've come to cook supper. And then perhaps we can play some quiet music on your Victrola." Lowering the bag to the floor she turned to face him. "I hope you like what I have in mind—ham and sweet potatoes."

"Like it? I'll love it." He pulled her close. "Thank you, Miss Syvertson, for being who you are. I really need your company right now."

46

Nate Hamilton stood, hat in hand. He bore the look of a man exhausted from hard labor. T. C. reached over to grasp his client's shoulder. "I know this session has been difficult but necessary. You now have some idea of the way you'll be treated when Garth Swain takes after you."

Nate's eyes were on his feet. "I don't know if I can handle it." Then he looked squarely at T. C. "But I'll do as you say. Tell the jury exactly what happened between me and Arnold Masters that night out there behind the hotel." He took a breath, held it, and then let it blow out. "And I'll do my damnedest to keep my temper under control. But it won't be easy if he's as rough on me as you've been this last hour."

T. C. gave Nate's shoulder a squeeze. "The treatment you got from me isn't even close to the treatment that you'll get from Swain." He released the squeeze and gave the shoulder a pat. "I understand you and your parents have hotel rooms for the night. That's good. Then there's no worry about getting to town in time for court tomorrow."

Spence spoke up. "Get some rest. But run your testimony through your mind once more before you sleep." He smiled at his ranch neighbor, his friend from childhood, now his client. "You'll do fine, Nate. I'm sure of it." With that last word of encouragement and a handshake, he issued his client out the door. Then he turned to his father with a sigh.

"I wish I was as confident as I want him to think I am. He nearly lost his temper when you pressed him, and you were only pretending to be his adversary. How will he hold up when Swain gets after him?"

T. C. ran his fingers through his hair, mussing it. "There's no question in my mind. He'll lose his temper, and when he does, he'll convict himself. But we've done all we can to help him. Let's hope it's enough."

"Any help at all from Albertson at the hotel?"

"He'll say that Cape did come to his door and say there'd been a ruckus out back—just a ruckus, nothing about a murder. And he'll say that Cape asked him to notify the sheriff, but only one time. He seemed confused in his memory and could change his story if we put him on the witness stand." T. C. rubbed his hand alongside of his face. "But I think we'd better do it. If he tells the jury even some of the things he told me, it could make Cape appear as even more of a liar."

"And if he confirms all that Cape said?"

T. C.'s smile was wan. "Then I guess I'll take the responsibility for the mistake."

"So, except for old Albertson, we're stuck with Nate's testimony and nothing else."

"That's it." A pained look clouded T.C.'s countenance. "And I just know he'll lose his temper."

47 Merci, seated in the first row behind Spencer, clenched both her fists and her teeth as the judge moved slowly to the bench. The time had come when Nate Hamilton, with the help of her brother and father, must save himself from prison or worse. God grant that Nate's temper didn't convict him.

After the usual scan of the courtroom and the recital that all participants were in attendance and in place, the judge faced the jury. "Last Friday court adjourned earlier than usual so that I could return home to my wife who was sickly. I'm happy to report that the sickness was short lived. When I left her yesterday evening she was back to her old self." Judge Crawford shifted in his chair to direct his remarks to everyone in the courtroom. "Thank you all for your forbearance. Now, we'll move forward with the trial." He turned his gaze to the defense table. "Mr. Bruce, you may call your first witness."

T. C., seated next to Nate with Spence on Nate's left side, rose promptly to his feet. Merci looked at her father with pride. Six feet tall, erect posture, dressed in a carefully tailored black suit with white shirt and black tie, and with a solemn countenance, he was the picture of a competent trial attorney. She turned her attention to Garth Swain. He was dressed, as always, in a slate gray suit and white shirt, accented by a dark, blood-red tie. Now, he rested comfortably at the prosecution counsel table, hands folded on its top, the picture of confidence.

"Your Honor, the defense calls Luscious Albertson." The hotel proprietor—old and somewhat stooped of posture—walked slowly up the aisle toward the working part of the courtroom. He wore a suit of clothes, years out of style. T. C. welcomed him with a smile and gestured to indicate where Albertson should stand to take the oath. Another gesture directed the man to witness chair. The lawyer waited a few seconds to allow Albertson to settle into the chair. Once he seemed comfortable, the older man looked to T. C. and nodded as though to say, "I'm ready."

"Please state your name and tell us where you live."

"I'm Luscious Albertson. I live in the hotel at Two Dot."

T. C. stepped around the counsel table to stand before the witness. "Mr. Albertson, day before yesterday you and I visited about some happenings in Two Dot. Did we not?"

"We did, Sir."

"Specifically, we discussed a knock that came to your door in the wee hours of the morning of the day that Arnold Masters' body was found on the boardwalk in your town. Is that correct?"

"That's what we discussed, yes. I told you that a tall man named Christopher Cape knocked on my door early that morning. I knew his name because that's the one he used when he signed the hotel register."

"What did Mr. Cape want at that hour?"

"He told me there'd been some kind of a ruckus out behind the hotel."

"What kind of ruckus, Mr. Albertson? Did Cape elaborate?"

"Well, he may not have used the word 'ruckus.' But he let me know that there'd been some kind of disturbance and asked me to call the sheriff."

"Did he say there'd been a murder? A killing?"

"Oh, no. Nothing like that. I thought it was just another bunch of young bucks having a scrap."

T. C. waited a second for the jurors to assimilate that remark, then asked, "Did you do that sir? Call the sheriff?"

"I tried but I couldn't get through to the operator at Harlo."

"What did Mr. Cape do then?"

"He just shrugged his shoulders, turned away, and left."

"Is that all?"

"That's all. He just left."

"Mr. Albertson, since the man asked you to call the sheriff, did you worry that something really serious might have happened out back of the hotel?"

"No, Mr. Bruce, I didn't. Young rascals are always drinking too much of Lippy Lippencott's booze. Then they cause problems for us—getting into fights, whooping, hollering, and making noise. Waking us up. I thought it was just the usual kind of foolish brawl, nothing more."

"What did you do after Mr. Cape walked away?"

"I just put it all from my mind and went back to sleep."

T. C. responded with a gentle smile. "Thank you, Sir. You've been most helpful." Turning to the judge, he added. "No more questions for Mr. Albertson."

Judge Crawford shifted his eyes to Swain. "Cross, Sir?"

Swain nodded. "A question or two." Without rising from his chair, he asked, "It's your testimony that Cape tried to get you to arouse the telephone operator in Harlowton?"

Albertson turned his head toward the prosecutor. "Yes Sir. That's what I said."

"The call was for the purpose of alerting the sheriff that there'd been a serious dispute out back?"

"I guess so. I don't really know what was on Mr. Cape's mind. I now understand he says he saw that man Masters get murdered. If so, why didn't he tell me?"

Swain frowned. Merci, watching and listening, couldn't help but smile.

"Mr. Albertson, is it the usual thing to have difficulty contacting the telephone operator in Harlowton?"

"Only sometimes and only at night."

Swain sat with his eyes on the hotel proprietor for a brief moment. Merci thought that for the first time he appeared to be at a loss. Finally, he looked from Albertson to T. C. and then to the judge. "I have no more questions for this witness."

Judge Crawford looked at the clock and then said to the jurors, "It's a little early, but we'll be in recess for fifteen minutes." A gentle bang of the gavel and court was in recess.

The time had arrived. "Call Nathaniel Hamilton, Your Honor."

Merci's mind had wandered. Spencer's voice brought her attention back to her lifelong friend. She felt a sudden sense of dread as Nate pushed away from the table, moved past Spencer, stood directly before the clerk, and raised his hand to be sworn. His voice was firm but not overly loud when he said, in response to the oath, "I do."

Nate, too, was properly attired in a dark business suit, the usual white shirt and black tie. His posture was erect as he moved to the witness chair. Once there, he sat squarely in its center, facing Spence. After a second, he turned—showing a sober but pleasant face—to look toward the jurors. Merci noted that most held his gaze although one of the homesteaders seemed to purposely avoid returning the look. After a second Nate looked again to his attorney.

Spencer, behind the counsel table, stood with clasped hands. "Mr. Hamilton, please state your name and address for the record."

"My name is Nathaniel Hamilton. I live on the Hamilton Ranch south of Two Dot."

"How long have you lived there?"

"All of my life. Except for time in the army during the war."

Spencer crossed his arms and then didn't speak for what seemed to Merci to be forever. She held her breath as she waited. At last Spence dropped his arms to his sides. His voice carried within it the seriousness of the question. "Mr. Hamilton, did you kill Arnold Masters?"

"No, Sir, I didn't." Nate turned to the jury. "I did not kill Arnold Masters." To Merci's relief it wasn't said with an attempt at sincerity that would have come across as fake. It was just Nate Hamilton, in his usual voice, making a simple statement. The jurors, watching him intently, appeared to accept it as such.

She looked at the prosecutor. Garth Swain no longer appeared relaxed. He leaned forward as though ready to leap to his feet to challenge anything Nate might say.

Spence continued. "You heard the testimony of Christopher Cape—the testimony in which he told the jury that he saw you kill Mr. Masters?"

"Yes Sir. I heard it."

"Was he telling the truth?"

"No, Mr. Bruce." Looking again at the jurors. "There was no truth in the things he said about me killing Arnold Masters."

Spence moved to the side of the counsel table. "Mr. Hamilton, you've heard all of the other witnesses who testified for the prosecution, have you not?"

"I have, Mr. Bruce."

"Let's review some of that testimony." Spence now stood before the counsel table, a few feet from the witness chair. "According to Sheriff Graves, you told him that you left the party early the night Arnold

Masters was killed, that you left while the party was still in progress."
He paused. "Was the sheriff's testimony correct?"

Nate didn't blink or show emotion. "It was."

"Was your statement to the sheriff correct? Truthful?"

"No, Mr. Bruce, it was not." Nate looked at Spence and not the
jurors as he spoke.

"If it wasn't the truth, why did you say it?"

Nate shifted an inch to the side of the chair—his first show of
discomfort. "Sheriff Graves came to the ranch and began yammering
at me that Masters was dead. I didn't know anything about the man's
death other than what the sheriff was saying." He glanced toward the
jury. "The way he was talking it was like he was accusing me of murder.
I didn't like it, and I had work to do. So I just told him I went home
early to get him gone."

Spence waited a second to let the jurors think about that statement. Then he began again. "Nate, may I call you Nate?"

Nate smiled. "You have since we were kids."

"Nate, is it true that you got into a shouting match with Arnold
Masters when he was dancing with Merci Bruce?"

"No, Sir. That's not true."

"How about when he was dancing with Irma Lewellyn?"

"Not any shouting match. I may have hollered something at him,
but if I did, I've forgotten it. The truth is that we were all just having
fun. There was lots of whooping and hollering going on."

"No one had to restrain you from charging at Mr. Masters?"

There was a small shake of Nate's head. "No. Of course not."

Spence stepped to one side and clasped his hands. "Mr. Lippencott
told the jury that you were out back after most of the others were gone.
He said that you not only yelled at Arnold Masters but threatened to
strike him. Did that happen?"

Nate turned toward the jury. "I was back there. And Masters and I did have words. But I didn't try to strike him or even threaten to do so."

Spence leaned slightly forward. "Words about what, sir?"

Nate turned back to Spence. "Masters had spent a lot of time in Olive's café—most of that time visiting with Irma Lewellyn. And he danced with her more that night than he should have. I didn't want him giving her any idea that she was more to him than a dancing partner. I've known Irma since we were kids. She's a nice girl who's had it tough. She doesn't deserve any more problems, especially from some guy that would soon be gone." Nate turned to face the jurors. "I admit it. I'd had a lot of Lippy's hooch that night and my behavior wasn't very smart."

Merci looked at the jurors. They each sat with a stony face, but they were all listening carefully. Out of the corner of her eye she could see Swain's lips curl into a hint of a smirk.

"So you and Arnold Masters had a confrontation behind the saloon and the hotel. What happened to end it?"

"Old Lippy came charging out there with his pick handle and told us both to clear out. Irma Lewellyn was there, too. He shook the pick handle at her and yelled at her to get back to her room." He gave a slight shrug. "It was time for me to get out of there anyway."

"What did you do when Mr. Lippencott told you to leave?"

"I headed back around the saloon. Arnold Masters kind of stumbled off in the other direction, down toward the railroad. Lippy stood there and watched us go."

"And Mrs. Lewellyn? What did she do?"

"When Old Lippy threatened her with the pick handle, she took off toward the corner of the hotel; but then she looked back to see that Lippy still had his eyes on us. The last I saw she'd stopped and just stood with her arms crossed."

Spencer stood for a moment before asking, "Did you see Chris Cape behind the hotel or anywhere near the place where all of this took place?"

Nate shook his head. "No, Sir. I never saw the man that night, not behind the saloon or the hotel or any place else."

"After you watched Irma Lewellyn stop and cross her arms, what did you do?"

"I walked around to the street, got in my auto, and drove home."

Spencer stepped back to lean his legs against the counsel table in an erect but relaxed posture. "Nate, you've seen the bayonet that was shown to the jury. What can you tell us about it?"

"It's mine. I took it from a dead German soldier." He looked at the jurors again. "A few months ago I gave it to Lippy to hang on his wall along with some other stuff he had there." Turning to Spence, he said, "The bayonet was out there that night. Someone took it off the wall and asked me about it. After that it was just handed around. I don't know where it ended up." He blinked. "Except in Arnold Masters' chest, of course."

Spence asked the clerk for the rope that was now part of the trial evidence. He held it loosely at his waist while he asked, "There's been testimony that you were doing rope tricks that night. Is that testimony correct?"

Nate smiled. "Yes. I like to spin a rope if there's an audience to appreciate the things I can do. I keep a cotton spinning rope in our car. I got it out that night and put on show for the ladies."

What kind of show?"

"Spinning the rope into big loops and little loops, around my shoulders, behind my back. Jumping in and out of a loop I was spinning down near the ground. That kind of show."

Spence handed him the short piece of rope he'd gotten from the clerk. "Do you recognize this as the rope you were spinning the night of the big party on the street of Two Dot?"

With the rope draped across his palm, Nate lifted it up for the jurors to get a good look. Then he grasped each end of the rope, spread his arms to pull it straight. "This just isn't long enough for any kind of rope tricks, let alone the kind I was doing that night." Nate dropped his hands and the rope to his lap. "In order to spin a rope the way I was doing it, the rope must be at least twenty feet long. This isn't more than six feet at best." He lifted the rope up again. Returning his eyes to Spence, he added, "I don't know where this rope came from, but it isn't mine."

"What became of the rope you were using for tricks that night?"

"I took it with me when I left. It's in our car right now. I can get it for you if you'd like."

"That won't be necessary." Spence retrieved the short piece of rope and returned it to the clerk. Back in front of the witness he stood quietly for a second. Finally, he leaned slightly toward his client. "Nate, did you have any reason to want Arnold Masters dead?"

Nate, erect in the witness chair, remained silent for a full ten seconds. When he spoke it was to the jury and in a quiet voice. "No. I hardly knew the man. The few times I was with him, he seemed pleasant enough. There was no reason for me to dislike him, much less hate him enough to murder him."

"You didn't kill him because he was spending too much time with Merci Bruce?"

Nate looked at Spence and shook his head. "No, Mr. Bruce. I did not kill Arnold Masters. For any reason." Another earnest look toward the jurors. "I just did not kill that man."

Spencer glanced toward his father who barely nodded. Time to end it. He stepped back to the counsel table and then turned to face the judge. "I have no more questions for the witness, Your Honor."

Judge Crawford eyed the clock and then the jury. "We'll recess now for half an hour this time. Remember my admonition. Don't discuss the things you've heard until I tell you that you may do so." With a bang of the gavel he vacated the bench.

As the jurors were parading to the jury room, Spence gestured to Nate. "Let's go where we can visit." In the small basement room, he grasped Nate's upper arm. "You did great! The way you handled yourself was almost perfect."

Merci chimed in. "The eyes of the jurors never left you. Your sincerity was obvious."

T. C. raised a hand. "All of that's probably true. But that was the easy part." He stared intensely at Nate. "As we've told you again and again, you must now maintain your composure—maintain it no matter what Garth Swain does. Got that?"

Nate took a breath and then blew. "I've got it. And I'll do my best. After all, it's my life that's on the line." He blew again and then said to Spence, "I'm just glad you got to ask questions first so I could get a feel for it."

Spence put his hand on the shoulder of his lifelong friend. "Answer the questions honestly, and don't lose your temper. Do that and you'll be fine." Dropping his hand he added, "Now, go to the restroom. Get that out of the way. Don't talk to anyone. We'll be here when you finish. If there are additional things we think of in the meantime, we can discuss them before court reconvenes."

Before Nate could take two steps, Merci grasped his arm and looked upward at his face. "You can do it Nate. I know you can."

He showed a real smile for the first time that day. "Thanks, Merc. I hope you're right."

Seated in his high-back chair, the judge intoned the usual monologue. "The jury is in the box and all of the principals are present." To Nate he said, "You are still under oath, Sir." He turned his eyes to Garth Swain. "You may begin, Sir."

Merci watched as Swain sat for a moment. When he stood at last, Merci thought his faced carried a crafty appearance. After a moment of silence, Swain moved around the corner of the table to speak to the witness. "Mr. Bruce called you Nate. May I do the same?"

Nate's eyebrow lifted ever so slightly, but his answer was in a calm voice. "If that's what you prefer, Sir."

"So—Nate—do you lie all the time? Or only when you think it suits your purpose?"

Merci held her breath. Here it comes. Nate will lose his temper.

But she was wrong. Nate blinked once but then maintained a neutral appearance. "I've truthfully answered all the questions asked of me today. It's up to the jurors. They will believe me or not, Sir."

For a second Swain seemed taken aback. Merci hoped the jurors could understand what had just occurred. Swain's attempt to rattle Nate hadn't worked. The prosecutor recovered quickly. "But we know you lied once. You've admitted to that. Correct?"

"Yes, Sir. I didn't tell the sheriff the truth about the time I left the party."

"So, you only lie on occasion? Is that your testimony?"

"Again, Mr. Swain, whether I've told the truth here today is up to the jury."

"Your tale of the doings out behind the Two Dot Hotel differs from that of several other people. You expect the good people on this jury to believe that you're being truthful and all the others are liars?"

Merci squeezed her hands together and held her breath. Hold it together, Nate. Don't let him goad you into a foolish response.

Nate looked to the jury for an instant before returning his eyes to the prosecutor. "Mr. Swain, I'll say it one more time. The jurors must decide which of us was being truthful."

Spence was on his feet. "Mr. Hamilton is correct, Your Honor. He's answered the same question more than once. Mr. Swain is now just attempting to badger him. I object to any more questions along that line."

Swain was quick in his response. "Not so, Your Honor. I've posed questions that can be answered with a yes or a no. The witness has yet to give us that yes or no. I have a right to continue to press for that response."

Judge Crawford leaned slightly forward. "I've heard your questions, Mr. Swain. They are not intended to elicit a yes or no. They're intended to bait the witness." He waited an instant for emphasis. "Now, Sir, continue your examination, but ask questions that you must surely know are proper."

Swain's nod in response carried just the correct amount of respect for the court without seeming to concede any wrongdoing. He shifted his attention again to the witness.

"Mr. Lippencott was lying when he said you were about to strike Arnold Masters. Is that your testimony—Nate?"

"I wasn't about to strike Arnold Masters at any time. Mr. Lippencott can say what he wants."

"So he's a liar. Is that your testimony?"

Nate turned to the jury. "Lippy said he saw me about to strike Masters. I've already told you that I never threatened to strike the man. You get to decide which of us to believe."

The prosecutor's impatience showed when he turned to the judge. "Your Honor, please direct the witness to answer the questions as he is obligated to do. And admonish him not to offer gratuitous statements to the jury."

Judge Crawford nodded his head once. "Mr. Hamilton, Mr. Swain is correct. You are here to answer the questions posed to you. Please do that in the future." He looked at Nate from the corner of his eyes. "Your attorneys will speak to the jury on your behalf. You are not to do it again."

Nate's response was given in a respectful tone. "I'll do my best, Sir." He paused. "But Mr. Swain is making it difficult."

Merci thought, "Score one for Nate!"

Swain scowled. "Lyndon Morgan said he saw you with a grip on the front of Masters' shirt, with your fist cocked ready to strike. Is he a liar, too?"

"I can't explain Lyndon's version of things. All I can do is tell the jury what I did or didn't do."

"That doesn't answer the question. Are you saying that Lyndon Morgan is a liar? Yes or No?"

"All I can tell you is what he said I did and what really happened aren't the same."

Swain's temper was beginning to show. "Nate. You stated that you didn't strangle Arnold Masters with a piece of rope. That was your testimony, Sir?"

"Yes Sir. That's my testimony."

"So you're asking the jury to believe your testimony? The testimony of a man who will say anything to save himself from a murder conviction? Asking them to believe you instead of all the other witnesses? Witnesses who have absolutely no reason to lie? Is that it?"

Spence called out, "Objection," as he rose to his feet, but Nate didn't wait. He looked directly at the prosecutor. "Yes, Sir. I'm asking the jury to understand and believe that I'm telling the truth."

Swain crossed his arms in a deliberate manner and stood cold faced and quiet for a long moment. Then he leaned forward as though for emphasis and almost snarled. "Well then, let's consider Mr. Cape. Mr. Cape who watched with his own eyes as you throttled Arnold Masters with a piece of rope. Mr. Cape who told the jury—in elaborate detail—exactly how the murder was committed." Swain stepped to the side so the jury could see his face clearly. "He's a liar, too. That's what you want these good people to believe. Is that right Sir?"

Merci could see that the badgering questions were beginning to wear on Nate's self-control. But, her friend waited, took a breath, and answered in the calm and respectful manner that Spence and T. C. had told him was essential—if there was to be a chance of an acquittal. He looked at the jury when he did so. "I want the jurors to believe that I've been truthful in my testimony. I hope they will do that."

Swain's face showed a disgusted look. "Your Honor, the witness has refused over and over again to answer questions—questions that only require a simple yes or no. In my years of practice no judge has ever denied me the right to a proper answer. Will you please direct Mr. Hamilton to answer simple questions with a yes or no answer? Beginning with the last question?"

Never so far in the trial had Merci seen such a fierce scowl on Judge Crawford's face. Spence began to stand to object but the Judge didn't wait. His voice when he spoke was equally as fierce. "Mr. Swain, if you have a quarrel with any of my rulings or other actions during this trial, report that to the proper authorities." He leaned forward over the bench and spoke in a more moderate voice. "As to the questions you've asked, they aren't intended to elicit a yes or no. They're only intended provoke the witness." After a long pause, he said, "And I believe the jurors know that, Sir. Now—continue your examination of the defendant—with proper questions."

Garth Swain gave no indication that the judge's mild scolding affected him in any way. He stood again, arms crossed, and stared at Nate Hamilton. His voice was soft when he began to speak but then rose in pitch and volume. "Why don't you just admit that you murdered Arnold Masters in cold blood instead of lying through your teeth in an attempt to save your miserable, worthless hide?"

Merci watched as the red coloring appeared at Nate's neck and then crept upward. He's going to lose it! He's going to lose his temper and say or do something that will spoil all he's achieved so far.

Nate clamped his grip on the arms of the chair so hard that his knuckles shown white. The muscles in his jaw tightened until they were clearly visible to those in the courtroom. He seemed to stop breathing, but after a second—a second that seemed to Merci to be an hour—the muscles relaxed. He slowly moved himself back in the chair. Once more, seemingly relaxed, he spoke quietly to the prosecutor. "Mr. Swain, if I were to say that I killed Arnold Masters I wouldn't be telling the truth." He waited for an eye-blink. "I've sworn to tell the truth today, and, Mr. Swain, that's what I've done."

Frustration flashed across the prosecutor's face. Then he turned to the jury, looked from one to another and shook his head as though to ask, "What can you do with someone who refuses to be truthful?" His movement back toward the counsel table was in slow deliberate steps. Once behind the table and in front of his chair he turned to the judge to say, "No more questions for the defendant."

Judge Crawford seemed relieved. "Redirect, Mr. Bruce."

"No, Sir. None." Spence paused for the briefest of moments. "And the defense rests."

The judge leaned back and glanced at the clock. "This has been a long session, but it didn't seem proper to interrupt the testimony by breaking for the dinner hour." To the jury he said, "The attorneys and

I have matters to address that don't require your involvement. They will take up a part of the afternoon. For that reason court will adjourn until nine o'clock tomorrow morning. At that time I'll read some instructions for you to follow during your deliberations. Then you will hear the attorneys' final arguments." The judge paused. "Please be here on time." He used the handle of the gavel to point for emphasis. "Remember my admonition to avoid discussing any of the things you've heard and seen during this trial. Don't do so with one another. And don't speak of it with any other person." He gave a kind of poke with the gavel handle for emphasis. "Understood?"

As expected, each of the jurors nodded a head in reply before the group cleared the court room.

Spence and T. C. met Nate as he descended from the witness chair. Each grasped his hand. T. C. spoke for both of them. "Let's get ourselves down to the hotel where we can talk in private."

As soon as they were in the private room at the hotel Amos reached for his son's hand. "You did good, boy." There was a choke in his voice. "You did good."

Merci placed her hands on Nate's upper arms and looked up into his face. "I'm really proud of you." She released him and stepped back. "But I knew you could do it—could show the jury the kind of person you really are." She offered him her most winning smile. "The jury is certain to believe you."

T. C. nodded his head in agreement. "I believe the jurors were impressed. Garth Swain didn't help himself when he tried to badger you instead of asking questions in a reasonable way. His whole manner was so offensive it may have upset the jurors. They must have appreciated how difficult it was for you to maintain your composure in the face of Swain's behavior."

Mrs. Hamilton didn't speak. She simply patted Nate on the arm one time. Her face showed neither smile nor frown. She understood exactly where the trial stood. While her son had performed well, there was no certainty the jury believed the things he said.

Spence gestured with a hand. "Let's eat. Then Dad and I have to get back to the courthouse." He directed his explanation to the elder Hamiltons. "We have to present our proposed jury instructions to the judge. Swain will do the same. The judge will go through them one by one, accept some, and reject others. We must be prepared to argue for the acceptance of all of ours. And argue for the rejection of some of Swain's." He moved to the table laden with the day's repast. "The rest of you may as well try to relax. There's nothing more you can do to help."

There were fewer arguments over the jury instructions than Spencer anticipated and they were quickly settled. Garth Swain hurried from the judge's office without a word to them or to even the judge. T. C. and Spence followed at a more leisurely pace. When the two were alone on the courthouse steps T. C. asked the question. "Are you ready? Ready to persuade the jury to acquit Nathaniel Hamilton?"

"No, Dad, I don't feel that I'm ready. In fact I'm scared to death." Spencer Bruce heaved a big sigh. "Right now I wish I'd never agreed to take on Nate's defense." Another huge inhalation and exhalation. "But I did. And now I'm stuck."

T. C. put his hand on his son's shoulder. "You've demonstrated good lawyerly skill so far in this trial. And for whatever it's worth, I'm confident of your ability to make a compelling argument, one that the jury can understand and accept."

"Thanks, Dad." Spence turned to face down the street toward his office. "I've been over the argument several times. But I need to review it once more. Then I'll put it aside. There's nothing more I can do to prepare for tomorrow."

His father smiled as he said. "Try to rest some and relax." His smile widened. "Perhaps Eunice will help."

"She already told me she's preparing the evening meal." Spence turned back to face T. C. "She's special, Dad. I'm awfully glad that I met her."

"As are your mother and I."

48

Merci understood why the prosecution—the State of Montana—got the first and last of the arguments to the jury. The burden is on the prosecution to prove—beyond a reasonable doubt—that the one accused of the crime actually committed the crime. She held her breath as Garth Swain moved around the counsel table to stand in front of the jury box. As usual he was impeccably dressed, all in gray. Seemingly relaxed and confident, his face showed a placid expression. Once again the thumb on his left hand was under his chin with the index finger resting beside his cheek bone, right hand resting on the left arm above the elbow. When he began to speak it was in a soft voice.

"Members of the jury, you've been most attentive throughout this trial. Each of you has listened both patiently and carefully. It's important that you have done so, of course, because your verdict must be based upon the things that transpired in this room. While there were physical exhibits entered into the record—and the production of those exhibits was important—it's the words spoken from the witness stand that tell you what really happened the night Arnold Masters was so brutally murdered. In essence, you must reach your verdict based upon the words of two of them: the words spoken by Christopher Cape and—" Swain pointed a long arm at Nate—"by Nathaniel Hamilton."

"Mr. Cape told of being out back of the hotel in Two Dot the night when the murder occurred. He described the scene in detail. You listened as he set forth the exact manner in which Nathanial Hamilton committed the crime. Hamilton attacked Arnold Masters from behind and threw him to the ground. Then, while sitting on the extremely intoxicated man so he couldn't resist, Hamilton throttled him to death with a length of cotton rope. There was no provocation by Masters. Others who testified to his condition and behavior prior to his death confirmed that he was not quarrelsome at any time. That made no difference to Hamilton. He simply wanted Masters dead."

Swain took a step back. "The reason he wanted Masters dead is obvious. Nate Hamilton is enamored of a woman." He turned to stretch his arm in Merci's direction and held it there for a long moment. "That woman. Merci Bruce." He slowly lowered the arm to his side and returned his eyes to the jury. "Masters posed a threat to Hamilton's hope —hope for a positive response from Miss Bruce to his amorous attentions—perhaps even agreement to marriage. Arnold Masters had to be eliminated. In his mind it was a simple decision. Christopher Cape told exactly how that decision was carried out."

Swain moved his hands up and face out, toward the jury, as though in entreaty. "Now, remember, together with me, the words spoken by Nathanial Hamilton." He lifted his arm to again point toward Nate. "That man walked to the witness chair and swore not only that he didn't murder Arnold Masters, but also swore that he wasn't behind the hotel at the time the murder occurred. In fact, he contradicted almost every word spoken by Christopher Cape and each of the others who testified. Who should you believe?

"Which of the two had a reason—a compelling reason—to lie? Was it Cape or was it Hamilton? The answer is obvious. Hamilton is facing a life in prison—perhaps even the gallows—if he's convicted of this crime. He had the most elemental of reasons to lie—to save his hide. And lie he did—over and over again. You will remember that he refused to answer directly to a single one of the questions that I asked of him, even after Judge Crawford directed him to do so. Why? Because to tell the truth would put him in prison—or worse."

The prosecutor's face and posture became more relaxed. "Now, consider Christopher Cape. What evidence was presented that would cause you to believe that he lied? Can you think of one scintilla of such evidence? There simply was none. The judge has instructed you that your verdict must be based upon evidence presented during this trial. It may not be based upon anything else—certainly not upon insinuation, no matter how artfully crafted. Evidence, gentlemen, only hard evidence.

"It isn't often that a jury in a murder trial gets to hear from a man who witnessed the killing, identified the murderer, and told exactly how the murder was committed. There can be no more compelling evidence than that.

"Mr. Bruce—one of them—will speak to you next. He'll try to explain away all the evidence that tells you his client is the murderer. He'll try to confuse you. That's his job. But just remember, either Christopher Cape or Nathaniel Hamilton is a liar. Hamilton had a very compelling reason to lie. Mr. Cape had none. His testimony is factual evidence sufficient for you to reach a verdict to guilty of murder in the first degree. I expect that you will do so."

Merci felt a chill as Garth Swain nodded once before turning to return to the counsel table. The man had never raised his voice, but the attention of each juror remained fixed upon him during the entire time that he was speaking. Even she found his argument to be persuasive. The members of the jury may have made up their minds before Spence even had a chance to speak.

Silence filled the room for a second or two that seemed much longer. When Judge Crawford spoke it was also in soft voice. "We'll be in recess for fifteen minutes. Then Mr. Bruce will speak for the defense."

Spence ignored those around him as he walked out the door of the courthouse, around the corner, and up the street to an alley. There, alone in the warm autumn sun, he collected his thoughts. The quiet, unemotional manner of Garth Swain's argument, as much as his words, seemed to impress the jury. With this quiet time to think, however, he knew that he could not let Swain's presentation affect his planned argument. He just hoped that the jury would listen to him as closely as they did to the prosecutor—and that he could be the more persuasive of the two.

His father met him at the door as he entered the courtroom. "The folks on the jury know you. Just be that person they know and they'll listen." Spence favored him with a weak smile.

49 The courtroom was jammed. Every bench was filled with people, crowded together to allow as many as possible to sit. Others stood along the walls. Merci, the Hamiltons, Felicity, and Eunice were seated directly behind the defense counsel table. Hiram Morgan sat near the middle of the room. Merci was surprised to see Lyndon next to him. T. C. must have given him the day off.

Arnold Masters' father was seated behind the prosecution counsel table. His countenance was fierce, and no one crowded the bench next to him. Roger Davidson, the county attorney, was on the bench behind him. Lippy Lippencott, one of those standing, leaned against the back wall with his arms crossed. His accustomed look of anger and defiance remained in place. The sheriff, acting as bailiff, stood against the wall near the railing that separated the participants from the spectators. Neither Chris Cape nor Irma Lewellyn was in the room.

Once again on the bench, the judge eyed the room before reciting the usual monologue, noting for the court record that all the participants were in place. Then he looked to the defense table. "Mr. Bruce, you may address the jury."

Merci squeezed her hands together and almost stopped breathing as her brother stood to speak. She admired once again his erect posture and clear-eyed countenance. Merci had noted that Garth Swain always stepped at a brisk pace. Spence, in contrast, had the unique and graceful movement of one who'd spent much time on horseback. That was evident as he walked around the end of the table to face the jury. Perhaps the jurors—the farmers and ranchers at least—would unconsciously recognize that he was one of their own. An air of confidence was reflected on his face. His voice, when he spoke, bolstered that impression. It was firm but not loud—the words clearly enunciated.

"Members of the jury, Mr. Swain told you that your verdict must be based upon the words of only two of the witnesses. Those two are my client, Nathanial Hamilton, and Christopher Cape. Mr. Swain and I are in near agreement with regard to that admonition—but not in total agreement. All of the evidence must be considered. The physical exhibits that were introduced are of importance, as is the testimony of each of the other witnesses who testified. They must be of importance. They were brought to you by the prosecutor. Let us consider why.

"First the physical exhibits. Mr. Swain brought to you a bayonet, a piece of rope, and a note printed on a piece of pasteboard. They were needed to give you an understanding of the situation the night that Arnold Masters was killed. They were presented in a way intended to link them to Nathaniel Hamilton and, thereby, lend credence to the argument that he was responsible for the killing. But did they do so? The bayonet admittedly belongs to Nate. He told you so. He handled it the night of Arnold Masters' death. He told you that, too. But how does that lead you to conclude that Nate committed the crime? The simple answer? It doesn't.

"So, too, with the rope. The rope was presented as the one that Nate used to spin as entertainment for others at the party on the night of Arnold Masters' death. In the end it surely must have been obvious to you, as it was to all the rest of us who watched and listened, that the piece of rope the prosecution says was used to kill Mr. Masters was much too short to be used for the rope tricks Nate Hamilton described. Not one single witness nor any other bit of evidence tied that particular short piece of rope to Nate Hamilton in any way. There was nothing to show that he ever owned it or even handled it on the night of the killing or at any other time. The rope, like the bayonet, does nothing to lead you to conclude that Nate Hamilton committed the crime of which he is accused.

"And finally, the note on the pasteboard. Remember? 'SHE'S MINE' it said. What evidence have you heard or seen that tells you Nate had anything to do with the pasteboard or the note? Think hard." Spence paused. "There was no evidence that Nate printed it. Certainly no evidence that he impaled it to the body of Arnold Masters. The note doesn't tie Nate to the killing in any way.

"Mr. Swain would have you believe that Nate's possession of a bayonet and a longer rope necessarily bolsters other things that might point to Nate as the killer. You should not make the assumption that Mr. Swain would have you make. The bayonet, the short rope, and the note do not in any way indicate that Nate is a killer.

Spence gently placed one hand on the top of the podium. He used the break in his monologue to move his eyes from juror to juror. He spoke again in the same firm voice. "There were several people who took the witness stand and provided testimony. What did we learn from the testimony of those beside Mr. Cape and Nathanial Hamilton? Did the words of any of them tie Nate to the killing? Let's review what each of them said, one by one.

"First, Sheriff Graves. You heard the sheriff describe his investigation. He told how Mrs. Olive Breen found the body, of sending the body to the office of Doctor Scanlan, of talking to various people who were at the party the night of the killing. And he told of his first conversation with Nathaniel Hamilton. During that conversation he asked Nate what time Nate left the party. Nate gave him an answer. The sheriff eventually learned that Nate didn't tell him the truth." Spence stopped and a hint of smile appeared at the corner of his mouth before he began again. "But remember the most important part of the sheriff's testimony. It was in response to this question, 'In your investigation did you find anything at all that tells you Nate Hamilton killed Arnold Masters?' His response? 'Why no. Nothing.' Think about it. The sheriff is the investigating officer. Nothing in his testimony offers even a scintilla of proof that my client is a murderer." He stood very still, hands at his side. "Do you wonder, as I wonder, why the sheriff never learned of the things that Chris Cape had to say?" He paused. "Maybe someone didn't want that known until Cape would take the witness stand."

Spence stepped nearer to the end of the jury box. "Next to testify was Leonard Lippencott." His eyes found Lippy in the audience. The eyes of every juror followed his. When Spence then spoke, their eyes quickly returned to him, each of them focused intently on his words. "Mr. Lippencott said many things, but his description of the happenings behind the hotel are of most importance. He told you he found Nate Hamilton and Arnold Masters in some kind of argument, or what he thought was an argument. After he got between them they both walked immediately and quietly away. He saw nothing to indicate Hamilton seriously intended harm to Masters." He paused. "Of more importance were Mr. Lippencott's words and actions relative to Ms. Irma Lewellyn. He yelled at her to get back to her room and he threatened her with his sawed-off pick handle."

Spence stood quietly for a moment—relaxed. When he spoke again he gestured in the direction of the audience—among them Lippy Lippencott. His voice had the same even tone but now it carried a more forceful quality. "Lippencott threatened Ms. Lewellyn. He admitted he was enamored of her. He admitted his concern that she was paying too much attention to Arnold Masters. You've heard of his violent disposition. What, do you suppose, was he willing to do so that Masters didn't interfere with his plan to marry Mrs. Lewellyn? I leave that to you to consider as you deliberate in the jury room."

Spence continued. "What, if anything, was there in Mr. Lippencott's testimony to convince you that Nate Hamilton committed murder? Search your memory. Unless you're willing to believe one man will kill another simply because of an argument, you won't find a single word of his testimony to convince you."

Spence stepped back, paused, and then continued in a quiet voice. "Then Irma Lewellyn testified. Ms. Lewellyn also told of being behind the hotel at the time when both Arnold Masters and Nate Hamilton were there. She was concerned about Masters who, she told you, had too much to drink and was sick to his stomach. In all of her testimony did she say one thing that would lead you to believe Nate Hamilton intended to harm Masters in any way? She did not. She said they were arguing, nothing more. What she *did* say was that Mr. Lippencott waved his pick handle and ordered her away. Her fear of Lippencott was obvious and that fear seemed justified. She told you that he'd threatened her on other occasions as well. Leonard Lippencott didn't like the time that Mrs. Lewellyn spent with Masters. Again I ask you, what was he capable of doing to put an end to it?"

Spence paused to allow the jurors to think about the question. He stepped to the counsel table to sip water from a glass. That done, he moved slowly back to stand as before, hands clasped at his waist. "Next to testify was Lyndon Morgan. Mr. Morgan told you only that he saw Nate Hamilton and Arnold Masters out back of the hotel. He said that Nate had Arnold by the shirt front and had his other fist doubled up. Then, Morgan said, Nate gave Masters a shove so that Masters fell to the ground." Spence let them contemplate that act. When he spoke again it was with one upraised finger. "But immediately after that came the important part of Lyndon Morgan's testimony. He said that Nate Hamilton walked off toward his auto. No argument. No threats. Nate just left." Spence stepped back one step. "I ask you, do the words you heard from Lyndon Morgan provide any reason for you to find Nathaniel Hamilton guilty of the killing of Arnold Masters?" He looked from one juror to another and then paused. "Hardly."

After another moment of quiet, he said, "So, of all the exhibits and testimony that we've just reviewed, what, if any, is of benefit to you in deciding this case? Very, very little. In fact, none."

Spence crossed his arms and stepped to his right. Merci realized he was doing it to create break to avoid losing the juror's' attention. "So Mr. Swain was almost correct when he said it is upon the testimony of Christopher Cape and Nathaniel Hamilton that you must base your verdict. Which of them told the truth?" After another pause he stepped farther back from the railing that fronted the jury box and turned so he could see both the jury and his client. With his face toward Nate he said, "Consider first the testimony of Nathaniel Hamilton. You will remember that he spoke freely—without hesitation or any apparent attempt at deceit. His answers to both the questions that I asked of him and those of Mr. Swain were straight and forthright. He often directed his answers to you, asking you to accept him for what he is, not a sophisticated individual from some place far away. A man of this community."

Spence gestured toward his client with open palm. "I'm asking you to believe that my client, Nathaniel Hamilton, told the truth here—in this courtroom—under oath." He turned to wave a hand in the direction of the witness chair. "But, you will remind yourselves, he confessed right there, on that witness chair, that he told an innocent lie to the sheriff. And that confession must, of course, remain in your minds.

Mr. Swain made much of that lie in his opening argument, and he's sure to come back to it when he speaks to you again. But remember, Nate explained exactly how the lie came about. The sheriff came to the Hamilton Ranch and began asking questions of Nate in a manner that Nate believed was accusatory. The insinuation that he'd committed a murder, when he didn't even know one had been committed, raised Nate's ire. So he told the sheriff that he'd left Two Dot long before the killing apparently occurred. That wasn't the truth and my client forthrightly admitted to it. Is it possible that anyone—any one of us—might have done the same thing in similar circumstances? Perhaps." Spence's face took on a look of dead seriousness. "Before you decide to convict Nathaniel Hamilton because he told one innocent lie, consider that another witness told a lie that made the entirety of his testimony unbelievable. That person was Christopher Cape."

Spence waited a whole fifteen seconds for the members of the jury to contemplate his last remark. When he began again, seriousness remained on his face and in his voice. "I won't take your time by reviewing all that Mr. Cape said under oath. I'm certain that you remember his testimony. Christopher Cape told you he stood and watched Nate Hamilton throw Arnold Masters to the ground and throttle him with a piece of rope. Of course you remember that." He paused. "And although he was standing only a few feet away, he made no attempt to interfere or stop the murder from occurring." He leaned slightly forward. "Would any grown man do that? Stand there, watch a brutal murder taking place, and do nothing—absolutely nothing? Not even call out to others for help. Is that believable?"

Spence stepped closer to the jury box. "What did Mr. Cape say that he did instead? He said that he rousted the hotel proprietor to call the sheriff, not once but twice. Remember that? Of course you do. But what did Luscious Albertson have to say? Mr. Albertson said that

Cape did, in fact, beat on his door to tell him there was some kind of ruckus out back—a ruckus, not a murder—and he should call the sheriff. Albertson did as asked but didn't get through to the operator in Harlowton. In that much Albertson and Cape were in agreement." Spence touched the railing before the jury box with one finger. "But— and this is the important part—Cape told you he returned and asked Albertson to try again. What did the hotel proprietor say about that? It never happened. Cape did not do the things that he told you he did. Christopher Cape lied to you. He lied to you when he was under oath and obligated to tell the truth."

Spence moved back and away from the jury box. "So, in reaching your verdict you have two witnesses upon whose testimony—according to Mr. Swain—you must base your verdict. They both told a lie. And the lie told by Nate Hamilton was given without any idea of its consequence—the weight that would be given to it here in this courtroom. Not so the lies of Christopher Cape. He told his lies while under oath, knowing full well his obligation to be truthful, and also knowing the testimony was given for the purpose of convicting another man of a heinous murder."

Merci noticed Spence's facial appearance, his posture, and his voice become more assertive as he said, "Which of the two, then, should you believe? Should you believe Nate Hamilton who told an innocent lie? Nate whose home is here among you and who spoke with the candor you would expect from someone from this community? Or should you believe Chris Cape? The man who told a tale of watching a murder—of standing almost within arm's reach as the murder was committed— and doing nothing to try to stop it. Of doing nothing more than ask someone to call the sheriff? A man who then went back to his room to peacefully sleep the remainder of the night away? That tale is so lacking in believability as to be almost beyond your consideration." He raised a hand, palm open. "Who is this man, Christopher Cape? You know from the testimony that he followed Merci Bruce and her Jenny airplane to Montana. You know—because he told you—that he was offended because Miss Bruce asked Arnold Masters to accompany her to Two Dot rather than ask him." Spence waited a full five seconds before asking, "Was he so offended by that slight that he took the life of the man he thought of as a rival?" He paused. "We simply do not know."

Now Spence moved close to the jury box. "What we do know is this. The only evidence, if it really is evidence, upon which you could possibly conclude that Nate Hamilton is guilty of murder are the words spoken by Chris Cape right here in this room. If you consider all that you saw and heard since the trial began you will find that there is nothing else. So—which of those words are the most important? His unbelievable story of watching a murder being committed and doing nothing to stop it? His blatant, outright lie about rousting the hotel proprietor twice to call for the sheriff?"

He leaned forward for emphasis. "Please do not convict Nate Hamilton based solely upon the words of Christopher Cape—words that were as contrived and as lacking in credibility as words can be."

Spence moved back and clasped his hands at the waist. "Nate Hamilton is innocent. He did not commit the crime of which he is charged. I can't tell you who murdered Arnold Masters. I wish I could. There were others who apparently had motives to do so. But only Nathaniel Hamilton is on trial here. You needn't attempt to decide who, other than Nate, committed the crime. You need only decide that Nate didn't do it."

Spence paused and looked from to another of the jurors. "After you've considered all that was said and all else that has transpired in this room over the past few days, please return a not guilty verdict. It's the right thing to do."

Spence made a half turn and a small hand gesture in the direction of the prosecutor as he showed a hint of a neighborly smile to the jury. "Now, Mr. Swain will speak in rebuttal. As he speaks, please bear in mind that it is to be rebuttal, not a time to introduce new argument. And please listen carefully as he tries to explain away the lie told by his principal witness. He will not be able to do so." After another moment of silence, the smile became slightly more pronounced. "I've talked long and you've been most patient and attentive. I thank you on behalf of Nate Hamilton and also for myself. I have complete confidence in your judgment and your desire to do the correct thing." Spence gave the jurors' a small nod before he walked slowly to his place at the counsel table. It was hard for Merci to resist the urge to stand and cheer.

Silence filled the room. It seemed that there was a collective holding of breath. The judge straightened in his chair. "Mr. Bruce has indeed spoken long." He looked upward at the wall clock. "Court could recess now for the noon meal, but I'm reluctant to do that. Mr. Swain deserves the opportunity to respond to Mr. Bruce's arguments without any intervening lapse of time. So we'll take another-fifteen minute break. After Mr. Swain has completed his remarks, we'll break for a meal. When you return, I'll give you a final charge. Then you'll adjourn to the jury room and begin your deliberations." Judge Crawford leaned far to the jury side of the bench and pointed with his four fingers. "Each time there's been a recess during this trial I've admonished you to refrain from discussing the things you've seen and heard in this courtroom. Even among yourselves. That admonition remains. Let me emphasize what I just said. You are not to discuss this matter among yourselves or with any other person until I tell you that you may do so. Don't be tempted to talk just because we're approaching the end." He rapped the bench with the gavel. "Court's in recess for fifteen minutes."

50

As they left the courtroom, Nate grasped Merci's arm and whispered, "Was it enough, Merc? Did Spence convince them?"

Merci turned her head to frown at him. "Not here. Wait until we get some privacy."

Halfway down the stairs to the small basement room, Spence stopped and leaned against the wall. He heaved a sigh before turning to his father. "I'm exhausted, Dad."

T. C. put a comforting hand on his son's shoulder. "That's understandable." He gave the shoulder a squeeze. "I'm proud of you. More proud than you can possibly understand. The members of the jury were as attentive as human beings can be. And they appeared to accept the things you said." He gave Spence's shoulder two gentle pats. "But now you're finished. There's nothing more you can do."

"My God, Dad, I just pray that it's enough."

In the small room his mother hugged him. Mrs. Hamilton spoke for herself and for Amos. "Thank you, Spencer. No one could have done more to protect our son."

Nate slumped onto a bench next to the wall. "Good God! Those twelve people have my life in their hands." He looked up at Merci and asked again in a voice now tentative and plaintive. "Tell me, Merc. Did Spence convince them?"

She dropped onto the bench next to her friend and put her right arm around his shoulder. "I'm certain that he did. The jurors listened to his every word. None of them showed any skepticism. They seemed to believe the things he said." She dropped her left hand to his knee. "But that man Swain gets another shot. He'll do his best to counter every single thing that Spence had to say." She removed the arm and patted his knee twice. "Your thoughts have to be positive, Nate. Mine will be."

Back on the bench Judge Crawford went through his usual recital. He looked to his right. "Mr. Swain?"

Merci held her breath as Swain walked with deliberate steps around the end of the counsel table to stand squarely before the jury box. His face lacked emotion as he stood for the briefest of moments without saying a word. Then he took two steps forward to put a hand on the jury box railing. "Well, our Spencer Bruce certainly is a glib young man, isn't he? In that long monologue he attempted to twist and turn all the evidence that you've seen and heard inside out and upon itself. That's what any defense lawyer does when the facts of the case clearly show that his client is guilty. And the facts of this case show that the defendant…" He turned to again to point a long arm at Nate. "is as guilty as it is possible to be."

Swain now placed both hands on the railing. "To accomplish his purpose, Mr. Bruce asks you to take the words of some of the witnesses and, from those words, conclude that a person other than the defendant killed Arnold Masters in cold blood. As example, just because Mr. Lippencott spoke sharply to Mrs. Lewellyn, he would have you jump to the conclusion that Lippencott is the one who murdered Arnold Masters. But where, in all you've seen and heard, is there anything other than those words to lead you to that conclusion? There just isn't any."

Swain removed his hands from the railing and straightened. "Or perhaps, Mr. Bruce said, it is Christopher Cape who's the killer. How does Mr. Bruce attempt to hang the crime on Mr. Cape? By attempting to make something out of nothing, that's how. He wants you to believe that Mr. Cape lied about his attempts to persuade Mr. Albertson, the hotel proprietor, to call for the sheriff. Mr. Cape told you he twice asked the hotel proprietor to call to Harlowton to inform the sheriff of the killing. Mr. Albertson agreed that Christopher Cape came to him with such a request. The only way in which their testimony differed is that Mr. Albertson said it happened only once."

Now Swain's face showed a hint of a smile. "But Mr. Albertson is long in years. He was wakened from a sound sleep. If he didn't remember that Cape bothered him twice it is easily understood. That old man was simply confused. Based on that simple misunderstanding it isn't reasonable to think that Cape deliberately told a lie. To then insinuate that Mr. Cape is a killer should offend your sense of decency.

Swain's face no longer had even a pretense of warmth. He half turned to face the counsel table where Nate sat between T. C. and Spencer. Merci, Eunice, Felicity, and the Hamiltons were in the first row of the spectator section directly behind them. With his arm outstretched, Swain barked, "There they are, the mighty cattle ranchers. Look at them. All gathered together in their desperate attempt to save one of their own. That's what the big landowners in this community and any other community do—protect their own at all costs."

The eyes of every juror followed the prosecutor's arm and shifted to look first at Nate Hamilton and at his lawyers. Next, almost in unison, they turned their eyes to Amos and Beatrice Hamilton and to Felicity, Eunice, and Merci seated directly behind them in the spectator section to see how the ranchers would react to the accusation.

T. C.'s impulse was to stand and object. Then he realized that to do so would only lend emphasis to Swain's outrageous statement. So he remained seated at the table with his son. A look of confident calm remained on both their faces.

If Swain and the jurors expected a reaction from Nate, they were disappointed. Over the course of the trial, he'd become inured to the things said about him. He maintained an appearance of calm. What he'd just heard didn't seem to register with him at all.

The Hamiltons, Eunice, and Felicity also remained unmoved and stern faced. Not so Merci. When she heard the accusation, she blanched, gasped, and almost jumped up to screech at the prosecutor. Only extreme self-control stopped her.

Swain, meantime, dropped his arm and moved forward to place his left hand on the jury box railing. "Who's the one most responsible for the death of Arnold Masters? Probably that young lady seated behind her father—Merci Bruce. She's the one who lured Masters to this community. Who knows what their relationship might have been. But then her old friend..." He paused for a long moment before continuing, "or was he more than a friend?" He waited another moment for the jurors to consider the implication. "the defendant, whether friend or more, took offense at the time and attention that Arnold Masters was receiving and decided to put an end to it."

At first Merci didn't believe the man had spoken the words. Such an unfounded and blatant accusation seemed beyond even a man so cold as Garth Swain. Her immediate thought was that someone had to protest. Merci reached for the railing that divided the audience section from the lawyers' tables. She would pull herself erect, point her own arm at that man Swain, and shout out that he was an incompetent, malevolent wretch. But a movement seen from the corner of her eye intervened. T. C. was on his feet.

His voice reflected none of the rage he felt. His words were spoken in a forceful but quiet way. "I object, Your Honor. Mr. Swain has gone beyond any of the evidence presented in this trial, the only evidence the jury is to consider. He has also gone beyond the bounds of human decency. His accusations are without any basis in fact and are nothing but the effort of a desperate attorney to achieve a conviction when neither the facts nor the law can support that conviction. I ask that the jury be directed to ignore every word of the accusation as well as its intended import.

Swain's response was immediate. "I'm not the one who's desperate, Your Honor. Mr. Bruce and his son have shown their desperation throughout this trial by asking the jury to find that someone—anyone other than their client—is the killer of Arnold Masters."

Bang! The judge's gavel smacked the top of the bench. "Enough! Both of you! That's enough." When the attention of both men was fully focused on him he added in a more normal tone. "First of all, Mr. Swain, Mr. Bruce is correct. Your remarks are way beyond acceptable argument to the jury. Accusations such as you've just made cannot be tolerated. There will be no more of it—absolutely none. Is that clear, Sir?"

Swain's facial expression did not change. "Yes, Your Honor."

The judge turned his attention to T. C. "Now, sir, I'm the one who will decide when and if there should be directions to the jury. Understood?"

"Yes, Sir."

Judge Crawford turned his whole body to squarely face the jury. "Mr. Bruce is correct. The remarks of Mr. Swain are not to be considered by you as having any validity insofar as the guilt or innocence of Nathaniel Hamilton is concerned. They were totally improper, and you must not allow them to enter your thoughts at all during your deliberations. Do you all understand what I'm saying?"

Each juror responded with a nod of the head.

Merci Bruce sat back, bit her lip, and scowled. Garth Swain deserved more of a scolding than he received. And fat chance that the jurors would not consider the things he said while they deliberated.

The judge's posture relaxed slightly as he spoke to Swain, "You may continue, Sir. But let there be no more such remarks."

To Merci, Swain always seemed to be without human emotion and remained so when he spoke again to the jurors. "The defendant killed Masters in cold blood." He turned, pointed once more at Spence, T. C., and Nate, and looked back at the jurors. "So what did they do? Merci Bruce's family gathered with their friends, the Hamilton family, and set out to protect the guilty one. And how can they hope to do that? Only by confusing you. Only by asking you to believe that someone other than Nathaniel Hamilton is the killer." The prosecutor's voice rose. "Don't let them do it. Don't let that little group of people cheat the others in this community out of a just and honest verdict. Don't let Nathaniel Hamilton escape punishment for the unprovoked, senseless, and vicious murder of Arnold Masters. When you are deliberating please remember these things. Nate Hamilton had a motive to kill Arnold Masters. The motive was jealousy. He had the means to do so. He was familiar with the use of rope. He had the opportunity when he was alone—or so he thought—with his rival for the affections of Merci Bruce out there behind the Two Dot hotel." A look of disgust appeared on Swain's face. "And most important of all, he's an admitted liar."

As T. C. began to rise to object. Swain turned and walked away from the jury box. T. C. dropped back into his chair. After two steps the prosecutor turned again to face the jury. "There is no one else." He pointed at Nate again. "That man did it. Now do your duty. Convict him!" He then walked, body erect, to his seat, acknowledging neither Bruce, father or son, nor the judge as he passed them by.

For what seemed to Merci to be an hour but wasn't more than a few seconds—there was nothing but silence in the large courtroom. The silence continued while Judge Crawford stared at Garth Swain in either astonishment or anger. The man had ignored his admonition. But after a moment of contemplation he seemed to reach a conclusion. Following a look at the clock, he turned to the jurors. His tone of voice seemed to convey relief. "It's one o'clock. We'll recess now for an hour and a half so you can get a midday meal. Please be back here promptly at two thirty. At that time I'll give you the final instructions. That finished, you will go to the jury room and begin your deliberations." He leaned toward them again for emphasis. "My admonition still remains. Don't discuss anything about this trial with one another or anyone else during this recess. You'll be able to discuss all of it freely amongst yourselves soon enough." He half stood. "Now, go get a good feed and be back here on time." The gavel banged as he added, "Court's in recess."

Everyone—spectators and trial participants alike—waited for the jurors to vacate the room. Then, before anyone else in the room could move, Swain hustled through the swinging gate in the railing. As he passed by Arnold Masters' father, Merci saw him wave a hand in a dismissive manner and heard him mutter in voice meant only for Warren Masters, "There! You got what you demanded. I hope it doesn't result in an acquittal." Masters made no attempt to reply.

Then the noise began as those in the audience section stood, stretched, exchanged comments, and began moving from the benches and toward the door. Among those who stood were Amos and Beatrice Hamilton as well as Felicity, Eunice, and Merci. Once on their feet, however, they remained in place.

Those at the defendant's counsel table didn't move. At last Spencer leaned toward Nate to say quietly, "Now we wait." He pushed himself to his feet and gestured for Nate to do the same. "We'll go to the hotel, get some dinner and then—after the judge gives his instructions—begin the waiting."

T. C., now standing, added, "Come along, Nate. There's no way to guess how long the jury may deliberate before reaching a verdict. And there's nothing more that any of us can do to influence them." He put a hand on the young rancher's arm. "So—Spence is right. We'll eat, come back, listen to the instructions, and then wait. And do our best to relax while we do it."

Nate, face crumpled in a way that showed his mental agony, shook his head as though to clear it. "God, man, how am I supposed to relax? I'm facing the hangman's noose!"

Merci reached across the rail for Nate's hand. "Come along, friend. Walk with me." Once he was into the aisle between the benches, she put her arm through his. "The members of the jury are reasonable people. They'll surely decide that you didn't kill anybody. Just keep that thought."

The little group straggled into the room at the Graves Hotel where they had gathered throughout the trial. The men assisted the ladies into chairs and slumped into chairs of their own. No one spoke. They all suffered from emotional exhaustion. At last Beatrice Hamilton said in a soft voice, "I think by accusing all of us of wrongdoing that man may have offended the jurors."

Eunice's voice was equally as soft. "I agree. At least a couple of them appeared to be disgusted by Mr. Swain's last remarks."

Merci was seated next to Nate, hand resting on his arm. "If so, and I think you are right, it should help them find Nate innocent. But, all that aside, I believe Spencer's argument was the more persuasive of the two. I'm confident they would reach a not guilty verdict even without any help from Swain."

"Thanks, Sis, for the compliment." The words were accompanied by a quick smile from Spence. "The jury will return at two o'clock. We should order now so we can finish eating and be back at the courthouse when court reconvenes."

Nate shook his head. "Nothing for me, Spence. I'd never hold it down."

5 1

The sheriff ushered the jurors back into the box as the little group entered the courtroom. Once again Nate, Spencer, and T. C. stood at the counsel table as Judge Crawford barged through the door. He rapped with the gavel and said to the room in general, "Please be seated." Next he addressed the jury. "Thank you for your prompt return from the meal." He picked up a sheaf of papers, shook them gently, and tapped them once on the top of the bench. Satisfied with their arrangement, he looked again at those sitting in the jury box. "I'll read instructions on the law to you. You will have the instructions with you in the jury room should you wish to review them as you deliberate."

That said, Judge Crawford began to read slowly through the instructions that the attorneys had prepared and argued the day before. Most important among the instructions was the requirement that the verdict must be unanimous. He finished by saying, "Go to the jury room, and choose a foreman. You are now free of my instruction that you not discuss the things you saw and heard during this trial. Just the opposite. You are now obligated to do so and do it in a responsible manner."

"We just have to wait." The two families had gathered some distance away from the crowd that had poured out of the courthouse. Spence felt his words were an inadequate response to Nate's plaintive question but there was no better one to give.

"But how long, Spence? How long do I have to wait?"

"Until they reach a verdict."

T. C. grasped Nate's upper arm gently. "There's no way to predict how long that will take. It could be a few minutes, if they're already in agreement. Or it could be several hours. There's not a thing we can do to hurry the process, so you may as well do your best to relax. "

"How am I supposed to relax? The people in that room could put a noose around my neck."

T. C. smiled at the younger man. "I understand, and I didn't mean to make light of it."

Before Nate could respond or T. C. could say more, Merci pulled on Nate's arm. "C'mon, friend. Let's go to the hotel. We'll order a parfait to help pass the time."

Beatrice Hamilton added, "Merci's right. There's little to be gained from standing here." She put her arm through that of Amos and began the trek down the street to the Graves Hotel.

All but Spence sat around the table with the ice cream before them.

Spence, standing near the door, said, "I left word with the sheriff that we would be here so he can let us know when the jury reaches a verdict. The judge wants us back in the courtroom right away when that happens. So don't leave unless it's really necessary. If any of you must leave, tell the others where you'll be." He opened the door. "I need to check at my law office. Other clients haven't gone away. If you get word that the jury has reached a verdict, pick me up as you go by the office."

His father was on his feet. "I'll go with you. There are things we should discuss."

T. C. sat across the desk from Spence. "If the verdict is adverse, we need to be prepared."

Spence nodded. "Move for continuance of Nate's release on bail pending appeal for one."

"That's what I was thinking of. Any others?"

"Prepare that appellate brief. I haven't been able to think of anything else yet. That's the real reason I'm here now, to look at some earlier cases for guidance. The trial hasn't given me time to do a proper job of it."

"Okay, I'll help. You take the Montana cases and I'll look to California." T. C. stood and pulled a volume from the shelves on the side wall. "Let's get to it."

Spence peeked at his watch. Four thirty had arrived with no word from the courthouse. He placed the book on the desk top. "Dad, we better get back to the courtroom to learn what's going on—if anything."

The group trudged slowly up the street. None of them seemed inclined to hurry. The sheriff met them at the courthouse door. "Just about to go looking for you. The judge wants everyone here."

Spence was surprised to see Roger Davidson, the county attorney, seated at the opposing counsel table. Where was Garth Swain? To his inquiring glance, Davidson only raised his shoulders as though to say, "I don't know, either."

Judge Crawford took his place and, as usual, scanned the room. He did a double take when he saw the county attorney where Swain should have been. "Mr. Davidson, may I ask what's going on?"

"All I can tell you, Your Honor, is that Mr. Swain stuck his head in my office and told me that I should take the verdict."

"Where's Swain?"

"I don't know."

The judge turned to the sheriff with an inquiring look. The sheriff shrugged. "I'm told that he caught the afternoon train going west, Sir"

Crawford wasn't pleased and seemed at a loss. He shifted one way and then another in his chair. He rubbed the side of his face. "Well, you are the county attorney. His appointment as a deputy county attorney doesn't deprive you of your authority." His question came with a bit of a frown. "Are you comfortable with the situation, Sir?"

Davidson's voice was calm. "It certainly is unusual, Your Honor, but I believe the taking of a verdict is something I can handle."

The judge stared at Davidson for a moment before turning to those at the defense table. "The jury sent a note saying they had a question for me. That's why I summoned you." He now turned to the bailiff. "Bring them in and let's see what they have to say."

The jurors straggled into their usual places except for Benton Kalberg who now took the seat in the front row nearest to the judge. Crawford asked, "Have you been chosen as foreman, Sir?"

Kalberg stood to reply. "I have, Your Honor."

"All right. I understand you wish to ask a question."

"We do." Kalberg took a breath. "What if we can't agree?"

The judge pursed his lips. A pained expression appeared briefly on his face. "Let me ask, have you made a serious attempt to resolve your differences?"

"We have Your Honor. Some of us…"

The judge stopped him with a raised a hand and a sharp bark, "Say no more. I don't want to hear about your deliberations." The fierce manner in which the judge spoke startled the jury foreman. His eyebrows popped up, and he involuntarily leaned backward.

Crawford, meantime, pushed his chair away from the bench and sat for a couple of seconds in thought. Then he leaned toward the jurors and spoke in a more gentle tone. "Well, you've not had long to deliberate." He looked up at the clock high on the back wall. "It's near to five o'clock. Ordinarily, I would send you home for the night, but once you've begun your deliberations it isn't proper to do so. Too much chance that someone may say something to you or something will happen to influence your decision. For that reason you must be sequestered. I'd hoped this wouldn't happen, but just in case I asked the sheriff to reserve a block of rooms for you at the Star Hotel. He will escort you to the hotel and see that you are situated. A room is reserved in which you can share supper. After you eat, return to your rooms. Breakfast will be served in the same room at eight o'clock in the morning. Then I want you back here at nine o'clock in the morning—well rested and ready to begin your deliberations once again."

The jury foreman spoke. "What if some of us need pajamas? Or a change of clothes?"

"Tell the sheriff what you need and who he should see to get it." He waved a hand at the sheriff. "Collect the exhibits as well as any notes or other writings that the jurors may have made and give them to the clerk for safe keeping." To the jurors, "Be gone. Get some rest. But be back here on time in the morning."

He then addressed Roger Davidson and the Bruces. "I'll see the attorneys in my office. Now!" A bang of the gavel as he announced "Court's in recess."

The old judge walked around the desk and slumped into his chair, his robe still in place. When the lawyers were settled, each in a wooden chair facing him, he leaned an elbow on the desktop and propped his chin in his hand. "All right, Roger. What's going on with Swain?"

The county attorney shook his head. "I can't tell you, Your Honor. He just told me to take the verdict. Then, as he reached the door to my private office he growled, 'I'm getting away from this miserable burg, and I'm never coming back.'"

"What brought that on?"

Davidson shifted around for comfort. "I don't know for sure. But the rumors around town have it that he and Warren Masters haven't been able to get along."

The judge raised his head and dropped his hand to the desk. "In what way?"

"It seems Masters hasn't been satisfied with Swain's handling of the Hamilton case. And he hasn't been slow to make that known to Swain—and others." Davidson leaned forward. "Apparently, he'd call or travel to Helena to tell his political cronies the things he thought Swain should do. Then Swain would get a call from the governor or the attorney general giving him orders to do as Masters said."

"Garth Swain changed his way of doing things on someone's orders?" T. C. asked. "Hard to imagine."

The judge showed a touch of a smile. "Indeed." Turning again to the county attorney, he asked, "How did Mr. Swain react to the orders?"

"As you'd expect. He and Masters would get into a shouting match. It happened in the house that Swain rented for an office. The neighbors could hear them yelling at one another."

Judge Crawford shook his head in apparent disgust. "Well, Swain's disappearance without informing the Court is unusual. It certainly is unprofessional." Then in a brighter tone he added, "But it shouldn't cause any problem. Roger, you've taken jury verdicts in my court before. Let's just hope the jury comes to a decision soon." The judge pushed his chair back from the desk and stood. "Be sure the sheriff knows where to find you. We don't want to keep the jurors waiting after they've reached a verdict." The lawyers were thus dismissed.

Spencer and T. C. found the others sitting listlessly—nearly in a stupor—on hard chairs in their gathering room at the hotel. At the sight of the lawyers they all straightened, inquiry showing on their faces. Spence spoke before they could ask. "The judge wanted to know why County Attorney Roger Davidson was sitting in the courtroom instead of Garth Swain. Roger told him that Swain has left town."

Nate's face showed puzzlement. "What will that do to me, Spence? What will happen now?"

"Swain's absence won't make any difference. The jury will decide upon a verdict. When they do, Roger Davidson, as county attorney, can take the verdict as well as Swain." His voice carried sympathy for his suffering client. "For now, we just wait."

Nate pushed away from the table. "Do I dare to go home to the ranch? I've got to get away from here, get out of this town."

T. C. was the one who answered. "That's probably a good idea. Just be certain to be here at nine in the morning. It would be the worst kind of mistake to show up late and antagonize the judge."

Amos pushed on the table to rise slowly from his chair. "I agree. Beatrice and I will take our son home. It'll be nice for the three of us to be at home together. We're just plain worn out." He turned to Spence. "I promise we'll leave the ranch early enough in the morning to handle any problem—like a flat tire. We'll be here at nine." He offered his hand to help his wife to her feet as he gestured for Nate to lead the way to the door.

Merci, who had been standing quietly next to Nate, put a hand on his arm. "I know it's almost foolish to suggest, friend, but try to put all of this from your mind and really rest. Just remember, the jurors are all good folks. They'll believe you."

Nate touched her hand. "I just hope so, Merc. I hope so."

T. C. extended his hand to Felicity. "We all need rest and some respite from the pressure of this trial. Let's do as the Hamiltons. Let's go home and put the last few days out of our minds."

Spencer, still standing, smiled at his parents. "That's good, Dad. You three go. I have matters that require my time at the office. But I'll get myself to my house early. I plan to get some rest, too." His face showed the beginnings of a smile. "Maybe Eunice will join me for some supper."

Merci put her arm through that of her father. "It will be good to sleep in my own bed." On the street in front of the hotel, Merci spoke to them all with emphasis, "I'm confident that the jury will reach a verdict early tomorrow morning, and the verdict will be that Nate is not guilty!"

Eunice arrived at Spence's house bearing a large cloth-covered tray. After placing the tray on the small kitchen table, she drew the cloth away to reveal a small pork roast, prepared to perfection. Browned potatoes and fresh green beans balanced the meat. Vanilla pudding provided a tasty finish. Later they sat side by side in two armchairs sharing quiet conversation. The hour's quiet time finally helped Spence relax in both mind and body. At eight o'clock Eunice stood and withdrew her jacket from the tiny closet near the front door. Spencer held it for her as she slipped her arms into the sleeves. At the door, he thanked her for the good food. Then, on impulse, Spence pulled her close, looked into her somber face. "Miss Syvertson, I don't know how I'd have survived these past days without your company and kindness."

Her somber appearance turned into a smile. "It's all been my pleasure, Mr. Bruce." She put both hands on his chest to push herself away. "But right now you need to get some sleep." Still standing near the door, she added, "Just knowing I've been some help to you will bring pleasant dreams to me."

Her soft voice whispered in Spence's ears until sleep came to him—at last.

52 The Hamiltons arrived at the law office at eight thirty the next morning. Spence, T. C., Felicity, and Merci were waiting for them. After the customary salutations and a trip to the bathroom by each of the Hamiltons, the five strode purposely up Central Avenue to the courthouse. The courtroom was already filling with spectators when they entered. Roger Davidson, hands clasped on the desk-top before him, was in the chair that had held Garth Swain throughout the trail. Warren Masters, sour-faced as always, was seated on the bench directly behind the county attorney. While he had not done it with Swain, Spencer felt appropriate to step over and offer a hand to Davidson. "Good morning, Counselor."

Roger stood to grasp the hand. "Good morning, Spence." He gestured with his head toward the jury box. "I expect the jury will reach a verdict before too much time goes by today."

Spence's face showed a kind of grimace. "Can't be soon enough for my client. This whole thing has been hell for him."

At that moment the bailiff called, "All rise." Spence scooted back to the defense counsel table as Judge D. D. Crawford climbed to his place. A tap of the gavel before he said to those in the room, "Please be seated," and turned to the bailiff. "Bring in the jury."

Merci looked carefully at the face of each of the jurors as they came through the door and paraded to their places in the jury box. None of them showed emotion. None of them looked toward Nate.

The judge spoke in a kindly manner. "I hope you all got a good night's sleep and are ready to continue your deliberations." His tone now changed perceptibly. "A great deal of time, expense, and effort has gone into the prosecution and defense in this case. It's important for that reason, if no other, that you reach a proper verdict. Each of you has an obligation to listen respectfully to the views of the others and to give them serious consideration. I'm not suggesting that you should defer your firmly held convictions to those of others. Were you to do that it would result in a miscarriage of justice." He paused. "You are all reasonable people. I'm certain, having had a night to reflect you will discuss the evidence with one another in a reasonable and respectful manner and then reach a proper and unanimous verdict. Go now and begin again to consider the evidence—both physical and verbal—presented to you during the trial. The bailiff will escort you to the jury room." The judge rapped the gavel. "Court's in recess."

Everyone stood silently as the twelve moved out of the courtroom to once again address their task.

Merci's eyes moved to her school hood friend. She realized, with a start, how much Nate's whole appearance and demeanor had changed over the course of the trial. Before, his bearing seemed to be one close to arrogance. Now, he seemed meek in countenance and behavior. His dark brow and other facial features were now nearly without life. She'd understood, of course, how difficult it must be to bear up under burden of the accusations that had fallen upon him. But she hadn't realized until that moment how beaten down his spirit had become. Her immediate thought was that she must somehow help him retain his sanity—no matter what the verdict might be. Dear God, she hoped it was an acquittal.

In the now all too familiar room at the Graves Hotel, each of the seven settled for the wait. Merci made an attempt at light-hearted conversation only to have it fall flat. Felicity summoned a waiter to ask for coffee and rolls. Those things, when they arrived, were addressed halfheartedly. There was nothing any of them could do but sit quietly with their thoughts—and wait.

At eleven thirty a sheriff's deputy knocked on the door to say the judge wanted them at the courtroom. Their trek up the street was at their fastest pace ever. Perhaps there was a verdict.

Once all the principals were assembled, Judge Crawford announced, "The jury had sent a note asking if they can break for the noon meal. I'm thinking of ordering the sheriff to have sandwiches, tea, and coffee delivered to them. That way they can continue to deliberate. Mr. Davidson, do you object to that arrangement?"

"I do not, Your Honor. It seems a reasonable thing to do."

"Mr. Spencer Bruce, how about you?"

"I agree with Mr. Davidson."

"Good. I'll return their note telling them of my decision." The judge looked toward the sheriff, "One of the restaurants should be able get some sandwiches ready in a hurry. Maybe some soup, too. Bring it as soon as possible. I don't want any of the jurors to get cranky just because they're hungry." He spoke again to the lawyers. "Anything else, gentlemen?"

Spencer Bruce and Roger Davidson answered in unison, "No, Your Honor."

"Then court's in recess until we hear from the jury again."

Felicity Bruce and Beatrice Hamilton could no longer bear to just sit in the dreary room. They left word that they could be found at the millinery shop.

Merci grabbed Nate's arm. "C'mon. We're going for a walk down in the park. Neither one of us has had much exercise lately." To her father she added, "We'll stay close to the road so the deputy can find us if word comes from the jury."

Spence was at his office with other legal matters to occupy his mind. That left only T. C. at the hotel. Someone had to remain there to wait for the sheriff's summons.

T. C. was the one to do the waiting—and do it alone. He paced the floor for a time before remembering there were magazines for sale in the hotel lobby. Thereafter, he entertained himself by reading stories from one called Ranch Romances, all the while wondering how he had arrived once again in a courtroom as a lawyer, after so many years.

The call to return to the courthouse came at four thirty. Davidson was at his place when Spence and the others pushed through the crowd that gathered once again. Having deposited his materials on the counsel table, Spence moved across to ask of Davidson, "Do we have a verdict?"

"I don't know. Like you, I was just told to appear. And here I am."

The room was quiet as everyone in it waited. When the judge appeared, his face, Merci thought, showed either anger or frustration. He rapped the gavel, said for the record that the principals were all in place, and then told the bailiff to bring in the jury. Merci, watching them closely, thought the faces of those twelve citizens showed nothing more clearly than extreme weariness. When they were seated, Judge D. D. Crawford said, "Mr. Foreman, you sent a note asking to see me."

Benton Kalberg used the arm of the chair to help himself to his feet. "We did, Your Honor." He inhaled, held it, and then blew with a whishing sound. "Your Honor, we've tried. We've really tried to agree, but we haven't been able to do so. We just can't agree on a verdict." Then he stood silent and waited.

The judge slumped back in his chair and remained there, eyes downward. Then he pushed forward and turned toward the jurors. "Is there any chance that another night's rest might be of benefit? Allow you to give further consideration to the expressions of those with whom you disagree?"

"No, Sir, it won't. We just can't agree, that's all. Each time we vote, the count is the same."

The judge raised a hand, palm out. "I don't want to know how you voted." The old jurist leaned back once again in his chair and sighed. "Well, if you can't agree we have a hung jury." He looked first toward Nate and the two attorneys seated beside him, then toward Davidson before saying, "I hereby declare a mistrial." He seemed to consider what to do next. Then he addressed Nate. "Mr. Hamilton, the state may decide to retry this case. Or the state may decide to dismiss the charges against you. Until that determination is made, the charges remain in place. You've been free on bond and that arrangement will continue. The bond and the conditions of your release remain as they have been. Do you understand?"

Nate followed Spence and T. C. to his feet. "I guess so, Sir."

"Well, if you have any questions, ask your attorneys. They will answer them."

Turning back to those in the jury box, he said. "You're discharged of your duties as jurors and may leave the courtroom to return to your normal activities. Thank you for your service. I know it has been difficult for you. You will receive payment from the county for the days you served." He shifted around in order to get to his feet, rapped the gavel, and announced, with some solemnity, "Court's adjourned."

Everyone in the room stood in silence until the jurors cleared the room. Then the noise level rose as the spectators began a slow exit. Most were talking, exchanging thoughts and some puzzlement with their neighbors. It all came to a halt when Warren Masters leaned over the railing to yell at the county attorney, "It's all been a setup, hasn't it? All you damn people taking care of one of your own." He leaned farther forward. "Well, by God, I won't put up with it. I'll bring in a lawyer with the guts and skill to retry this case, and bring some justice for my son. He'll tear this whole burg and all of you yokels apart." Masters wheeled and rammed his way to the exit, shoving people roughly aside to do it.

Nate and his two attorneys were standing like the others. Stunned by the tirade, they remained still until Masters was out of the room. That's when Nate collapsed back into the chair he'd filled throughout the trial. "Oh God, Spence, I can't stand this any longer. I just can't!" It came out as a guttural choke.

Spence could think of nothing to say that would comfort his client. T. C. put a hand under Nate's arm in an attempt to help him to his feet. Nate jerked angrily away. Merci, watching from the front row of the audience section, dashed through the gate and around the table to face her old school-hood friend directly. "Come with me, Nate. We'll get out of here." Nate's eyes flew upward. He stared at Merci for a moment, then relaxed and nodded his head. She reached for his hand. "Both you and I need to get out of this town. Your folks will take you home. I'll go home with my parents." She dragged him along to the gate in the railing. There she stopped, thought a moment, then looked at him from the corner of her eyes and grinned. "Do you remember when we were kids and were both sent to check salt in the pastures where the ranches join? We got to that old tumble-down homestead building at the same time. The building was full of pack rats that scared me." Her grin broadened. "You wanted to show me how brave you were by throwing rocks at the rats. Be darned if you didn't hit one and kill it. Remember?"

Nate's face relaxed at the remembrance. "You sure were mad at me for that."

"Well, climb on some old pony tomorrow and ride over to that building. I'll meet you there. And I'll bring a lunch. Want to bet you can't kill another rat?"

Nate dropped his eyes to his hand, opening and closing the fingers as though testing them. With a hint of a grin, he said, "I can. And I'll prove it tomorrow."

"Not a chance." Merci punched him on the upper arm. "See you tomorrow." She wheeled back through the swinging gate and on toward the exit door, leaving Nate to trace her path with his eyes.

53

Felicity was awakened by the pounding. For a moment she couldn't figure out what caused the noise in the dark of the night. Then she clambered out of bed, pulled a robe around her shoulders, and hurried to open the back door. Mrs. Morgan stood hunched over and shivering in the chilly night air. The homestead neighbor blinked at the sudden light and then pushed her way into the rear hallway. She grasped Felicity by both upper arms and sobbed, "Wake Merci! And call your son, Spencer. Have them come to our house as quickly as they can. And tell Spencer to bring the sheriff."

"Why? What's wrong?"

"It's Lyndon. I don't know what's come over him. He's acting crazy. That boy never was one to drink, but he brought some liquor home from town." The sobs became more pronounced and tears streamed down the woman's face. "He's been drinking that vile stuff ever since he got home last night. And he's staggering around and talking to himself." Mrs. Morgan pulled a cloth from the pocket of her coat and wiped at the eyes and then at her nose. "Mrs. Bruce, he keeps muttering about Chris Cape. And he's been mumbling that he has to see Merci. And also that he has to tell Spencer the truth. Just now, he spoke directly to me for the first time since he came home. He said, "Get Merci Bruce right away.""

"And he wants someone to get the sheriff?"

"That's what he said. But the thing he was saying over and over as I left was. 'Get Merci to our place. Hurry.'" She choked out another sob and released Felicity's arms. Tears kept coming. "As I was leaving he took that jug and his rifle and headed off on foot somewhere up the side of the Two Dot Butte." She shook Felicity's arm. "I'm terrified. I don't know what he's done that has him acting this way. My son seems to be out of his mind."

T. C. finally wakened enough to hear noises from the back of the house. He shuffled into the kitchen, a robe over his pajamas, just in time to hear Mrs. Morgan's last remark. "Out of his mind? Who's out of his mind, Mrs. Morgan?"

"Lyndon. My son, Lyndon, that's who." The distraught woman turned her attention from Felicity to T. C. "Mr. Bruce, please help my son. Something is terribly wrong." And then she repeated all that she had said to Felicity.

At the end of her monologue, T. C. straightened. "We'll help." He touched Felicity's arm. "Rouse Merci. Then get on the phone and see if you can raise the storekeeper to call Harlo. Tell him you must reach Spence's house right away. If you get through, tell Spence to pick up the sheriff and get to Morgan's house as fast as he can."

"It's three o'clock in the morning. I'm not sure if I can raise Mr. Steiner, but I'll try." Felicity pulled a chair away from the table and said to her guest, "We'll do what we can. Please wait."

As his wife hurried toward the phone that hung on the kitchen wall, T. C. looked down at Sophia, who'd slumped into the chair. "I'll get dressed and head for town. If Felicity doesn't get through on the phone, I'll fetch Spence and the sheriff. And I can drop you off at your place on the way by." He started for the bedroom, then turned back to ask, "Where's Hiram?"

The distraught woman shook her head. "He's campaigning." She looked pleadingly at T. C. and added, "I think he's out near Martinsdale somewhere. He said he was going to visit the ranches in the west end of the county to look for votes."

From her bedroom Merci heard the clamber. She appeared, fully dressed, at the door. "Dad, if I can take the Runabout, I'll go to Morgan's right now. If Lyndon needs to talk to someone I'll listen."

T. C. said, "Go."

Merci turned to Lyndon's mother. "Can I give you a ride back to your house, Mrs. Morgan?"

"Yes, please. Maybe my son will be back."

While leading Sophia to the auto, Merci muttered, "Let's hope so." One pull of the crank and the engine of the Runabout sputtered to life. It turned to a rumble as Merci sped out the gate.

Within minutes T. C. strode, fully dressed, from the bedroom. Felicity called over her shoulder. "I've raised the storekeeper. He's trying to get through to central in Harlo."

"Good." T. C. opened the door before calling back to his wife, "See if you can get through to the storekeeper in Martinsdale. Maybe he can locate Hiram and tell him he's needed at home right away." The sound of the Packard as he drove away was a growl.

Merci knew where to find Lyndon. Thankful for the light of the almost full moon, she tramped up a narrow cattle trail south from the Morgan house, up along the slope of the Two Dot Butte; between rocks of all sizes and around stands of wild rosebushes. At last, she reached the upwind side of a boulder the size of a house, put one hand against the rock and followed it around to the downwind side. A small flow of water crept from under the rock and trickled a short distance down the slope before it died away into the ground.

Lyndon Morgan sat with his back propped against a nearby smaller rock, one hand on a jug that glinted in the moonlight. The other was wrapped around the stock of the rifle. He didn't move when the young woman rounded the boulder. She spoke in a quiet voice. "Lyndon, it's me, Merci."

The man still didn't move. As she got close, she saw his glassy, unblinking eyes seemingly staring at the Snowy Mountains in the far distance. His breath was so shallow that it first seemed that he wasn't breathing at all. Merci took another step closer. "You told your mother you wanted to talk to me. And to the sheriff. Well, I'm here and the others are on the way." When there was still no movement from Lyndon, she asked, "Do you hear me?"

Lyndon seemed to rouse and focus. He blinked twice and then pulled the rifle close. After a second of concentration he gathered himself to sit in a more erect position. The weak smile he cast in Merci's direction carried little humor. "Yes." After a long pause, he mumbled in a slurred voice. "Yes, Merc, I hear you. And I need to tell you what I've done."

"How about we go back down to your house and you can tell everyone there?"

Eyes wide, he yelped, "No," with a quick look in the direction of the house. "No! I don't want my mother to hear."

"Well then, I'll just sit down here with you and listen. How's that?"

"That's what I want. I just want you to listen until I'm finished. Don't interrupt."

She perched on a smaller rounded rock. "All right, let's hear it."

Lyndon tipped the jug for a long pull. The besotted man dropped the hand with the jug down to the ground next to his leg before he looked directly at Merci. "You remember what I said when Spencer asked me questions in the courtroom?"

"Of course. What about it?"

"I didn't tell the truth."

You didn't tell the truth? About what?"

Lyndon peered off into the distance once again. At last he blinked and focused on Merci. "I lied about what happened back of the bar that night."

Merci frowned. "What do you mean?"

"Do you remember that I said I heard Nate Hamilton threaten Arnold Masters?"

"Of course I remember."

"That wasn't true."

Merci's frown deepened. "Why did you say it, if it wasn't true?"

Lyndon turned a frown to her. "Just let me tell it, okay?"

She put out a hand face down toward him to indicate she understood his need. "Of course. I'm sorry for interrupting. Go ahead. Tell me."

"Here's what really happened." Lyndon took a deep breath. "I was back there in the brush to do my business when I saw Nate Hamilton and Arnold Masters arguing. But I never heard Nate threaten to kill Masters. I was kind of behind some brush and too far away to hear anything they said,"

Merci inhaled to speak but Lyndon held up hand. His voice had a bite when he frowned. "I said, let me tell it." She nodded and relaxed as best she could while seated on the hard rock. Lyndon continued. "Masters was there and Lippy Lippencott was there and Irma Lewellyn was there and they all seemed to be yelling at one another. Irma stopped yelling to listen for a minute. Then she kind of shrugged and walked away. Lippy hollered something and shook his club at Masters one more time before he hurried back toward the saloon." Lyndon stopped as though to recollect. "Nate Hamilton wasn't even there then. He'd already gone back to his truck." He was silent for a moment, and Merci waited. "Masters kind of staggered off farther down the creek toward the depot. He didn't get very far." Lyndon's eyes widened and glinted in the moonlight. "Irma hadn't gone to her room like Lippy'd ordered. She cut around the brush and met Masters near the depot. I wondered what she was up to so I kind of crept through the brush that way." He paused. "I heard Irma say, 'Come on, Arnold. Let's get away from this town and go somewhere together.'"

"What happened?" Merci asked when Lyndon stopped talking.

"Arnold laughed. He just threw back his head and laughed a drunken laugh. When he finally stopped laughing he leaned over and kind of choked. Then he told Irma that she meant nothing to him. He said he was just passing time with her."

"What was Irma's reaction?"

"She stood with her hands on her hips. I think she was kind of shocked. Then she asked, 'Then why did you tell me you loved me while we were in bed together?' Arnold laughed some more—more like he giggled and said, 'I don't know. It just seemed like a good idea.'"

Lyndon's eyes widened. "It was pretty dark, so I couldn't see Irma's face very well, but I could see her eyes go wide and then her mouth go all twisted. An unearthly growl come out of it, and her hands come up fast. She hit Arnold in the chest with both of her hands. He started to fall backwards but kind of twisted around to land on his hands and knees. Before he could move, she jumped on his back." Lyndon looked at the ground and shook his head slowly all the while he described it. "Where Irma got the rope, I don't know. But she had it in her hands and wrapped it around that man's neck in a flash. He jerked his body and thrashed around, trying to buck her off." Lyndon's head stopped moving and he looked directly at Merci. "Irma's a powerful woman. She just kept twisting that rope until Arnold finally collapsed on the ground and stopped moving." Lyndon gulped once and then dropped back against the rock.

Merci, speechless, stared silently at the drunken, despondent man. What was there for her to say?

When Lyndon finally spoke again his eyes were wide in remembrance. "Then she stood up and kicked him."

Merci straightened. "My God! What did you do?"

"I was terrified. I turned to sneak away through the brush toward the saloon." His voice caught, but then he continued. "I hadn't gone more than ten steps before I felt that rope around *my* neck. I thought it was Irma." Lyndon shoved the rifle aside and rubbed his hand at his throat. "I don't know where Chris Cape came from, but he was the one with the rope. He pulled it tight and growled at me, 'Say one word about what happened just now and I'll kill you!' The man kept tightening the rope. I was choking so I did what Masters had done. I tried to get my fingers under the rope. Couldn't do it."

"But he didn't kill you."

"No. What he did was tell me to testify that I'd heard Nate threaten to kill Arnold. He said he'd know what I said when the trial took place and if I didn't say the right things, I'd be dead."

"What did you do?"

"I tried to nod my head to let him know I'd do it, but he just kept tightening the rope. Finally, he let one end of the rope loose and grabbed me by the shoulders and jerked me around to face him. God, that man's powerful strong!"

"Then what?"

"He shook me like I was a little child and told me I'd better do what he said. Then he threw the rope away and went to Irma. She seemed to be in some kind of shock. I guess she realized what she'd done. Cape put his arm around her shoulder and said, "Don't worry. We can take care of it." Then they walked off toward the depot together. That's the last I saw of either of them that night." Lyndon heaved a huge sigh and sagged against the rock.

Merci asked, "What did you do after Cape left?"

"I just stood there for a long time. Too scared to move, I guess. I don't even know where Cape came from," he repeated. "I hadn't seen him anywhere. He just suddenly appeared out of the dark." Lyndon was quiet as his head fell forward. When he spoke again, his voice was almost inaudible. "Finally I looked at Masters' body. It just didn't seem right to leave it lying there. I checked to be sure Cape was long gone. Then I grabbed Arnold by his armpits and dragged him through the opening between the saloon and the house next door." He looked again at Merci. "I know it was stupid, but I'd been drinking. Between Lippy's hooch and Chris Cape, I was almost out of my mind." He reached for the rifle again and pulled it close. "So I dragged your friend around to the front of the saloon and kind of spread him on the boardwalk."

Merci couldn't stop herself from asking, "But the bayonet?"

"Yes, the bayonet. It was lying there next to the saloon where someone had dropped it while the party was going on." Lyndon stopped speaking and shook his head slowly from side to side—over and over again—as though in disbelief. He was staring at the ground when he spoke again. "Well, there was piece of old cardboard lying there next to the bayonet. And I began to think about you, Merc." Looking up at her once and then quickly lowering his eyes, he mumbled, "You're always on my mind. You're the most wonderful person in the world. I know you hardly see me even when I'm standing right next to you." He peeked at her again. "But I daydream about you, and you're in my dreams at night." Lyndon paused and sighed. "That's when I decided to do it. I had an old pencil in my pocket so I printed the message on the cardboard and placed the cardboard on Arnold's chest. After that I picked up the bayonet and rammed it through the cardboard and through him." He shook his head. "It went through a lot easier than I thought it would." Lyndon sighed, took a pull from the jug, and clutched the rifle even closer. Then the distraught man lapsed into silence, his head hanging down on his chest.

Merci could neither move nor speak. She was wide-eyed and rigid in shock.

54

When Spence got the call he dressed in a hurry. It took precious time to drive to Sheriff Grave's house and raise the officer from his sleep. The two men were on the road west to Two Dot by five o'clock. The darkness was beginning to fade in the east when Spence pulled his Hudson to a stop at Morgan's gate. The sheriff clambered out to open it. The Morgan house stood at the end of a track about four hundred yards away. Sophia Morgan was waiting at the front door to meet them.

Without preamble, she pointed southward toward the rocky slope of the Two Dot Butte. "Lyndon walked that way. I haven't any idea where he might have gone, but he's up there somewhere. Merci went to look for him."

Sheriff Graves didn't move. "What's going on, Ma'am?"

"It's Lyndon. He's not himself, Sheriff. He's acting crazy. And he's been saying he needed to talk to Merci. And to Spence. And then he said he wanted to talk to you, too." She wiped at her swollen eyes. "I'm terribly afraid. He's been drinking and he has a rifle." She pointed again to the butte. "Please go and find him before he does something terribly bad."

Spence pulled at Grave's arm. "C'mon, Sheriff, Let's go. I think I know where to find Lyndon. I'll bet Merci's with him. We'll ride in the car until we get into the big rocks. After that we walk."

With his hand still on the sheriff's arm, Spence caught a glimpse a Model T going west along the road to Martinsdale that ran south of the Bruce Ranch buildings and close to the landing field. He thought, "Who's that, so early in the day?"

About a quarter mile from the Morgan house Spence pulled the car to a halt among a cluster of large rocks. Spence looked at the sheriff. "From here on we go on foot."

The two men began a shallow climb up a hillside that steepened as they moved along. The sheriff, soon winded, stopped and sat down on a rock. Spence stood at his side as Graves rested. "There's a small spring not too much farther up this hillside. It flows from under a huge boulder—a boulder as big as a small house. When Merci and I were children we rode our horses around behind it and pretended we were outlaws hiding from the sheriff. I've told Lyndon about it. I'll bet that rock is where we'll find him." When the sheriff wiped at his brow with a cloth and didn't move, Spence said, "You wait and rest. I'll go on ahead and see if I can locate him."

The sheriff stuffed the handkerchief into his back pocket and used one hand to push off the rock. "No. Let's go. I'll keep up."

Spence took them to the top of a low rise. There he pointed. "See that big boulder? Next to that rock is where we'll find Lyndon."

Sheriff Graves took a deep breath. "Then let's get to it."

Merci was startled when Spence stepped from behind the rock, the sheriff at his side. She quickly came to her feet and moved close to her brother to whisper, "Lyndon needs help—lots of help."

The presence of Spence and the sheriff didn't register with Lyndon. He was staring into the distance after taking another drink from his jug. Their presence penetrated his mind when Spence reached a hand toward him. "Your mother said you need to see us. We're here."

Lyndon shrank away from Spence's hand and jerked the rifle close. But he looked upward. "I've already told it all to Merci."

"Told her what?"

Lyndon didn't respond. Instead he turned to Merci as though expecting her to relay his confession. He didn't shrink away when she put her hand on his shoulder to say, "You've got to tell it all again. Both Spencer and Sheriff Graves need to hear it from you."

"God, Merci, do I have to?"

"Yes. You must. Right now."

And so, Lyndon Morgan sat by the rock, jug and rifle in hand, and laid it out for the lawyer and the law officer. He told them how Arnold Masters met his death. And how the bayonet came to be impaled in the body.

From time to time during the telling, the sheriff muttered in astonishment, "I'll be damned!"

When Lyndon finished, however, there was silence. The others were too shaken to speak.

That silence was broken almost immediately by the far away sound of an airplane beginning a takeoff run. Merci acted first. She ran around the rock to peer into the distance at the Bruce Ranch airfield. Her Jenny, appearing toy-like in the distance, sped along the ground on a takeoff run and then rose slowly to the air.

The sound roused Lyndon, too. He struggled to his feet to stagger next to Merci. A look of horror spread across his face at the sight of the airplane climbing to the west. For a moment he was frozen. He dropped the jug and grabbed Merci by an arm "Jesus, Merc! You've got to stop him." She didn't seem to hear him. "Listen to me." He jerked at her arm. "I wasn't at work yesterday. I just couldn't do it. So I rode the train to Harlo to get away. I was in the Beanery at the depot for a cup of coffee. Chris Cape and Irma Lewellyn were there but they didn't see me. Chris Cape asked Irma if she'd like an airplane ride—before they left town for good." He peered at the airplane as it turned to the south and climbed higher into the air. Merci still didn't seem to be listening. Her eyes were following the Jenny. Lyndon jerked at her arm. "He said he'd take her in your airplane if she wanted to, and she giggled and said, 'Why not?'"

Merci jerked her arm loose as she watched the Jenny pass above them—climbing as it went. "What the hell is Chris Cape up to now, for God's sake?"

Lyndon grabbed at Merci again. "You've got to stop him, Merc! You've got to!"

Merci scowled at the distraught man who was pulling at her arm. "How am I going to do that?"

Lyndon let go of her arm and whirled around as though to find someone to help him bring the airplane back to earth. Then he grabbed her arm again and almost yelled in her ear. "We've got to do something!" After that, his body slumped and he moaned, "My God, what have I done?"

Merci took her eyes from the Jenny to focus a scowl on Lyndon. "What do you mean?"

Lyndon pulled the rifle up next to his chest in a kind of hug. "After I got back, I thought of the things that Irma and Cape had done. She'd murdered Arnold Masters, and he'd threatened to kill me. And they were going to take your airplane for a flight this morning. So I walked over to the hangar where you keep the airplane and took a file with me. I filed nicks in some of the wires that hold the wings on the airplane." He almost whimpered as he continued. "Irma killed Arnold! I decided she needed to die, too. And I decided to get rid of Chris Cape at the same time. Then, he couldn't threaten me any more." Lyndon was breathing hard. "I thought maybe one or more of the wires would break when he got your Jenny into the air. Then the wings would come loose and the plane would crash." Lyndon stopped to look upward at the aircraft that was now high in the air over the town of Two Dot. "That would be the end of both of them. I wouldn't have to worry about the things I'd said at the trial ever again."

Spence, hearing it all, gasped. "Jesus Christ, Lyndon!"

Graves, who'd been listening from nearby, started for Lyndon. "You damn fool! You could kill them both."

Lyndon saw the sheriff move and turned the rifle in his direction. "Stay away!"

Graves halted and put out a hand. "No need for that." Their eyes met. But the whine of the aircraft pulled their attention toward it.

The Jenny was now so high in the air that it appeared more like a toy than the real thing. It seemed to be holding together, so maybe the wires weren't as damaged as Lyndon thought. Merci and the three men watched as it completed one more circle over town. The aircraft banked steeply to the right and rolled into a shallow dive. As the speed of the Jenny increased, the sound of the motor rose until it became a howling scream. The Jenny's dive gradually became more shallow. As they watched, the aircraft leveled off and began to curve upward into the beginning of a loop.

That's when it happened. The right lower wing broke away first, and then the upper wing. As the two folded upward, the Jenny began to roll and then to drop nose first toward the ground. The machine made two complete turns with the loosened wings, still harnessed by the un-damaged wires and flapping at the side of the fuselage. The sickening sound of the impact, when the Jenny struck the ground, could be heard plainly by those on the hillside—those who watched in horror.

For an instant, Merci was paralyzed. The scream that came from her throat after that instant told of her anguish. Her next reaction was to shove Lyndon aside and race down the slope in the direction of the crash.

Lyndon was staggered by the shove. His eyes were open so wide that the whites seemed to bulge outward. He moaned, "Oh, God! God help me!"

Sheriff Graves had been focused on the airplane. He turned to Lyndon with a growl, "You murdered them. That's what you did!" He took a step, reaching for Lyndon's rifle.

Too late.

Lyndon jerked the rifle next to his body, pushed the muzzle up and under his chin, and pulled the trigger—all in one movement. The sheriff found himself watching as blood and tissue flew into the air. A body still stood before him, a body without the top of its head. A body that remained erect for an eyeblink before crumpling to the earth.

T. C., returning from Harlo, was first to the wreck, four hundred yards south of the place where Merci had first coaxed the Jenny into the air. He found the remains of two bodies amidst the wood, fabric, and metal that had been the Curtis JN4. One body was that of Chris Cape, the other of Irma Lewellyn. It was obvious from their mangled condition that nothing could be done for either of them.

Merci arrived within minutes. She scrambled from the Runabout and began a run toward the wreckage. T. C. stepped in front of her with his arms spread wide. When Merci tried to push by, her father grabbed her around the waist and held her until she stopped struggling. "It's not something you want to see, child."

55

Merci stood next to her horse, one hand on the saddle horn, staring at the debris that had once been the Jenny. Nate Hamilton stopped the lumbering Model T truck some distance away, stepped from the cab, and stood with his hands hanging at his side. Merci turned slowly from the wreckage. "What are you doing here, Nate?"

"I saw you here. Thought I should check to see if you're all right."

"No. I'm not all right. The Jenny's demolished. And I'm responsible for the deaths of four people. Why would I be all right?"

Nate moved half the distance between them. "It's not your fault those people are dead, Merc. You didn't make any of them do what they did."

Merci led the horse to Nate's truck where she settled onto the front bumper with her elbows on her knees, eyes on the ground. "Easy to say. Not so easy to live with."

Nate leaned one hand against the hood of truck. "A lot has happened in the last few days." After a moment, he changed the subject. "I hear that Spence might propose to Eunice."

Merci squinted upward at Nate. "I'm certain that he already has. And I'm just as sure that she's accepted. Eunice will be good for him." She dropped her head back down. "The most important thing is that Judge Crawford dismissed all the charges against you."

"Spence said the judge didn't have much choice after he heard the all the things Lyndon confessed to." He drew some lines in the dirt with the heel of his boot. "To have that behind me is an unbelievable relief, more than you can ever know. I was terrified I'd wind up in prison—or dangling at the end of a noose." He sat on the ground, back against a tire, one leg up, one leg stretched out. "Do you know what the worst part was? I couldn't do anything to help myself. I had to depend on your brother and your father to take care of me." He looked sideways at her. "I'm not used to depending on someone else, Merc."

Merci continued to speak to the ground. "That's done and gone."

"Not really. There will always be some who think I got away with murder."

"The jury was split ten to two for acquittal." She peeked at him from the corner of her eye. "That should be enough for anyone to accept your innocence.

"I wish it were so."

Merci said, "I wish I could have seen the look on Garth Swain's face when he heard it all. He was so cocksure of himself."

"And Warren Masters. What of him?"

"Roger Davidson hasn't heard a word."

Nate shifted for comfort. "Tell me about Irma's family. And Cape's."

"Spence sent wires to all of them. Irma's folks sent a wire back telling Spence to bury her. Not much feeling for their daughter."

"Some kind of services for her?"

"Tomorrow at the mortuary. I hope a few people show up. Irma wasn't a bad person. She just had a tough life, short as it was."

"I'll be there. So will my folks."

"Chris Cape's father arrived day before yesterday and arranged to ship his son's body back to California for burial."

"And the Morgans buried Lyndon yesterday."

"Yes. It was good of you and your parents to come to the cemetery. As you know, there weren't very many there." Merci looked westward toward the Morgan homestead. "They're leaving on the train for Indiana. Dad bought their automobile and machinery. Hiram's so distraught he can hardly talk. The poor man's in tears most of the time. Sophia's broken hearted, too, but she made all the arrangements."

They sat in silence as Merci used her own boot to scuff out the lines Nate had made in the dirt. Eyes still on the ground, she asked, "Tell me, Nate, why would Irma kill Arnold? It just doesn't make sense."

"It makes all the sense in the world. She couldn't stand the fact that she'd been used—again."

"But why did Chris Cape try to protect her?"

"Same reason Arnold Masters was kind to her. She was someone he could use for entertainment—while he waited for you." After a long silence, he said, "He was just like some of the rest of us."

Merci turned her head to him. "What do you mean?"

Nate slowly stood. "Merci, without you these last months, I would never have survived. I was terrified the entire time—with the gallows always in my thoughts." Before she could respond, he changed the subject by gesturing toward the wreckage of the Jenny. "What will you do now? That airplane's gone for good."

Merci shifted the bridle reins from one hand to the other. "The men from the ranch are coming tomorrow to begin hauling what's left of it away. Dad's been wondering if the motor could be used to power a water pump or something." Merci stroked the horse's nose. "Right now it's hard to think about much of anything except those who are dead. Arnold Masters was a nice man who would never intentionally hurt anyone. Poor Lyndon Morgan. He wouldn't hurt anyone, either. Irma Lewellyn just wanted a decent life with some nice fellow to provide for her. How did she become a plaything for uncaring wealthy men?"

She stood with one fist on her hip and stared at the jumble that, only days before, had been an airplane. "If I live a hundred years I'll never understand Chris Cape. He had everything in the world. Why did he do what he did?"

Nate stood near her without touching. "He wanted you, Merc. And he was willing to do anything to get you. But he wasn't willing to be without companionship until you came around." After a minute of silence, he looked down at her. "No chance you might change your mind about me, I guess."

"No, Nate." She reached up and ran a finger across his cheek. "You really are a fine man. A good catch for any woman. So find yourself a nice girl who wants to live on a ranch. When you find her, make her happy and be happy yourself." She turned to the horse, grabbed a stirrup, and swung into the saddle. "I just came to take one last look at what's left of the Jenny." Merci reined the horse around to face west toward the Bruce Ranch, but shifted in the saddle to look over her shoulder at Nate. "After watching Spence and Dad in court, I decided to enroll in the law school at the university in Missoula. Spence says we can practice together after I graduate."

"They'll let a woman in the law school?"

"It's a new world." She flashed her radiant smile at Nathaniel Hamilton. "Find that nice girl, Nate, and forget about Merci Bruce."

With one kick to the side of her mount, she headed west for the Bruce Ranch without a backward glance at the remains of her once precious Curtis Jenny.